torn

Also by

Chris Jordan

TRAPPED
TAKEN

Chris Jordan

torn

Recycling programs for this product may not exist in your area.

ISBN-13: 978-0-7783-2575-8
ISBN-10: 0-7783-2575-X

TORN

www.MIRABooks.com

Printed in U.S.A.

To Lynn Harnett, with love.

PROLOGUE

The Pinnacle
Conklin, Colorado

He awakens with no memory of who he is, or how old he is, or why he should be in this palatial chamber. No, not so much a chamber as a grand hall, with one distant wall formed entirely of high, soaring glass, beyond which magnificent mountains rise from a stark landscape.

Men have gathered at his bedside. Doctors? Attendants? No, they are more like acolytes, for their eyes defer to him in supplication. Is he a prince? A king? A movie star?

He feels like a movie star. The enormous, glass-walled space, with its high curved ceiling melded into shadows, it has the look of a set, something designed for film. But if he's a movie star—the star of this scene, surely—why can't he recall his lines? Where have all the words gone?

"Good morning, sir," says one of the acolytes, looming over the bed. A homely gnome of a man who looks vaguely familiar. "How are you feeling today?"

He searches for the words, wanting to respond, but the only thing readily available is one simple syllable.

"Ha," he says, suddenly aware of the dryness in his mouth, a thickness in his throat that makes it hard to swallow.

"Bring water!"

A straw appears. He refuses, taking direction from his body, an instinctive recoiling from anything that must pass his lips. And then his mind catches up, slowly unfolding in all its complexity, and with a shudder he remembers that someone is trying to poison him. It is poison that thickens his throat and slows his mind. Poison that traps him in this bed.

He struggles but the poison has made him weak. A needle slips into a vein and the poison drips into him. A subtle, insidious, undetectable toxin that seeps into the cells of his brain, interfering with synaptic response. The bag appears to be harmless saline solution, but it cannot be. The notion that he's being slowly poisoned is something that he has deduced, rather than proved. The theory is highly probable because it's the only explanation for his condition: under no other circumstance would men like this—mere drones attending the queen—dare to treat him in this fashion. Unless they had betrayed him.

The drone with the homely face dares to speak for him, as if interpreting the words that clot in his throat.

"Stand clear. He wishes to see the mountains."

He has issued no such command—what does he care of mountains?—and then the rising sun strikes the peaks in just such a way, as if etching them into the sky, that his labored breathing catches. He knows it is only reflected light glancing off stone, ever so briefly imprinted on his retinas, but the image has the power to bring tears to his eyes.

He remembers, then. For a fleeting moment he regains a sense of who he is. Not a king, exactly, and certainly nothing as insignificant as a mere movie star. He is like the mountain and these lesser beings seek to erode him. They scratch and fuss and block him from the light. They drip their pathetic poisons like rain upon the mountain and like the mountain he will prevail, he will survive, in the most fundamental way, long after they are gone and forgotten.

The drone looks away, as if aware of the greater man's thoughts and ashamed for his own. He glances at an expensive wristwatch, feigning patience, and when the sunrise ceases to color the mountains he calls for a screen to be drawn around the bed.

Nurses attend to him, changing his catheter, evacuating his bowels. Sponging him down, patting him dry, as if he was some mewling infant and not…whatever he is. He struggles to hold a sense of self. Who is he? Who? A great man in a glass room, beset by lesser species, suffering various indignities. Indignities soon forgotten, absorbed by the scent of baby powder. Beyond that he does not recall.

Nothing holds, nothing stays.

Drip, drip, drip.

"Sir? Your wife is here. Would you like to see her?"

With great effort, fighting up through the silky gauze that swathes his mind, he musters a single "Ha."

A woman who claims to be his wife floats into view, and if he could laugh, he would. Because it is beyond a bad joke. The woman is old enough to be his mother. Regal, beautifully preserved, expensively coiffed, and obviously very wealthy. But old.

As if he would marry a woman like that! He finds the

notion so absurd that it's hard to hold her words in his mind and sort them into something meaningful.

"Arthur? Can you hear me, darling? Blink if you can understand. I've done exactly what you requested. What you spelled out months ago. I followed your instructions precisely, do you understand?" She studies him, then announces triumphantly to the others, "He blinks! He understands!"

He understands only that she must be an elaborate fraud. An aging actress contracted to play a role. She may be in league with the fawning acolyte. Whatever she is, whatever her motives, he cannot trust anything she says.

"You have the best doctors, my darling. The very best in the world. We are not giving up on you, do you understand?" She leans in close, wafting the scent of lilies, and whispers words meant only for him. "You can't die, Arthur. Not now, not ever. Whatever happens, you must come back to us. One way or another, you must live forever."

Then she draws away, dabbing at her eyes, and vanishes from his sight line. The scent of lilies. For a moment he knows with absolute conviction who he is and how he has come to be in this place.

He is the one, the Ruler of Rulers, he is all minds in one.

A moment later he begins to drool.

Part I
Humble, New York

1. A Simple, Ordinary Life

The day before my son's school exploded, he asked me if heaven has a zip code. We're having breakfast, me the usual fruit yogurt, Noah his mandatory Cocoa Puffs, cup of 'puffs' to one-half cup milk, precisely. He licks his spoon, gives me that wide-eyed mommy-will-know look, and asks the big question.

"Not a real zip code," he adds, "a pretend zip code, like for Santa. Like for writing a letter to Dad. Just to say hello, let him know we're okay and everything."

It's a strange and wonderful thing, the mind of a ten-year-old child. Last night, as we read our book before bed—the very exciting *Stormrider*—Noah had asked, out of nowhere, "How we doing, Mom?"

We'd both known exactly what he meant by that—the slow, painful rebuilding of our world—and without missing a beat I'd responded, "We're doing okay," and he'd filed it away in his amazing brain and twelve hours later, out pops the idea of writing a letter to his dead father.

"You write it," I suggest, "I'll find out about the zip code."

"Deal," he says, and grins to himself, mission accomplished.

Then he calmly and methodically finishes his cereal.

My husband, Jed, used to say that Humble, New York, was well named, but only because 'Hicksville' was already taken. Humble being a small, one-of-everything town thirty miles outside of Rochester. One convenience store, one barber/beauty shop, one police station, one firehouse, one elementary school. At last count there were more farm animals—mostly dairy cows, cattle, and sheep—than people.

We moved here shortly before Noah was born and my first impression wasn't exactly positive. I'm a New Jersey girl, a mall rat at heart, and the idea of living upstate in sight of a cornfield wasn't exactly my dream come true. Postcards are meant to be mailed, not lived in. But Jed was convinced a small town would be safer than Rochester, where he'd just been hired, and which has the usual problems with poverty, drugs, and empty factories, so when he found the 'perfect old farmhouse' on the Internet there was no way I could say no.

Not that I ever said no to Jed. What he wanted, I wanted. We agreed that we had to get out of the city, had to make a new life for ourselves, as far away from his crazy family as possible. It was all good, and for a while—nine wonderful years—we lived the American dream, or as near as real people can live it. Not that everything was perfect. Sometimes Jed brought home his job tensions—he was an electrical engineer with a struggling company, lots of pressure there. Sometimes I let my resentment—how did *his* family situation get to run my life?—overpower my own good sense.

Sure, we squabbled now and then, all couples do, but we never went to bed angry. That was our rule. Arguments had to be settled before we hit the sheets. I'd grown up in a family that fought—my parents divorced when I was in high school—and Jed's parents had been, to say the least, dysfunctional as human beings, and therefore more than anything we'd both longed for normality. A normal family in a small town, living a simple, ordinary life. The fact that Jed's family was far from normal no longer mattered, because we were making our own family, our own life, far from them.

Along the way this suburban Jersey girl got pretty good at stripping old plaster, hanging new Sheetrock, painting and wallpapering, the whole nine yards—whatever *that* means. My old posse would just die if they knew prissy little Haley Corbin had learned how to solder leaky pipes, unclog blocked drains, refinish old kitchen cabinets. With Jed working so hard, and being dispatched as a troubleshooter to distant locations, much of the 'perfect old farmhouse' renovation was left to me. I had no choice but to take off my fabulous custom-lacquered fingernail extensions and get to work. *This Old House* and HGTV became my gurus. I attended every workshop offered at the nearest Home Depot.

I took notes. I paid attention. I learned a thing or two.

My personal triumph, after studying a chapter on home wiring repairs and puzzling over a diagram, was wiring up a three-way switch for a new light in the foyer. Jed was truly amazed by that little adventure. I mean his jaw dropped. Claimed my body had been taken over by alien electricians. I offered to flip his switch, and did, right there on the stairs with Noah fast asleep in his crib.

Life was good. No, life was great. We'd done it. We'd managed to escape from a really bad scene and get a new start. Then it ended, as sudden as a midnight phone call, and the kind of hole it left cannot be plastered over, not ever. The best you can do is push your way through the days, concentrate on being the best mom possible, even if you know in your bones it can never really make up for what's missing.

Lately Noah seems to be faring better, which is good. He's not acting out in class quite so much. He's testing me less, a great relief. That's the thing about kids. When the impossible bad thing happens, they accept it. Eventually they adapt, and, as the saying goes, 'get on with their lives.' One of those clichés that happens to be true. But really, what choice do we have?

"Mom?" says Noah, holding up his wristwatch. A gift from his dad he has never, to my knowledge, taken off.

"Ready?"

"Like five minutes ago. You were noodling, Mom."

Noah doesn't approve of me 'noodling' because he thinks it makes me sad. He may have a point. I feel better when I'm busy, focused in the moment. Not wallowing in daydreams.

Moments later we're out the door, into the car.

Noah never takes the bus to school, not because he wouldn't like to—he has made his preference known—but because of the seat belt thing. No seat belts in buses, which drives me nuts. We're legally required to strap them into car seats until they shave, make sure they wear helmets while riding bikes and boards, but school buses get a pass? What's *that* all about?

Jed always thought I overreacted on the subject and maybe he was right, but I can't help picturing those big yellow buses upside down in a ditch, or in a collision, small bodies hurtling through the air like human cannonballs. So I drive my boy to Humble Elementary School—distance, three point four miles—and see him inside the door with my own eyes. And when school gets out I'll be right here waiting to pick him up and see that he gets home safely.

A mother can't be too careful.

2. Waiting For The Voice

Roland Penny watches from behind the filthy windows of his 1988 Chevy van as the children enter the school. The little brats with their backpacks and their enormous shoes. Probably need the big shoes so they don't tip over from the weight of the backpacks—they look like miniature astronauts stomping around in low gravity.

Strange, because when Roland himself attended this very same school, he, too, had big fat shoes with Velcro fastenings and a Mickey Mouse backpack, which he thought was cool at the time. Now he knows how small and ridiculous he must have looked to the adult world. How pitiful and partially formed—barely human, really. A lifetime ago, long before his mind was successfully reprogrammed with an understanding of the forces that rule the universe. Before he understood the fundamentals. Before he evolved to his present phase.

The cell on his belt vibrates. Very subtle, almost a tickle, but there it is. Incoming, baby. He touches the phone, hears the bright voice in his headset. A rich, persuasive voice that always seems to be perfectly in tune with his harmonic vibrations.

He listens intently. After a moment he responds.

"Yes, sir. I'm in place, on station."

The Voice, his own personal guidance mechanism, helps him keep focus. Centers him in the vortex. Reveals the secret rules and structures. Shows him the way. The Voice calms him, guides him, persuades him.

The Voice thinks for him, which is a great relief.

"Yes, sir, understood. Wait for the chief. Will do."

The connection is severed, causing him to wince. It's a physical sensation, losing connection to The Voice. Like having the blood supply to his brain cut off. But he has trained for this day for the past four months, guided every step of the way, and he knows The Voice will come to him exactly when he needs it, and not a moment before.

Roland Penny sits back in the cracked, leatherette seat of his crappy van and smiles at the thought of the new vehicle he's going to purchase when this mission is successfully concluded: a brand-new Escalade with all the options! Sweet. For now The Voice tells him that his old van is good cover. Patience. Complete the mission, then savor the reward. The Humble police chief is due at the top of the hour. Doubtless he will be on time, but if not, remain calm. Roland understands that he must not panic, must not deviate from the plan. If he deviates in any way, The Voice will know, and that would be bad.

Very bad.

3. Prime Numbers

Noah loves his homeroom teacher, Mrs. Delancey. Mrs. Delancey is kind and smart and funny. Also, she's beautiful. Not as beautiful as his mother, of course—Mom is the most beautiful person on the entire planet—but Mrs. Delancey is pretty in a number of interesting ways. Her hair, which she keeps putting back in some sort of elastic retainer thing, the way her dark eyes roll up in amusement when something funny happens, and her nice, fresh vanilla kind of smell, which Noah finds both familiar and reassuring.

The most attractive thing about her, though, is the smart part. At ten years of age Noah Corbin is an uncanny judge of intelligence. He can tell right away if an adult is as smart as he is, and Mrs. Delancey passes. In fourth grade there's no more baby stuff, no picture books or adding and subtracting puppy dogs and rabbits. They're learning real science and real math, complicated stuff that teases pleasantly at his brain. Mrs. Delancey isn't just reading from the textbooks or going through the motions—not like dumb-dumb Ms. Bronson who just about ruined third grade—Mrs. Delancey really understands the concept of factors and multiples and even prime numbers.

In Noah's mind, prime numbers glow with a special kind of magic. Almost as though they're alive. Alive not in the human way of being alive, of course, but in the way that certain numbers can have power. When he thinks of, say, 97, it seems to have a pulse. It's bursting with self-importance—look at me!—as if it knows it can't be divided. Because dividing by one doesn't really count. That's just a trick that makes calculations work, but everybody who understands knows that what makes prime numbers prime is that they can't be cleanly or perfectly divided. They remain whole, invulnerable, no matter what you try and do to them. Primes are like Superman without the Kryptonite. Which is actually how Mrs. Delancey described them on the very first day of math, totally blowing him away. What an amazing concept!

Yesterday Mrs. Delancey gave him a special tutoring session during recess. Noah had not wanted to go out on the playground at that particular moment—it just didn't feel right, he couldn't explain why—and lovely Mrs. Delancey had opened up a *high-school-level math book* and explained about dihedral primes. Dihedrals are primes that remain prime when read upside down on a calculator. How cool is that! Mrs. Delancey knew all about dihedrals and even more amazing, she knew he'd understand, even though it was really advanced.

Noah, having stowed his backpack, sits at his desk, waiting for the class to be called to order. At the moment mayhem prevails. Children run wild. Not exactly wild, he decides, there is actually a sort of pattern emerging. His classmates are racing counterclockwise around and around the room, a sweaty centrifuge of fourth-grade energy, driven mostly by the Culpepper twins, Robby and Ronny, who have been selling their Ritalin to Derek Deely, a really scary fifth grader who supposedly bit off the finger of a gym instructor in Rochester, where he used to go to school. Necessitating that his entire family escape to Humble, where they're more or less in hiding. That's what everybody says.

Noah finds it perfectly believable that a kid would bite off a teacher's finger. He's been tempted himself, more than once. Although that was mostly last year, when everybody thought that feeling sorry for him was the way to go. Like Ms. Kinnison always trying to hug him and 'check on his feelings.' Which really should be against the law, in Noah's opinion. Feelings were personal and you weren't obliged to share them with dim-witted adults who didn't know the first thing about aerodynamics, momentum effects, or dead fathers.

"Take your seats! Two seconds!"

Mrs. Delancey hasn't been in the room for a heartbeat and everything changes. Two seconds later every single child has plopped into the correct seat, as if by magic. As if Mrs. Delancey has waved a wand and made it so. While the truly magical thing is that she has no wand—Noah doesn't believe in magic, not even slightly, not even in books—but has the ability to command their attention.

"Deep breaths everyone," she instructs, inhaling by way of demonstration. "There. Are we good? Are we calm? Excellent!"

As Mrs. Delancey takes attendance, checking off their names against her master list, Noah decides that she is the living equivalent of a human prime number. Indivisible, invulnerable. Superteacher without the Kryptonite.

4. The Cheese Monster

The amazing thing, given his family background, is how normal Jed turned out. Okay, my late, great husband was brilliant—after he died, his coworkers kept saying he was some kind of genius, the smartest guy in the company—so maybe having a brilliant mind isn't exactly normal, but in all the usual normal human ways Jed was normal. He loved me unconditionally and I loved him back the same way. We wanted to make a life together, raise children, do all the normal kinds of things that normal people do. And we did, so long as we both shall live.

Not that it wasn't a challenge. And luck played a role, right from the start. It was luck that we ever met. Blame it on Chili's. Jed was working his way through Rutgers—he'd already cut all ties with his family—slogging through four-hour shifts at a local Chili's three days a week and full-time—often twelve hours per shift—on weekends. Forty hours busing tables, thirty hours in lecture halls and labs, another thirty hitting the books—it didn't leave much time left over for things like sleeping, let alone meeting mall girls from South Orange who just happen to be at a Chili's celebrating a friend's birthday, downing way too many Grand Patrón margaritas. Mall girls who get whoopsy drunk and barf in a tub of dirty dishes. Mall girls who are then so humiliated they burst into tears and cry inconsolably.

Well, not inconsolably. I wasn't so drunk I didn't have the presence of mind to take the dampened napkins the hunky busboy provided to clean up with, or let him walk me outside so I could get some fresh air. He was so sweet and kind, and so careful not to put his hands on me, even though I could tell he wanted to. And when I came back the next evening, cold sober, to formally apologize, we sat down and had a coffee and by the time we stood up I knew he was the man for me. The very one in the whole wide world. All the other boys—hey, I was a hot little mall girl—all the others were instantly erased, gone as if they'd never existed. My heart beat Jedediah, and it still does.

Jedediah, Jedediah, can't you hear it?

* * *

After dropping Noah off at school I stop by the Humble Mart Convenience Store for a loaf of bread and some deli items—the selection is limited but of good quality—but mostly to hear the latest gossip being shared by Donald Brewster, the owner/manager. Called 'Donnie Boy' by everyone in town, which dates from his days as a high school football hero. Donnie Boy Brewster keeps a glossy team photo up behind the deli counter, blown up to poster size. When the customers mention it, and they do so frequently, Donnie Boy rolls his eyes and chuckles good-humoredly and says who is that kid? What happened to him, eh?

The 'eh' being the funny little Canadian echo some of the locals have, from living so close to the border.

Anyhow, Donnie Boy is one of the nice ones, a local kid who made good by staying local. He obviously loves his store, keeps it spiffy clean and well stocked, and he knows everything that's going on in the little village of Humble and, best part, loves to share. Even with recent immigrants like me.

"Hey, Mrs. Corbin!"

I've given up trying to get him to call me Haley. All of his customers are Mister, Missus, or Miz, no exceptions. On the street he'll call me Haley, but when he's on the service side of the counter, I remain Mrs. Corbin. Donnie Boy's rules.

Donnie in his little white butcher's cap and his long bulbous nose and radar scoop ears, going, "We've got that Swiss you like. No pressure."

"No, no, give me a quarter. It's Noah's favorite."

"Coming right up," he says, placing the cylinder of cheese in the slicing machine. "Thin, right?"

"Thin but not too thin."

"Not so thin you can read through it. Got it. D'ja hear about the dump snoozer?"

Why I come here, to hear about mysterious local events like dump snoozing.

"Old Pete Conrad. You know, out Basel Road? The farmhouse with the leaning tower of silo?"

Happily, I am indeed familiar with the 'leaning tower of silo.' Nice old farmstead, with the main house kept up and painted and all the other buildings, barns and sheds in a state of disrepair, including a faded blue silo that's seriously out of plumb. I don't know Mr. Conrad personally, but have seen him at a distance, fussing at an ancient tractor.

"Pete's out the dump—excuse me, the recycle center—in that old Ford, and it's parked there most of the day before anyone notices Pete's not in the freebie barn, which is where he usually hangs out. They're about to lock the gate when somebody thinks to check his truck, and there's Pete, lying on his side, obviously dead."

"No!"

"That's what they thought. So they call Emergency Services, the ambulance and crew arrive, everybody is hanging around, reminiscing about the deceased, when all of a sudden Pete sits up and demands to know what's going on."

"No!"

"Sound asleep! Said his wife's snoring kept him awake all night and he came out the dump to catch a few winks. He finds garbage peaceful. Lulled to sleep by the sound of front-end loaders. Which is apparently a whole lot less noisy than Mildred snoring."

"What a riot," I say, chuckling.

"Anyhow, that's my cheesy gossip for the day," he says, handing the neatly wrapped Swiss across the counter.

"Thanks, Donnie."

"*De nada,* Mrs. Corbin. Noah's in for a treat today, eh?"

"He loves his cheese."

"No, I meant Chief Gannett. He's giving his talk to the elementary school kids. For D.A.R.E.?"

"Really? Is there a drug problem in the elementary school?"

"Not that I know of. And Chief Gannett will tell you that's because he starts early. He gives a wonderful presentation, very entertaining in a this-is-your-brain-on-drugs kind of way. Fire and brimstone but sort of funny, too, you know?"

I leave the Humble Mart with a smile on my face. Fire and brimstone, but sort of funny, too. Perfect. Plus Noah will have a treat when he gets home from school. He likes to take little bites around the holes, pretending they are black holes in the universe and he's the cheese monster, one of the many nicknames given to him by his doting father.

Ruggle Rat, Crumb Stealer, Noah-doah, The Poopster, The Cheese Monster. When I pick him up at two-thirty, no doubt full of excited, exaggerated stories about the visiting police chief, that will be the highlight of my day. And I wouldn't have it any other way.

5. Killing Yourself To Live

The van windows are so dirty and pitted it's hard to see inside, but when the cop car eases into the school parking lot Roland Penny nevertheless slinks down in his seat, to avoid being recognized. Can't be too careful. The chief knows him, and may recall certain events in Roland's teen years, and that might prove awkward, or even lethal. Later, once events have been set in motion, there will be time for recognition.

Hey, Q, remember me?

'Q' came from 'cue ball' because longtime Humble police chief Leo Gannett is bald, completely hairless with alopecia totalis, a condition considered comical by many teenage boys. As funny as being retarded or crippled or, for whatever reason, hideously uncool. Yo, Q! shouted on the street as the cruiser rolled by was guaranteed to get laughs from your buds. Or the derisive snorts of those you wished were your buds.

Whatever. That was over. That was the old Roland, before he emerged from his chrysalis.

Eyeballing the scene in his rearview, Roland watches the familiar figure of the tall, paunchy cop get out of his cruiser, straighten his uniform, and set his lid on his shiny head. Roland knows that big city police officers refer to their regulation hats as 'lids' because he watches lots of cop shows on TV. Just as they call their uniforms 'bags,' supposedly. And how they like to sum up situations by saying things like 'code four,' which means 'everything is okay,' and 'code five,' which means there's a warrant out on a suspect, and 'code eight,' officer calling for help.

Hey, Q! Code eight coming right up, sir! Roland chuckles, amazed by his own ability to think humorously, wittily, at such a critical juncture. Obviously he has developed nerves of steel, strengthened by training and practice. Amazing that when the big moment finally arrives he experiences no uneasiness, no fear, just a pleasant feeling of anticipation. Various tasks to be performed. The next level to be attained. Homage paid to the Profit.

Not the prophet. Never the prophet. The Profit. Crucial difference.

Once the big, bald cop is safely inside the school, Roland emerges from the van. He opens the creaky rear door. His tools are inside, neatly laid out. First to be removed is the small janitorial cart, rattling as it hits the pavement. Inside the cart he places a ragged string mop, intended for show—look, I'm a janitor cart!—and then, very gingerly, a zippered gym bag. The bag is heavy, more than fifty pounds heavy.

Careful, careful, don't want that little sucker activated before the time comes.

Then, clipped to the inside of the cart rim, just out of sight, a canvas holster, quick release, containing a Glock 17, modified with a reduced-power spring kit for the lightest possible trigger pull. Perfectly legal and not, as the kit warned, for self-defense. Point and shoot without even having to squeeze, that's how soft the pull—the gun will practically shoot itself.

Before setting off with the cart, Roland places the white earbuds in his ears and activates the iPod. The Voice has instructed him in the use of the iPod, a device that does not respond well to his clumsy, insensitive fingers. Roland prefers buttons, switches, triggers, not wimpy touch screens. Still, he learned, he practiced until he got it right, and it's not as if he has to scroll through the selections. The only playlist is a comp of Black Sabbath, specifically selected by The Voice. Even in the heaviest throes of his metal phase, Roland was never a Black Sabbath fan. Way too old. Geezers in wigs. Pathetic. His taste tended more toward classic Megadeth tracks, or if he was really twisted, anything by Municipal Waste. Thrash? Don't mind if I do. The fact is he hasn't listened seriously to metal since he began to evolve—nearly a year now—but The Voice specified Black Sabbath, and once he has the Ozzified itch of "Killing Yourself to Live" buzzing in his ears it's okay, strictly as a kind of soundtrack to the sequence of events that have been so painstakingly rehearsed and memorized.

Roland can see the task list in his mind's eye, clear as day. Start from the top, follow the numbers, execute each task.

1. Gain Access

A wheel spins out of kilter as he pushes the cart across the parking lot, approaching a side door marked Exit Only. Although it is not marked as such, this is where the school takes deliveries. Roland knows this because he worked, ever so briefly, for custodial services. Ring the delivery buzzer and they will come. The buzzer sounds in the coffee room—little more than a closet—and the duty custodian will grudgingly put down his cup, amble out to the door, maybe cadge a smoke from the truck driver making the delivery.

Roland presses the button, waits. Counts to ten, pushes it again. Lazy bastards.

It seems to take forever. His heart pounds like a boxer's padded glove hitting the canvas bag, but in less than a minute the fitted metal door yawns open.

"Hey, hey," says Bub Yeaton, his usual salutation.

Roland figured old Bub would be on duty. Not that his presence is crucial to the plan. Any warm body will do, so long as the door opens. But seeing Bub start to squint, as recognition dawns—his watery eyes tracking from the cart to Roland, looking comically quizzical—having Bub in his sights is pretty sweet, all things considered.

"Roland? Hey. Um, what are you doing here?"

"They give me my job back," says Roland, reaching into the cart.

"I don't think so," says Bub warily. "Nobody told me."

"Check with him," Roland says, pointing at the empty corridor.

Bub turns to look. Pure instinct—if someone points, you turn to look. And as the elderly custodian turns his head, Roland withdraws an eighteen-inch length of lead-filled iron pipe from the cart and smacks old Bub on the back of the skull, midway up. Exactly as he has rehearsed, practicing on ripe watermelons.

The only sound the custodian makes is a flabby wet thump as he hits the hard rubber tiles of a floor he recently cleaned, waxed, and polished.

2. Subdue Custodian.

Roland turns up the volume and grins to himself as Sabbath bruises his eardrums. So far so good.

6. Eva The Diva

The sun has barely cracked the horizon in Conklin County, Colorado. Dawn oozing up over the eastern edge of the mountains like a tremulous egg yolk charged with blood. Blood is on the mind of Ruler Weems, who has been wide-awake and manning his operations desk for many hours. His work hampered by the fact that he dare not use cell, e-mail, or text in the certain knowledge that his adversaries—mostly notably the Ruler security chief, Bagrat Kavashi—have broken his personal cipher and are monitoring all electronic communication coming from the Bunker.

All of which makes it difficult to marshal his forces, keep them informed. Difficult but not impossible. Back in the day, when Rulers were few, none of those media existed, and yet still he helped build an enterprise whose power and influence extended from Wall Street to the upper echelons of government. And now the entire organization is in grave danger. The county, the village, the institute itself—everything he's helped forge, build, and create could be destroyed by the willful actions of one woman, in league with her ruthless security chief.

Weems rises from his command post, goes to the window slit, allows himself to be bathed by the slash of sunlight pouring through the two-foot thickness of the concrete bunker. He has many flaws, but physical vanity is not among them—he's keenly aware of a homeliness that has not improved with age. At sixty-three his hatchet nose, wattled throat, and severe underbite make him look like an old tortoise without a shell. The curvature of his upper spine, naturally drooping shoulders, and dark, deep-set eyes add to the effect.

Long ago he accepted his ugliness, learned how to use it to his advantage. Blessed with a resonant voice, he honed his speaking abilities, perfected his courtly good manners, his natural deference. So that, despite an aspect that can make people cringe at first sight, he tends to make a favorable impression in the long run. Those who offer loyalty are always rewarded. Those who misjudge him do so at their peril.

The woman has misjudged him. But that doesn't mean she's not exceedingly dangerous, that the inevitable implosion of her ambition might not be powerful enough to destroy all those around her, the innocent and the guilty alike.

Behind him a vault door slides open.

"Evangeline," he says without turning.

"You rang, sir?"

His tortoise head swivels, dewlaps quivering.

"That's a joke, Wendall," she informs him. "*The Addams Family,* I think. That makes you Lurch the butler. Take away his chin, there's a distinct resemblance."

Weems happens to know she just turned fifty-five, although you'd never know it. The miracles of nip and tuck, priceless ointments, personal trainers, and a low-calorie diet composed, from what he can see, of little more than twigs. Twigs and malice, for never has he known a woman who harbors so many self-sustaining resentments. Her blood must be acid by now, and her eyes, still large and beautiful and hopelessly compelling despite surgical tightening, have, at a closer examination, the sheen of cold anthracite. Animal eyes peering out through a lovely human mask.

She plops down in his chair, smiling as she takes possession. "Kind a *Star Trek* thing you've got going here," she observes. "'Ruler Weems on the bridge, sir!'"

"You seem to have vintage television shows on your mind," he says. "TV will rot your brain, Eva. It may already have done so, if what I hear is true."

The smile chills.

"You've put us all in danger," he says. "Terrible, destructive, senseless danger. Are you crazy?"

The smile stays frozen, but the beautiful eyes are

amused. "You know what, Wendall?" she says, somehow swiveling her hips and the chair in the same subtle motion. "You need to grow you some gonads. Doing nothing is not a policy. It's not a strategy. It's simply doing nothing."

"He wouldn't want this."

"And how would you know what Arthur wants?" she says, taunting. "He hasn't spoken to you in months."

"I visit his bedside many times a day," Weems responds, defensive despite himself. "He speaks to no one. That part of his mind has been damaged."

"He speaks to me," she insists.

"Prove it," he suggests. "Make a digital recording."

"It's more a mind-meld kind of thing," she says with a seductive smile, shaping her recently plumped lips. "I look into his eyes and I know what he wants. I know it as deeply and as surely as if he's spoken. Arthur is beyond words now. He wants me to act as his voice to the world."

Weems sighs, puts a hand to his forehead, intending to shield the flash of cold rage in his eyes. "If it was only speaking, that would be one thing," he says, in his most reasonable voice. "But to hatch this lunatic plot? Endangering God knows how many children? To put us all at risk of arrest? Not to mention what it will do to recruitment and revenues if the truth comes out. It's insane, Eva. And whatever our differences, I never doubted your sanity."

"There is no God."

"What?"

"You just said 'God knows how many children.'"

"It's an expression, Eva. Don't try to change the subject. You reached out, willful and shameless in your ambition, you set loose a man you know is capable of murder, and now terrible things are going to happen in some little town that's never done us any harm. If your hand is found in this, and surely it will be, we'll all be destroyed."

She laughs. "Wendall, don't be so dramatic. You sound like some old fruit from a daytime drama. 'Dear me, we shall all of us be destroyed!' You're being ridiculous. No one will ever know—Vash will see to that, and when it's all over, Arthur's wish will have been carried out."

"And you'll take control of the entire organization. You, speaking for Arthur, with the help of that thug Kavashi."

"Pretty much, yeah."

"And where do I figure in your great plan? Me and those I represent?"

She shrugs. "You don't. Retire. Write your own book. Start another enterprise. It makes no difference to me. You and all your friends ride off into the sunset, that's the bottom line."

"Which you think will happen because why? Because you want it to?"

"No, Wendall. Because *he* wants it to."

Weems shakes his head. They've had variations on this conversation before, never settled anything. "You lie so well," he says, almost with admiration. "If I didn't know better."

"When it comes to lying, I stand on the shoulders of giants."

"Naked ambition," he says.

She stands up from his custom-built command chair, strokes her hands on her hips playfully. Poisonously. "What are you saying, Wendall? You want to see me naked? Does little Wendy have a woody for pretty wittle Eva the Diva?"

"Get out," he says.

She gives him an air kiss as she passes him by. "You'll try and stop me," she whispers huskily. "You'll fail."

7. The Bad Clown

Most of the kids, as they stream into the bleacher seats, contrive to sit with friends. The teachers remain at the aisles, directing traffic, making sure the individual homerooms don't get blended. Order must be maintained or, as Mrs. Delancey is fond of saying, all heck will break out.

All heck. Noah loves the way she says it—the twinkle in her eye—and also her other favorite phrases like "think smart and you'll *be* smart" and "one fish doesn't make a school," which she had to explain to some of the slower kids wasn't about school construction but the way fish—and people—react to other fish and people.

Although most of his classmates find Noah interesting or at least entertaining, he doesn't have any particular best friends—friends who might ask about personal stuff—and so his goal upon entering the gymnasium is to end up sitting as close as possible to Mrs. Delancey. Preferably a spot, an angle, where she won't be aware that he's keeping an eye on her. Because Mrs. Delancey is very careful about not playing favorites, and she's already giving him special time, what she calls 'one-on-one' sessions, when he's supposed to be out on the playground.

One-on-one. He likes that phrase because he sees it as one raised to the first power, or one times one, or one divided by one, all of which result, amazingly enough, in one. You can't escape *one*—no matter where you go, it leads you back. It stands alone but takes care of itself. According to the book, one is not a prime, although Noah hasn't quite figured out why not, if it is only divisible by itself and by one, which it is. That's the first definition, right? So why make an exception? Mrs. Delancey explained that once upon a time the number one *was* considered a prime, but in modern math the primes begin with two, the only even prime number.

Noah intends to pursue this further, the next time he has a chance. The next time he has Mrs. Delancey one-on-one. Right now she's concentrating on getting her students seated and behaving.

"Bethany! Christopher!"

That's all it takes, just their names announced with a certain tone, and both kids stop what Mrs. Delancey sometimes calls 'skylarking.' Skylarking being okay at recess, even at certain times in class, but never at assembly.

Noah has often been guilty of skylarking, or worse—right here in the gymnasium, in fact—but this morning he vows to behave himself, not wanting to embarrass his homeroom teacher in front of the principal, Mrs. Konrake. Often called Mrs. K. Who stands by the gymnasium doors in her dark mannish suit, her prim, pursed mouth a little pink O, as she oversees the assembly. What she lacks in stature—in heels she's not that much taller than the biggest fifth grader—Mrs. K makes up in voice power.

If most people have voices like car horns, Mrs. K is a big truck. An 18-wheeler. When she honks, you pull over just to get out of the way. First graders have been known to wet their pants upon being sent to her office. There are even rumors of a spanking machine, something with paddles and a big crank handle. Noah, who has spent some considerable time in Mrs. K's office, has never seen such a machine and knows from his own experience that when it gets down to one-on-one—those magic numbers again—Mrs. K is actually pretty nice, and her office voice is much less threatening than her hallway voice. As if she has different horns for different places.

When all of the students have been seated, Mrs. K raises her right hand for silence and waits until all one hundred and fifty-seven students have raised their hands to indicate compliance. Aside from the squeaking of the wooden plank seating, the resulting quiet is remarkable. As Noah's dad used to say, you could hear a germ fart.

"Thank you," says Mrs. K. "As was explained to you in your homerooms, this morning we have a very special event. Chief Gannett has taken time out of his busy schedule to give us his presentation for the D.A.R.E. program. He'll be telling you about drug abuse resistance education, and the new Web site for kids, and a lot of very interesting stories from his own experience as a police officer. Let me stress that this is very important and that we are very fortunate to have Chief Gannett with us today. I'm confident that you will give him your full attention, and that when the time comes for questions you'll be polite and respectful. So without further ado let's put our hands together and give our guest a great big Humble Elementary welcome!"

The chief has been waiting patiently, looking very somber and formal in his dress uniform. He's the only man Noah has ever seen who wears white dress gloves. It reminds him of a cartoon character, because in cartoons the hands look like gloves. Thinking of the chief as a variation on SpongeBob or Goofy makes Noah smile. His secret, you'll-never-guess-why-I'm-laughing smile. He stares into his folded hands, grinning to himself and fighting back a giggle.

The giggle wins when the clown suddenly enters the gymnasium. Noah knows he's not a real clown—there's no rubber nose or makeup—but like all of the other children he can't help but laugh when the man with the little janitorial cart bumps through the gym door. Because at that precise moment the police chief has stepped behind the podium and is testing the microphone by tapping it with one of his white-gloved fingers. Tap, tap, tap. There's something comical about the contrast between the somber, formally dressed policeman and the disheveled-looking man hurriedly pushing the little cart right out onto the gymnasium floor. The man pushing the cart has a pinched look on his face, as though he's smelling something bad. A fart maybe. That's funny. He's wearing earbuds and bobbing his head to the beat, and that's funny, too, because no one else can hear the music. Even the mop sticking up from the cart looks comical, as does the fact that one of the cart wheels is spinning wildly around.

The children laugh uproariously.

Noah notes that Mrs. Delancey is smiling, too. So maybe the sudden entrance of the funny man with the cart is part of the D.A.R.E. presentation. That's how it looks. The puzzled expression on the policeman's round face appears to be exaggerated, as does Mrs. Konrake's look of stern consternation. It's all part of the entertainment, like at a circus or a TV show, with everybody playing his or her part.

The funny man reaching into the funny cart for some sort of funny prop. The nice policeman reacting hastily, awkwardly, fumbling at his belt.

A loud popping noise like a balloon exploding, or a really loud party favor.

Noah is studying Mrs. Delancey when it happens, so at first he has no idea why the shrieks of laughter have turned into shrieks of screaming.

8. A Very Dangerous Word

I'm in the library discussing books with Helen Trefethern when the first siren goes by. Helen runs our little two-room public library with a velvet fist, and she almost always has suggestions on what books Noah and I might enjoy reading together. *Stormrider* was her idea.

"There's a bunch more books in that series," she tells me. "And if he gets sick of spy stories and wants something funny, you might try *Hoot.* Really smart and sassy, and it will make you laugh out loud. I think Noah will like it—he's a tough one to pick for—but I'm certain you'll love it."

Helen is about my mother's age—or the age my mom would be were she still alive—and a real Humble native with family roots that extend back a century or more. Unlike most of the local best and brightest who go away to college—in her case Syracuse—she had returned to marry and raise a family. Her husband had passed away a year or so before we lost Jed, so that was another thing that bridged the age difference and made me think of Helen as one of my trusted local friends. As opposed to my old New Jersey posse, who have no idea why I vanished, or where I might have gone.

"So how's he doing?" she asks. With her it's not a casual question—she really wants to know.

"Better," I tell her, with great relief. "New year, new teacher, it's really made a difference."

Last year Noah went through this disruptive behavior phase, mostly by acting the clown. They told me—very pointedly—that you can't teach a classroom of children when they're howling with laughter because my son has attached erasers to his ears like headphones, or when he is making ghostly noises from inside the air ducts. He always had the tendency to go his own way, right from kindergarten, and for a couple of months after the accident it got worsc. Much worse. There were many calls from the principal requesting that I take Noah home, which of course I did. What I would not agree with was the advice offered by the school district's child psychologist, who thought my son's behavioral problems could be improved with psychotropic drugs. A cocktail of Ritalin and Paxil. As if grief can be erased by a pill. And even if it can, would you really want to?

The psychologist pushed, but I stood my ground and this year has been better. This year Noah has a crush on his homeroom teacher, and if you think that makes his mother jealous, you've no idea how relieved I am that my brilliant little boy has been trying to impress Mrs. Delancey with his good behavior.

It helps that Irene Delancey has a graduate degree in mathematics. No doubt she could be making a lot more money as an actuary, or whatever else math types do when they focus on making money. Instead of chasing the bucks, Irene decided to teach in public schools, this being her first year at Humble. I find her a bit cool and cerebral—she's one of those unflappable types—but she's been devoting a lot of extra time and energy to dealing with Noah, and for that I am grateful.

It's the second siren that finally gets my attention. Two sirens in less than a minute. Must be an accident. Traffic or farm—and around here farm accidents tend to be the most horrific.

Helen says, "Humph," and ambles over to a window overlooking the street. "Haley? Those were troopers."

I join her at the window. "Not local cops?"

"State police. Must be serious. Escaped prisoners, maybe?"

The nearest prison is in the next county, fifty miles distant, but we Humble residents worry because four years ago Mildred Peavey was tied up and gagged and had her car stolen by one such escapee. The really tragic part is that Mildred lived alone and it was several days before anybody missed her. By then she'd died of a stroke, still bound and gagged. So the notion of an escaped prisoner is our local boogeyman.

Here comes another siren, a shrill wee-waw wail from a light-flashing ambulance. And this time we're both able to see it take a left turn onto Academy Road.

"Oh my god," says Helen, stealing a look at me. "The school."

By the time I get there, half a dozen state cop cars have arrived, as well as the ambulance. A young trooper with a bright pink face is frantically trying to control the incoming traffic.

Hopeless.

Parents, mostly mothers, are converging from every direction. Most are not bothering to find a parking space, but are abandoning their vehicles and running toward the school, eyes wide with concern, or panic—both.

I'm one of them. Under normal circumstances I'm a pretty calm and rational person. But this is not normal. You can feel it in the air, pick it up from the way the young cops don't want to look us in the eye. Something terrible has happened.

There's talk among the moms about panicked phone messages from inside the building. From teachers and also from a few students who apparently ignored the ban on cell phones. Something terrible has happened but no one seems to know what, exactly.

All I know for sure is that Noah doesn't have a cell phone. Since when do fourth graders need such things?

Since right this very minute.

What kind of mother am I, not foreseeing the need?

"Get them out!" someone shouts.

The crowd surges forward, and me with it.

Uniformed state troopers armed with shotguns are barricading the school entrance.

"Nobody gets in! Stay back!" one of them bellows, his voice cracking.

"What's happening? What's wrong?"

That's me, pleading. Sounding like a frightened ten-year-old, and feeling that way.

The young trooper with the big voice and the baby-blue eyes shakes his head reluctantly, as if he's under orders not to divulge information. "You'll have to get back!" he repeats, pointing a finger at me.

Beside me, a furious, tubby little woman ignores the

shotguns and the big shoulders barring her way, and attempts to burrow through the troopers, screaming, "They've got the kids! They've got the kids!"

It's Becky Bedlow. She has a boy in Noah's class, a shy little guy, small for his age. And when she says *they've got the kids* in that desperate tone of voice we all know what it means.

Mad bombers, terrorists, Columbine. Every fear we've ever had, every nightmare news story, has come careening into our little school. It's like the entire town is having a panic attack. Mothers are shouting, demanding to be let into the school. The troopers look shocked and maybe a little frightened by the raw passions being expressed—some of it scatological—but refuse to back down.

"Establish a perimeter!" one of the older troopers bellows. From the way they react he's the big boss, the man in charge.

"What's happening! Somebody tell us what's happening!"

The trooper in charge—he's got a jaw as big as a clenched fist, eyes as pale as gray ice—wades into the crowd, holding up his hands, palms out like a traffic cop.

"Stop it!" he commands. "Stop right there!"

Amazingly enough, he's rewarded with a cessation of shoving. As the volume lowers, I can hear women weeping. I'm one of them.

"We have a hostage situation!" the big trooper explains. "Man with a gun, barricaded inside the gymnasium with most of the children and teachers."

"What about the children? What about the kids?"

"As far as we know, no children have been harmed. But

if anybody tries to force their way inside, that may change, do you understand? You'll only make it worse, maybe get somebody killed. So allow us to establish a perimeter. Allow us to do our jobs. Please!"

It takes more persuasion, but within a few minutes he has managed to get us all back behind a flimsy barricade of yellow crime scene tape that has been hastily erected at the far side of the parking lot.

Before I can get my breath I notice a nearly hysterical Meg Frolich waving around her iPhone. Evidently she's just received an image from her daughter's cell phone, somewhere inside the school. "Look at this!" she's screaming, trying to get a beleaguered state trooper's attention. "They shot Chief Gannett! He's dead! They killed him! Oh my god, oh my god, oh my god!"

I try to get a glimpse of the tiny image on the iPhone screen, but someone else wrestles it away. Can it be real? Does she have it right? Could the child have misunderstood whatever it is that's happening inside? Maybe this is all a scary mistake, a group panic kind of deal. But it seems so real, this strange gravity of fear that thickens the air somehow, making it hard to breathe.

Not knowing is killing me. It feels as if icy fingers are clawing at my insides. The way it did when they told me Jed's plane was down with no survivors. An end-of-the-world sensation, as though I'm falling and falling and it will never stop. The vertigo makes me so dizzy I have to sit down on the grass and cry until my eyes are blind with tears.

Noah, Noah, Noah. I know he's in there with all the other children, with his teachers and maybe even the principal, but in my head he's all alone.

9. An Angry Blur

Whatever the cops know, they're not sharing it with us. Not beyond "man with a gun in the gym."

Most of what I learn is secondhand at best. An uncertainty that somehow adds to the fear. For example, Megan Frolich had her iPhone seized by the state troopers, with vague promises of getting it back once the images have been downloaded. So we have to rely on what she recalls of the pictures and the accompanying text message from her eleven-year-old daughter.

"I know what she was trying to say," she insists, her normally pretty eyes looking like overinflated pink balloons. "*Bd,* that's 'bad' and *m-n,* that's 'man'—*s-t* has to be 'shot' and *c-o-p* is 'cop,' that's obvious. 'Bad man shot cop.' Then *c-a-n-t* and then *m-v,* must be 'can't move,' right? And *A-f-r-d* is 'afraid.' I know it is! She repeated it three times. Afraid, afraid, afraid. Bad man shot cop. Can't move. Afraid, afraid, afraid."

The accompanying image, as Meg remembers it, is a slightly blurred snapshot of the gymnasium floor, as seen from the stands. On the gym floor is what appears to be a blue plastic tarp. Not lying flat, but jumbled, covering something. And in proximity to the mysterious blue tarp—that very disturbing blue rectangle—Meg recalls a young man who looked, she says, vaguely familiar. Someone local maybe. Meg hadn't actually seen a gun in the man's possession—only part of him was on-screen—but she formed the impression he was agitated.

"It was the way he blurred," she says, trying desperately

to grasp whatever meaning had been imbedded in the image. “An angry blur, does that make sense?”

We all agree that it makes perfect sense. An angry blur, a frightened girl. Afraid, afraid, afraid. We’re all afraid, frightened out of our wits, and the sense of anxious dread exuding from the cops—state, local, and county—doesn’t do anything to allay our fears.

We’re waiting, all of us, cops and parents, for whatever comes next. Wrestling with the awful notion that the world as we know it, our little patch of it, may be coming to an end. That from this moment on our lives will be altered. Unbearable. I’m gritting my teeth so hard my jaw aches. All around me desperate parents are calling family and friends, and it occurs to me, with a body-wrenching pang of sorrow, that I have no one to call. Jed is gone. I have no siblings. My mom died in her late fifties of breast cancer. My father, twelve years her senior, passed a year later. My old New Jersey homies have no idea where I am these days and I have to keep it that way. And my new, local friends already know about the situation at the school because by now the whole village has heard about it. Indeed most of the population seems to be on-site, milling around the parking lot and athletic field in a state of shock and anxiety.

This can’t be happening. Bad things happen to good people, I know that, but do bad things *keep* happening? Isn’t it enough to lose a husband so young? What will I do if something happens to my precious boy?

I somehow force my eyes to focus on the school. Noah’s school. It looks so peaceful. A cheerful little elementary school, carefully constructed of cinder block and brick to keep our children safe. A typical, totally normal public school found anywhere in suburban or small-town America. The main building is one story with a flat roof and plenty of glass to make the classrooms airy and filled with light. The boxy, windowless gymnasium at one end, higher than the rest of the building.

The gymnasium is where the bad thing is happening. Men in various uniforms swarm around the base of the gym. A wiry, long-limbed deputy from the county sheriff's department begins scaling the wall, inching up a drainpipe like a black spider. As he hunches and turns I catch the white letters emblazoned on his padded vest.

SWAT.

Oh my god.

"Haley?"

It's my librarian friend Helen, crouching in the grass, reaching out to touch my tear-soaked chin, a look of sorrow and concern on her open face. Next thing, we're hugging and it's all I can do not to call her 'mom,' the sense of maternal concern is that strong.

"Easy now," she says, trying to comfort me. "They'll get them out. It will be okay, you'll see."

"You think?" I respond, trying to smile.

"I heard it was Roland Penny. He's harmless, Haley. Roland would never hurt the children."

"Who?"

"Roland Penny. Kids used to call him 'roll of pennies.' Local boy. The cops have pictures from inside. Cell phone images. They recognize him."

I want to believe her, that everything will be okay, but something in me can't. Something in me expects the worst.

"Someone got shot," I say. "That's what we heard."

Helen nods. "They think it was poor Leo Gannett. He's been chief for years and he's got a long history with Roland Penny, from when Roland was a kid."

Just listening to her, my heart starts to slow, approaching something like normal. "How do you know all this?"

Helen smiles, her eyes crinkling with affection. "My sister's boy, Thomas. He's with the State Police Emergency Response Team. That's him over there by the ambulance. Isn't he a handsome boy? Listen to me, Haley. They've got it under control. They know who they're dealing with. That's what Thomas says and I believe him."

"They're going to start shooting, aren't they?"

More men with SWAT lettered on their backs, a whole team armed with deadly looking rifles is assembling near one of the emergency exit doors.

"Not unless they have to," Helen assures me. "They know about all the children, Haley. They won't risk hurting the kids."

"What does he want, this crazy man? What does he want?"

Helen shakes her head and sighs.

10. Can You Help Me Occupate My Brain?

Nobody warned him about the smell. Pack a hundred and fifty little kids in a gymnasium, scare the pee out of them, and you get these nasty, eye-watering fumes. Roland has been to the old Yankee Stadium exactly once in his life, on a church-sponsored outing for troubled youths, and the stadium lavatories smelled a lot like this, overflowing with urine and puked-up beer. No beer stink today, so it could be worse. And if the little brats are weeping and wailing—

and many of them are—he can't hear a thing, thanks to the Black Sabbath tracks bruising his eardrums. Turns out to be a good idea, the iPod, providing a useful soundtrack to events that have been ever so carefully orchestrated. Helps him concentrate. *Leave the earth to Satan and his knaves.* Yeah. Go Ozzy.

As to the plan, so carefully conceived by The Voice, so far so good. The essential action, taking out the cue-ball cop, had proved even easier than Roland had imagined. He's destroyed the man thousands of times in his imagination, sometimes roasting him alive, but this had been as simple as raising the weapon and applying the slightest pressure on the customized trigger. What with the music pumping through his earbuds, he never even heard the pop. And old cue ball went down like a puppet with cut strings. Roland was expecting him to be blown backward, like in the movies, but the reality was he simply dropped where he stood, dead before he hit the floor.

True, there was a disturbing amount of blood, but Roland managed not to obsess on that, and whipped the blue tarp out of his handy little cart, covering both the body and the blood, exactly as he had been instructed. Out of sight, out of mind. Besides, it felt really good, knowing his old nemesis was no longer in the world. And when he saw the stricken looks of shock and horror coming from all those little faces in the stands, and the teachers recoiling in fear, man, he got pumped. What I'm talkin' about, dude! Carpe diem like the book said. Seize the day. Make it your own. Establish who you are and what you desire. Ignore all contrary voices, tune them out, find your inner voice and concentrate on what you want. Visualize it. Make it so.

And he'd done it, he'd made it so. Told the stubby little principal to take the chains and padlocks he'd provided. She had followed his command, chained the exit doors, and then when a glimpse of defiance flashed in her beady little eyes, he promptly cuffed her with the late cue ball's own official cop cuffs and commanded that she sit down, shut up, or get tarped. After that she was compliant, didn't have the courage to look him in the eye.

"Listen up, toadstools! Anybody moves, I open fire, okay? And when the clip is empty, I detonate the bomb! Did I mention the bomb? No? Well, I got a bomb. And it's really cool. Fifty pounds of C-4, which is enough to turn you all into jelly beans!"

Roland is unaware that with the music blasting, he's shouting in a way that makes him sound like a raving madman. A babbling, out-of-control psycho. But that makes him all the more effective. None of his captives doubt that he will kill again at the slightest provocation.

"So stay in your seats!" he shouts. "Don't move! You want to use your phones, make a few calls, go ahead! Let 'em know I got it under control!"

He raises his other hand, showing off the Sony TV remote he has cleverly modified, guided by The Voice. "See this! It's a detonator! Tell all your friends! Press this button, we all go boom!"

Roland and The Voice had debated the cell phone issue when the plan was being formulated. At first Roland thought he should confiscate all the phones, take control of communication, but The Voice reminded him how difficult that might be. Many of the teachers would have cells, a lot of the kids might have them stashed, and texting made it easy to send messages without being obvious. One man couldn't search all those kids and teachers, not by himself, and the whole purpose of the plan was that he do it alone, his own personal one-man show. Thus proving that he was ready to move on to the next level.

So the idea was, embrace the captives' ability to communicate with the outside world. No need for Roland to use his own cell, or share his own identifying vocal patterns with the authorities. Let little Kelly or Timmy make the call. That way he can concentrate on managing the situation, not get distracted by some dippy hostage negotiator. *Excuse me, Mr. Penny, would you kindly step into our telescopic sights?* No way. The Voice was right. Let the communication flow. Concentrate on the plan. Execute.

And whatever you do, don't look at the tarp, or what seems to be flowing out from under it.

"People think I'm insane because I'm drowning all the time!" he shouts, unaware that he's singing along with the heavy-metal lyrics pounding into his head. "Can you help me occupate my brain?" he screams. "Oh *yeah!*"

He's right. Everybody in the gymnasium, students and teachers, and staff, they all think he's totally insane.

11. The Calculus Of Heaven

Noah is pretty sure what it means to be turned into jelly beans. That's what happens when a bomb goes off. You get blown into pieces no bigger than jelly beans. Not that he intends to explain it to the other kids, many of whom are confused about what the crazy bad man said. Jelly beans? Is the bad man going to give us candy?

Noah is not even slightly confused by what has happened. He gets it. He understands that none of this is pretend. The bad man is not a funny clown; he's a killer. It's all very real. The bad man really shot the white-gloved policeman and then quickly covered the body with a blue tarp. The bad man made Mrs. K lock the exit doors, weaving bright new chains through the push bars. The bad man keeps waving his ugly black gun, alternating between making threats and singing along with his stupid iPod.

One other thing Noah understands. The crazy bad man is getting worse, more crazy. He's shouting things about Satan being inside his brain. He's raging about cell phones, and the importance of letting the whole world know what's going on, and some of the other kids are madly texting, as if the act of communicating what the bad man says will save them. Noah isn't so sure about that. He thinks the bad man might really do it. He might press the button and turn them all into sticky red jelly beans. Then all of them would go to heaven—or not—Noah hasn't decided yet about heaven, whether it really exists or whether it's like Santa Claus, to make people feel better. He likes to think of his father as being in heaven, but if his dad was really in a place like that, wouldn't he find some way to let his son know? Unless there are rules, and Noah supposes there might be, rules about not talking to those left behind. Rules as complicated and hard as calculus. He knows calculus exists because Mrs. Delancey has a book about it in her desk and Noah sneaked a look, and to his surprise could not immediately understand the contents. Whatever it is, calculus is more than arithmetic, more than algebra, more than geometry—it's all of them mashed together, making something completely different, but at the same time tantalizingly familiar. Differentials? What are those? The formulas and symbols looked intriguing, as if they might contain all the answers about everything there is to know, including whether heaven really exists.

More than anything else, Noah wants to live long enough to understand calculus, and have his mom read him a bedtime story, and get up and have breakfast, and go to school as if nothing bad had ever happened. So he's thinking really hard about what to do. How to get away without being turned into jelly beans, or doing something that will turn Mrs. Delancey into jelly beans.

Meanwhile the bad man rages at them.

"I see a black moon rising and it's calling out my name!" he shouts, bobbing his head and pretending to strum an air guitar like on Guitar Hero. Then the bad man seems to correct himself, like a funny skip on a DVD. "Text the world, I want to get off! They'll be coming round the mountain, boys and girls!" Then, shouting so loud he spits: "Don't move! I swear to the prophet, I WILL BLOW THIS BITCH!"

Now he's waving around the detonator button, pointing at it with his gun as he grins, showing all of his small yellow teeth. He holds the pose for a few beats, as if he knows that his picture is being captured on cells.

"Noah?"

Somehow Mrs. Delancey has slipped along the bench and is beside him, a comforting presence, a still point in the chaos of fear and confusion that radiates from everybody in the gym, including the bad man. She pitches her voice for him alone, her mouth a mere inch from his ear. "I want you to go and hide," she whispers. "Hide in the air duct, Noah, like you did before. Can you do that for me?"

"I'm scared to move."

She hugs him. At this moment, in this place, she smells like home. Like flowers and bread and home. And so he doesn't want to leave her side. Doesn't want to risk doing something wrong. Something that will make the bad man press his crazy button and send them all to heaven.

"Listen to me, Noah," Mrs. Delancey says in her beautiful, lilting voice. "He's not focused on anything but himself. All you have to do, slip down through the space between the benches, like you did before. He won't be able to see you. Hide, Noah, please? For me? Hide in the air ducts, okay? I'll come to find you when all this is over."

"You promise?"

"I promise. Now go."

As the bad man raises his fist, shaking the detonator and screaming something about children of the grave, Noah slips under the bench, through the narrow gap, into the stands. Into the familiar geometry of the supports and trusses that hold up the benches. The last time he did this, slipped away into the space under the stands during an assembly, he got in a lot of trouble. Mrs. K was really upset with him then, told him he might have been injured and nobody would have known where to look for him. Noah thought it was pretty funny, the way he'd run along under the benches, tugging at dangling feet to make the girls giggle and shriek. Mrs. K didn't think it was funny at all and his mom had to come to the school and take him home. But that was last year. Things were different last year. He was younger then and he didn't have Mrs. Delancey. Mrs. Delancey who understands him, and wants to save him.

Hiding in the air ducts sounds like a really good idea. It will be snug and cozy in there. Noah discovered the attractions of the ducts last year, when he brought an adjustable screwdriver to school, removed a metal grate, and then shinnied around on his tummy, just as he'd seen in the movies, where air ducts were often a means of secret escape. The big difference was that the ducts at school were way too small for anybody even slightly larger than he was—Matt Damon wouldn't ever fit, no way!—and they didn't really go much of anywhere useful. Retreat a few feet and you ran into a fan, baffle, or filter system. So basically they were good for hiding in the classroom and making spooky echo noises to amuse your classmates. *This is the booger monster and I'm coming to get you ooh ooh ooh!* Even Mrs. K couldn't keep a straight face when she marched him to the office. *Booger monster?* she had said, breaking up. *Where do you get this stuff?*

What Noah knew from his previous experience, and what Mrs. Delancey obviously knew, as well—there were a couple of fairly large duct openings under the stands. Part of the circulation system for the sock-smelling gym. He hadn't attempted to access the ducts at the time—it was too much fun tugging on dangling feet—but once he climbs down to the floor beneath the stands—there's *pee* dripping down from the benches, ick!—he makes a beeline for the wall, locates one of the ducts.

The duct is, like all the others, covered by a metal grate. The problem is, he no longer carries the adjustable screwdriver. Because of his previous 'behavioral problems,' the screwdriver set has been forbidden. Too much like a weapon, they said. He might poke out somebody's eye. To which his mom had said all he needs for that is a pencil. Wrong answer. For a whole week they didn't let him have pencils and he had to fill in the answers with a crayon, like a baby! And his mom was so mad she cried.

Noah has some change in his pockets, but none of the coins fits the special slots on the screws that hold the metal grate in place. He's hurrying because the crazy bad man is shouting again. Scary shouting that doesn't make sense.

"Don't mess with success! Heed the prophet! I bite the heads off bats! Leave the earth to Satan and his slaves! Into the void, boys and girls! Into the void!"

A moment later there are gunshots, and children screaming. Teachers, too. Is that Mrs. Delancey? Has something happened to Mrs. Delancey? Has she been punished for helping him escape?

Fighting his fear, Noah creeps to the front edge of the gymnasium seating on his hands and knees and looks out through a slot between the benches.

The crazy man is running around in circles, firing his gun straight up in the air. He looks as frightened as the screaming children. Smoke is pouring out of his little janitor cart. Huge amounts of thick black smoke, billowing over the floor and into the stands.

The crazy man kicks at the cart as if he wants the smoke to stop, as if he doesn't understand what's going on. That's the really weird thing. He looks genuinely puzzled. He looks scared.

When the smoke begins to filter under the stands, enough to make him cough and make his eyes sting, Noah retreats back to the air duct.

Stupid people taking away his screwdriver! He hooks his fingers into the metal grate and yanks with all his might.

To his surprise the grate swings open on its hinges. He climbs inside just as the whole building begins to shake and the air goes black with smoke.

12. Out Of The Smoke

When Jed proposed, he sealed the deal with his grandmother's wedding ring. A thin band of gold set with a diamond about as big as a grain of sand. But if I'd ever had any doubts—and who doesn't have a few?—that little old ring blew them away. A man you love more than anything, more than you can possibly describe, he drops to one knee with tears of joy in his gorgeous eyes, and he offers you not only a place in his heart, but a place in his most precious memories.

A girl just has to say yes. Actually I didn't stop saying yes for about half an hour, and by then we were in bed, and, come to think of it, I was still saying yes. But that's private. You don't need to know.

What really matters was that Jed trusted me without reservation, holding nothing back. The proposal of marriage came with an escape clause. He was going to tell me a secret, a terrible secret, and if I wanted to back out, forget the whole thing, he'd understand.

And that's the thing about Jedediah; he really would have understood. Because it wasn't just the secret, it was what it meant about our future together. Marriage would mean leaving everything behind—friends, family—and making a new life.

First thing I asked him, joking: you mean like the witness protection program?

He'd nodded gravely and said yes, a little bit like that, except we'll be totally on our own. No U.S. Marshals to protect us. Nobody to give us new identities or settle us into a new life. It will all be up to us alone.

So who did you kill? I asked.

He'd rolled his eyes at that—he got a kick out of what he called my 'smart-mouth jokes'—and said, it's nothing I did, it's who I am. Who my father is.

So who's your daddy? Tony Soprano?

And that's when he told me who his father was, and what that meant, and after he was done, as he waited gravely for my answer, I kissed his eyes and said, didn't you hear me the first ten thousand times? The answer is yes.

Saint Francis of Hoboken, patron saint of New Jersey, he said, regrets, I've had a few. Not me. Even after all we went through, I have no regrets. Not about saying yes. Not about loving Jed. Not about the life we lived, the baby we made, the time we had together. What would I be if I'd never met Jedediah? Another person, surely. Not Noah's mother, that's for sure.

And if I'd known Jed would be gone in twelve years, snatched away in one terrible instant? If instead of an unforeseeable fatal accident he'd had, say, a disease that would shorten his lifespan. Something we knew about from the start. Would I have said no and saved myself the loss, the pain? No, no, no. No matter how you make the calculation—and all of this has raced through my mind a million times, in every possible variation—I would never choose to erase those years. Would never, ever wish

I had taken another path. You can't truly love someone and make a choice based on how long he might live. Love isn't something that can be rated by *Consumer Reports*—go with the Maytag or whatever, because it will last the longest with fewest repairs. That's not how it works. We like to think we're rational creatures but we're not. And besides, when you're twenty, twelve years seems like an eternity. It seems, indeed, like a lifetime well worth having.

And it was, it was. I swear on my wedding ring. So forgive me if I admit that when the smoke starts pouring from the building, my first reaction is that I'd rather die than endure this again. I simply can't do it. If Noah doesn't come out of that gym alive, I want my heart to stop beating. I want to go wherever he's gone.

It starts amid the swarm of uniforms. The county SWAT team, the state police tactical units. Deputies, firefighters, all positioned around the gym like bees desperate to return to a hive. I'm on my feet by then, with my friend Helen providing moral support, gathered with the other parents just beyond the bounds of the police barricade.

Until that moment I thought 'gnawing on your knuckles' was just an expression. It's Helen who gently draws my fist away before I draw blood.

"That's Tommy crouching by the exit doors," Helen says with obvious pride. "He's the unit expert on surveillance devices. He's threading a fiber-optic device through the door frame, so they can see what's going on inside."

"You can tell all that from here?" I ask, my eyes still blurry and swollen.

She squeezes my hand. "Just my assumption, dear.

That's what Tommy does, so I assume he's doing it now. Plus I saw him with an electric drill in his hand."

I'm not reassured. "Remember what happened at Columbine? They waited and waited and waited. Kids bled to death while they waited."

"They've learned a lot since then," she says soothingly. "Tommy's unit studies Columbine. They won't make the same mistake."

"Or they'll break in too soon and he'll set off his bomb."

"Your little boy will be okay." She gives me a quick hug. "You'll see."

I can't blame her for believing that her nephew can work miracles, and I've no doubt he'll try, like all of the others swarming the building. They have one thing in mind, to save the lives of our precious children. But I can't help fearing the worst.

God help me, what I fear most is that Noah will make himself the center of attention. Which is what he tends to do when he's unhappy or under stress. He tries to relieve the tension by doing something silly. Which would be exactly the wrong thing to do around a violent, insane individual.

Please, Noah, don't make a joke. Don't hang erasers on your ears, or scratch under your arms like a monkey. For once in your life blend into the background. Be invisible. Your mother is begging you.

That's just about when the smoke starts coming out from under the doors. At first just a whiff, barely there. But smoke, definitely. Was anybody else seeing it? Are my exhausted eyes playing tricks?

Beside me, Helen mutters, "Oh, no," and then covers her mouth with her hand, her eyes bright with fear.

"Oh my god, there's a fire!" someone shrieks. "He's lit the school on fire!"

The crowd begins to keen. Even Helen, my rock, is crying. And me, I'm running through the barricade, spinning away from outstretched hands, with a single purpose in mind. I'm going to smash open an exit door with my own body and get inside.

As it happens, Helen's nephew Tommy and his fellow state troopers are way ahead of me. They know what smoke means, too. Before I get anywhere near an exit door a couple of big guys smash through with a battering ram and a moment later about a dozen tactical officers run into the smoke wearing headgear and full-face masks.

Then I'm down, tackled and held by the ankles; all I can do is watch as great billows of black smoke pour from the opening. Behind me the whole crowd is screaming and shouting, but it sounds like background noise because all of my attention is focused on the exit door. On wanting Noah to come racing out of the smoke.

There are a few popping noises. Gunshots. Just a few. Maybe they got the guy and it's over. Or maybe it wasn't a gunshot. Maybe something exploded in the fire.

They breach another pair of doors and firefighters race into the smoke dragging hoses. Shouting orders, directing the rescue efforts—*Over here! Pressure up! Full mask SCBAs! Bring in the air caddys!*

The smoking doorways are thick with emergency responders. All of them diving into the dark, no hesitation. Doing all that can be done, that's obvious even to a desperate, overwrought mom like me.

Please, God, please. Let Noah be safe. Let all of them be safe.

An eternity passes and then suddenly, miraculously, children begin to pour out of the building. They come through the smoke like little football players ripping apart a dark, billowing banner, eager for a game. Or eager to find their mothers, their fathers.

Child after child emerges from the smoke.

Whoever has me by the ankles finally relents and I'm up, staggering to the gym with all the other parents—there's no holding us back now—and child after child is swept up into loving arms. Most of the kids are crying and some of them are coughing, but the smoke, for all its ropy thickness, doesn't seem to be all that bad. Worse on the eyes than the throat. And it doesn't smell of fire, which is strange.

I'm calling out for Noah. At the top of my lungs, I don't doubt. But I might as well be shouting into a raging hurricane because my voice can't rise above the din. Noah! Noah! Noah!

Watching as the kids, by some amazing instinct, seem to gravitate like little iron filings to the magnet of their mothers' arms. Like all the others, I have my arms out, waiting for them to be filled with my little boy.

I wait and wait and wait and still he does not come. The only people still coming out of the gym are firefighters and cops. Have I somehow missed him? Is he back there in the parking lot, absorbed into the joyous crowd?

"My son!" I scream at a startled firefighter. "Where is my son?"

He rips off his mask, tells me the gym is clear. "We got

them all," he assures me. "There isn't any fire, just a smoke device of some kind. Not even toxic," he adds. "So he's got to be out here somewhere. Come on, let's find him, you and me. It'll be okay. I promise."

A young, earnest fireman with a farm-boy face, anxious to help and pumped because the rescue went off like clockwork. All that training paid off. He seems so assured, so certain that all the children were rescued, that I let him steer me away from the exit doors, heading back to the crowd.

We're thirty yards or so from the gym when it explodes in a ball of fire, blasting me into darkness.

Part II
Mad Mom

1. Six Weeks Later

The bank teller thinks I'm nuts. It's there in her eyes. Which means she's heard about me. The crazy mom from Humble, the one whose son got blown up in the school. The one who won't accept reality, who keeps handing out pictures to strangers. The one folks will cross the street to avoid, if at all possible.

"How would you like this, Mrs. Corbin?"

"A bank check would be fine," I tell her.

She doesn't want to make eye contact. As if looking me in the eye might somehow be dangerous. As if crazy is catching. "Who should I make it out to?" she asks warily.

"Make it out to 'cash.'"

"Cash? That, uh, that means anyone can endorse it."

"I know what it means."

She's troubled by the transaction and goes off to confer with her supervisor. Who glances over at me and shrugs. I'm no lip reader, but it's pretty obvious what she says to the nervous teller: *It's her money.*

Two minutes later I'm out of there, check in my purse.

Which leaves me plenty of time for the twenty-three-mile drive back home. Plenty of time for me to think about what I'm going to say to the man after giving him the check.

Wondering how much time ten thousand dollars will buy me.

He's expected, having called not ten minutes ago, looking for directions. But still the doorbell makes me jump. Everything makes me jump these days—cars backfiring, thunderclaps, loud whistles, whatever.

A glance in the peephole confirms my visitor's identity. Randall Shane, retired Special Agent of the Federal Bureau of Investigation, now working as a civilian consultant, if you can get him. Type *missing child hopeless case* into Google and up pops Mr. Shane. Legendary in law enforcement circles, supposedly. Gets results when no one else can. A blurry head shot on a Web site gave me a vague idea of what he looks like, but nothing has prepared me for the man on my front porch pressing the bell.

He's huge. Lean but large.

When I crack open the door he introduces himself and then says, "You must be Haley Corbin. If I've got the right place."

"You've got the right place.... Come in."

He ducks his head as he comes through the doorway. The farmhouse ceilings are low and he doesn't clear the old fir beams by all that much.

"Good thing you've got a crew cut," I tell him. "Another inch you'd be bumping your head."

Startled, he looks up and touches a big hand to a beam.

"Nah," he says gently, "plenty of room. You've got seven feet at least. That leaves me five or six inches. All the room in the world."

"It might be better if you sit down," I suggest, indicating a pumpkin-pine leaf table in the kitchen. "Coffee?"

"Coffee would be great."

I get busy with the coffeemaker. "Was it a long drive?"

"Not so bad," he says, carefully settling onto a spindle-back chair as if he's afraid it might collapse under him.

"Must have been six hours, if you came up through Binghamton."

"Seven," he says, touching a hand to a neatly trimmed Vandyke that's delicately streaked with gray. "I stopped for lunch. More like a late breakfast, actually. They have a nice diner there, in Binghamton. Danny's Diner, on Main Street. It's an old Sterling."

"Excuse me?"

"Sorry. A Sterling diner," he explains. "Manufactured by the J. B. Judkins Company. I'm kind of a diner fan. They evolved from lunch wagons. I like lunch wagons, too, but there's not many left."

"Here you are. Cream or milk?"

"Just black," he says. "That way I know what I'm getting."

We smile at each other as he sips the coffee. He's trying to smile as though it's every day he drives all the way across the state of New York to chat with a crazy mom. I'm trying to smile as though I'm not actually deranged and therefore he won't be wasting his time.

"Very good," he says, tipping the cup.

"I've got the check I promised you," I tell him, fumbling in my purse.

He sets the cup down. "This is a courtesy call," he says firmly. "No retainer necessary. I thought I made that clear."

"Take it," I insist, more or less blurting it out. "Ten thousand dollars if you'll listen to my story. Really listen."

I place the envelope on the table between us. He leans forward, ignoring the envelope. "No charge for listening, Mrs. Corbin."

I take a deep breath. "Just so you know, money isn't a problem. My husband had a million-dollar rider on his life insurance. Plus what the airline paid after the crash. All of it's available, if that's what it takes."

"We're not there yet," he says.

There's a distinct vibe coming off the big man. I get the impression that money is never Shane's prime concern.

"You read the media reports?" I ask anxiously. "Clicked on the links I sent you?"

He nods. His eyes are an unusual shade of pale blue. Clear and cool and liquid, the color of melting icicles. According to the brief bio I found on the Web, he's in his late forties. But broad of shoulder, long of limb, he looks remarkably fit for any age, and I'm pretty sure my first impression was correct: he's a little shy, physically, maybe overly conscious of his size. A big guy who would by nature prefer to blend in, but can't. A gentle giant type.

Let's hope not too gentle. I need a warrior, someone who will stand up and fight against overwhelming odds.

"So," I ask, "what do you think?"

Now he's the one to take a deep breath. "It all seems pretty straightforward. Your son was killed in an explosion. His remains have been identified. A DNA analysis from a reputable lab confirms the finding."

I nod carefully, concentrate on keeping my cool. Knowing that a meltdown will send him packing, taking with him all hope of ever seeing my little boy again. "That's what it says in the reports. That there's no doubt."

"But you have doubts."

"More than doubts," I say, adamantly. "Certainties."

"Sudden death is always difficult for the survivors," he points out.

"When my husband died, I accepted."

"The death of a child is different. It goes against all the rules."

"They never found his body. Did you read the coroner's report? All they found were a few bits of tissue, a few drops of blood."

"Bombs are the worst, Mrs. Corbin. Sometimes there's almost nothing left."

I know all about nothing left.

"When my husband's plane crashed it hit the ground at three hundred miles an hour," I tell him. "That's what they estimated. Collision with a small plane sheared off one whole wing of an Embraer 190. Spinning down at three hundred miles an hour, can you imagine? The fuel tanks exploded on impact. The wreckage was strewn for half a mile. They had to identify his body through dental records."

He nods, grim-faced. "That's pretty standard."

"Dental records," I repeat. "So even after a plane falls two miles and explodes into the earth there were still teeth to identify. An intact lower jaw. That's why they went with the dental records."

"What a terrible thing," he says softly, as if he has

some idea what it must have been like, making that ID. "I'm so sorry."

"Teeth, a jaw," I say, listing the gruesome details. "Enough to identify, enough to convince me. But there was nothing left of Noah. Nothing. Not a hand, not a finger, not a tooth. Not a fingernail, for that matter. The coroner said he must have been right on top of the C-4 when it detonated. He'd never seen anything like it, not in thirty years as a coroner and medical examiner. They found enough of Roland Penny for positive identification. Same for Chief Gannett. But not one identifiable body part that would be linked to Noah. Until the DNA results came back."

He sighs, grimacing behind his short, salt-and-pepper beard. "DNA analysis is definitive, Mrs. Corbin. The odds are a million to one."

"More like a billion. Unless they've been faked."

He gives me a searching look. Not dismissively, but as if he really wants to know. "Why would the results be faked?"

"To make it look like my son has been killed, when in fact he's been abducted."

To give him credit, Mr. Shane does not break eye contact. He's not obviously repulsed by what most have judged magical thinking. The grieving mom can't cope with losing her little boy and so her poor addled brain creates scenarios wherein her child somehow remains alive, against all odds, against all reason.

"Go on," he says, not needing to add *convince me.* That's a given. That's why he has traveled all those miles. To hear me out. To be convinced he isn't wasting his time.

"It has to do with my husband," I begin. "Who he was and what he told me a year or so before he died."

Shane sits up a little straighter. I already had his attention but now he's focused. "Go on."

"Jed lived under an alias since before we married. His real name was Arthur Jedediah Conklin. 'Corbin' wasn't much of a change but it was enough to hide his real identity."

"And why did your husband feel the need to change his identity?"

"Because his father is Arthur D. Conklin."

It takes a moment for the name to register, but when it does his eyebrows twitch. "The Arthur D. Conklin?"

I nod.

"Well, that changes everything."

2. The Promise

Randall Shane stands up, rubs the back of his neck.

"I need to make a call and then I need to stretch my legs and think," he announces, his manner formal and coolly polite. "I'll take it outside."

Arms crossed, I hunker down in my chair, a blacker mood descending. All this hope centered on one person, a person I've never even met until minutes ago, and already he's about to walk out the door. What did I expect? That he'd instantly take my side? That he'd believe me when everyone else thinks I've been demented by grief?

Did I really think this man, supposedly a legend in law enforcement, would take up my cause like some knight in shining armor—or in his case khaki slacks and Topsiders? I don't know whether to laugh or cry, but come to think of it, laughter is not in the cards for me lately. I can't recall what it actually feels like. As for crying, sorry but I've dried myself up. Tears are now a luxury I can't afford.

Perhaps sensing my frustration, the big man pauses at the door and says, "I don't mean to sound like the Terminator, but I'll be back. Promise."

"After you make your call," I retort through gritted teeth.

He shrugs. "I need to consult with someone I trust."

"Because you're afraid of Arthur Conklin and the Rulers."

Shane doesn't exactly deny it. Instead he carefully explains, "More wary than afraid. All I know about Arthur Conklin and the Rulers and the Conklin Institute is whatever makes it into the media—that whole reclusive billionaire thing—like it's public knowledge that his followers treat him like some sort of god or prophet. I'm aware he employs a huge team of attorneys and is famous for suing just about anybody at the drop of a hat. Anyone who *isn't* wary of a litigious, wealthy cult leader isn't thinking clearly. I need to think clearly or I can't be of help. Also, I really need to stretch my legs—I get cramps from sitting too long in the car. Give me ten minutes, Mrs. Corbin."

"Fine," I say. "But take this with you."

I open my purse and hand him a picture of Noah. A cheerful school photo taken at the beginning of the semester. I've printed up hundreds, handed them out in every village, town, and city within a five-hour driving radius, my name and cell number on back. Which so far has proved about as useful as those pictures of lost kids you see on milk cartons.

He looks at the photo thoughtfully and carries it with him, out the door.

I watch from the kitchen window, willing him to believe. It must be my heightened mothering instincts kicking in, because despite my frustration and anger—I saw the doubt in his eyes!—my first thought is that he's not appropriately dressed for the weather. No coat or hat, and a thin flannel shirt that barely cuts the wind. And we get a wicked wind in the North Country at this time of year. The dark days of December, when the sun rises late and begins to fade like a dimmed-out lightbulb by midafternoon. You need insulated boots, not deck shoes. You need to cover your ears. At the very least you need an insulated vest.

At least most of us do. The big man's breath steams as he talks into his little phone, but other than that he doesn't seem aware of the cold air. Not so much as a shiver. Nearly noon, the warmest part of the day, and it's barely thirty-one degrees.

He's aware I'm watching and raises a friendly hand, smiles at me while he talks.

Yeah, I got a sad case here. Crazy as a bedbug. Thinks there's been some big conspiracy because she can't find enough of her kid to bury.

Some variation of that. He won't be the first law enforcement guy to try and let me down easy. Usually they suggest I 'see someone.' Meaning get yourself fitted for a strait-jacket, honey. Take some pills, zone yourself out. One of the New York State Police investigators who came around at my insistence put it bluntly: *Sorry, ma'am, but blown-up isn't the same as missing. Missing means there's a chance the victim is still alive, however remote. Blown-up with positive DNA match means you need to talk to God, not me.*

I did talk to God, you bet I did, but God didn't respond, being too busy directing typhoons, earthquakes, epidemics, and ethnic cleansing. So currently I'm no longer speaking to Supreme Beings, and I refuse to take comfort in pretty notions like heaven. Not when I know in my soul that my little boy is alive somewhere. Alive and missing me almost as much as I miss him.

That's what I believe.

After pocketing his phone, Randall Shane circumnavigates the house. Eating up yards with his long legs, swinging his long arms. Ignoring the dusting of snow on the partially frozen ground. Might as well be walking a warm beach in the sunshine instead of this cold, soggy reality. As he comes by each window he smiles and waves as if to say, look at me, I'm stretching my legs, just like I said.

Trying to figure out how to make his excuses, beat a hasty retreat.

I have the front door open as he comes around the house for the third time.

"Enough," I say, and he enters, somewhat sheepish.

"The air is good up here. Gives you a real clean feeling in the lungs."

"I'm *not* crazy or delusional," I announce, marching around the leaf table the way he marched around my house. Hugging myself to force calm as I make my argument. "I know children can die. It may go against nature but it happens all the time. Disease, accidents, even murder. It happens. But it didn't happen to Noah. It just didn't."

"Mind if I get some water?"

"Help yourself," I say, gesturing at the glass-fronted cupboard.

He pours a glass from the tap. Drinks it, every drop. "Good water, too. I can see why folks live up here, this close to the North Pole."

"Say what you've got to say," I urge him. "I can't stand this. Not knowing if you'll help."

He leans against the sink. "*Help* is a big word," he says, very carefully. "I'm going to look into something but it may not help. You should know that."

"Look into what?"

From his hesitation I pick up that he's not sure whether or not he should be specific, to safeguard my feelings. Finally he nods to himself and goes, "The lab. I made a call. Confirmed that the DNA lab the State Police used has an excellent reputation. State-of-the-art facility, supposedly. Very unlikely they've been compromised or somehow got it wrong."

"But possible," I insist. "If Noah is alive they could plant a sample of his blood, right?"

Shane looks skeptical. "We'll see. If I'm satisfied the lab work is correct, and your son was killed in the explosion, that's the end of it."

"It will never be the end."

"Let me ask you this, Mrs. Corbin. If your son was hit by a car crossing the street, would you blame the grandfather or his cult followers? Bad things happen sometimes, regardless of wealth or connections."

"You don't have to tell me that! I know that! But if Noah was hit by a car his body would still be here!" I point out, aware that my voice has gone high and loud. "Noah *wasn't killed* in that explosion. Nobody believes me, but I know he wasn't."

"Okay," he says.

"You want to know how I know?"

He nods.

"Because of what Jed said. Months before the plane went down he said if he ever disappeared, ever vanished without an explanation, it would be because of his father. Because he'd been taken."

"Your late husband knew your son was in danger?" he asks, looking startled.

"No. No. Jed meant if *he* disappeared. Jed himself. Then he laughed, because it was such a crazy idea, that he'd be abducted because of his own father. That the Rulers would want him, of all people—a man who disinherited his own father, cut all ties. What would they want with him? But it wasn't crazy, was it? Jed died and they took Noah instead—Arthur Conklin's only living descendent. And they did it in a way that means nobody will look for him. Nobody but me. I know it sounds like a fantastic conspiracy, sending a madman into a school to blow it up so they can steal a child. But it happened. They did it."

Oh yes, I'm aware of how it must all seem, the paranoid rant of a mother driven mad by loss. But give him credit: Randall Shane didn't flash me that look. The look I'd seen on the faces of so many cops and detectives. The look that said, best get away, leave this one to her misery.

Instead he nods and says, "I'll look into it, Mrs. Corbin. Whatever I find, I won't lie to you. Good, bad, or terrible, I won't lie to you. That's all I can promise."

3. Letter Of Proof

A few minutes later he's driving away in his black Lincoln Town Car. A big boat of a vehicle that tacks slowly out of my long, unpaved driveway, bumping carefully over the frost heaves before finally turning onto the main road and vanishing around a long curve.

Anybody else, I'd figure he's gone for good. But Shane looked me in the eye and promised that whatever he decided he would return and tell me in person.

Which gives me something to cling to. He said it would take a day or so to check out the lab. So I've got one more day's worth of hope. Hope that he'll find something, maybe just a hint that maybe the crazy mom is onto something.

He did say an odd thing before folding himself into the big car. "You sure your husband told you the truth? That Arthur Conklin really was his father?"

My first reaction, knowing Jed, was to blurt, "Why would he lie?"

The big guy shrugged. "People have their reasons. Rich, famous people, it's not exactly unusual when someone makes a claim to be related. They may even believe it. It happened with Howard Hughes, James Brown, JFK. Lots of famous and powerful people. I'll bet, you go back far enough, it happened with the pharaohs."

"Jed didn't *want* to be related to that horrible man. He was trying to get away."

"Have you ever been contacted by Conklin or his organization? Any of his so-called Rulers?"

Shivering in the cold, I shake my head.

"Something to think about," he says before powering up the window.

Hours later that's all I can think about.

Midnight finds me in the attic, going through boxes. Not in a frenzy, nothing like that. I'm being very cool and methodical. Some rational, robotic part of me has taken over and begun conducting a search for evidence that Jedediah hadn't invented his connection to the father he sometimes called Monster Man. Monster Man not because Jed had ever been physically abused, but because his father had such monstrous ideas about human behavior.

There will be no recent correspondence, no original birth certificate, of that I'm almost certain. Jed burned all of that, his little hoard of what he called "sick memorabilia," before we moved upstate. Eventually he obtained a legal passport—he had to have one for his job—but the required birth certificate had been altered from Conklin to Corbin. And that document he had forged before we met, while he was still attending Rutgers, already planning for a complete break with his cold and domineering father and the devoted followers who called themselves Rulers. According to Jed, no contact had been attempted in years. Not from his father or any of the Rulers. Certainly not since Noah was born. So it's not as if we had saved Christmas cards from dear old Dad.

Jed had wanted a clean break and part of it was giving up the things that linked him to his past. But he hadn't thrown everything away, because shortly after he proposed, after confessing to be the son of Arthur Conklin, *the* Arthur Conklin, Jed had read me a letter the legendary man had written to him years before, when Jed was twelve years old. A letter that pretty much explained what happened between them, although the actual, final break didn't come until several years later, after Jed's mother died and his father remarried.

The letter certainly existed at the time, of this I am certain. I have a clear image of it in my mind. It was creased, well-worn, resided in a tattered, folded envelope.

For a long time Jed carried it in his wallet, as a reminder of why he'd made the break. That much I recall, Jed flapping it around as he read—come to think of it, he had it pretty much memorized—offering it as proof positive that cutting himself off from his famous father was something he had to do. Within the last few years he'd stopped carrying the letter. I know this because I bought him a nice ostrich skin wallet for his last birthday and watched as he transferred all his cards and cash, and I recall thinking to myself, he's finally put away the letter, that's good.

Unless he threw it away. But somehow I don't think so. Somehow I think that if it ever came up with Noah, why he'd never met his grandfather, Jed would have wanted to show him, just as he'd shown me.

One o'clock in the morning comes and goes. Amazing how much stuff we've stowed in the attic. Boxes of canceled checks, bills, credit card receipts, tax forms. Tons of my own family junk, from broken dolls to obituary notices for both my parents, plus all the condolence cards, neatly sorted and bound with elastic bands. Which had, no surprise, disintegrated in the summer attic heat. The elastic bands, I mean, not the cards. Hallmark greetings live forever, apparently. Plus every sketch and coloring book Noah had ever made, from day care on.

I spend hours going through Noah's drawings, reliving kindergarten, first grade, second grade, and so on. Right up to the last, furious drawings he'd made of a black plane falling from the sky. Not crashing—never crashing in Noah's drawings—but falling like an angry leaf.

Eventually I get back to the task at hand, and just after dawn it finally reveals itself.

Jed had tucked it into one of the graphic novels he collected as a teen. *Batman: The Dark Knight Returns.* Of course, I should have known. Although he'd carried the letter as an adult, it dated from his boyhood, and so he'd stowed it away with something else that made a big impression on a twelve-year-old, namely Batman.

I hold the thing reverently, this tattered, wrinkled, finger-smudged envelope. Jedediah's name and address is handwritten, inscribed in a firm hand. The boarding school where he had been sent against his mother's wishes, and where he had been, for the first several months, miserable and homesick. Enough so that he had written to his imperious father begging to be allowed to come back home. This letter, the letter he saved as a reminder, is in response to that request.

> Jedediah—Let me be crystal clear: the answer is no. You are to remain in school. During holidays and summer break I have given instructions that you will be boarded either on campus, or, when that is not possible, elsewhere. In your letter (there are a number of misspellings, by the way) you profess to loving your parents, in particular your mother, but this is merely reflexive and typical of an as-yet-unformed mind. As an expression of self, the bonding instinct we mistakenly call love can be a powerful tool for success, but in its lesser form, as an emotional attachment to others, love tends to weaken self-interest, thereby weakening the whole. Your mother now agrees that her connection to you is only biological, mere reproduction. Therefore she does not 'love' you any more than I do. Do not attempt to contact us again until after your

> 18th birthday, by which time your brain will have matured to its final adult form, and you may finally be ready to evolve into a fully developed Ruler. Until then, any attempts at contact will be rebuffed. Phone calls will not be taken and letters will be returned unread. In the meantime, work on forming your protective carapace. Form your adult self. When in doubt consult the manual. All answers lie within. The Rule of One is the One Rule.

That's it. No formal closing, no *yours truly* or *sincerely yours*. But the handwritten signature is clear enough: *A. Conklin.* Not *Dad* or even the more formal *Father,* because terms of affection and familiarity are signs of mental weakness.

The manual he refers to is his bestselling book *The Rule of One.* All answers lie within. No ego at work there, eh? Jed almost always referred to the book itself in sarcastic or derogatory terms. *The Sociopath's Bible,* or *How to Be Selfish and Justify Your Greed in 900 Hard-to-Read Pages.* Wisecracks covering the pain. He'd grin and roll his eyes, but deep down he meant it. He'd been a late child and an only child, born after his father had already become a reclusive cult figure, and in any case the old man believed that children were meant to be observed and perhaps, if they exhibited interesting behavior, studied. But not loved. Never loved. That had been made clear.

I have to fold that horrible, inhuman letter away quickly, store it back in the envelope before my tears dissolve the only physical proof I have that Jedediah didn't lie to me about who he was and what he'd been through.

It's a relief, really, to find that I can still cry.

Randall Shane might not consider the letter proof of anything because letters can be forged, but I know it's real because I know where Jed hurt. Exactly where, and how to heal it, too.

You can't fake a thing like that, not for ten years.

Not for ten seconds.

4. A Few Drops Of Blood

According to Shane's in-dash GPS navigator, GenData Labs, Inc. is located in one of the new high-tech industrial parks situated a few miles west of the Greater Rochester International Airport. Which means it takes Shane, who habitually drives four miles an hour below the speed limit unless being chased or chasing, a little more than an hour to get there. An hour in which he listens to most of Herbie Hancock's *River* album and tries not to think about how he'll deal with Haley Corbin when he will undoubtedly have to return with the bad news.

For all he knows her little boy really was Arthur Conklin's grandchild—he'll run that down later, if need be—but her theory about the kid's survival is so far-fetched that it strains the imagination. Wealthy, powerful families, however dysfunctional, can still be victims of random tragedy. Terrible events are not necessarily spawned by vast conspiracies, no matter who is involved. For instance, no one fed Governor Nelson Rockefeller's son to cannibals in New Guinea—he got there all on his own, no conspiracy necessary. Joe Kennedy Jr., scion of the powerful Kennedy clan, risked his own life flying an insanely dangerous mission, like thousands of other brave pilots in WWII, and paid the price. No conspiracy necessary, or likely.

Sometimes a person is just in the wrong place at the wrong time. Breakfasting at Windows on the World on the wrong sunny morning in September. Shopping at the Santa Monica farmer's market when a befuddled elderly driver steps on the gas instead of the brake, killing nine, injuring more than fifty. On holiday in Phuket when a tsunami rolls in without warning. Being struck and killed by a neighbor's car. Total accident, just one of those things, even if you are the child of crime boss John Gotti. No conspiracy necessary. Bad luck doesn't discriminate on account of income level or social connections or, in this case, because the victim may have a family connection to a reclusive, charismatic billionaire with a long history of getting what he wants, no matter the cost or consequence.

Okay, Mrs. Corbin has a point, it is unusual to have so little of the remains recovered after an explosion. Unusual, but by no means unheard of. Off the top of his head Shane can think of several exceptions, including a South Carolina fireworks factory and a gas leak in a Newark tenement, each of which turned several bodies into mere molecules. Forty pounds of C-4 doesn't have the explosive power of ten thousand pounds of black powder, but it could certainly turn a small boy into blood and tissue, awful as that is to contemplate.

Not that he thinks Haley Corbin is delusional. She's a nice young woman beset by random tragedy—her husband and now her son—and she's grasping at straws and unlikely scenarios.

One thing gives him pause. In his years in the Bureau,

and especially since he left, Randall Shane has seen enough exceptions to know that rules really can be broken, conspiracies can sometimes happen, and even paranoids sometimes have real reasons to fear. So he will check out GenData and satisfy himself that the lab got it right, that Noah Corbin is no more, and that will be the end of his involvement.

That's what he keeps telling himself.

The first thing he notices, upon entering the large, one-story facility, is that security looks first-rate. Metal detector, armed guards with the sharp, neatly pressed uniforms. The guards restrict entrance to a single stream of visitors who must apply for a pass at the reception desk before attempting to enter the main building. Not that the place is inundated with visitors—at the moment there's a FedEx guy with a trolley of small boxes—samples, one assumes—and Shane himself, who smiles and makes small talk as he gets wanded.

"All the lab workers come through here?" he asks amiably.

"Sorry, sir, we can't discuss security."

"Nah, sure, course not. Just professional curiosity. I'm guessing there's another entrance for the employees. Got to be."

"You're good to go, sir. Show your pass and ID at Admin, they'll guide you to your destination."

The security seems overelaborate, actually, but he assumes it's all part of the package. Assuring the legal system that forensic samples and items going through GenData are not contaminated or tampered with. No break in the chain of custody.

After another courteous inspection of his time-stamped

pass and his driver's license, Shane is waved into a bright, cheerful office with a view of a snow-dusted field and the woods beyond. He paces along one wall, checking out the framed degrees. Very impressive indeed.

A moment later he's joined by a bright, cheerful woman who seems to be a perfect match for her office. Knee-length pleated skirt, a plain but elegant blouse, and a crisp cotton lab jacket—a 'white coat'—that somehow looks good with the ensemble. Short blond hair, pixie cut to compliment small but lovely features and big green eyes not the least obscured by very stylish glasses. Might be forty but looks years younger. All she's missing is the stethoscope and she could be a surgeon guest-starring on *ER,* the one who has a brief fling with the handsome but troubled pediatrician.

"Hilly Teeger," she announces, offering a perfectly manicured hand. "Hilly is for Hildegard, so you know why I go with Hilly. You must be the FBI guy that called ahead."

"Retired," he reminds her. "I'm a civilian now."

"I bet everybody wants to know if you played basketball. Or was it football."

"It comes up," he admits. "Neither. Not after high school."

"Do you mind taking a seat so I don't get a crick in my neck?"

Shane sits, keeps a pleasant, nonaggressive smile in place, well aware that his size can be intimidating, and that this isn't a situation where intimidation would be helpful. He can't shrink, but he can slump in his seat, make sure his voice remains on a light register.

"Pretty impressive bunch of degrees you've got there, Dr. Teeger," he begins, glancing at the wall. "Harvard, McGill, Johns Hopkins."

She waves away the compliment and leans back in her chair, keeping the desk between them. A desk that appears never to get used. "Hopkins was just a research fellowship. Lucky to get it."

"So GenData doesn't fool around. They hire a lab director, they go for the top tier."

"We do our best," she responds evenly. "This is just one of thirty-eight labs nationwide. How may we assist?"

Shane gets the distinct impression that somehow she's taking his temperature. A very careful woman and, from what's hinted in the wall display, vastly overqualified for her position. According to Google, the GenData corporation owns and runs a chain of testing facilities and does not engage in research. It's basically a lucrative, high-tech factory, processing samples. Curious that it would employ a person with her qualifications. Research fellowships not being easy to come by at Johns Hopkins, where he's pretty certain that little is left to luck.

"As I mentioned over the phone, I'm inquiring on behalf of Mrs. Haley Corbin, whose son's remains were—"

"I know who she is, Mr. Shane," she says. "The poor woman. What a horrible thing."

"Then as you know, Mrs. Corbin is concerned that the results might have been wrong. That a mistake could have been made."

"Hmm," says Hilly Teeger, not sounding even slightly surprised. "May I ask in what capacity you're representing Mrs. Corbin? Are you practicing law by any chance?"

"I'm not a lawyer. I'm a retired Special Agent."

"Ah," she says airily, as if amused by his response. "Once upon a time most FBI agents had law degrees."

"Before my time," Shane says, keeping it affable, non-threatening. "Are you concerned that Mrs. Corbin may be contemplating a lawsuit?"

"It crossed our mind. Our minds—mine and others in the company. GenData, the national entity, not this lab specifically, let me just say there have been lawsuits, okay? And not only in the forensic arena. Someone doesn't like their BRAC analysis, or how the results are presented, they think that's a basis for a lawsuit. It's not, but sometimes they think it is. This is America, after all."

"BRAC analysis?"

"Accounts for almost thirty percent of our business nationwide. We sequence DNA upon request and determine if there are mutations shown to indicate a genetic propensity for breast and/or ovarian cancer. It's an early warning system of sorts."

"This isn't about cancer, Dr. Teeger."

"That was just an example. People sue for all kinds of reasons. That's their right under the law. It's just we like to know if that's what we're dealing with."

Shane sits back, thinks about it. Something is going on, he's not sure what. "So far as I know, Mrs. Corbin is not planning a lawsuit at this time. Or any time. She simply wants to know if a mistake could have been made in the identification of her son's remains."

Hilly Teeger gives him a bright smile. "That's great about no lawsuit being contemplated. Welcome news. Let me ask you, Mr. Shane, are you an expert in genetic identification? Is that why you're representing Mrs. Corbin in this matter?"

"Not an expert, no," Shane says. "I *have* worked with

labs and with DNA identification experts in the past, while investigating crimes and also in preparing expert testimony. So I know just enough to get myself in trouble."

"But you're more or less current with lab protocols?"

He shakes his head. "No, I wouldn't say that. Tests and procedures change so quickly it's hard to keep up. Excuse me, Dr. Teeger, but was there a problem? You seem to know a lot about this particular case right off. Enough to be concerned about lawsuits."

She sighs and gives him a pained look. "I've spoken to Mrs. Corbin personally. Several times. As recently as last week, as a matter of fact. I assured her, as I'm going to assure you, that I'm one hundred percent certain that the blood spatter we tested is a match for the little boy's blood. The genetic markers are identical to a slide sample that was taken when he had his tonsils removed two years ago. Perfect match. We also tested against Mrs. Corbin's DNA, at her request—and at no charge, by the way—and again determined that the samples taken from the crime scene are from her biological son. So even if the comparison sample from the hospital had been tainted or misfiled somehow, we still know that the samples taken from the gym belong to her son, no doubt about it."

"So the blood is a slam dunk."

"I'm not crazy about sports analogies in criminal matters, but yes. Slam dunk."

"Same for the tissue?"

The beautiful doctor hesitates, covering her uncertainty with a wry smile. "Not so much," she admits. "If this ever came to trial, and I don't see how it could since the perpetrator died, we'd have to exclude the tissue match."

Shane sits up straight. The time for slumping is over. "Excuse me?"

"That's why we've been unable to comply with Mrs. Corbin's request that we retest the tissue as well as the blood."

Shane nods, wanting to give the impression he knows all about the retest request. "Yes," he says. "And why exactly was that? Retesting is pretty routine in criminal cases."

"This is embarrassing," Hilly Teeger says, studying the top of her empty desk, avoiding eye contact. "After the initial test, which showed a match, the tissue samples were accidentally incinerated. We fired the tech, of course. Obvious violation of protocol, no excuse. Fortunately the blood spatter remained intact and we have in fact retested those samples. Twice."

"But the tissue collected at the crime scene, that was incinerated?"

"Yes, it was."

"So no tissue samples remain?"

"None."

"Just a few drops of blood."

She nods, a glum look dimming her beauty. "We're very sorry," she says. "It's inexcusable, but accidents do happen."

Randall Shane isn't very sorry. Not in the least. He leaves GenData with a veritable bounce in his step. Thinking, I'll stop by the motel, do a little exploring online, and then I'll go see Mrs. Corbin and tell her the news.

How good or bad the news will be depends on what he finds in the next few hours.

5. An Indispensable Man

In Conklin, Colorado, Evangeline has an early-morning appointment with the devil. That's how she thinks of Vash, full name Bagrat Kavashi. But really that isn't his full name because he's got all these impossible-to-pronounce clan names, too, plus the various cover names he used while running his own private militia back in the old country. Whatever, there's no denying that he has a devilish smile, a way of holding his lips in a little pout that makes her feel all gushy inside.

Well, not gushy, exactly. More like horny, to be honest. Those big shoulders, those slim hips, the cocky confidence, and, yes, the deep streak of cruelty. Not that she's allowed mere physical attraction to compromise her position as the voice of the Profit. That would never do. Tongues would wag and then, inevitably, tongues would have to be removed, one way or another. And Vash, as chief of security, would have to remove them. No, no, don't go there. And certainly not before Arthur makes his final exit.

Still, she can't resist standing against the light of the rising sun when he enters her suite. Her legs apart so that he can glimpse her trim, well-toned figure through the thin fabric of her white silk robe. It will be obvious that she's naked under the robe. Letting him have a peek at heaven, just to keep him interested.

"'Scooze me," he says in his cute little accent, eyebrows raised at her attire. "Am I the early bird? Apologies!"

"No need to apologize, Vash, dear. You and I, we needn't stand on ceremony. Welcome back."

She extends her slender hand, knowing he will do that

Eastern European thing, not quite clicking his heels as he kisses the back of her hand, two fingers resting lightly upon the inside of her palm. Lingering just long enough so that she registers the soft imprint of his lips. Vash with his blue-black curl of Superman hair flopping playfully on his forehead, and the dark, calculating blaze of his eyes, she can practically hear his greedy little brain humming. Calculating the odds, counting his money, improving his status.

"Tell me everything," she breathes.

As always, he takes her literally. "No worries. Perp is dead. No evidence to follow. So state police give up on school investigation."

"I know about that, baby doll," she says, containing her impatience. "What about the lab? And the private investigator?"

"Miss Hilly Teeger knows which butter to put on her bread, no problem. This Shane you warn me about, turns out he's old guy, retired, he's got no legal power. He'll find nothing and go away very soon. If not, we take care of him, okay? For sure no problem."

"What about the woman?"

"The crazy mother? That's beautiful, because everybody, they think she really *is* crazy, you know? All the time she's talking conspiracy this, conspiracy that, everybody out to get me, sure sign of crazy. But if crazy mother gets to be big problem, we make her stop. Probably she's suicide. She puts head in oven, or maybe pipe from exhaust, something like that. Terrible tragedy. Very believable."

"She was supposed to die in the explosion, looking for her son," Evangeline points out, feeling petulant.

"Yeah, yeah, I know. But this thing happen," he says, not the least bit sheepish. "Nothing goes completely the right way, okay? Important thing, we can fix if necessary. I got people in place, no problem."

Evangeline smiles. "That's what I love about you, Vash, dear. You always have people in place. There's always no problem."

He flashes his wolflike grin. "Helps when you own big company, yes?"

"Oh yes," she says, sidling an inch or two closer. "That helps."

6. Proof Of Sanity

I'm watching the tube at ten in the morning when Randall Shane finally returns, a laptop case in one hand and a big grin on his face.

The TV has been on since I came down from the attic. Something to make background noise, keep me company. Now and then I zero in on something—Regis and Kelly are upset about *Captain Underpants*—but mostly it's a comforting drone, the soundtrack to the flash of images in my brain. Jedediah holding me when I was sick at Chili's—stupid girl!—except I know he never actually held me, not then, but it's nice to pretend he did, it helps me with the grief. And Noah looking up from his Cocoa Puffs, asking about zip codes and the black pulse of the bomb going off, over and over, endless loop.

I'm having a bad day. A bad day in a bad life, that's how it feels. I thought finding Jed's letter would make me feel better. Wrong.

Randall Shane smiling, though, that has to be a good thing.

"What?" I ask, whipping open the door, my voice pitched like a broken whistle. "What?"

"Something fishy's going on," he says, striding into the kitchen and placing the carrier case on the leaf table. "Got any coffee?"

A few minutes later we're both seated at the table, sipping high-test. There's something very different about this version of Randall Shane. The big man is more animated, there's a light on behind his pale blue eyes, and oddly enough despite the palpable excitement there's something more relaxed about him. As if he's stopped holding his breath, feels free to inhale deeply.

This is the guy I read about on the Web. The guy they raved about on missing person blogs. The guy who makes things happen, who finds kids that can't be found. This is the self he didn't want to reveal until he was convinced there was a shred of hope to cling to.

I feel like weeping, but don't. This is a time to show strength.

"Impressive lab," he begins. "Just opened in the last six months and already they're getting work from most of the state agencies, plus tons of stuff from the private sector. Apparently there's something called BRAC analysis that's really big right now. These folks can find DNA on the head of a pin, literally. They've got protocols in place that make the old FBI lab look like something in Boris Karloff's basement."

"Boris Karloff?"

"Old movie dude. You're too young. Once played Frankenstein's monster."

"I thought that was Robert DeNiro."

"Later, much later. Anyhow, the lab is state-of-the-art and they pride themselves on transparency. That's what the lab director told me. Dr. Hilly Teeger—she has a truly amazing number of advanced degrees in medicine and biology. I believe you've spoken to her."

"Three or four times, yeah. Wasn't much help. Very polite and trying to sound like she cared, but she wouldn't say 'yes.' Just all that stuff about protocols."

"Sensitive topic. Because they violated their own protocols, not to mention local, state, and federal protocols. Dr. Teeger never mentioned this?"

"Not like that. All she kept saying was, the original results were confirmed, they couldn't run the tests again."

"Yeah, well, that's because they messed up." Shane stirs a teaspoon of sugar into his cup, explains that he needs the energy. "Didn't sleep last night, the sugar helps."

"You say messed up? How did they mess up?" I ask. "I kept calling, they kept saying 'results confirmed.' Like there was nothing more to be done. Then I asked to have the, um, tissue returned, so I'd have something to bury. They said that couldn't be done, because of protocol. Always with the protocol."

"You wanted the tissue back to bury? Or to have tested elsewhere?"

"Tested someplace else," I admit. "That's not Noah."

"The blood spatter was a match," Shane points out. "They matched to the samples taken when Noah had his tonsils out. Plus they reveal genetic markers that confirm you are his mother, from the oral sample you provided."

"But you said something was fishy. What? Why are you smiling?"

He nods eagerly. "Sorry. I'm a bit wired, not explaining things in the right order. There's no doubt the blood spatter is a match. But when you requested another test, the tissue samples turned up missing. I phoned the lab technician who handled the material—who by the way has been terminated—and he seems completely baffled. He has no satisfactory explanation of how the tissue sample vanished from the lab, other than to assume it was somehow diverted to the incinerator. Which totally should never happen."

"But it did."

"Absolutely it did. That's why they kept stalling you. You've got the basis for a major lawsuit and they know it."

"I don't care about a lawsuit. I just want them to admit that Noah wasn't killed in the explosion."

Shane shakes his head. "They won't. They've retested the blood spatter and come back with a perfect match. That's their only concern—identification—not proof of life or death."

"I don't get it," I say, feeling even more helpless than usual. "What's good about this? What made you change your mind?"

Shane reaches across the table, gently touches my tightly folded hands. "It's relatively easy to contaminate a scene with a little blood spatter. Blood can easily be drawn from a living person. Cut your cuticle, you've got blood. But tissue is more difficult to fake. The details are gruesome and we needn't go into them, trust me on that. But we've seen people trying to fake their own deaths by squeezing out a few drops at a crime scene. It happened after 9/11, if you can believe it. A guy planted his own blood in the Trade Center wreckage, a few days later his 'widowed' wife files for a big payoff. They almost got away with it, too. The jerk got himself arrested at a stripper bar a few months later, which pretty much proved he was alive."

"So you think Noah is alive."

Shane gives me a startled glance, leans back in the chair, which creaks ominously. "I didn't say that. We don't know that yet. All we know is that the tissue samples collected at the scene were, at the very least, compromised. Which warrants further investigation."

"That's it?"

"That's a lot, Mrs. Corbin. Yesterday I thought this was going nowhere."

"But you looked so happy coming to the door! You were *smiling,*" I say in an accusatory tone. It feels as if his smile was some sort of betrayal.

"That's because of the other thing," he says.

"What other thing!" I demand.

"I was just getting to it," he says. "The other thing I found out. That's what kept me up all night last night, running it down. Took me hours to work back through all the companies and legal entities. But what I finally determined is that the holding corporation that owns GenData and several other related enterprises is in turn owned by a private equity firm controlled by legal representatives of Arthur Conklin and his organization. The Rulers."

"Oh my god," I say again, heaving a huge sigh of relief. While at the same time there's a chill creeping up my spine.

"I told you I wouldn't lie to you," Shane says, concerned. "This is an interesting and possibly very important development, but it doesn't prove your son is alive."

"Maybe not," I tell him, unable to focus through tear-blurred eyes. "But it proves I'm not crazy."

7. Driving Mr. Shane

The new Randall Shane—the energized version fueling himself on caffeine—waits for me to mop up my tears, get myself together, and then opens up his laptop and starts to take notes, typing rapidly. He wants to know everything, all of my suspicions, all the things that convince me Noah somehow survived.

But first he wants me to share what I know about Arthur Conklin.

"I know he's a coldhearted bastard," I tell him, and produce the letter Jed saved for all those years.

Mr. Shane carefully unfolds the worn pages and reads. He sighs and shakes his head once or twice and when he's done he carefully folds it up, hands it back to me. "I'd say your assessment is generous. Plus it fits with what little I know. Egocentric professor writes famous book about how to get rich by being selfish, follows his own advice."

I put the letter away. "The amazing thing is, even after all that, Jed didn't really hate him. He needed to cut himself off, but he never really hated him. Said his father couldn't help being who he was, that something was missing. Believe it or not, he felt sorry for him."

"So you never met Arthur Conklin?"

I shake my head. "We assumed he didn't even know I

existed. Or about Noah. I thought we succeeded in starting a new life. We both did."

The big man nods to himself. "Okay. I get it why your husband wouldn't want anything to do with his father, but why did he feel the need to take a new identity? Why didn't he just stop going home for Christmas?"

"It wasn't just his father," I explain. "It was the people around him. They treat his stupid book almost like the Bible. So to them Jed was sort of like the son of God. Except they don't believe in God, so that doesn't really make sense, does it? Whatever the reason, they were always trying to draw Jed back in. As if they could use him somehow. That's what he was afraid of, why he changed his name, started over. He always said they'd put him in a cage. A golden cage."

He looks puzzled. "Did he mean an actual cage?"

I shake my head. "More like they'd keep him in luxury, give him everything he wanted, except they'd never let him go. Never let him be himself."

"And he walked away from all that. Wealth and power."

"He didn't walk away, he ran. And I ran with him."

Mr. Shane clacks away, typing in his notes. "Okay," he says, looking up. "I'll see if the FBI cult experts have any helpful insights. But first I want to get a handle on exactly what happened here in Humble. The events leading up to the explosion. You mentioned a state policeman who knew the suspect?"

"Yeah, Trooper Thomas Petruchio, with the ERT. Sweet kid. He's the nephew of our town librarian, that's how I know him. He went to school with Roland Penny."

More notes. Again he looks up. "What's this about a schoolteacher you haven't been able to contact?"

"Irene Delancey, Noah's homeroom teacher. He adores her. I spoke to her briefly a few moments after the explosion. She told me that while they were all being held hostage, Noah slipped down below the seats for a while, but she was sure he was with the rest of his classmates when the smoke started. It was crazy in there, a panic because of the gunman and the smoke, and nobody could see a thing. They all linked hands but somehow Noah got separated. One second he was there, the next he was gone. She was devastated, said she could never go back into the school without thinking of Noah. I think she blamed herself."

He checks his notes. "So she quit her job and left town, is that correct?"

"Yes. Once I was thinking straight—and that's up to question, I guess—I tried to contact her but had no luck."

He folds down the lid of the laptop. "Okay, several leads with potential. That gets us started. Can I ask you one more thing?"

"Sure."

"How are your driving skills?"

The last and only time I've ever been in a Town Car was on the way to Newark Airport for a spring break extravaganza. Me and the mall girls heading for a wild weekend in Cancun, or so we thought. Only we never got out of Newark because the chartered flight got canceled. As it turned out, a scammy Internet travel agency had taken our money and promptly gone out of business. So the limo excursion to the airport was a giggle fest, but the bus ride home was very subdued.

Obviously I wasn't driving the hired car that day, so I had no idea how wide the Town Car is compared to, say, my Subaru wagon, which you can probably fit in the Lincoln's trunk. Big or not, it still has a steering wheel and a couple of pedals, so I know how to drive it, more or less.

"When in doubt, slow down," Mr. Shane cautions.

Turns out he's a nervous passenger, always touching the invisible brake on his side, but assures me I shouldn't take it personal. It's not me, it's him.

"I never allow myself to drive when I haven't had a good night's sleep," he explains. "That's how accidents happen."

I didn't sleep much, either, but decide not to share. Twelve ounces of strong coffee and I'm good to go. Driving has never been one of my problems or anxieties, I'm always happy to take the wheel, and within a few miles the Townie and I have come to an understanding.

First stop is the state police barracks in Montour Falls, just south of the Finger Lakes. An hour on the road, winding through some lovely countryside, and when Randall Shane finally decides I'm not going to run us into a tree he concentrates on his laptop. Funny to see such a large man hunched over such a small machine. He can cover the keypad with either hand, which makes it look awkward or even comical, but he nevertheless has a delicate touch and seems to be very comfortable navigating from site to site. If only he were that comfortable navigating on the open road.

"I saw that!" he exclaims, barely looking up from the screen. "Was that a dog?"

An animal has just shot across in front of us, a furry blur. I barely had time to tap the brakes before it was gone, and am surprised he noticed. Must have great peripheral vision.

"Fox," I say. "It made it."

"Bad luck, running over a fox."

"No doubt. But the fox is fine, she's hunting mice by now."

Mr. Shane glances up from the laptop, gives an odd look. "You know what fox prey on? I thought you were a New Jersey girl."

"Plenty of fox in New Jersey," I protest. "But you're right. In my other life I never paid attention. Up here, all you have to do is look out the window. Nature beckons."

He looks pleased at my explanation. "I like that—nature beckons."

"So you live in Connecticut, right? I bet they have fox in Connecticut."

"Yeah, they do. A few."

"And deer."

"Lots of deer. Deer have become a problem."

"Wife, kids?"

"Excuse me?"

"The bio stuff on the Web didn't mention family, but I'm guessing you have a wife and kids."

He glances away, looks out the side window. "Once upon a time. No longer."

He says it in a way that convinces me he didn't lose his family in a divorce. Something bad happened. Is that why he's made such a name for himself, recovering missing children, because he lost someone close? My instincts tell me not to press the point, that he'll tell me about it in his own time.

The GPS advises us to bear to the right, confirming what I already know, and a few minutes later we're cruising into the village, which isn't much larger than Humble in population, and Mr. Shane is sucking in his breath and going, "Wow!"

"Pretty impressive, eh?"

I slow to a stop so he can get a gander at the Falls, which come steaming out of Lake Seneca and drop a hundred and sixty-five feet at the end of Main Street.

"So that's why they call it Montour Falls," he says.

"Yep. The Indian name of the waterfall is Chequagua. But the village is named for Catherine Montour, who was a Seneca chief, so I guess it counts."

Shane grins at me. "And you know this how?"

"Wikipedia. Noah did a report on old Catherine, she's very famous in these parts. Our local Sitting Bull. Plus Helen and I drove out here to see Tommy."

"Trooper Thomas Petruchio."

"Helen calls him Tommy. So does his mother."

"Yeah? What do they call him at the barracks?"

"They call him Trooper."

"Good to know," says Mr. Shane, satisfied.

As I'm turning into the Finger Lakes Troopers headquarters, he clears his throat and goes, "We haven't discussed this, but it's better if I see Trooper Petruchio on my own."

"No problem," I say with a shrug. "Man talk, eh?"

Mr. Shane gives me a look. "More like there may be things he'd rather not discuss in the presence of a victim's mother. Especially one who's a friend of the family."

"Like I said—man talk. Don't worry about it, Mr. Shane. I'll do what you need me to do, and you'll tell me what I need to know, right?"

"Absolutely," he says. "And it's just Shane, please. No mister."

8. Answer Me That, Batman

Shane loves that spit-and-polish smell of the barracks. Reminds him of his own days at the FBI Academy in Quantico, when he was young, desperate to impress, and invigorated by the competition. Unlike a lot of the recruits, that was as close as he ever got to the military. Although an argument could be made that the academy ordeal was every bit as difficult as regular army boot camp. He'd loved the endless running, the obstacle courses, the forensic science labs, the intensive classes, even studying for the exams—everything but the indoor firing ranges. Not because he had anything against guns—he's always loved the oiled, mechanical satisfaction of a well-made firearm—but because for whatever reason he was a lousy shot and struggled to make a passing grade. Which may have had something to do with the turn his career took, come to think of it. More toward software, gadgets, and technical intelligence gathering than shoe leather on the street.

He'd been making up for that since leaving the Bureau. More street, less software. And the only gadget he truly relies on these days is his own brain. He still knows his way around a computer, of course, but his most reliable hard drive is between his ears. And that brain is nagging him right at the moment, questioning his judgment, telling him that despite a couple of puzzling coincidences there is really very little chance that Mrs. Corbin's child is still among the living.

So why chase ghosts? Better to concentrate on helping her accept reality, and then move on to a case more likely to produce positive results. The mother-and-child reunion is what he's all about, after all, the satisfaction of making things right in a deeply flawed world. One thing he knows for certain: his considerable skills don't include raising the dead.

Trooper Thomas Petruchio is currently on shift, but after some minutes of back-room discussion, his commanding officer agrees to make him available for a brief interview. Special circumstances, he says. Implying that it's not Shane's connection to the Bureau that's allowing him to get a foot in the door, it's a local courtesy being extended to a grieving parent.

"I appreciate it," he says as he's led down a corridor so clean it squeaks under his boat shoes.

The young trooper is running through a gear checklist for his squad—an inventory of assault weapons, various surveillance devices—and pointedly lets Shane know they'll have to cut it short if the unit is dispatched. "You know how it is," he says, offering a polite but unenthusiastic shake of the hand.

The young trooper—it's hard for Shane not to think of him as a kid—is lean and long of limb. Hair closely cropped and thin, pink-tinged ears that jut out from a boney, high-cheeked skull. He's nowhere near as tall as Shane, but there's enough physical similarity that he's reminded of himself at that age. Similar dedication and intensity of purpose. Similar skepticism, too. The trooper's attitude is not exactly filial. More like, show me why I shouldn't hold you in contempt.

Shane has an inkling where the 'tude' comes from and realizes he must deal with it if he expects to get anything from Tommy Petruchio.

"You mind if an old man takes a seat?" he asks.

The trooper snorts derisively. "You're not exactly an old man, sir."

"Old enough," says Shane, who often chooses to sit down so he doesn't tower over interviewees. "No 'sir' necessary. *That* really does make me feel old."

"Yeah? So how is Haley doing?" the trooper asks pointedly. "Is she hanging in there?"

"Seems to be," says Shane. "I understand you know her through a family connection?"

"Yeah, my aunt Helen. They're book crazy, both of them."

"You're aware that Mrs. Corbin believes her boy wasn't killed in the blast?"

Tommy Petruchio nods slowly, thoughtfully, obviously distrustful of the former agent's motives. "Yeah," he says. "I'm aware."

"Mrs. Corbin is out in the car. I asked that she not attend this interview because I wanted you to be able to speak freely."

"I'd never lie to the lady. Sir," he adds pointedly.

"No, but you'd spare her feelings," says Shane. "Anybody would. You don't have to worry about sparing my feelings."

Tommy grunts. "You got that right."

Shane nods to himself, smiling his little smile. "Okay, Trooper, I get it. I do. You think I'm wasting my time, investigating what has already been thoroughly investigated?"

"I do, yeah. Among other things. Sir."

"Call me Shane, please."

"They got a positive match from the DNA. Sir. Sorry, force of habit."

"No problem. You're probably right about this being a waste of time, but I've agreed to look into this for Mrs. Corbin. To satisfy her mind. She's adamant that it be done. If not me, I'm afraid it might be an unscrupulous person, one who might be interested in draining her of money instead of clarifying things. Do you understand what I'm saying?"

Tommy's expression is devoid of sympathy. "You're not interested in her money? Really? That's kind of odd, sir, because I heard she cut you a big check."

Shane sits up straight, looks him in the eye, holding steady. "I'm not interested in money, Trooper, other than how it may be useful in finding and recovering a missing child. Your sources are correct. Mrs. Corbin offered me a generous retainer, but I haven't yet taken it."

"Oh yeah? And why is that?" asks Tommy, still deeply skeptical.

"Because it wouldn't be right. Not unless I can determine that her son is somehow alive. Satisfied?"

He shrugs. "Yeah, I guess. If you say so."

Shane opens his wallet, hands Tommy a card. "Check me out. Your concern is appreciated—the lady does need someone looking out for her best interests. But right now I'd appreciate your full cooperation, despite any reservations you may have about me personally."

Tommy thinks about it, shrugs. "What do you want to know?"

"Mrs. Corbin tells me you knew the perpetrator. Let's start with your impressions of him."

Tommy grimaces at the recollection. "Roland Penny was a loser. Not a nice loser—a sneaky, lying, mean-ass loser. He was that way in first grade and he was that way when he murdered poor Leo Gannett and scared the pee out of a bunch of children."

"So you knew him for most of his life."

"Yeah. Except not so much the last few years. Roland dropped out in tenth grade, soon as he turned sixteen. Small town you're always aware of everybody your own age, but he was into drugs. I was into football. Different worlds. Plus I never liked him anyhow. Fifth grade he got suspended for torturing Billy Beribe. Billy's got Down syndrome."

"Torture?"

"Roland locked Billy in a dark broom closet, shoved his hands in a bucket of cold deer guts. Literally scared the shit out of poor little Billy."

"He had a history of violent behavior?"

"I guess. He had a lot of grievances. Whatever he screwed up, it was always somebody else's fault. Thought he should be somebody important, somebody successful, even though he never did much of anything. You know the type—not very smart himself but he assumes everybody else is stupid? That's Roland."

"He was smart enough to make a bomb," Shane points out.

"Probably found plans on the Net."

"Your impression is that he was organized? Capable of planning?"

Tommy shrugs. "Nah, not Roland. That wasn't my assumption. My assumption was the dude couldn't have planned a one-car funeral procession. But obviously I was mistaken."

Shane makes a few notes in a small reporter's notebook he carries for just such occasions. "I understand you managed to get a surveillance camera on-site."

The young trooper brightens when the subject turns to equipment. "Yeah, we got a tactical fiber optic with a sixty-inch reach. Got a real good look at old Roland, strutting around and waving his gun. You know what that sick son of a bitch was doing? He was singing! At the top of his lungs! Like this was some kind of karaoke deal he had going. Ozzie—can you believe it?"

"Ozzie?"

"Ozzie Osbourne. Black Sabbath. Roland was singing along to Black Sabbath. 'Paranoid.'"

"He was paranoid?" Shane asks, writing it down.

Tommy chuckles. "Man you really are old. 'Paranoid' is a song. A famous song written way before I was born. Like the most famous metal song ever recorded."

"Sorry. I was more into Dire Straits."

"'Sultans of Swing.' Ugh."

"Hey, I was clueless. My other favorite was Supertramp."

Trooper Tommy Petruchio laughs so hard he spits drool. "Dude!"

"Is Ozzie Osborne the one who ate bats for breakfast?"

"Yeah," says Tommy, wiping his eyes with the back of his hand. "On his freakin' Cheerios."

"So Roland Penny was a heavy-metal fan."

"I guess. Must have had it on his iPod."

Shane stops with his pen above the page. "The perp was wearing a personal listening device?"

"Yeah," says Tommy. "And he had it cranked. I could tell he had it cranked. I remember thinking, you little weasel, you'll never hear the shot when it comes. You'll never know we're busting in until you're already dead."

"So the iPod was like what, a soundtrack to his suicide?"

"That's the theory. Not that anybody really cares."

"You don't care?"

"Not about Roland. He's dead. What difference does it make what songs he had playing in his sick mind?"

Shane makes a note. "Okay, you had audio and visual on the guy until what, the smoke started?"

"Yeah, that was weird."

"How so?"

"Why bring a smoke bomb to the party when you've got a real bomb set to blow a few minutes later? What was the point? And when the smoke started coming out of that cart, Roland looked like he was freaking."

"So he didn't ignite the smoke generator?"

Tommy shrugs. "I guess he must have. Or maybe it went off earlier than he planned. Whatever, once the smoke started we no longer had visual contact. We forced entry, concentrated on getting the kids out of the building."

"You lost sight of Roland."

"Man, it was thick smoke! Like you wouldn't believe. No viz at all. We were grabbing little kids just by reaching down, feeling around."

"Any indication Roland was equipped with a gas mask or any sort of smoke protector?"

"Not that I saw. But it happened so quick."

"So you surmise that he remained in the center of the gym while you and your men evacuated the building?"

"That's the theory."

"Were shots fired, once the building was breached?"

Tommy shakes his head. "Nope. The only shot he fired was to the back of Leo Gannett's head, and that happened first, before we got there."

"So he never reacted?"

"No."

"He never attempted to flee the scene?"

"He was within a yard of the C-4 when it detonated," Tommy says, folding his arms resolutely, confident of his opinions. "That's what they determined. We found pieces of Roland all around the gym, consistent with him being that close. We figure he activated the bomb by hand."

"How so?"

"Because the remote control he was waving around, threatening all those poor kids with how he'd turn 'em into jelly beans—that was just a regular Sony TV remote. Totally harmless."

Shane pauses. "I hadn't heard about the dummy remote."

"I don't guess it matters how he triggered the detonator. We know he triggered it somehow because it blew him and Leo to pieces."

"And little Noah Corbin," Shane reminds him.

"Yeah, poor little guy."

"Any theories on the smoke? Why he was packing a smoke generator, what he hoped to accomplish?"

Tommy shrugs. "He was nuts, obviously."

"It occurs to me," Shane says carefully, "that smoke is a pretty good diversion, as well as a cover."

"Yeah, but for what? Roland wasn't trying to escape. He blew himself up."

"Or somebody else did, using another remote detonator."

Tommy snorts. "Yeah, that was a theory for about five minutes. Trouble is, there's no physical evidence indicating he had an accomplice. Nothing. Nada."

"But that smoke, the smoke bothers me. It's a tactical

strategy. It's what you deploy if you want to confuse the situation. If the whole crazy scene with Roland was somehow staged, or he was put up to it. The smoke confuses Roland. It confuses everybody. So maybe the smoke was for a reason."

"Oh, you mean the kid. Could somebody have snatched him."

"Could they?"

"Doubtful. I mean, who? It was just us in there. My unit and the teachers and the kids."

Shane looks quizzical. "I understood some of the firefighters helped out."

"Yeah," he allows. "They were grabbing kids, too."

"And Roland waited until all of you were safely out of the building before he detonated the bomb."

"Yeah," says Tommy. "That was lucky."

"Except for the kid."

"Except for the kid."

Shane pauses. They share the quiet for a while. Trooper Tommy Petruchio scratches his nose and finally breaks the silence. "You know what bothers me?"

Shane waits.

"The Escalade."

"Escalade?" asks Shane, genuinely puzzled.

"A week before it all went down Roland Penny put three grand, cash, down on a new Escalade. We found the receipt in the glove box of his old van. He never paid the balance, never took delivery, but still. I told you Roland was a loser. He was also unemployed and without any obvious source of funds. So where did he get the money for the down payment?"

"Any theories?"

"The detectives in charge figured maybe he was dealing."

"And was he?"

"No hard evidence either way. And if he did get the money from dealing, why'd he spend it on a car when he was planning to blow himself up in a few days? Answer me that, Batman."

9. What The Moon Is Made Of

The last time I was in a diner it was probably a Johnny Rockets at a mall somewhere. In other words, a nostalgic substitute, not the real thing. No cracked linoleum counters, no worn vinyl booths lovingly polished by generations of ample bottoms. No heady perfume of sugared doughnuts and sizzling bacon. No short-order cook who looks to be in the final stages of alcoholism, eyes peering out from a ruined face as he chops peppers and onions for an omelet that never ends.

Shane has found us a prime example of a real working diner, or so he says, located just north of the Finger Lakes. This is my first visit to the city of Auburn. Shane calls it a 'nice little burg' and I see no reason to disagree, even if the burg's main claim to fame is that Abner Doubleday took up residence for a time, and no doubt dreamed of baseball. Oh yeah, and according to the helpful historical notes included on the menu, the first-ever execution by electric chair took place at the local prison in 1890. So the place has a lot going for it if you happen to be a fan of baseball or capital punishment.

As to diners and lunch counters, I can taken 'em or leave 'em, whereas Shane is clearly smitten.

"This is a Jerry O'Mahony," he says, looking around. "Early 1950s. They were well into the stainless steel period by then. O'Mahony was one of the major manufacturers, out of Elizabeth, New Jersey. They helped make stainless diners fashionable in the 1940s. Before that it was barrel tops."

"Whatever you say."

He's waiting for a slice of pie and a glass of milk. I'm not hungry.

"Barrel top was the original style. First it was horse-drawn carts with rounded tops, to give them more headroom. Then I guess what happened is, the lunch carts started parking in one place. Maybe put a little foundation under the cart, add on a wing for more room. So the folks building the carts got bigger, too. Voilà, the American diner is born. People think they're all shiny and stainless, but the early versions were more like old boxcars with a rounded top."

"So this is your hobby?" I ask. "Not bowling or fishing or golf?"

"Just an area of interest," he says with a small, tight smile.

"Sorry."

"No. You're right. Who cares about diners? Boring."

"Now you're pissed."

He chuckles, shakes his head. "No, no, absolutely not. Here I am, rattling on, when what you want to know is what happens next. Where we go from here."

"The down payment for the new car," I say eagerly. "It's proof, right? That somebody paid Roland Penny to do what he did?"

The pie and milk arrive. As she sets down the glass and plate, the uniformed waitress checks him out with hungry eyes.

"Getcha anything else?" she asks, all innocence, hovering so he can get a shot of her ample ta-tas if he cares to look.

"I'm good," he says, oblivious.

After she slinks away I whisper, "She wants to jump your bones."

Shane makes a face, clearly thinks I'm being ridiculous. Not a clue. He digs into the pie. He's a neat, methodical eater, has it in four bites. Dusts his hands with a napkin, then drinks half a glass of milk in one swallow. "Sorry," he says, setting down the glass and for some reason looking guilty.

"Proof," I remind him. "Somebody paid Roland and he thought there was more to come, enough to buy an Escalade. Plus the smoke. That never made sense, save to give them cover to snatch Noah."

"Them?" He pats his lips with the napkin, makes sure his beard is crumb-free. "We're getting ahead of ourselves, Mrs. Corbin. The down payment is interesting, given what we know about the perpetrator, but it proves only that he came into a little money somehow. Not who gave it to him or why. Maybe Tommy's wrong and he made it dealing. Maybe a rich uncle died."

"And maybe the moon is made of lemon meringue pie."

He smiles. "Sure you don't want a slice?"

"You don't want to give me false hope, is that it?"

Shane stares at me with pale blue eyes that have seen a whole lot of sadness. "That's it exactly. Tommy the Trooper already assumes I'm scheming after your money. He won't be the only one. And they have a reason to be concerned."

"But you wouldn't take the check."

"Others might. There are private investigators out there who specialize in bleeding parents dry. They come up with tantalizing little clues, some new slant, persuade the frantic mom and dad to sell the house, empty their bank accounts. And they walk away when the money runs out."

"You wouldn't do a thing like that," I say.

"No."

Just a word, a simple word, but I believe him. For no other reason than instinct and gut feeling, the same kind that makes me believe my son is still alive in the world.

"So what next? Where do we go from here?"

Shane flips open his laptop, scrolls through a few screens. This isn't exactly Wi-Fi territory, so he's not cruising the Net but his own research files. "The Humble Police Department," he says. "Serving your rural community with competence, courage, and integrity. Not a bad motto."

"They've been very nice. The investigation was run by the State Police, but the local cops are good folks, even if they don't know much about what went down."

"I'll bet they knew Roland," Shane says.

10. Follow The Money

The day Noah's school exploded, I really did lose my mind for a while. It felt like my brain was spinning like a mad gyroscope and I had to spin with it or lose my mind altogether. Mostly I remember running. Running around in circles in the parking lot, trying to scream but nothing coming out. Running past the distracted firefighters and cops and somehow finding my way into the ruined gym. It was smoky, of course, and the lights had been blown out, but part of one cinder-block wall had collapsed and a beam of sunlight poured through the hole. At first I thought the air was alive with butterflies, some miracle of light and goodness that would guide me through the wreckage to Noah. But it was thousands of tiny bits of paper fluttering in the utter stillness that followed the detonation. Homework, lesson plans. The smell was awful but at the same time strangely intoxicating, like a whiff of ammonia when you've fainted, and for a time it slowed the spin in my head.

I must have been shouting for Noah, but I don't remember that part. What I remember is the large scorched area where the bomb went off. Like an enormous version of the mark left when boys set off firecrackers on the sidewalk. I remember climbing into the splintered wreckage of the gymnasium seats, looking for my little boy. Crawling through the twisted steel, looking, looking, as if the force of a mother's eyes could make him reappear.

It was so lonely inside that wreckage, so lonely it hurt to breathe, but I couldn't leave, not without Noah. Eventually I became aware that people were shouting at me, trying to persuade me to come out. I recoiled from the grasping hands—didn't they know I couldn't leave, that staying here would make my son come back?

The man who eventually persuaded me out, and then covered me with a blanket until the EMTs could take charge, was Troy Hayden, one of the local cops. What made me relent—I was gripping a steel support beam with both hands and refusing to let go—was his promise that they'd find Noah for me. That he hadn't been able to keep that promise could be why he's always so kind and polite when I come storming into the station with some new theory about that day.

It was Troy who first suggested checking out private investigators, so it makes sense that he's willing to cooperate with Randall Shane.

"Hi, how are ya," he says, giving the big man a formal handshake and showing us both into his small, windowless office. What used to be Leo Gannett's office. Troy is now acting chief, and everybody expects that he'll eventually be appointed chief.

"Doin' okay," says Shane. "I understand from Mrs. Corbin that you've been very helpful and generous with your time."

"Least we can do," Troy says. Compared to the late Leo Gannett, who was pretty imposing, he's a slender little guy, only a few inches taller than me. His lack of height has never seemed to bother him, maybe because he's a miniature hunk and has never lacked for female attention. Think Kurt Russell circa *Escape From New York* and without the eye patch. Helen calls him 'Troy The Beautiful Boy,' but she means it in the nicest possible way.

Shane hands him a business card. "I put my credentials on there strictly for disclosure. We both know being a former FBI Special Agent doesn't give me any special privileges. I'm not a licensed private investigator. I'm acting in a civilian capacity as a consultant to Mrs. Corbin in the matter regarding her son, just to be clear."

Troy grins, which makes him look about fifteen. "You're famous, dude. At least on the Internet. When Haley told me, first thing I did was run a Google search on you."

"Don't believe everything you read on the Net."

"You saying you don't actually walk on water?"

Shane smiles. "Ever seen Wile E. Coyote attempt to walk on water? That's me."

"Nah, nah," says Troy with a dismissive wave. "Bet you can do it when you need to. I read all about that deal in the Everglades, where you found the girl in the swamp? Everybody else gave up, but not you."

"Not her mother, either," Shane says, with a glance to me. "She never gave up."

"Anyhow, I'm real pleased you're looking into Haley's case. Fresh eyes."

"Thanks. Please understand this is preliminary. I'm still looking into the possibility that Noah Corbin survived, and have reached no final conclusion. Not yet."

"Yeah," says Troy, shooting me a look. Wanting to know how I'll react. Understandable. He's seen me at my worst.

Both men seem concerned that I'll freak out if they say the wrong thing. What they don't seem to understand is that once you've been to the worst place, once you've confronted the unthinkable, talking about it doesn't make it worse. If I freak out—and I might, you never know—it will be on my own time, for my own reasons, and not because someone mentions the possibility of Noah being dead. I live with that possibility every moment, awake or asleep.

"I'm hoping you'll tell me everything you know about the perpetrator," Shane is saying, leaning forward. "Past history, habits, rumors, whatever. Your personal impression."

"That's easy. He impressed me as a weasel."

"Mrs. Corbin says he had a long history with your department."

"Mostly with Leo, yeah," Troy says. "I didn't grow up

around here, so I didn't know Roland when he was a kid, or when he first got in trouble. But Leo always said he was a sad case. Mother a tweaker—excuse me—a methamphetamine addict, father in prison. To be truthful I never saw the sad part of Roland. What I saw was a mean-spirited, self-centered creep who for some reason thought he should be treated like a celebrity. Famous-in-his-own-mind kind of guy. For what reason I could never figure out."

"He'd been picked up numerous times?"

"Yeah. Charged twice, convicted once for possession of less than a gram. Meth, just like Mom and Dad."

"Incarcerated?"

"Naw. Slap on the wrist. Probation, I think."

"He was a dealer?"

Troy makes a face. "In his dreams, maybe. Following in the footsteps of dear old Dad. But no, we never saw indicators of dealing. Leo used to stake out Roland's trailer now and then, but there was never enough traffic to indicate dealing. Nobody trusted the guy enough to front him."

"Was he cooking?"

"Roland? Cooking up meth? No way. He didn't have the means or the skill."

"But he had the means to obtain a significant quantity of C-4 and construct a bomb?" Shane points out.

Troy sighs, studies the ceiling. "I know, I know. It doesn't fit. Roland going nuts with a gun, shooting Leo, I get that. Didn't see it coming, but it fits. The bomb, the smoke machine, that's what puzzles me, Mr. Shane. That's why I thought it was a good idea, bringing a guy like you in to have a look around. Like I say, fresh eyes."

"I assume the plainclothes have been thorough? In your estimation?"

"The state police detectives? Oh yeah. Real pros. Departments this small, we don't have the facilities or the experience to investigate major crimes. The trooper investigators handle it, that's in their charter. And I got no real complaints on that score. They were all over it. But once they got the DNA match it was case closed, on to the next. Who really cares what motivated Roland Penny? He did it and he acted alone, that was their conclusion."

"But not yours?"

He glances at me before responding to Shane. "I haven't come to a conclusion," he says uneasily. "Maybe Noah was killed in the explosion, maybe he wasn't. I'm keeping that possibility open in my mind. But for sure something is off about Roland Penny being the big bad master bomb maker."

"You think he may have had an accomplice?"

"It's a possibility. Yeah."

"Any likely candidates?"

"No leads toward one. And I can't think of one. And I've tried, believe me."

Shane takes a break, goes back over his notes. To fill the void, Troy attempts to reassure me with a smile. He's been so nice, so cooperative, I can't hold it against him that he thinks my son is dead. He says otherwise, about keeping an open mind, but I can tell. A mother can always tell.

"Any thought on where Roland got three grand to put down on a new car?"

Troy sits up straighter, keenly interested in this particular subject. "It wasn't dealing, I'd stake my life on that. Even if he was dealing, which I highly doubt, he'd have been small-time. A hundred bucks here or there, five at the most. This guy lived hand to mouth. No way he'd get his hands on three grand all at once, let alone the rest of the fifty or sixty grand."

"So you checked it out?"

Troy shrugs. "I was curious. Figured no harm, no foul, follow the money like they say."

"Even though the troopers were investigating. Had come to their own conclusions."

"Yeah. Happened on my watch, right? Even with the Staties in charge, I still got an interest. So I drove over to the dealership, checked it out. Strange thing, the salesman who took the down payment couldn't identify Roland."

"A bad memory? Too many customers? I'm not really surprised."

"Yeah, but he did remember the guy who put the money on that particular vehicle. Because the salesman has been trying to unload it for months, it gets about what, two miles a gallon? It's just he doesn't remember Roland, he remembers a guy with a dark mustache, had an accent."

"Yeah?" says Shane, perking up. "He say what kind of accent?"

"That's where he gets vague. Maybe Russian, maybe Greek. Could have been Polish. He really had no idea."

"His impression was a mustache and a foreign accent. Maybe."

"Yeah, which is why it's not really helpful. All he really knows, he's positive it wasn't Roland. A dude that scruffy and slimy would have made an impression. He said the guy with the accent was handsome, like a movie star or something. And Roland was no movie star, believe me."

Shane makes more notes, writing firmly in a legible hand. "I assume the troopers searched his domicile?"

"That dump of a trailer?" Troy scoffs, his nose wrinkling in disgust. "Yeah, they tore it apart, looking for more explosives. It was clean. No trace of C-4 or detonators or any sort of bomb-making equipment. They went over the place with a chemical sniffer. All they got was the fumes off Roland's dirty socks. The detectives told me wherever he put the bomb together, it wasn't there."

"Anything on his computer?"

"You mean, did he download an instructional manual, something to show him how to wire up the C-4? Maybe, but not on his home computer because he didn't have a home computer. I dunno, he could have used a library computer, or gone to an Internet café in Penfield or Rochester or somewhere. Nobody knows, and at this point nobody really cares. Other than, you know, us," he says, catching my eye again.

"So there was no computer in Roland's trailer?"

"Nope. And no phone lines, either. He had a cell, not a landline. No cable hookup, no satellite. So no Internet connection, even if he did have a laptop stashed somewhere. Which I find highly doubtful."

"Why is that?" Shane asks.

"Because Roland wasn't a laptop kind of guy. He just wasn't."

When we get up to leave, Troy waits until Shane clears the door and then gives me a thumbs-up and a nod of approval. He thinks I made the right choice, bringing in the big guy. In contrast to Tommy Petruchio, who scorns the notion of outside investigators.

One out of two. I'll take those odds.

11. The Door Swings Open

Up to now, the only laws I've ever broken have to do with traffic. Speeding and a few parking tickets. I never even shoplifted when that was a 'thing' with my old Jersey girl posse. It wasn't a moral reservation at the time—can you have moral reservations about The Gap?—more a fear that I'd get caught, be publicly embarrassed.

So I'm surprised at my own reaction when Shane proposes breaking the law. No hesitation, I'm all for it.

"Okay, but I don't want you in the vicinity," Shane cautions. "Even if you don't actually enter the premises you could still be held as an accessory."

"For checking that nasty old trailer? You said it doesn't have a proper lock on the door, so it's not exactly breaking and entering. Just entering."

"Entering a private domicile without invitation is, at the very least, trespassing," Shane reminds me.

"Is trespassing a serious crime?"

"Depends on the circumstances. It can very serious if there's an intent to burglarize."

"Are we going to burglarize?"

"Depends on what we find."

"Good," I say. "Let's do it."

"Really, Mrs. Corbin, it's best if you leave this to me. You can bail me out if I get caught."

He makes getting bailed sound so routine that I have to ask, "Have you ever been arrested?"

"I've never been charged or convicted," he says, somehow making it sound dignified.

"So you *have* been arrested."

He shrugs. "More like taken into custody. Hazard of the job. Pushing to locate a missing kid, sometimes you go over the legal line. It happens."

Eventually we agree that I'll drop him off and drive away and he'll call me on the cell when he wants to be picked up. Which sounds very sane and reasonable until I pull into the rutted, unpaved driveway to turn around and catch a glimpse of Roland Penny's broken-down old trailer glinting in the setting sun.

I can't resist. Throwing the big Town Car into Park, I grab my purse, get out. "Screw it," I tell a startled Shane. "If they want to arrest a grieving mother for checking out the rat hole of the man who blew up her son's school, let them."

"Mrs. Corbin, really, I think it would be better—"

"Are you coming?" I ask, striding off through the ankle-deep snow.

"Okay then," says Shane, shortening his gait to keep pace with me. "When did it snow? Last night?"

"Early this morning."

"No footprints," he points out. "So nobody has been poking around here recently."

The rock the creep lived under isn't exactly a classic Airstream. It's a battered old construction trailer left over from some long-ago project, plunked down on a parcel of land once exploited for gravel pits. A power line was brought in years ago, but not much else. According to Troy, Roland was paying a hundred a month to an absentee owner, and from the look of things he wasn't getting any bargain. One of the aluminum side panels has been kicked in, revealing a thin stuffing of dirty, waterlogged insulation, and some plastic water pipes that must by now be frozen solid. There's only one small window, the cracked glass held together with a strip of duct tape. The door hangs on broken hinges, propped closed with a cinder block.

We saw this much from the paved road. It looks even less appealing close-up. Shane removes the cinder block. The door swings open, screeching back at the cold wind that's just now stirring.

"After you," I say, losing some of my conviction. "Don't bump your head."

The air temperature is dropping quickly with the sun. The old trailer is an icebox that never warmed up and because of the low headroom Shane has to remain in a crouch as he fumbles for a flashlight. No surprise, the power has been shut off. No heat, no lights, and we have to wade through the bottles and cans and rubbish that Roland left behind. It's doubtful the state police search could have made things worse. This has the feeling of long-term disorder, and the cold stench of rot and frozen mildew is all-pervasive.

If this is how the monster lived, how he was raised, then for the first time I have a twinge of sympathy. A very small twinge. Living in circumstances as wretched as this must be truly awful, but it doesn't mean you get to take it out on innocent children.

In addition to being disgusting—to say the man lived like an animal would be insulting to most animals—the place, basically one small room with a nonfunctioning toilet, the place is *spooky*, okay? You can feel him here, and understand why he might have welcomed violence as an alternative to an unbearable reality.

"So what are we looking for?" I ask, my voice a little shaky.

"I'll know it when I find it," says Shane. "Maybe."

"You've seen places like this before," I say, picking up on his vibe.

"Believe it or not, I've seen worse."

The flashlight beam sweeps through the debris underfoot. Everything seems to have ended up on the floor, possibly as a result of the police search. Or maybe because gravity is trying to suck the place back into the earth.

"This explains why Troy was so sure Roland didn't have a functioning computer," I say. "He didn't have a functioning anything. Not even a TV set."

"And yet he had an iPod," Shane muses.

"Anybody can buy an iPod," I point out. Keeping my hands in my pockets so I don't have to touch anything. Trying not to breath mold spores through my nose.

"You still need a computer to put songs on it," Shane reminds me. "You need, at the very least, an Internet account, and there's nothing to indicate he did. He didn't have a credit or debit card. He didn't have credit, period. So where did he get his music and how did he sync it to the iPod?"

"Maybe somebody gave it to him fully loaded—no Internet or computer required."

"Exactly," Shane says. "Like the three grand."

"You know what?" I say suddenly. "I'm going to wait out in the car."

"Good idea," he says, shuffling carefully through the discarded junk, prodding it with his flashlight. "Hold on!"

I freeze in the open doorway. The first thought, an almost electric cascade of raw nerves, is that he's come upon a booby trap. A trip wire or timer. Another bomb that will blow me into darkness, again.

But it's not a bomb, it's a book. A thick paperback swollen with absorbed moisture. The cover has been torn off and the title page is missing. Shane holds it up, illuminating the stiff, water-damaged pages with the beam of his flashlight.

"*The Rule of One,*" he says, squinting. "Isn't that Arthur Conklin's famous book?"

12. What Shane Sees

After we bought our dream house Jed and I spent all of our free time trying to make the dream part come true. First thing you need to know about old farmhouses is that they are old. Old means the sills have rotted, a sizable undertaking to repair, best left to contractors who specialize in that sort of thing. Old means it isn't properly insulated, especially upstairs under the eaves, and that means taking down the crumbling lath-and-plaster walls. When the plaster is finally gone, the wiring is exposed, so you might as well bring it up to code. Once the new gypsum-board walls are painted you start on the floors. Stripping, sanding, repairing, refinishing. Oh, and don't forget the ancient lead-sealed plumbing, left over from the Romans, apparently. Best to remove all that nasty lead if you're planning to get pregnant and you don't want the baby to have two heads.

Jed pitched in for the first few projects, but then he got very busy at work and had to do a fair amount of troubleshooting, which took him away for days at a time. So I became a Haley-of-all-trades, no job too small, and I must say I did one heck of a good job. The house is as tight as a tick—a phrase picked up from the old-timers at Home Depot—and stays warm and cozy even when the Montreal Express comes wailing down from Canada and batters us with freezing forty-mile-an-hour winds.

The one thing I've never been able to repair is the creaking. When those big winds blow, my beautiful dream house moans and protests. Its old bones and beams creak ominously. The new windows shudder in their rebuilt frames. The chimney whistles mournfully. Jed always said the old place was talking to us. As part of our routine I'd dutifully ask, so what's it saying, Jedediah? And he'd grin and go, it's saying put another log on the fire and pour yourself a drink.

In those first crazy days after the school blew up I threw away all the alcohol in the place, refusing to numb myself to the pain, so the best I can offer Randall Shane is a mug of hot cocoa. Real cocoa topped with real whipped cream, the way Noah likes it.

"That'd be great," he says.

"Throw another log on the fire," I suggest.

He glances at the Hearthstone in the kitchen, which is already flickering merrily. "Really?"

"Kidding. It's gas, not wood. Much cleaner. I meant you could turn up the thermostat if you're cold."

"Nah, I'm good," he says, rubbing his big hands together. He listens for a moment. "That wind," he says.

He makes small talk about the weather while I prepare the cocoa. Seems amazed that I bother to whip up the cream—haven't I heard of Reddi-wip?—but then admits my version tastes way better than the canned stuff. Mug in hand he leans a hip against the counter, claiming he'd rather stand than sit, he's had enough sitting for the day, thank you. Standing means I have to look up at him to respond, and suddenly it seems so strange to me, to be here in my familiar kitchen with the wind moaning and a tall handsome stranger in a leather bomber jacket, smiling at me with whipped cream in his mustache. My late husband had a jacket like that. There's nothing going on, no actual sexual tension—swear on a Bible—but the casual intimacy of sharing a counter gives me such a pang of longing for Jedediah that I have to put my mug down and turn away and pretend to fuss with the Hearthstone.

"So where are we?" I ask after clearing the lump from my throat.

"We had a busy day, didn't we?" Shane says cheerfully. "I learned a lot."

"So you believe me?"

He speaks carefully. "I believe there's a strong possibility that Roland Penny didn't act alone, whatever the result."

"That's something, I guess. More than I ever got out of the state police detectives. So you'll take the check? You'll help me find my son?"

He holds up a cautionary hand. "We're not quite there yet, Mrs. Corbin. I need to consult with a couple of experts before I make that decision."

"What experts?"

"Former associates still employed by the FBI. I'll make a quick trip to Washington, consult with them, and then get back to you."

I'm not sobbing or anything, there are no convulsions of crying, but all of a sudden the tears are flowing freely and I have to brush them away or risk blubbering. "Get back to you," I say, my voice thick. "That's what they say when they reject you for a job. They'll get back to you. They never do."

"I will get back to you," he promises.

"You'll call. It's easier to walk away by phone."

He shakes his head. "No phone calls, I promise. Swear on my life. I'll come back here, to this house—my car will be waiting at the airport, remember—and we'll discuss the options in person, face-to-face, whatever I learn in Washington."

"But what about the book!" I wail. "He had the book! That proves he's one of them!"

Shane remains utterly calm, hands me a tissue to blot my tears. As if it's a common occurrence, witnessing a mother cry her heart out, and for him I suppose it must be. "The book is why I'm going to Washington," he explains. "I know very little about Conklin's followers, or how his organization functions. I need to learn more."

"Rulers—that's what they call themselves. Like they're rulers of the universe," I add bitterly.

Shane takes the swollen paperback from his pocket. "Twelve million copies in print," he says, glancing at the back cover. "And this is an old edition, so it must be more by now. Did your husband talk about this book? What it means? What they believe?"

"A little. Not much, really. It's about being selfish, he said. How it's good for the individual to be selfish."

"Guess I'll have to read it on the flight down."

"Good luck," I say. "I tried to read it once, so I'd have some idea what Jed went through as a boy, but to me it was all mumbo jumbo. This tedious stuff about bees and insects and parallels to human behavior, and the differences between hive minds and drone minds. None of it made sense to me, so I quit. When Jed found the book he threw it away. Said it made him uneasy to have a copy in the house. When I told him I didn't understand it he laughed and said nobody did, not really. That was how his father made all that money, because people paid him to explain what the book really meant. Joining the Rulers means you keep paying them for more and more explanations, for as long as you live, because it takes a lifetime to understand what it really means, *The Rule of One.*"

Shane takes it in, considers his reply. "Just because Roland Penny had a copy in his trailer, it doesn't mean he read it. Maybe he tried like you and then put it down. There are twelve-million-plus copies out there."

"But that was the only book there, right?"

"Only one I could find," Shane admits.

"So maybe Roland really did read it and it made him mental. Like those loonies who think *The Catcher in the Rye* is telling them to shoot people."

Shane grunts and shakes his head. "*The Catcher in the Rye* doesn't make you shoot people. I loved that novel."

"You know what I mean."

"Yeah, I do." He tucks the book into his jacket pocket. "Listen, this is a bit awkward, but I have a favor to ask."

"Anything, if it means you'll look for Noah."

"Could you drive me back to my motel? In my car? It would mean taking a taxi back here."

I shrug. "Sure, why not? But what's really going on? What's the deal with not driving? You drove all the way from Connecticut. Six hours on the highway."

He sighs, grimaces. "It's boring, but I suffer from a

sleep disorder. What I have is more than common insomnia, which can be pretty bad. When I'm unable to sleep—and I haven't slept now for thirty-eight hours and counting—my brain does funny things."

"Yeah? What kind of funny things?"

"It's called wakeful dreaming. It means I sometimes see things that aren't really there. Which makes it very dangerous to drive."

The big man sounds deeply embarrassed, and I get the impression he wouldn't be sharing unless it was absolutely necessary.

"That's why you left the FBI," I say, realization dawning. "You're disabled."

"I hate that word.... But yeah."

"Okay. So I drive you to your motel. How will you get from there to the airport?"

"I'll be fine by morning," he explains. "Tonight I'm taking a pill. It'll knock me out for five or six hours and then I'll be okay to drive."

"What caused it?" I ask. "You didn't have this all your life or you'd never have gotten into the FBI in the first place."

"You don't miss much, do you?"

"Is it a secret, what happened? Some mission you were on?"

"Nothing like that. I was off duty at the time. It was a vehicular accident. A bad one. I sustained brain injuries that may or may not have triggered the sleep disorder, nobody can tell me for sure. Some doctors think the cause is organic, others think it's purely psychological."

He finishes his hot cocoa, rinses the mug in the sink,

sets it on the drain board. I hand him a tissue, indicate the whipped-cream mustache. He looks embarrassed, doesn't want to meet my eyes.

The whipped cream isn't what makes him look away.

"What do you see?" I ask. "When you're, what do you call it, wakeful dreaming?"

He winces, as if jabbed with a pin, keeping his gaze averted.

"You said you wouldn't lie," I remind him.

He nods, admitting as much. "The doctors call them artifacts. Images from my memory so distinct they look real. It can be very…distracting."

"What do you see?" I insist.

He looks directly at me with eyes that have witnessed an eternity of sorrow. "Sometimes I see my wife and daughter," he begins. "They died in the accident."

Part III
Rumors

1. Kaboom Means Never Having To Say Goodbye

He's thinking it's amazing how young the SAs are nowadays. Some of them look like teenagers in adult costumes, although most Special Agent applicants are in their late twenties by the time they get the minimum college degree, plus law enforcement and/or military experience. He was what, twenty-eight before he finally qualified for the FBI? Something like that. But he never looked this young. No way.

It's kind of a kick, hanging out in the concrete fortress of the Hoover Building, just observing. *In the lobby, agents come and go, speaking of Mafia gigolos.* Actually he's in the mezzanine, not the lobby, and there's probably less chat about the mating habits of mobsters than there was back in the day. The main mission now being terrorism, both domestic and international. But the old place still has the same feel, the same thrum of energy from ambitious kids wanting to break the big case. They come in all colors and ethnicities, but they have in common the desire to be heroes, to get the job done, no matter the risk.

Most will burn out, that's a given. Some will leave angry and cynical, disappointed that they hadn't been able to change the world. Others will take an early out, the result of physical or mental traumas suffered on the job or off. Not that you're ever off the job. Not when you hold the badge.

"Mr. Shane?" A young, pleasantly chubby lab tech peers at him through small, stylish eyeglasses that give her the look of a pretty goldfish. "Dr. Newman will see you now."

Shane laughs. He can't help it, but the lab tech looks startled, and then slightly offended. "Sorry," he says. "For just a second there, it was like Dr. Newman was my proctologist, and this was an appointment. You know?"

The lab tech says, drily, "You better hope he's not your proctologist."

"Actually, I don't have one."

"Excuse me?"

"A proctologist. Charley's an old pal of mine. He didn't mention?"

"I'm filling in, his regular's on maternity leave."

She marches away on squeaky crepe soles, leading him through security, waiting as he's wanded, collecting him on the other side, taking him to a different part of the huge building—Hoover's labyrinth. Charley Newman's lair has obviously been moved since the last time he looked in.

Shane worries that maybe his old friend has been demoted, but that isn't it. As the Bureau's senior expert on explosive devices, he's finally gotten a bump up to bigger and better digs, courtesy of al Qaeda. He actually has an office with a window now, not a glorified closet shared with two assistants and a secretary.

"The prodigal son!" Charley cries, bounding out of his

padded chair to grab and shake his hand. He stands back, takes a good look at Shane, appears satisfied. "Your eyes are clear. You've been sleeping."

"Like a log," Shane replies. Which is not quite true. With the help of pills he did render himself unconscious for several hours the night before. And then on the shuttle leg down from LaGuardia he actually fell asleep unassisted. Okay, twenty minutes of snooze time in a fully reclined exit-row seat isn't going to make an entry in *Ripley's Believe It or Not,* but for Shane it's something of a breakthrough.

"Interesting stuff you sent me," Charley says.

"I was hoping you might have some thoughts," Shane says.

"Thoughts or answers?"

"At this point, I'll settle for whatever you've got."

Charley shoos away the temporary lab tech, whose antennae have risen—what are the bad boys up to now?—and drags Shane into an adjoining room. Not, as expected, a workshop, but more like a conference room, equipped with a long table, a projection screen, and an old-fashioned chalkboard upon which is scrawled the enigmatic phrase, *Kaboom means never having to say goodbye.*

Tall and thin, though not quite as tall as Shane, and with narrow, bony shoulders rounded by years peering into microscopes, Dr. Charles Newman, who traded his three-letter school—M.I.T.—for a three-letter agency—FBI—seems as engaged and energetic as ever. When they were both young and full of mustard some of the SAs took to calling Charley 'Doc Brown,' for the Christopher Lloyd character in *Back to the Future.* Despite the thinning, wavy hair and the big proud honker of a nose—and the fun he had blowing things up out at his containment bunker in Quantico—Shane never saw the resemblance. To him Charley is and always will be The Chalk Man, a character all his own. Never a Special Agent himself, he's one of the Bureau's many overqualified, underpaid civilian employees. Long married to his high-school sweetheart, he and his wife, Trudy, had been godparents to Shane's daughter. Death hasn't broken that bond. Nor has Shane's bad habit of not making contact for months at a time, and usually only when he needs to pick his old friend's large and well-stocked brain.

As is his habit, Charley heads for the blackboard and starts thinking with chalk, the dust from which will soon adhere to him from forehead to foot. "Okay," he begins. "The device was placed in a janitor's cart, one of those wheeled jobs. Estimated forty pounds of military-grade C-4. So assume the center of detonation is between ten and fourteen inches from the floor. That's consistent with photos of the blast mark. Sound about right?"

"You're the expert."

"Yeah, but I'm working from e-mailed attachments. You were at the scene."

"Negatory on that," Shane tells him. "The gym was bulldozed a week after it was released."

"What?" Charley looks stunned.

"It was determined the damaged structure was a danger to the adjoining school. Which maybe it was. So as soon as the state police released the crime scene, down it went. I got the impression that everybody involved wanted to see it gone. Didn't like having all those kids walk past the wreckage every day."

"They maybe have a point," Charley admits thoughtfully. "Still, I was hoping to have your on-site impressions."

"Sorry."

The Chalk Man chuckles. "That was just to be polite. I was going to ignore whatever you said. The scene was very well documented, no problem there."

"Good. So you figured it out."

"Nah, I made calculations. Which I then converted into a three-dimensional rendering in my handy-dandy, blow-it-up software."

"Kaboom."

"It seems like an appropriate name, no? The foam goes up, the stains go down."

"Huh?"

"As seen on TV. In addition to being the pet name for my dimensional-force software, Kaboom is also the brand name of a toilet-bowl cleaner."

"Charley, Charley, Charley."

"The Chalk Man will have his fun, even if it means bathroom jokes."

Shane shakes his head, grinning.

"As to your question, can one small boy be effectively atomized by that quantity of explosive, in the circumstances described? Kaboom came up with an answer—my software, not the aforementioned cleaner—where was I? Right, okay, the big answer from Kaboom is *no.* Almost certainly *no.*"

"Almost?"

"Nothing is certain in this quantum-haunted world," Chalk Man admits with a sigh. "Not even with a fairly standard chemical combustion explosion. But aside from the physics, we have the evidence of the other two victims.

Both bodies severely damaged in different ways. The cop was prone at floor level, the perp standing upright within a few feet of the blast center. You will have noted in the crime scene report that significant skeletal and bone fragments were recovered from both adult victims. The perp's head was more or less intact. Separated from the rest of his body parts, granted, but nevertheless identifiable. You saw the grisly pictures, bro. He was still wearing his earbuds."

"Strange things happens when stuff blows up."

Chalk Man scratches his big honker. "That could be the title of my memoirs. Indeed, strange things do happen, not all of them predictable, no matter how good the software, and Kaboom is very, very good."

"I have no doubt."

"Bottom line, all things considered, and a dew-moistened finger up to the mystical wind for luck, The Chalk Man says it wasn't the C-4 that made your boy vanish."

"That's what I was hoping to hear," says Shane. "Thanks, Charley, you're the best."

"Is this an overnight? Can you do dinner? Trudy'd love to see you."

Shane regretfully declines. He has another expert to consult, and miles to go, and promises to keep.

2. When The Phone Trills

"He promised to come back, no matter what he decides."

"And you believe him," Helen says. "That's good."

Keeping my voice low, I make my case, wanting my friend to share my sense of confidence, my renewed sense of hope. "He found out more in two days than I have in six weeks," I tell her. "That's pretty amazing, right there."

Helen beams. We're in the library, her domain, and a hushed murmuring comes from the children's reading nook, where a book is about to be 'talked' by one of the volunteers for the Every Day Reads program.

The daily book talk is Noah's favorite part of a visit to the library. If I close my eyes I can almost hear him among the eager children, struggling to keep his voice down. It hurts, but no more than usual. I haven't gotten used to the pain, but have come to expect it as a constant presence in my life. The fact that someone is finally following up on my suspicions has helped immensely—I'm no longer quite so alone.

"What's he like?" Helen wants to know.

I shrug. "Kind of retro, I guess. Fortysomething. Get this—his hobby is visiting diners."

"Diners? Are you serious?"

"As serious as pie à la mode. He loves those funky old roadside diners, what can I say?"

"Okay, a diner maven. What else? I heard he was really tall. Basketball player tall."

"More like football player tall. Hey," I ask suddenly, "what do you mean you heard? What did you hear?"

Helen smiles, her gray eyes alight with mischief. "Troy's dispatcher has a five-year-old," she explains, nodding at the reading nook. "That's all she had, a physical description. Tall and yummy. Her words, not mine."

Yummy. Sorry, but I don't think of Shane that way. Any more than you'd be assessing the yummy factor when a fireman is carrying you out of a burning building. Later, maybe, after you're safe.

I'm a long way from safe. Safe will be when I have my little boy back, then I can decide whether or not Randall Shane is yummy. Until then, all that matters is, is he willing to run into a fire?

"You said he doesn't care about the money," Helen prompts.

"Doesn't appear to. Won't take a penny until he's convinced he can help me find Noah. If that's part of a con, it's a really good one. Plus, I think for him finding missing children is more of a life mission than a way to make a living. What happened, he lost his wife and daughter in a road accident."

"Oh my god."

"Which explains his sleep disorder," I add.

"Excuse me?"

"Just before he left, the big guy finally revealed some of the gory details. How he and his wife and daughter had been coming back from Washington, D.C. How Shane was nodding off so his wife took over driving on the Jersey Turnpike, and that's when they got hit by a truck whose driver was asleep at the wheel of his big rig. Car crushed, Shane the only survivor, waking up to find them both gone, his life forever changed. Sleep and death are now associated in his mind, hence his aversion to normal sleep. Or that's what the shrinks have told him."

"What a terrible thing," says Helen, her eyes glistening.

"Yeah," I agree. "You want to know an even more terrible thing? He tells me that, and my first reaction is to be glad it happened, because if it didn't, he wouldn't be helping me now. Isn't that awful?"

Helen pats my hand. "No, my dear, it's not awful. It's

human. We're all human. Even your big, yummy knight in shining armor is human."

"Not too human, I hope," I say.

Home again, home again, where I'm not quite bouncing off the walls. Brain humming with all the recent facts and details... The bomber's expensive new wheels, provided by person or persons unknown. The mysterious disappearance of the supposedly matching tissue samples. From a lab owned, however distantly, by Jedediah's father. Whose famous book was found in the bomber's wretched trailer. All of it more or less confirming my gut, that the whole terrible siege of the school had been a smoke screen—a literal one in those final moments—for whisking Noah away.

But why? For what purpose? What Arthur Conklin might want with a grandson he'd never met? Can't bear thinking about that. Was it possible that the old man never knew the boy existed until Jed died? Was it the plane crash that set off a chain of events that turned me into the madwoman of Humble, wandering the streets in search of her lost son?

Possible, yes. From everything my late husband alluded to, his father would not be constrained by what we mere mortals consider right or moral, good or bad. What he wants he takes. No apologies. No consideration for the normal attachments of parent and child.

Okay, maybe the old man really doesn't have a conscience. But even so why go to the enormous, complicated trouble of making it look like Noah was dead? Why not just kidnap him? Why go all Tarantino on it? Conklin had to be getting old, late seventies at least—maybe he thinks his grandchild is destined to take his place. But why not make contact? See if they could draw me into the fold? Make me a true believer? Surely they don't think a ten-year-old boy can run their empire? And even if they do, why not go to court, seeking custody? With all their high-powered lawyers, no doubt they could find a way to make me look like an incompetent mother if they tried hard enough.

Calm down. Think clearly. There has to be something else. More going on than a man simply wanting to take control of the last of his estranged family by any means possible. Some madness at the root of the old man's cult, some crazy *thing* they believe. Something I don't get because I don't understand—don't *want* to understand—the philosophy or religion or whatever it is that made him such a selfish, greedy monster to drive a truly decent man like Jedediah from his heart.

Really, it's more than I can stand to think about, because if I think about that I'll start obsessing on where Noah is this very instant, what they've done to him, are doing to him. And that way lies insanity. So I fire up my iMac—Jed preferred that operating system for some reason—and resume my search for Irene Delancey, the teacher Noah had such a crush on.

I shouldn't blame her for quitting, but I do. No doubt some of it was guilt on her part. She was the only teacher in the school to lose one of her students, and it couldn't have been easy, dealing with the boy's bereft mother. Not that I ever blamed her for what happened. She said he was there when she gathered up the kids and led them out through the smoke and that somehow he vanished between the seats and the exit door, and I believed her. It was panicked and crazy in there, losing track of a child in the blinding smoke would have been so easy. But in those first few days after the blast, when I saw quite a bit of her and the other children, she seemed to have withdrawn, tightened up somehow. She avoided looking me in the eye, as if one look would pass on the madness of grief. As if she didn't dare make contact, couldn't bear to deal with the raw emotions, or with me.

And then she was gone. Resigned: trauma and stress. No forwarding address left with the school district. No word left with her fellow teachers, or any of the parents, including me. She and her husband just packed up and split. Through various search engines I'd been able to find a few references to Michael Delancey, a day trader who worked from his home office. Until their move to Humble he'd been employed by a Wall Street firm, belonged to a couple of professional organizations, and since Irene wasn't popping up anywhere new, I'd been concentrating on the husband. My assumption being that he'd keep in contact with his investment banker cronies. So far no joy there—most of my inquiries were ignored, a few were downright rude because the recipient assumed I was a phisher, trolling for salable numbers, bank accounts and so on. One flaming response had accused me of being some "puffy geek in his pajamas, pretending to be a bereaved parent so he can steal someone else's hard-earned money" and threatened to report me to the FBI. I responded by begging him to report me, hoping the FBI would take an interest. That's before I found Randall Shane mentioned on a missing-kid Web site—a mom raving about how he'd done the impossible—and located his phone number in the White Pages. Before things finally began looking up.

I don't blame Irene Delancey for what happened, truly I don't, but I do have a few questions. Some of the kids in Noah's class seem to think he'd slipped beneath the seats and wasn't with the group when she led them out through the smoke. If so, why didn't she mention that to me or the various detectives investigating the crime scene? Was she ashamed, guilty, what? Or did she witness something that frightened her even more than a crazed, gun-waving lunatic? Something going down that made her want to run away and forget she'd ever been here?

That kind of question. But first I had to find her. She didn't strike me as the type who would be comfortable or even capable of changing her identity—not like Jedediah, for instance—so some trace of her had to be out there somewhere. New vehicular registration, new phone number, new credit application, something. Trouble is, it's only been six weeks and some of this stuff takes months to get on a database, so for now Irene Delancey is a phantom, there but not there.

Still, it gives me something to do, a project I can handle on my own. A point of focus that insulates me from the anxiety of waiting on Randall Shane. Who says he'll be back in a day, two at the most.

I really and truly believe him, I do, I do. If Noah can be found, he'll find him. Cling to that. Own it.

When the phone trills, cell not the landline, I'm sure it's Shane.

"Yes?"

"Haley Corbin?" asks an unfamiliar voice.

"Yes, who is this?"

"Um, I'm, ah, not sure I should give you my name,"

says a young male, practically stammering. "But it's about your kid. What I saw."

He has all of my attention.

3. Two And A Half Wows

Shane waits on the curb, eyeballing the traffic on Route 29 in Fairfax City, Virginia. On the lookout for a Diamond cab conveying his late lunch date from the district. Late and getting later every minute that passes. Probably gridlock in the capitol, road construction, maybe even a presidential motorcade. If he had a lick of sense he'd have skipped the nostalgia trip and arranged to meet closer to where she worked. Some trendy latte café or maybe the Willard, she always liked the Willard.

"Hey, handsome, looking for a good time?"

Shane jerks around, finds her standing behind him, grinning.

"Cabbie made a wrong turn," she says. "So I walked a block or two."

"Maggie! My God, what happened!"

Maggie Drew, ten years his senior, lifts her fragile, damaged hands and executes a pirouette, showing off her slender legs. "Amazing, huh? Look, Ma, no canes. No limp. No pain."

Shane stares and stammers. He's never seen her so healthy, so mobile. "It's…it's a miracle," he says, believing it.

She giggles. "Oh yeah. I crawled the last mile at Lourdes."

"No," he says, fighting to contain his astonishment.

"Okay, ya got me. It wasn't Lourdes. It's a miracle of modern medicine."

"What happened?"

"Buy me lunch, I'll tell you all about it."

She links arms, a bit awkward because of the difference in height, and he walks her to the diner. She remarks that it has been years, and it has. Too long. Back when he'd been active with the Bureau, he and Maggie Drew had been a pair. She, limping around on two canes, determinedly cheerful; Shane, a devotee of her brilliant mind, her caustic sense of humor, her insights into human behavior. Maggie a civvie, Shane an SA without portfolio, drifting from one posting to another, a bit of a lone wolf. Maggie joked about being his work spouse, but jokes aside, there was some truth to it, their mutual affection and comfort level, how they looked out for each other.

Now, and he finds this hard to believe, a decade has passed and Maggie Drew has to be in her fifties, except she has somehow gotten a youthful glow that makes her look younger than she did in the bad old days when her body was racked with rheumatoid arthritis.

They take a booth, Maggie looking around, remembering. "Hasn't changed a bit," she says. "The first time you took me here? We were working the Branch Davidians, just before it all went south, which had me a bit distracted, so that's my excuse for a brain malfunction. I thought you were taking me to some romantic little restaurant away from the big city, maybe you had a motel in mind."

Shane blushes.

"You haven't changed, either," she says. "Still blushing like a stoplight at the merest hint of flirtation. Don't worry, I was planning to let you down easy. Compete with that gorgeous wife of yours? Never entered my little brain.

And I got over it quick when I saw this joint. Don't get me wrong, I love the old 29, but romantic it ain't."

29 Diner, a landmark of sorts, dates from the late 1940s and clings to the past with attitude. Or, with attitude and a righteous royal cheeseburger and a ten-buck T-bone. Back in the day, when the job got to him he'd trek out here, have a milk shake. It calmed him down—his own personal Prozac. And he shared it with Maggie.

"So how'd you do it?" he asks, staring at her healthy self. "Join a rejuvenation cult?"

Her smile is impish, secretive. "We need more of those, but no. I did it the old-fashioned way. I found me a new doc, he's a bit of a stud, actually, and he put me on a new drug. A TNF blocker. Tried 'em before, but this is a new version and this time it worked. I skin-pop the stuff every two weeks and so far the RA is in deep remission. It doesn't hurt to sit, it doesn't hurt to walk, it doesn't hurt to be alive. Can't do anything about the joint damage to my hands, but other than that, I'm good to go."

"Oh, Maggie."

"Don't you dare cry on me, Randall."

Nobody calls him Randall. He grins, eyes glistening. "I'm so happy for you."

"It's amazing, it really is," she says eagerly, her pixie features lighting up. "I had no idea what it was like, walking down the street without my sticks. The weird thing is, sometimes I even miss them. You know, when I want to club a baby seal or whatever."

That gets Shane laughing, and something that has been tight around his heart for years lets go. "Wow," he says, hand on his chest. "I'm getting a contact high."

"There's only one cure for that," says Maggie, lifting her menu. "A Cheeseburger Royal."

They order, eat, reminisce, catch up. An hour passes and Shane is having so much fun he doesn't want to spoil the reunion by bringing up current business. She knows this, of course, has anticipated his hesitation, and apparently finds it endearing, or at least familiar. She waits until he fingers up the last crumb of piecrust, then leans in, her voice low and seductive.

"Still no motel, huh?" she says, batting her long lashes. "The only reason you call is to pick my brains. Some girls would consider that an insult."

"I love your brains," he says. "Is that so wrong?"

"Relax, Randall. I got the goods for you. Everything you ever wanted to know about the Rulers and were afraid to ask."

"Dazzle me."

Maggie Drew never reads from notes. She's always had an uncanny ability to absorb and retain pretty much anything she reads. Retain, evaluate, reason through, she's able to sift through the chaff, locate the kernels of truth, and explain it all in a way that makes sense to the big bosses and also, generously, to lowly SAs looking for guidance. Which is how she and Shane first crossed paths.

"How much do you know?" she asks. Not an idle question.

"The very basics. Guy writes a self-help book, makes a mint. The book turns into a cult. He makes even more money. He becomes an eccentric recluse. Howard Hughes without the airplanes."

"Cute."

"Got it from *People* magazine. An old issue."

"It would be old," she says. "The Arthur Conklin organization has ongoing lawsuits with every popular magazine, most tabloids, network and cable news organizations, and poor little Wikipedia. Basically if you publish a word about him that isn't from an official Conklin Institute PR release, you'll be sued. God forbid if you say something critical about him or the Rulers or what they believe in. Repeat a rumor, mention an allegation that can't be substantiated in court, libel lawyers descend from the heavens like intercontinental ballistic missiles, nuking your ass into bankruptcy."

"Which explains why I can't find anything solid on the Net."

"Yep."

"And why I need to consult with the foremost cult expert in America."

"You flatter me," she says, obviously pleased. "Although it happens to be true. There are young pups nipping at my heels, but I've forgotten more than they know."

"And you don't forget anything."

She shrugs, admitting it. "What can I say? Understand, for the last few years my department has been focusing on the international side. Mostly suicide bomber cults. Not much focus on the domestic cults, unless they happen to utter a chant to Allah. I just got back from Birmingham, England. I'm writing a paper on how Islamists persuade native-born lager louts to don very fashionable explosive vests and blow themselves to bits. On loan to MI5, more or less. So I haven't had a look at the Rulers recently."

"Whatever you've got."

"Okay. Let's start with the basic history. In 1969 Arthur Conklin is a forty-five-year-old professor of entomology at UC Berkeley, married to a former student twenty years his junior. Nice for him. His special interest is bees. He's widely published on hive behavior. A tenured professor, well respected in his field, but something happens—there was a lot of radical stuff going down that year at Berkeley, chaotic behavior he took exception to, he's a pretty conservative guy, is Professor Conklin—and he resigned from his professorship and severed all ties with the university. He and his wife—they have no children—move to a rural area of Colorado, where they live in a remote cabin in the mountains while he writes his famous book."

"They have no children?"

"Not then. After the book is published his wife gets pregnant and they have one child, a boy. Bit of a miracle baby because Professor Conklin has a very low sperm count, result of a fever when he was a child. They name the miracle baby Arthur J. Conklin. Different middle name so he's not a junior."

"*J* for Jedediah."

"Correct. Very good. So Professor Conklin writes his book, gives it a catchy title *The Rule of One.* The book lays out his theory about how human beings can learn from the example of insects and reorganize the brain for success. It's all very complicated—unreadable nonsense in my never-humble opinion—but aside from improving your brain power, the book promises to make you rich. Conklin published the book with a small but legit publisher and that first year he sold less than five hundred copies. So he decides to take back the contract and publish it himself.

Good move on his part. He expands the title to *The Rule of One: How to Unleash the Hidden Powers of Your Mind.* He sets up seminars—get this, he charges to explain his own book, then sells it to you. And he doesn't sell you one copy, he sells you a hundred and tells you how to make money selling it to your friends and neighbors, and how they'll get rich selling it to *their* friends and neighbors."

Shane chuckles and shakes his head. "It never changes, does it? The old scams are the best."

"True," Maggie agrees, "but Conklin added a few variations of his own. Pretty soon he's moving up to ten thousand copies a week in hardcover. Then nearly a hundred thousand copies a month in the trade paperback edition. He's advertising on cable TV, buying thirty minutes at a time, promoting his book, his secret system for accumulating wealth. He gets very wealthy. Some of his devout readers become his followers and take to calling themselves 'Rulers.' They call Conklin the 'Profit,' as in *making a profit.*"

"I heard that," says Shane. "I thought it was a joke."

"No joke. Believe me, these folks are very serious. At this point, the late 1970s, his organization has all the makings of a nascent cult, with the author as the charismatic leader, but it's not quite there yet. *The Rule of One* has a core philosophy—the individual transforms himself by tuning into what he calls 'hive think,' or group intelligence, and then utilizes newfound brain power to dominate the unenlightened. The average saps that Conklin calls 'drones.' That's all very much standard cult, but what the Rulers lack is the origination myth associated with most religions. Conklin has nothing whatever to say about a supreme being, no theory about how the universe began.

He does not promise an afterlife—indeed he discourages any such beliefs. For Rulers, the only thing that counts is the here and now."

"Greed is good."

Maggie smiles. "Not quite. Conklin believes that greed is an effective stimulant for the higher evolution of the mind. He has no particular use for 'good' or 'bad.' But he very effectively uses greed to bind his followers together. Many of the original Rulers, the first few hundred, they also get rich, mostly by running seminars that charge upward of five thousand dollars per person, more or less guaranteeing that true believers will turn that initial investment of five grand into fifty thousand in six months or less. And many of them do."

"A Ponzi scheme?"

"Looks that way, doesn't it? But no. That's what's different about the Rulers. Conklin isn't into ripping off his people. He uses his own accumulated wealth—basically a very private hedge fund—to help the Ruler elite get rich, and stay rich. By elite, I mean those who rise through the ranks, true believers who have proven their understanding and unconditional acceptance of his theories. By this time Arthur Conklin has founded the Conklin Institute and established a strictly controlled hierarchy within the Rulers. He begins to enforce the notion of 'sharing-in,' which means that when you join the club and become a full-fledged Ruler, they access your net worth. From that moment on, you must pledge to return twenty-five percent of any increase in your net worth to the organization."

"You're kidding," says Shane, sitting up straight. "Wow."

"That would be two and a half wows," Maggie says.

"Many churches encourage a more voluntary tithing, donating ten percent of your earnings to the church. Conklin helps you get rich, then takes twenty-five percent of your newfound wealth and returns it to his own coffers. Which means that whatever else they are, the Rulers are made of money. The Conklin Institute is an immense and efficient cash machine. At this point we're talking billions. Invested in real estate, U.S. treasury bonds, and in several holding companies that own or control scores of small, mostly high-tech corporations. Believe me, they're a power on Wall Street. Savvy, deeply secretive, and feared."

"So he really is like Howard Hughes."

"There are certain parallels," Maggie concedes. "Shall we get back to my thumbnail history?" she adds with a grin.

"By all means."

"By 1980 Arthur Conklin is no longer making personal appearances at seminars, at least not live—his image is featured in their presentations, of course, and his voice is on the Ruler indoctrination audiocassettes. By 1985 he's gone from self-help book promoter to full-fledged cult leader and is rarely seen in public. The day-to-day operation of the empire is overseen by his CEO, Wendall Weems. If you think Conklin is secretive, then say hello to Mr. Weems, if you can find him. In 1991, Conklin's wife dies—breast cancer—and he marries Evangeline Dowdy, one of his many accountants. Thirty years his junior—Arthur likes 'em young. The word is that Eva the Diva wields considerable influence within the organization, and has long been resented by Mr. Weems. In 1992 the institute purchases two hundred square miles of remote land in Colorado, establishes their own tightly controlled county government, and builds what amounts to a college campus with a surrounding village called, you guessed it, Conklin."

"So the man doesn't suffer from lack of ego."

"No indeed. And for a while there in the nineties it looked like his cult would go the paranoid route. That's why we were paying special attention, because the more inward and paranoid a cult, the more potential for bloodshed and self-destruction. At the time, the Rulers seemed to be closing ranks, developing a siege mentality. Almost apocalyptic. Not unlike the unfortunate Branch Davidians, but without the religious component. But they were acting like they expected to be attacked, developing a bunker mentality."

"But that changed?"

"It did, yes. Apparently Arthur Conklin had some sort of revelation, or maybe he really did get smarter, because he changed his attitude in a fundamental way. Less inwardly paranoid, more outward recruitment of new members. It worked—the paying membership tripled in size. Conklin—the town, I mean—went from being a bunker-mentality refuge to being what is in effect a ski resort without the skiing. Condos, lodges, all owned by wealthy Rulers. They built a very attractive campus for the institute. All that being said, it remains a very private place—you have to be invited in, and needless to say you pay for the privilege. Seminar fees start at five thousand and go up, the higher you advance within the organization."

"How big is the place?"

"We think the population fluctuates between three and six thousand, depending on who is in residence, but it could be more. As I mentioned, in some ways it functions like a very expensive resort, with members buying time-shares. Virtually all the residents and students are devout Rulers, or those who wish to become Rulers. Anybody else they bring in, mostly maintenance and construction crews, must be issued visitor permits that are akin to visas. They even have their own private security force."

"Like the Vatican."

"I think the Catholic Church would be very offended by the comparison, but yes, a teeny, tiny, little bit like the Vatican, with Arthur Conklin as the pope. In that scenario, Weems and Eva would be rival cardinals, I suppose."

"That old *People* article said it was like Scientology without the science fiction."

Maggie rolls her eyes. "Again, I'm quite sure that Scientologists would be offended by any comparison to the Rulers. Scientology has become a mainstream religious philosophy. Unlike the Rulers, who still operate in the shadows, Scientologists live public lives, and openly defend their beliefs."

"Tom Cruise, John Travolta."

"And Will Smith, Kirstie Allie—the list goes on. I *loved* Travolta in *Hairspray,*" she adds, brightening.

"Missed it," Shane admits, expressing no regret whatsoever. "So tell me, is it plausible that Arthur Conklin would hatch an elaborate scheme to kidnap his own grandson?"

Maggie shifts in her seat, as if uncomfortable with the thought. "Not Conklin himself, I seriously doubt that. But there have been rumors of late."

"Rumors?"

"Only rumors, not substantiated," she cautions. "We do have a few disgruntled Rulers who occasionally pass on information. Lower level types, I'm afraid. Like I say, the agency isn't putting a lot emphasis on tracking non-

Muslim domestic cults of late, unless there are charges of, say, child molestation. Then everybody gets very excitable. Anyhow, the word is that Arthur Conklin is presently incapacitated, and has been for months. A stroke or possibly a neurological disease, nobody seems to be quite sure. What they are sure about is that a couple of factions are struggling for control of the organization."

"And all that money. Billions."

"Yes. This is typical for charisma cults. What happens when the charismatic leader dies? Who takes charge? Power schisms within cults are often resolved by violent means. The word is that the establishment—that would be Wendall Weems, the acting CEO—is in conflict with Evangeline and her faction. Eva's followers include the Ruler security chief."

"What do you know about him?"

"Quite a lot, and it's not good. His name is Bagrat Kavashi, affectionately known as 'Vash.' Dashing-looking fellow with a black mustache, quite vain. Mr. Kavashi hails from the Republic of Georgia, where as an ambitious teenager he ran a private militia that was really a criminal enterprise—extortions, abductions, murders, you name it. When it got too hot, he took his loot and split for good old America, land of opportunity. That was years ago. Apparently Evangeline discovered him, took him under her wing—and possibly into her bed—and set him up in the security business. Turned out to be a good move on her part. BK Security is now third or fourth behind Wackenhut."

Shane says, "Now that I think of it, I'm pretty sure there were BK guards at the lab that processed the remains.

So this Kavashi dude is her pit bull, is that what you're saying? He does the dirty work?"

Maggie nods. "My sense is that if Eva the Diva decided that controlling Arthur Conklin's only living descendent will help them hold on to power, Mr. Kavashi wouldn't hesitate to arrange an abduction, maybe even blow up a school to cover his tracks. But that's all speculation. There's not a shred of physical evidence to support it."

Shane leans forward, his hands folded on the table. "So given what we know about the players, Haley Corbin might not be a paranoid delusional? She might be right? That's your professional opinion?"

Maggie looks him in the eye. No flirting, no fooling, just the facts. "Absolutely," she says. "And if I'm correct, she's in danger, too."

4. Into The Cold And Black

Route 31 isn't exactly a superhighway. Heading west it adds and subtracts lanes at a whim, stops for the occasional traffic light, winds through small towns like Palmyra, Macedon, and Egypt. Farm country, peppered with a few commuter developments, but as far as I'm concerned, on this particular evening it might as well be the yellow brick road to the Emerald City.

After six weeks of pure hell, things are finally clicking, moving faster and yet spinning less. Mad mom has got it going on. Suddenly I'm operating on two fronts. My big guy is in D.C., consulting with experts, and I'm on my way to meet up with the nervous, prefers-to-be-nameless dude who claims to know something about my son's disappearance.

Not that he would tell me much over the phone. Just that he "saw something go down" at the Rochester International Airport the day after Noah's school exploded. What, exactly, he won't say because "they might be listening." I get the impression he works at the airport but he won't give me any particulars, not over the phone.

Mr. Paranoid. A face-to-face, that's the only thing that will make him feel safe enough to speak. I'm more than willing to oblige. A thirty-mile trek is no problem—I'll drive to the ends of the earth, if that's what it takes. Besides it gives me something to do—something with a purpose—while I wait for Shane to return.

On a section of the road that runs parallel to the old Erie Canal, my cell chirps. I snap it open without looking—sorry, I don't do headsets—thinking it might be Mr. Paranoid with more nervous instructions.

"Mrs. Corbin? Is that you?"

"Shane!"

"Are you at home?" he wants to know.

"On the road."

He insists on me pulling over. And not just the side of the road, a proper parking lot, to avoid getting rear-ended. Considering what happened to his family, I give him this one. So I pull in at a feed-and-grain store, closed, and leave the headlights on, illuminating the empty, snow-strewn parking lot.

"Okay," I tell him. "All safe and sound. So what's the verdict?"

Making it sound cheery, like how's the weather, but well aware that his decision may change my life forever.

"You know how I said I'd come back and tell you, no matter what I found out? I'll still be doing that. I'm waiting to board as we speak. But I thought why not let you know, that's what phones are for."

"So you're taking the case," I insist, having decided not to take no for an answer.

"Oh absolutely," he agrees. "Didn't I say that?"

"Not exactly." The blood seems to drain from my head in a pleasant way, leaving me happy and a little light-headed. "But thank you, Shane. Thank you, thank you."

"Sorry, doing two things at once herc. Laptop and phone. The thing is, Mrs. Corbin, an associate has entrusted me with some very interesting data. Everything the FBI has accumulated on the Rulers, including a list of their current members, which is supposed to be a closely guarded secret. Anyhow, first thing I ran a couple of names. Guess who comes up?"

"Roland Penny."

"No, actually, Roland isn't on the list. But get this, a Michael Delancey has been a regular contributor to the Conklin Institute for the last seven years, and his wife, Irene, is on the books for the last five years."

It takes a moment for the names to register.

"Mrs. Corbin?"

"Oh my god," I say in a small voice. "His homeroom teacher!"

"Yeah. That pretty much decided me, right there. One coincidence too many. Following your lead about Mr. Delancey working on Wall Street, I did a little more checking, and last year at this time *both* of the Delanceys were working on Wall Street."

"Both?"

"She worked under her maiden name. So yes, they were employed as investment bankers, managing currency portfolios. A power couple making, one assumes, the big bucks. Next thing, they're in Humble and she's suddenly the kindly schoolmarm, taking a special interest in your son."

"The *bitch,*" I hiss. "I can't believe it! She seemed so nice!"

Shane makes sympathetic noises. "She probably *is* nice, on some level. But she was in on it, the whole scene, she had to be. That seems clear. Every compass is pointing to the Rulers."

"I *knew* it."

"You did, you did," he agrees. Then his voice thickens with concern, and he sounds a teeny bit hesitant, as if not wanting to impart bad news. "Listen, Mrs. Corbin. I've, ah, been consulting with the Bureau's expert on cults and cult behavior, okay? I won't go into the details now, but in her expert opinion there's reason to believe that you may be in danger from these people. Not just your son, you personally."

"They already did their worst," I say. "What more can they do to me?"

"I'll explain it all when I get there," Shane says, speaking quicker. Noises in the background make it sound like he's on the move. "For now I want you to go home, lock the doors, and don't open for anyone but me. Not even for folks you think are friends. If the Rulers planted a member in the school system, they might have somebody else in a position of power or influence. I'll need to run names against the list, see if anyone else pops." He waits a beat, wanting my reaction. "Mrs. Corbin?"

"Soon as I get back, I'll lock the door, promise," I tell him and then explain how someone has finally responded to my find-this-missing-child flyers, and that, as it happens, I'm already on my way to the airport to meet Mr. Paranoid.

Before I can give him the details, he interrupts forcefully. "No! Absolutely not! Turn around, Mrs. Corbin, go home. Please! I'll check the guy out when I get there."

"I don't even know his name," I protest. "His phone number was blocked. How could you possibly find him?"

"You say he works at the airport? I'll find him."

"No, no. That was just my impression, that he works there, okay? He never actually said whether it was the airport proper or in the vicinity. All I know for sure, he has something he wants to tell me about Noah and he's scared to do it over the phone. So I'm meeting him at the car-rental lot."

"He implied he witnessed something?"

"That's what he said. All I know for sure, he's nervous and worried and if I don't show up, I doubt he'll ever call again."

"Do not do this alone," he says, pleading. "Go home. Lock the door."

"It's a rental-car agency," I remind him. "There will be people around. There will be lights, surveillance cameras, airport security. Plus I've got my pepper spray. First sign of anything scary, I'll blast away, promise."

Shane sighs, obviously exasperated by my response. "You're a very stubborn woman, Mrs. Corbin. If you're determined to go ahead with this, do me a favor, okay? After you meet with this guy, whoever he is, don't leave the airport. Find the most public place, a cafeteria or a ticket counter, waiting lounge, whatever is open. Someplace where people congregate. Wait for me there. I'll find you. I'll be on the ground in less than two hours."

"So now you don't want me to go home? What changed?"

"Thinking it through. This could be nothing, just a guy who thinks he saw something, but it could be a ploy to get you out of the house. So find a safe, public place and stay there until I find you. Promise me you'll do that?"

"Yeah, okay. Wait for you at the airport."

"Good, great. Gotta go. We're boarding. I'll see you in less than two hours."

Taking unnecessary risks is not my thing. Never has been. Bungee jumping, skydiving, extreme sports, that's not me. My idea of danger is taking a chance on a new furniture polish. But there's no way I'm going to let Mr. Paranoid walk away. This might be a waste of time, in fact probably is. I know that. Maybe the guy saw another kid who reminded him of Noah, an honest mistake. Maybe he's off his medication. Maybe he's scheming to collect a reward. Maybe he's one of those sickos who gets his kicks messing with worried parents. Whatever, I'm going to find out. Because it's also possible that he's the key, that something he witnessed will lead to my son.

How can a mother *not* take that risk?

My destination, the Budget Rental lot, is on the loop at Airport Road, within sight of the terminal complex. Plenty of lights blazing, but to tell the truth, it feels way more remote than I expected. When I pull up to the rear of the lot as instructed, my little Subaru wagon shivers, buffeted by great blasts of wind from the runways and open fields.

Wind from the north we usually blame on Canada. This is from the east, so I guess Vermont must be at fault. Or maybe Albany. Whatever, I wish it would stop. Surely no one will be wandering around in weather like this, not even Mr. Paranoid. Peering through the slightly blurred windshield, all I can make out are bright security lights, stark shadows, and row upon row of partially frosted vehicles. Small, vivid whirlwinds of snow dancing like tight-hipped ballerinas through the lanes between cars, then suddenly collapsing, as if exhausted by the cold, sucked back into the earth.

He's not going to show, whoever he is. Something spooked him. Come as soon as you can, he'd said, as if he'd be there, regardless. As if he worked here. Doing what? The exit barrier is automatic, and if there's someone manning the return booth, no more than a cubicle, he's keeping out of sight, below the window line. Asleep perhaps?

Should I honk the horn, announce myself?

Inches from my head, a frozen claw rakes ice from the side window. My heart clenches as I jerk around to see a ski-masked face studying me up close, eyes watering.

Not a claw, but a plastic ice scraper. He gestures with the scraper, wanting me to lower the window.

Mr. Paranoid.

I lower the window a few inches, right hand in the pocket of my parka, clutching the canister of pepper spray.

"Haley Corbin?" he asks.

A boy's voice, younger in person. He peels up the ski mask, his breath steaming. A bony, feral-looking face, bad skin, uneven gaps in his teeth. High school or thereabouts—under twenty for sure. The puffs of steam carry the smell of cigarettes and beer.

Mr. Paranoid is drinking on the job. Maybe to calm his nerves—he's a jittery little guy, dancing beside my car.

"In the van," he says, gesturing with the plastic scraper as if it's a light saber. "We'll talk there. Not out here."

Looking around, very furtive, so nervous and flighty I have to remind myself that he could be a threat. He might smite me with the little scraper, breathe toxic fumes at me, gnaw at me with his brittle teeth.

Okay, he looks harmless, more scared of me than I of him, but my hand stays on the pepper spray.

"Keeping the windshields clear, that's my job," he says, suddenly chatty as we squeak through the cold snow. Leading me toward a white Budget Rental van, motor running, windshield steamed. "Every vehicle comes with a scraper, but sometimes that ain't enough. So we got, you know, deicing spray and stuff."

"Like the airlines."

"Yeah," he says. "Like that."

"What's your name?"

"Um, I, ah, rather not say. No names, okay?"

"You know mine."

"Yeah."

I stop a yard from the van, holding my ground. Hand still in my parka, but ready. "I'm not getting in there with you," I announce. "What if you decide to drive way?"

"Why would I do that?" he asks, sounding stunned by the idea.

"What do you know about Noah?" I demand. "What did you see? Did you see my little boy?"

His hands start waving around his head, as if he's being assaulted by bees. "No! Not out here!" he cautions. "Inside. You can sit in the driver's seat. Take the keys if you want, I ain't drivin' you nowhere."

He stamps around the van, gets into the passenger seat, slams the door. I tap at the window. He shakes his head, points at the driver's side.

I slip inside, holding the spray canister in my lap. He stares at the dashboard, his bony face all knotted up, as if he's tasting something unpleasantly sour.

"Okay, here I am, like you wanted. So what about my little boy? What did you see?"

Mr. Paranoid turns to me, his expression still nervous but now also sorrowful.

"Sorry," he says plaintively. "I really needed the money."

Before I can react, something rises behind me.

A strong hand clamps a wet rag to my face.

Dizzy, swirling. Fumes in my eyes.

I'm screaming into the rag when the darkness pulls me down, into the cold, into the black.

5. Strolling Like Kanye

Randall Shane cools his heels in a small, windowless room deep inside the airport terminal. The room is furnished with a small laminated table, three molded plastic chairs, and way too much incandescent lighting. The bilious green walls can't be an accident. Probably some Homeland Security consultant with a theory about color-induced confessions. Sick-making color schemes being about as effective, in Shane's not-so-humble opinion, as blasting loud music at suspects. Turn down the Snoop Dogg, I surrender! Right. Tell it to the Branch Davidians.

An hour creeps by, ever so slowly. Deprived of his cell, laptop, and notes—all connection to the outside world—

he has nothing to occupy his thoughts but an examination of what has transpired since his plane touched down. Whatever mistakes or errors in judgment he may have made, beginning with his decision to go to Washington when, in hindsight, he should have been looking out for the lady. His thoughts keep roving back to that awful moment of tightly controlled panic when he realizes that his worst fears have come to pass: his client is nowhere to be found, not in the airport or vicinity, not at her home. Haley Corbin is gone. First her husband, then her son, now her.

A burly, sour-faced man enters holding two steaming Starbucks cups. He kicks the door shut behind him. "Hey, Randy, thought you might want a coffee."

"Randy?" says Shane, lifting an eyebrow.

"Just trying to be friendly."

"Ah," says Shane without inflection. "That explains it. You were just being friendly when you locked the door."

Preston Chumley, a forty-four-year-old senior investigator with the New York State Police Bureau of Criminal Investigations, feigns an innocent look. "The door was locked? My apologies. That was an oversight. You're not being detained. You're not under arrest."

"I'm also not a suspect," Shane points out. "The sooner you confirm that to your own satisfaction, the sooner you can concentrate on finding Mrs. Corbin."

"Thanks for the advice. We're doing our best, in our simple, bumbling way."

Shane sighs, studying the man, decides his eyes are too close together, that's the problem. Makes it hard for him to see the obvious. Plus his beefy neck bulges over his collar, causing him to resemble a pale, overstuffed sausage.

Maybe it's the too-tight clothing—your basic cheap plain-clothes suit—that makes him irritable and suspicious. Why else detain the very man who reports a woman missing?

"Did you call my contact numbers?"

Chumley shrugs. "I called the first one. Monica whatever."

"FBI Assistant Director Monica Bevins."

"Yeah, her. I left a message. Assistant Director, that's a really high-ranking individual."

"That's right. She reports to the Deputy Director."

"I'm impressed. Thing is, she hasn't got around to returning my call. So either she doesn't know you, doesn't respond to inquiries from state investigators, or she's busy with some really important FBI stuff and can't be bothered. Which pretty much leaves us back where we started."

"Me reporting a crime."

"You reporting your suspicion—I believe you called it a 'gut instinct'—that a woman was abducted from this airport."

"Or nearby."

"The car-rental lot, yeah. Happens to be on airport property."

"Have you found her vehicle?"

Instead of answering, Chumley chews on a torn cuticle, spits it out. Cuticle chewing in public is, in Shane's opinion, a felony offense, but the investigator doesn't seem the least ashamed of his rude, disgusting behavior. Probably talks on his cell while urinating; he's that kind of guy.

Shane tells himself to cool it, that the more personal this gets, the less he'll accomplish. What matters here is Mrs. Corbin, not minor bruises to his own ego.

"If you think I've been interfering in an investigation, I apologize," Shane says. "It won't happen again."

Chumley shrugs lazily. "Oh yeah? I know how you operate. You're all over the Internet. Testimonials from grateful parents. Very moving."

"Don't believe everything you read on the Net."

"Oh, I don't. All that stuff about Randall Shane never giving up, taking the law into his own hands, gathering evidence without warrants, impersonating a law officer, making local investigators look like clowns. You really did all that, you'd have been prosecuted and I checked—you haven't. So the testimonials are bull. The big deal former FBI Special Agent, that's bull, too, isn't it, Randy?"

"If you say so."

"I mean, come on, it's not like you were out there recovering kidnap victims when you were with the agency. You weren't exactly kicking down doors, right? You were, quote, developing print recognition software, unquote."

"That's right."

"A computer geek. Big guy like you? My guess, they discovered you were useless in the field so they stuck you back at the lab, gave you your very own pocket protector."

Shane nods agreeably. "I still have it. The pocket protector. Better than a flak jacket."

"My point exactly," says Chumley, attempting to loosen his collar with a plump pink finger, bleeding around the torn cuticle.

"It's true," Shane says, shamefaced. "I'm a complete fraud. I've been taking credit for work done by real police. I'm completely out of my depth. That's why I reported Mrs. Corbin missing, because I didn't know what else to do."

Chumley's piggy little eyes brighten. "So you admit

you misrepresented yourself to the attendant at the car-rental lot?"

"Not intentionally, no. I'd never do that. But he may have gotten the impression I was an active agent, rather than retired."

Chumley sits up straight. "You badged him?"

"I don't have a badge. I showed him a leather folder holding my business card. You have that, along with my wallet."

"Guy thinks he saw a badge."

"It was snowing. I woke him up. He fell asleep listening to the shopping channel. There was alcohol on his breath. You probably noticed that, being a senior investigator and all."

"Don't smart-mouth me, pal. Yeah, the guy is a drunk, that doesn't mean he didn't see a badge."

"Double negative, I think."

"What?"

Shane sighs, tries to look ashamed. "You got me, Trooper. I put all that stuff on the missing children forums myself, the testimonials, the pictures of kids reunited with their families. I'm in it strictly for the money, taking advantage of grief-stricken parents. When I was with the agency I hid behind a desk because I was afraid to kick in doors. I faint at the sight of blood. I suck."

"I knew it," says Chumley. He has the hungry, can't-wait-another-moment expression of a man about to gobble up a big juicy jelly doughnut.

"But in this particular instance I didn't break any laws," Shane adds, almost sorrowfully. "I did not impersonate an officer of the law. I no longer own a badge, not even a commemorative or courtesy badge, and if I did I wouldn't use it because that would be illegal and I'm a coward and afraid to go to jail."

The trooper sucks his teeth, looking irritated. "She's rich and crazy and you took advantage of her. How much you get?"

"Nothing yet. We hadn't agreed on a fee."

"Oh yeah? Is that your story? Maybe I never worked for the feds, but we got our sources, and I happen to know that Haley Corbin withdrew ten grand in cash within the last few days."

"Wouldn't give it to me," Shane says. "Showed me the cash, said I had to produce results. Very hard-nosed lady, Mrs. Corbin."

"It's illegal to pose as a private investigator."

"I'm a consultant. That's legal."

"Where I sit? All you fake P.I.s and unlicensed P.I.s and so-called consultants, all you do is take advantage of folks don't know better. Vultures."

"You got me. I'm scum of the earth. Did you locate her vehicle?"

"I'm asking the questions here, and so far—"

He's interrupted by a brisk knock on the door. A young, uniformed trooper leans in. "Sir? Major Seavey on the landline."

Chumley scowls, gets to his feet. "Stay where you are, please," he says to Shane, exiting.

The lock on the door clicks.

Shane leans back with his fingers laced behind his neck, feeling much better, thank you. From the sound of it Major Seavey would be Chumley's boss at the Bureau of Criminal

Investigation, the troopers plainclothes division. A wiser mind, no doubt, or he wouldn't have risen to such a high rank at the BCI. At that level he'd have had many dealings and links with various federal enforcement agencies, be less inclined to react like S.I. Chumley, nursing his resentments.

That, or he'd order Shane be formally held on a trumped-up charge until the BCI boys could sort it out. Fifteen minutes tick by with the alacrity of paint drying on a rainy day. Shane studies his fingernails. Wishing he had his laptop, or failing that something to read. Newspaper, magazine, novel, cereal box, whatever.

Centuries pass. Eventually S.I. Chumley reenters the room with a new attitude. From his expression, one might assume the new attitude has been achieved by having his fingernails extracted.

Shane relaxes.

"Follow me," says the newly forlorn investigator.

Shane follows him out of the interrogation room, down a series of narrow, windowless hallways, to a room not much larger than the one he's just vacated. Chumley holds the door, says nothing as Shane passes. The room is crammed with small surveillance screens, floor to ceiling. Flat-screen LCD monitors, and most have been divided into four separate feeds from video cams positioned throughout the airport. He doesn't bother counting but there have to be more than a hundred cameras in the system.

"Impressive," Shane says to his silently brooding host.

It isn't particularly impressive, but he's trying to be nice. No sense rubbing the man's nose in the mess he made. The practice rarely works with puppy dogs, never with humans.

Without meeting Shane's eyes, the burly investigator

explains. "Assistant Director Bevins has requested that you be afforded full cooperation. My supervisor has ordered me to comply."

"I do appreciate it," says Shane.

"Figured you for a fake," Chumley continues, pulling the words out as if they're as deeply imbedded as bullets. "Feds say you're not…my mistake."

"Not a problem. What did you find?"

Chumley heaves a deep sigh, nods at the surveillance screens. "The vic's vehicle. Ground level in the long-term parking garage. Empty."

"You conduct a search?"

"Not without a warrant, no. But we did a thorough visual. It's a wagon, fully visible, no place to hide a body, if that's what you're thinking."

"That's what I'm thinking," Shane admits, the clench in his belly relaxing somewhat. "You get her on film, parking the car?"

"No film," says Chumley, a little huffy. "This is a fully digital operation."

Shane waits. Film is just a figure of speech, and Chumley knows it.

"Not her," the inspector finally explains, words thick in his throat. "The kid who parked it."

Shane is instantly fully alert, blood humming. "Show me," he says.

Chumley cues up the MPEGs, indicates that Shane can run the little joystick if he so desires. The first segment, four seconds or so in duration, is from the automatic ticket dispenser at the south entrance to the long-term parking garage, across the street from the terminal. As the driver runs down the window he averts his head. Down jacket with the hood up, total concealment of the face. Shane gets the same youthful impression Chumley mentioned, but all he can really identify with any certainty is the slim hand plucking the ticket from the dispenser.

"Caucasian."

"White guy, yeah."

"He knows about the cameras."

"Anybody who pays attention knows about the cameras. We don't hide 'em."

"Maybe he's an employee."

"Maybe."

Shane takes his time, plays the file through in slo-mo, and then one frame at a time. Nothing pops. Nobody in the background behind the driver. Passenger seat appears to be empty. No indication Haley Corbin is on board. No revealing reflections in any surface, glass or mirror. He scrolls forward to the next file segment. The main feature, fourteen seconds in duration. Opens as Mrs. Corbin's Subaru wagon wheels into a compact car slot. Seen from the rear at a distance that takes in the entire row of cars. The Subaru door opens almost instantly, but the driver has trouble exiting the vehicle because he's parked too close to the next car.

Drumroll, Shane thinks, expecting the panicked driver to do something stupid. But what he does is smart, in that situation. He backs out of the door butt first. Obviously keenly aware of camera placement, because not only is he backing out, he's using his left hand to hold the hood in place. Manages to keep his head fully averted from the camera.

"Watch for it," Chumley cautions.

In that instant a gust of wind invades the parking garage and blows back the hood. For a moment the young man remains frozen, as if uncertain of what to do, but it doesn't matter: he's wearing a ski mask. Once free of the car, the masked and hooded man quickly vanishes into the shadows, out of camera range.

"Hood and mask," says Chumley. "That's a perp wears rubbers over his boots. Mr. Careful."

Mr. Paranoid, Shane thinks as he plays the little movie to death, but again nothing pops.

"What is with the way he walks?"

"Hip-hop," says Chumley. "Lots of white boys adopt the hip-hop walk."

"That explains it," says Shane with a nod. "Like he's a little bouncy. I assumed it was nerves, but you're right. He moves like a rapper."

"Very common," says Chumley, sounding pleased with himself. "Half the kids in Rochester, the white kids, I mean, they stroll like Kanye."

"Who?"

"You never heard of Kanye West?"

"If I did, I forgot."

"Yeah, well."

"I'm more Van Morrison, J. J. Cale, Bonnie Raitt," Shane explains. "Although I do like a couple of Amy Winehouse songs. That old R & B feel, you know?"

"Not exactly. I got a fifteen-year-old thinks Kanye is God. That's why I know."

"Okay then," Shane says, getting back to it. "We both agree he's young, twenty-five or under, white, probably likes hip-hop. That about it?"

"He didn't steal the car," Chumley points out, sounding a defensive note even as he posits a worthwhile statement. "Means he was part of it."

"The probable abduction of Haley Corbin?"

"What I said. He comes upon an abandoned car, he's got a couple of options—report it or steal it. Putting the vehicle out of plain sight by hiding it in a parking garage, that's more like he's following orders."

"Part of a conspiracy."

"I hate that word. The grassy knoll and all that shit."

"A small, contained criminal conspiracy to abduct a woman. She's lured to a particular destination, probably the car-rental lot she mentioned, they grab her and get rid of her car. Wouldn't take more than two or three people if they were well organized."

"Conspiracy in the legal sense."

"Exactly," says Shane. "You, me, and our buddy Kanye agree to rob a bank. That's conspiracy, agreed?"

"Sure, yeah. So who took her, if indeed she got snatched?"

Shane thinks carefully, decides not to share more than necessary. Not at this juncture, and not with S.I. Chumley. "Unknown. She believed she was meeting with someone who had information about her son."

Chumley has recovered enough to look Shane in the eye. "This is the fatality in Humble, right? The school?"

"Mrs. Corbin believes that her son survived the explosion."

Chumley's jowls tremble as he clears his throat. "She did, huh? What do you think?"

Shane's smile is tight, giving nothing away. "I think Mrs. Corbin is missing."

6. Darker Than Sleep

I wake up weeping because in my dream Noah is curled up next to me and I'm stroking his hair and want the dream never to end.

The sense of aching loss feels as if it will stop my heart.

I had him back! Spooning his little body against mine as we did when his father died, both of us seeking the welcome amnesia of sleep. Part of me knew it could not last, that waking would make him vanish. But it seemed so real. He was there. I smelled his hair. Felt his pulse beating in time with my own.

Losing a child is like losing a limb. You know the limb is gone but when you close your eyes you can still feel it. The connection remains intact, nerves to brain, blood to heart, soul to soul. And so I remain curled in a fetal position, clenching my eyes shut, willing him back to me. Just for a moment, God. Just long enough to sense his warmth.

After a while the weeping slowly fades and I realize that my eyes are no longer closed. And yet somehow the darkness remains. A darkness darker than sleep. A darkness pressing me from all sides.

My hands fly out, connecting with a hard, plastic surface.

The Budget Rental van, the jittery boy saying he was sorry, he needed the money. Something rising from behind, the wet rag over my mouth. It comes back all at once, like a punch to the guts: *I've been abducted.*

Kicking out, or trying to, I discover why I'm in the fetal position, curled up knees to chest: there's not room enough to stretch my legs out. Breathing deep, forcing calmness, I use my hands and feet to find the limits of my confinement and discover that I'm surrounded by heavy plastic, the surface riddled with holes. Vent holes. There's a slippery steel grate just beyond the top of my head and some sort of padded rug under me.

I know what this is. A dog crate. One of those big plastic things. My friend Helen has a big, honey-colored Lab who prefers to sleep in his kennel. Raised that way from a puppy, he thinks the kennel is his den, feels safe inside it.

Someone drugged me, shoved me into a dog crate. Is the crate in the back of the van? Is that why the darkness is so absolute?

In the darkness the crate begins to move. Faster and faster and faster.

I scream and scream and scream.

7. The Hip-Hop Kid

An hour or so later Shane is back at his room at the Comfort Inn, a few miles from the airport. He's in the shower, bending down so the hot water can stream over the top of his head, when his cell goes off, dancing across the porcelain. Fully shampooed, he has to blindly reach for the phone, patting the entire sink area the way he'd pat a dog. So by the time he has the thing up to his ear, the message has gone to voice mail.

Good news. The hip-hop kid is in custody.

Senior Investigator Preston Chumley's superiors have decided that the suspect should be interrogated on the airport premises, under the legal auspices of the Homeland

Security Administration, rather than at the nearest local police station. HSA having sweeping powers of detention, namely the legal authority to detain virtually anyone for any behavior deemed suspicious, the actual 'suspicious' component being very carefully undefined in the statute.

"Basically they can yank you out of line for chewing gum the wrong way. Or in this case what we're calling a 'distinctive gait.'"

"Walking the wrong way," Shane says.

"And not chewing gum at the same time," Chumley adds with a grin.

"However you did it, that's mighty fast work, cowboy."

"Nothin' to it," the trooper says, affecting a western drawl. "Started with rental company employees, found him almost before we started looking."

"And you're sure he's the one?"

"If there's another skinny, hip-hop-walking white boy working the rental lots, I haven't found him. Has to be him," Chumley adds, "because he's so ready, you know?"

"He wasn't surprised you picked him up?"

"Not in the least."

The deal is, as a former Special Agent with an interest in the case, Shane will be extended the courtesy of witnessing the interrogation, but will not be allowed to ask questions. Not directly.

"I ask you, you ask him?"

"That'll work," says Chumley, who seems to have decided that things will go easier if he makes nice with the former FBI agent.

The suspect has been deposited in the same small, windowless room where Shane was so recently entertained.

Sitting there with his chin on his narrow chest, eyes heavily lidded, revealing no surprise or anticipation as the two men enter. Arms folded, knees cranked wide. The sullen, knowing posture of a troubled youth with wide experience in the criminal justice system. Shaved head, baggy pants, a blurry ninja tattoo on his neck, the whole career delinquent package.

Except, curiously, Gordon Kurtso, nineteen, has never before been arrested or detained. Not even a traffic ticket.

The state investigator slides his chair close enough to smell the boy's breath. "Hey, Gordon. You hanging in there?"

The boy does not react.

"Sorry we had to drag you out of bed. You've got a cold, right? That's why you left in the middle of your shift?"

No reaction.

Chumley turns to Shane. "Picked him up, he said he had the flu. Must be a throat flu, affecting his voice. You know what the cool thing is with Mr. Gordon Kurtso? He goes by G-Man. That's his gangster nickname or his street name or whatever." Chumley turns back to the suspect, cocking his head sideways as he tries to make eye contact. "You make that up yourself, Gordon? G-Man? 'Cause the funny thing is, we got a real G-man with us. This big dude is former FBI Special Agent. Special Agent with a special interest, you might say."

The boy speaks. "I want a lawyer."

"I want lots of things," Chumley says agreeably. "Wanting keeps you focused. You better focus, G-Man. Tell us everything you know about that little Subaru. Where you found it. Why you parked it. Everything."

The boy shrugs. "It wasn't me."

"Yeah, it was."

"I want a lawyer."

"Okay, maybe you didn't actually abduct the lady yourself. Maybe all you did was move the car. If that's how it went down, say it, we'll go from there."

"I want a lawyer."

"Okay, if you insist we can go in a different direction. Maybe keep you under detention while we get a warrant, search your domicile, see what we find. Top to bottom search, looking for cash, drugs, whatever."

The boy snorts. "Fishing. You'll never get a warrant. I want a lawyer."

Chumley tries to look casual and relaxed, mostly succeeds. "I dunno, terrorist activities, you'd be surprised how easy it is to get a warrant."

"I ain't no terrorist and you know it. Do I get a lawyer or what?"

"Woman possibly abducted at an international airport? That could be construed as terrorist activity. They give us pretty wide latitude, Gordon, when we're working with Homeland Security. Believe me on this."

"I believe you're lying," the boy says, staring at the floor. "I want a lawyer."

"Let me sketch out your situation, Gordon. A young mother agrees to meet with a stranger who claims to have information about her, um, missing ten-year-old boy. The mother is now missing, presumed abducted. No doubt we'll be able to trace your call to her. The call that lured her out here."

The boy shakes his head, looking smug and confident.

"Used a throwaway, did you? No problem, we can enhance the parking garage video, use heat sensors to map your face. We can prove it's you. Didn't you ever see *CSI?* Technology is on our side."

"Bullshit," the boy sneers.

"Worst case, we recover Mrs. Corbin and she identifies you. Then you're part of a conspiracy to abduct—that's a federal offense. No parole for a federal conviction, did you know that? Just time off for good behavior, maximum fifty-four days per each year served. Kidnapping? If the victim survives, they might go light, you could get as little as thirty years. Figure you'd serve twenty-seven, provided you're a good little boy. If she dies? The least you'd get is life. No time off for good behavior on a life sentence. You spend the rest of your days behind bars."

"So," the boy asks, "am I arrested? Are you pressing charges?"

Chumley rolls his piggy little eyes. "We're discussing your options, kid. You want to be arrested, is that it?"

"I'm requesting a lawyer. The Homeland Security angle is crap. You gotta get me a lawyer if I ask."

"You sure about that?"

"You're a sworn officer of the law, right? When I ask for a lawyer that means you have to stop with your bullshit questions and get me a lawyer."

Chumley sighs, stands up.

"Coffee break?" he says to Shane.

Outside, the investigator makes a face. "That went well, huh? You believe that kid?"

"He watches a lot of TV. That's where he picked up the tough-guy act. Probably *The Wire.*"

Chumley rubs his jowls, looking exhausted. "Wire

schmire, he knows the law. HSA lets us detain and question him on a hunch or because he looks wrong. But unless he's identified as a known terror suspect he has the right to counsel. He asks for a lawyer, he gets a lawyer, that's the way it works."

"Within a reasonable time frame."

"Which is flexible, yeah. But only if we got a major player. You and I know he's the guy, but I'll never be able to charge him based on his hippity-hop styling. All we got is the hunch—we both know that. Apparently he knows it, too."

"You're letting him walk?"

Chumley grimaces. "Hell no. Not until I've grilled him like a bad hamburger."

"Enjoy," Shane says, picking up his briefcase. "You might have better luck on your own."

"Maybe so," says the investigator wistfully. "I really thought he'd take one look at the size of you and pee his pants."

"The little shit is waterproof." Shane offers his hand. "Thanks for this. Sorry we got off on the wrong foot. My personal observation, you're good police."

Chumley shrugs. "We'll see about that."

8. MC Popsicle

They kick him loose at dawn, twenty minutes after his public defender drags her saggy, underpaid butt onto the premises. No arrest, therefore no hearing, no bail. Nothing more than a stern warning not to leave the area.

Right.

"Why would I leave?" He smirks on his way out, not

even bothering to thank the P.D., who stands there with her jaw slack and her eyes still sleepy.

Screw 'em both. Cops and lawyers, two sides of the same stupid coin. Why should he be grateful? Because she mumbled a few words, did her job?

F-bomb that.

G-Man's very jaunty as he strolls into the big bad world, heading for his wheels, his breath coming in cold little puffs of steam. Thinking he will have to quit his job, stay away from the airport. Hanging around, taunting that pig of a cop would be fun, but he's no fool. Out of sight, out of mind, that's the way to go. Also he needs to be careful with the money. His crew finds out he's green, they'll be all hands out gimme some of that love.

The money is for personal use. It'll buy him four or five sessions in a real studio, let him find the right beats, put down his flow, do his own slim shady thing.

His wheels, a faded box of dents that used to be a Chevy Impala, waits in the employee lot under an inch-thick dusting of fluffy snow. He's thinking if the mutha won't start he can always ask the public defender bitch for a jump start.

G-Man unlocks the door, creaks it open as fluffy snow cascades to the ground. Cold and dark in there, he's thinking, but before he can climb behind the wheel something happens. Something big crushes him into the seat. Hands like steel grappling hooks shove his face so deep into the cold, tattered foam-stink of the seat that he can't breath. Steel hands that lock on his jaw and squeeze so hard that he feels the lower half of his face dislocating, creating an explosion of pain so totally awesome that he wants to scream like a girl, if only he could.

Twenty seconds later he's wrapped like a mummy in silver duct tape, arms pinned to his sides, everything but his eyes and one nostril slathered in wraps of adhesive. Then he's rudely flipped into the backseat, crashing faceup, unable to do anything but squirm in a writhing panic.

"My advice, don't fight it," suggests the big dude, looming over the seat like a neatly bearded monster, all angry eyes and flashing teeth. His big steely hands encased in surgical gloves. "All your air has to come through one little nostril. Concentrate on that. Fight it and you'll smother."

The big dude chilling next to the fat cop, didn't say much. Big dude holding up the roll of duct tape.

"Love this stuff," he says. "Better than cuffs. Way more effective. With handcuffs the victim can still scream, maybe even bite. Did you know the human bite can be more deadly than a dog bite? Fact. Comes to biting, your average human being is more dangerous than your average pit bull."

G-Man bucks and shivers, getting nowhere. Strangled little yelps coming from deep beneath the duct tape.

"Gordon," says the big dude. "Calm yourself. You have limited air. Just enough to keep your brain conscious, not enough for a struggle. Besides, the struggle part won't work."

The big dude tears off a strip of tape.

"See this? This is the final frontier. If you don't stop squirming, I'll tape up your last nostril and that will be that. The only remaining question, will they find your dead body before it freezes solid. G-Man, The Human Popsicle."

Unable to control his fear, G-Man bucks and whimpers for a while. Then he stops. The stench of urine permeates the already rancid interior of the old Impala.

"It happens," the big dude says with a shrug. "Sphincter's next, if you don't relax, concentrate on getting all the air you can through that one little nostril. Try it. See? Better already."

G-Man weeps as he carefully inhales through a single, snot-encrusted nostril. It's like sucking air through a too-small straw.

"Here's the deal," says the big dude, in words that fall like shards of ice. "You're going to tell me what happened to Haley Corbin. The lady with the missing kid. The one you called. The one you set up. You'll be giving me all the details. Every little thing."

The big dude slips a hand around G-Man's neck. "Are you ready? You'll notice I have really big hands and you have a really small neck. Feel that? That's me squeezing just a little. If you scream when I pull back the tape, I'll squeeze a lot."

The big dude peels back the duct tape. G-Man tries to scream.

The big dude pastes the tape back down over his gaspy little mouth, heaves a deep sigh of disappointment.

"I was hoping you weren't a slow learner," he says. "Oh well. We'll just have to take our time."

9. Did I Mention The Really Comfy Leather Seats?

"Sorry about the dog kennel," the woman says, not even pretending to sound apologetic. "It's all we could think to do."

My captor is a slightly built, extremely nervous female with a tidy little mop of curly, dyed-blond hair and small, darting eyes that never seem to settle on anything. She's crouching at the locked grill of the kennel, exuding an air of ironic detachment, like isn't it faintly amusing that we, two women of the world, find ourselves in this position, you inside the cage and me outside laying down the rules?

Me, I'm not feeling ironic. More like enraged and terrified and helpless and more enraged, that combination, in that order. Keenly aware of how a trapped animal must feel, caged and in motion, unable to see where its tormentors are taking it. When the bumpy acceleration first threw me to the back of the kennel, I assumed I was in a runaway van, about to smash into something at high speed—as if my captors were staging a fatal accident. Then, abruptly, we were airborne and rising rapidly, and my trip-hammer heart began to ease.

I was in a plane, probably in the cargo compartment. I had assumed it must be a commercial airliner, something big enough to have a special place to stow pets, but when Miss Ironic crawled in and turned on the lights, it became obvious that I was aboard a relatively small aircraft.

"Gulfstream G-450," she tells me. "Owned, not leased. In this configuration we can carry six passengers, three crew. Tonight all we've got is me and Eldon and the one pilot, with the cockpit door sealed from the inside. So if the pilot has like a stroke or something we're all screwed. Eldon thinks he could fly the thing, because he helped develop this flight simulator software? But really he couldn't. And besides he can't get through the cockpit door with the pilot down, can he? No way."

Still not quite looking at me as she chatters away, naming various options on their aircraft, as if it were a luxury automobile. Leather seats, individual climate control, exotic hardwood trim, even "a totally amazing wine chiller that also works on champagne bottles." Mostly staring at her shoes as she babbles on. Blahniks, slightly scuffed, which is probably a crime in her zip code.

"Who the hell are you?" I finally demand, hooking my fingers in the cage door. Resisting the impulse to bare my teeth like some rabid canine. "Where are you taking me?"

My captor studies her nails and sighs. "Colorado. Ever been? They have these mountains, really serious mountains. Eldon likes to conquer mountains. Me, I could care less."

Colorado.

"You're Rulers," I suggest.

My captor giggles nervously. "Well, duh! Where else would we get fifty million bucks to buy a little old airplane? Not that it's old. You know what I mean."

"Let me out of here!"

My captor runs a frail hand through her mop of curls. Looking like an elfin version of Harpo Marx. A female Harpo who can't stop running her nervous mouth. "Yeah, well that's what I'm here to discuss. Maybe letting you out if you're cool with it. Eldon thinks I should negotiate, you know, girl-to-girl or whatever. Did I mention the really comfy leather seats? If you'll promise to behave you can come into the cabin, which is way better than first class. You can even have a glass of wine if you want."

"I promise."

"Yeah, but you would, wouldn't you? Promise anything to get out of this doggy thing? I know *I* would. It must suck in there, you don't have any legroom at all. The thing is, we're like totally on your side."

"You're on my side?" The woman must be deranged. They drugged me, jammed me into a dog kennel, and they're on my side?

She nods, serious as a heart attack. "Totally. We're trying to facilitate the situation."

"What does that mean?"

"The whole succession thing, it's gotten totally out of control. The whole point of being a Ruler—well, one of the points—is we don't attract attention from government drones. Like we make tons and tons of money—Eldon made almost half a billion last year, isn't that amazing?—but we always pay our taxes. So they leave us alone. But this," she adds, indicating my cage, "stuff like this, they might get the wrong idea."

I'm speechless. The wrong idea?

"Because the thing is, we're going to help you get your son back," she says. "That's what you want, right?"

"Oh…my…god," I gasp, convulsing.

"You knew he was alive, right?" she says, sounding concerned. "Oh wow, I guess maybe you didn't know for sure. Well, he is. I haven't seen him myself, but everybody says he's really cute and smart and everything. Are you okay? You're not going to puke are you? You need to like, take a breath or something."

She unlocks my cage.

Part IV
Rulers

1. What Noah Knows

Evangeline stands at the leading edge of the glass atrium that juts out from the Pinnacle like the prow of a great ship. Far below, dense clouds roll in slow, majestic motion. Waiting for her loyal faction of Rulers to assemble, she sips a healing potion of rare green tea from a paper-thin porcelain cup. The tea is outrageously overpriced. Evangeline should know—she owns the company, an herbal remedy outfit that promises to cure all disease, reverse aging, and delivers, well, a cup of pretty good tea. Five thousand dollars an ounce, and legal. Why deal in illicit drugs when unregulated herbal remedies generate more revenue, without the risk? For years she has invested heavily in high-end herbal products, as well as a successful chain of luxury rejuvenation spas. She knows the market. Money flows to Evangeline, and she believes that wealth buys her health. It pays for the exotic emollients that soften the faint scar lines of her numerous cosmetic surgeries. Surgeries which make her look decades younger, as seen from a middle distance. Close-up her complexion has the quality of a theatrical mask, an effect of which she's keenly aware. For that and other reasons, she confines her appearances to video whenever possible. As Arthur so clearly understood, video imagery, which can be endlessly repeated and manipulated, has always been the key to indoctrination and mental dominance.

A gentle gong sounds. It is time. She glides across the atrium, enters the private studio that was originally designed for her husband. A thronelike chair with a back-screen projection of mountain peaks at dawn. A simple, powerful image inspired by the designs of Leni Riefenstahl, who knew a thing or two about the triumph of the will. Long ago, Evangeline learned how to control the lighting and cameras, enabling her to dispense with a crew and give her complete control. She positions herself in the throne, checks the resulting image in the studio monitor, and then strokes the touch-screen, activating the connection to the secure video conferencing room where her faction has gathered.

"Greetings from the Pinnacle," she purrs. "Together we face the new day with a new mind."

The ritual greeting, originated by Arthur Conklin, often shortened to "new day, new mind" by his followers. Evangeline prefers the complete phrase, a subtle reminder that she alone speaks for her husband. Gazing at the conference-room monitors, she names those in attendance, noting their generous contributions to the cause. Seven of the most successful Rulers, all originally recruited by Evangeline herself, and rewarded for their loyalty with key positions within the hierarchy. Four males, three females, each keenly aware that the organization is about to undergo traumatic change. Each determined to emerge with more power, more wealth. True believers, every one of them.

"The great mind still lives," she assures them. "We spoke not an hour ago, and once again he has made his wishes clear. First, he insists that the truth of his condition be shared with his most trusted followers." Evangeline pauses, takes a deep breath. "Needless to say, this information must not be passed on to those at a lower level. As some of you are already aware, Arthur's body is failing. The years of dialysis have taken their toll, as we all knew they must, and he has decided not to undergo another transplant. In my weakness I begged him—" She pauses wiping a nonexistent tear from her eye. "I begged him to live, to survive at whatever cost, but as always, Arthur knows best. He wants you all to know that he does not fear physical death. He experiences no pain, and contrary to certain malicious rumors his brilliant mind remains clear. He remains focused on the future and he believes absolutely that soon he will truly face a new day with a new mind."

She pauses, letting her words sink in, reading the faces. Of course they already know about Arthur's condition. Several show signs of relief, having heard the malicious rumor that the founder is virtually brain-dead. And so he is, to all intents and purposes. The true state of affairs matters not; so long as Evangeline claims otherwise, they will choose to believe her.

"I've called you together this morning to impart great news," she says, her reedy voice lifting. "Like Arthur's true condition, this information must not be shared until the time is right. Hear me and share my joy. Even as the founder and the one true Ruler fades away, his successor is amongst us."

With a great flourish she keys the video feed from a secret, highly secure location called the Nursery. A live image appears on their screens, triggering gasps of astonishment from the faction. One of the females is seen to shriek and can barely contain her exuberance.

"You are looking at the new form of Arthur Conklin," Evangeline informs them. "By DNA, by blood itself, the boy is two generations removed. In the primitive way of thinking, he is a grandson of our founder. But the bond is much, much closer than mere DNA. As so often happens, true genius seems to have skipped a generation. Our tests confirm the boy has Arthur's level of intelligence, and Arthur's amazing talent for mathematics, and many aspects of Arthur's unique, charismatic personality. Given the correct environment, he will evolve into the One True Voice that guides us, our Ruler of Rulers."

The live video feed reveals the boy seated at a small desk in a sunlit room. The colors are warm, soothing. The boy has been fitted with headphones and appears to be listening intently as his slim, blond-haired tutor, seated nearby, takes notes. The boy's expression reveals little. He might be aware of the concealed cameras covering his every breath and move, he might not, hard to say. But the resemblance to boyhood photographs of his grandfather—iconic images revered by all true Rulers—is uncanny and produces exactly the effect Evangeline has anticipated.

As Arthur himself might have said, in one of his more ironic moments, there is joy in Mudville. The conference room is abuzz. Her mighty seven can barely contain themselves. They have many questions—some are shouting themselves hoarse at the muted conference microphones—

but Evangeline has decided that today's presentation, like almost all of Arthur's many presentations, will be strictly one-way. She speaks, they listen.

"The boy has been with us only for a short time," she explains, "and yet already he has begun to absorb some of his grandfather's revolutionary theories of human thought and social organization. At this very moment he is listening to Arthur's first recorded lecture from *The Rule of One.* You may be thinking, he's only a child, how much can he understand of this difficult text? I can tell you only this—you'd be amazed how much he comprehends. Even so, we expect the learning process to take a number of years. After all, most of us have been studying Arthur's thoughts for a lifetime, and still we have much to learn."

On the screen the boy seems to look directly into one of the many cameras monitoring his every movement. It is the face of a child, soft and not yet fully formed, but his eyes have an intensity rarely seen in a child of ten.

"This concludes the session," says Evangeline with a frosty smile, using the phrase that her husband employed at the conclusion of all of his lectures. "Over the next few days I will be contacting each of you individually. There is much to do."

Her lacquered nail strokes the touch pad and she vanishes from the screen.

In the Nursery, Noah sits quietly at his desk, pretending to listen to the annoying drone in his headphones. Mrs. Delancey says the voice is his grandfather and that it doesn't matter if he doesn't understand at first, the words themselves will be recorded deep inside his mind and will slowly improve his brain from the inside out.

Noah doesn't want to have his brain improved, but he knows he must bide his time. He knows Mrs. Delancey is a big fat liar, liar with her pants on fire. He's keenly aware that even though everybody seems very nice, and treats him as if he's really special, they're holding him against his will, which is the same as kidnapping. He knows all of this and one thing more: they're lying about what happened to his mother when the school exploded. He knows in his head and his heart and his bones that Mom didn't die there, like they said, and that someday soon she will come to get him, and when she does Mrs. Delancey and all the others will be in big, big trouble.

That's what Noah knows.

2. The Man With The Beautiful Eyes

The thing about being afraid is that after a while it makes you tired. At first the fear is like fire in your blood, and all your senses seem enhanced. Smell, color, sound—everything is more vivid. I suppose that must be the adrenaline, keeping you wide-awake, ready for anything. And then as time passes it just gets so exhausting that all you want to do is close your eyes and go away.

Minutes after the plane lands, I'm sound asleep. No idea how long I'm out, but when I finally do wake up it's to find myself in what at first glance looks like a dimly illuminated luxury hotel suite. Heavy drapes cloak the windows. The furniture is low, ultramodern, and for some strange reason—something to do with my dreams?—looks vaguely sinister.

The next thing I notice is that I've been dressed in cotton pajamas—who do *these* belong to?—and then something clicks in my head and I'm sitting bolt upright shouting, "Noah! Noah! It's Mom!"

A moment later the woman with the flouncy mop of Harpo curls appears by the bedside, eyes almost comically wide, her mouth a pink O of surprise. "Hey!" she says, looking as panicked as me. "Hey! Calm down!"

It's the petite little woman who let me out of the cage, who told me Noah was alive. My captor, my savior, whatever, my only direct link to him right now, and I can't help myself.

"Where is he?" I demand, grabbing her wrists, pulling her close. "I want my son!"

Frightened by my iron grip, she cries out in a high voice, "Eldon! Eldon!" and a moment later a slightly larger male version of herself appears, looking equally startled.

The husband. I must have glimpsed him when they transferred me from the jet to the van, because he looks familiar, and not just because of the physical similarity to his wife. This is the Eldon that "made half a billion last year, isn't that amazing?" The man behind the plan to lure me to the airport, knock me out, stuff me in a dog kennel, and whisk me away in his fancy private aircraft. My enemy, no doubt, and maybe, if his wife isn't completely off her rocker, my friend.

"You said you had my son!" I remind them, letting go of her and focusing instead on him.

"Not us," he responds, carefully backing his wife out of range, as if I'm a grenade.

"Who, then? Where is he?"

Eldon can't bring himself to look me in the eye. "We think we know who took your son and why. We think we know where they're keeping him, okay? At least the general vicinity. At the moment we can't do anything about it, but we're on your side, lady, I promise."

"Prove it!" I demand. "Take me to Noah! I want to see him with my own eyes, right now!"

Husband and wife exchange a glance.

"Not possible," Eldon says. "How about some breakfast, you must be starved," he suggests, in what he intends to be a soothing voice.

"I don't want any fucking breakfast—*I want my son!*"

They exchange another mysterious glance, come to some sort of silent agreement, and then quickly withdraw from the room without another word.

The door, no surprise, is locked and solid as a bank vault. Pounding on the door gets me nothing but a sore fist. Windows! Go for the windows. If it's not too high maybe I can jump, or scream loud enough to get somebody's attention. But when I draw back the drapes, I discover that the windows have been covered from the outside with heavy aluminum storm shutters, blocking out light and sound.

I'm still in a cage.

Time passes, maybe an hour. Hard to tell under artificial light, without benefit of clock or watch. I'm starting to deeply regret refusing breakfast when the lock on the door clicks softly.

I'm right there, ready to bolt through the opening, but my new visitor has anticipated my eagerness and sweeps me away with a strong arm and shuts the door firmly behind him, all in one smooth move.

Thrown off balance, I fall to the carpet, landing on my butt.

"I do apologize," says the visitor, looking down at me with what can only be described as a benevolent expression. "You're being confined for your own protection. Your host family has asked me to explain the situation, and I shall. But first we need to get some food into you. Did you know you're trembling and that your teeth are chattering? That's not the air temperature. That's because you're hungry. Even a healthy person like yourself has to watch the blood sugar."

His appearance is enough to stun me into silence. Standing over me, dressed in simple black like a priest devoid of collar, is perhaps the homeliest human being I've ever encountered. Not ugly—ugly can be scary or threatening—but painfully, exquisitely homely. The man has a hunched spine, a protuberant little belly, and no chin. His spindly neck is heavily wattled, his prominent nose looks like a fat, crooked finger, and his asymmetrical ears could be borrowed from Mr. Potato Head. To make matters worse, all of his features are slightly askew, as if he was somehow blurred at birth, and the effect is to make me want to look away. Which I would happily do, except for his eyes.

His eyes, set deep beneath a jutting, simian brow, are strangely, compellingly beautiful. Old and deeply wrinkled, but nevertheless beautiful, although I couldn't say what color. Not blue or green exactly, but somewhere in that range.

"Take a good look," he encourages me, attempting a smile with his misshapen mouth. "I'm used to it. Arthur used to say I was the ugliest creature on earth, and he loved me for it."

"Arthur Conklin."

"Himself." He nods, looking somehow both wise and tortoiselike. "Our founder and my one true friend."

"Your one true friend stole my little boy," I remind him, getting to my feet.

He shakes his head. "No, never. Absolutely not. Arthur would never have done such a thing. Not when his mind was his own, and certainly not now. There are other forces at work. Dangerous, greedy people who will stop at nothing."

"Who?"

"If you'll take a seat and try to relax, Mrs. Corbin, food will be brought in. You must eat—you're shivering from hunger—and then I'll try to explain exactly what's going on and what we're going to have to do to get your son back."

Ordinarily I'm not big for scrambled eggs, but when Eldon and his bookend wife scuttle in with a tray of food, the smell of eggs and buttered toast makes me ravenous. Side of home fries, small dish of warm, cinnamon-tinged applesauce, more of the amazing toast slathered with jam. I probably consume enough calories to last a week. As my visitor predicted, the shivering stops and my head seems to settle firmly upon my shoulders.

The homely man is Wendall Weems, and if Arthur Conklin is the pope of the Rulers, then he's the cardinal who serves as the Vatican Secretary of State. Or, that's how he's begun to describe himself.

"Though that's actually a terrible analogy," he concedes, sipping from a glass of water as I mop up the last of the scrambled eggs. "The Conklin Institute is not a religious organization. Far from it. In all of Arthur's writings there is no mention of God or soul, or of any necessity for a spiritual life, or indeed of a promised afterlife. For which, by the way, he has been branded an atheist, a charge I consider profoundly unfair as well as beside the point. In his many works Arthur has never denied the existence of a supreme being—he has simply never chosen to discuss the possibility. Spirituality and the prospect of eternal life are outside of his purview. Instead he concentrates on improving the human mind by rewiring the way we process thoughts. That's the essence of what we do—teach people to control their thinking. We're all about self-improvement."

"I thought Rulers were all about making money."

"A misperception," Weems responds, sounding utterly reasonable. "Once raised to the next level, a Ruler's improved brain power will almost inevitably result in the acquisition of substantial wealth. We would say that wealth flows toward Rulers as magnetic waves flow through a charged device."

"So Rulers are all about magnets?"

He smiles, looking almost impish in his homeliness. "You mock us, Mrs. Corbin, but that's okay. You haven't been brought here for some sort of grand conversion to our way of thinking. No, no. For you this is not the road to Damascus. It is the road to being reunited with your little boy."

"And you'll help me do that?"

"Absolutely," he says, bathing me with the warm light of his beautiful, ancient eyes. "That's my mission."

The people Weems insists are my hosts join us at his invitation, still looking slightly nervous. He presents them to me as if we're being introduced for the first time at a business meeting, or a Chamber of Commerce get-together.

"Haley Corbin, these two courageous individuals are Eldon and Missy Barlow. Eldon is a brilliant gameware designer with many patents, and Missy is, if I may say so, brilliant at managing their resources. The point is, at my request they took a great risk bringing you to sanctuary in their own home, and the circumstances were such that you may have felt threatened at the time, unfortunately."

I snort. "They knocked me out and put me in a dog kennel."

Weems studies me, not unkindly. "Would you have accompanied them willingly?"

"No way."

He leans forward, which increases the curve at the top of his spine, making him look almost hunchbacked. "There were indications that your life was in immediate danger—it still is, by the way—and we had no time to lose," he says. "Had the Barlows not taken action, it is entirely possible that you would already be dead."

Eldon and Missy nod in unison, seconding that opinion.

"Yeah? Who wants me dead?"

Weems clears his throat, makes a little smile. "Evangeline, Arthur's second wife," he says with some measure of distaste. "Her loyal faction, her followers."

"Jed's stepmom wants to kill me? Why?"

"There is an unfortunate situation developing in our little community. You are the mother of Arthur Conklin's only grandchild, therefore you threaten Evangeline's dominance."

"Because of Noah?" I say, recoiling. "But that's insane!

You people steal my son, make it look like he died—and somehow it's my fault?"

"Not at all. You are entirely blameless."

"So you admit it's your fault."

"Not me, nor those I represent," he responds, sounding endlessly patient. "As I mentioned, my great friend Arthur Conklin is incapacitated. A series of strokes have so damaged his mind that he suffers from dementia. He is dying, Haley, and his wife wants to seize control of the organization."

"Let her. Why would I care who's the boss of your cult or community or whatever it's supposed to be?"

"We're not a cult," pipes up Eldon Barlow, looking to Weems for approval.

"Unfortunately, Evangeline is a force beyond my control," Weems admits, looking a little shamefaced. "She represents a small but ruthless faction who believe that our founder has mystical powers. If she has her way, the institute really will become a cult that worships Arthur as a kind of god. For the last few years, since Arthur's decline began, this group has gained traction because Evangeline claims to speak for her husband. In effect, she puts words in his mouth, and that can only work as long as he remains alive. She has taken extraordinary, and in my opinion, exceedingly cruel steps to keep the poor man alive, including a number of transplants. In the past few years, against all rational medical advice for a man his age, Arthur has received a new heart, a new kidney, and a partial liver. Now his poor body is failing, and nothing more can be done to prolong his agony. It's a matter of weeks, perhaps days. That's why Evangeline chose this moment to kidnap your son. She believes, or professes to believe, that Noah will in effect become the reincarnation of Arthur. And of course she will continue to speak for him. Your son will become, if she has her way, a sort of puppet under her command. Which is why she wants you to vanish from the face of the earth."

I feel faint, and must look it, because Weems quickly hands me a glass of water.

"I know it's a lot to absorb," he says apologetically.

When the dizziness passes I tell him, as forcefully as possible, "You really want to help me get my son back? Call the police. The FBI. If this woman has done what you say, she's a criminal. Criminals can be arrested."

Weems sighs, and for the first time he looks uneasy, as if he's not comfortable with what he's about to say. "I'm afraid it's not that simple, Mrs. Corbin. If a phone call to the authorities would free your little boy from her clutches, I'd make the call, believe me. But you're talking about Conklin, not Kansas."

"What does that mean?"

Weems looks up at the ceiling, steeples his long fingers as if in prayer. "That's part of our present difficulty, I'm afraid. Our community is controlled by the institute that Arthur founded. We own the county, the village, the campus—everything. We are therefore a political entity as well as a business and real-estate entity. There is no civil police force in Conklin, at least none answerable to the state of Colorado. Security is provided by a private security firm, and that firm is controlled by one of Evangeline's most rabid followers: BK Security, owned by Bagrat Kavashi. Mr. Kavashi is an exceedingly dangerous man. Smart, brutal, and utterly without remorse. According to our sources, Kavashi has been given orders to make you disappear. That's why we took such elaborate measures to bring you all the way to Colorado undercover, and why we must keep your precise location a secret."

"So call the FBI," I suggest, cheeks heating up. "Kidnapping is a federal crime. Being a gated community with some nasty rent-a-cop in charge won't protect them from the FBI, not when a child has been taken!"

Weems glances at my so-called hosts, who both look stricken by my outburst. He sighs deeply and with a palpable sense of melancholy. "We considered that option, Mrs. Corbin. But I'm afraid that Conklin is much more than a gated community, and Mr. Kavashi is much more than a mere rent-a-cop. If we're correct, Evangeline has your son hidden somewhere in the Pinnacle."

"Am I supposed to know what that is?"

He shrugs, as if in apology. "I thought you might. Apparently your husband never mentioned it. No matter. The Pinnacle is a very large and very secure enclave—it could be described as a kind of fortress—located high in the mountains. Virtually inaccessible to outsiders."

"I don't care where it is. Take me there. Let me see him."

"I'm afraid that's not possible. If Evangeline suspects that some legal entity like the Colorado State Police or the FBI is about to put her in jeopardy, she will destroy the evidence of her crimes. My understanding is that such a contingency plan is already in place."

"Destroy the evidence?"

"Without hesitation."

"You're saying she'll kill my son if the cops get too close."

"Unfortunately, yes," he concedes. "If she gives the

word, if she believes the integrity of the Pinnacle is about to be violated, your son will be made to disappear. No trace of him will ever be found. She's a fanatic, Mrs. Corbin. Those who threaten her have a tendency to disappear, utterly and completely."

I stand up from the table, my whole face hot, eyes wet with anger. "You know what I think? You're all a bunch of crazy psychos! Why should I believe anything you say? *You're* the ones keeping me prisoner!"

In the face of my outburst Weems remains utterly calm. "You may be correct about Evangeline. She may indeed be a psychopath. But if we truly didn't care about what happens to your son—to my dear friend Arthur's only grandchild—then I'd make that call to the FBI myself. In the end, after the raid and the inevitable battle and the eventual investigation, Evangeline would at the very least no longer have the boy as leverage, whatever happened. She might or might not be prosecuted or convicted—she has an army of lawyers to defend her—but one way or another our position would be improved. So despite what you think of me—of us—I do have a conscience. If I didn't, you wouldn't be here. You wouldn't even know for sure that your son is alive."

"I know," I tell him bitterly. "I always knew."

Weems reaches into a pocket, hands Missy a shiny silver disc. "Put that in the machine, would you, dear? Thanks."

Missy obediently trots over to a flat-screen TV, happily punches buttons on a slender DVD player as she feeds in the glittering disc.

"In the end the choice has to be yours," Weems is

saying. "If you decide to call in the FBI, and manage to convince them that your son is being held somewhere in Conklin, and they stage a raid to try and recover him, we will not stand in your way. We will not impede you or the FBI. But first you better take a look at this."

Weems points the remote and Noah appears on the screen, big as life.

3. Maggie Makes Her Case

Shane can't help it, he keeps looking up. Not because he thinks the sky is falling—not at the moment, anyhow—but because there's something about the wild roof that draws his attention. The architects who designed Denver International Airport call it a "tension fabric construction," intended to echo the peaks of the Rocky Mountains, but to Shane it looks like the inside of a mad white circus tent.

As airport designs go, DIA is crazy and kind of cool, but he decides he wouldn't want to be standing under that roof when a blizzard dumps a few million tons of snow on top, filling the gaps between the swooping peaks. If the fabric fails it would be like being trapped in a man-made avalanche.

"You'll hurt your neck, big boy."

He looks down to find Maggie Drew smiling up at him. That's the first thing he notices, the warmth of her smile. The second thing he notices is the cane.

Today she's using her cane.

"Little flare-up," she explains, making light of it. "It happens. Touch of the old rheumatiz in my wee little ankles. Nothing to fret about."

"You made it." He bends to kiss her cheek. "All the way from D.C. as a favor for a friend. Thank you, thank you."

"You said something about buying me a cup of coffee," she says airily, nudging him with the knob of her cane.

He'd already picked out a relatively quiet little café on the mezzanine level of the concourse, overlooking the fountains, but now is worried she'll have trouble on the escalators. "I'm fine, lead on. View's better up there—closer to heaven."

He pretends not to notice the twinges of pain that flicker across her face as she limps toward the escalator. It's slow going, but eventually they're seated in an out-of-the-way spot he scouted while awaiting her flight. The ambient noise of the fountain will make it hard to be overheard, supposing he's been followed, which he's certain is unlikely.

Old habits die hard.

Shane hands Maggie a menu—it's self-serve—but she waves it off. "I ate on the flight, believe it or not."

They both know that chronic pain kills the appetite, and she doesn't want to talk about the relapse of her rheumatoid arthritis. Maggie is clearly determined to be brave, and Shane prays that it really is, as she claims, just a flare-up.

He drinks strong coffee, not having slept in two days, and she sips delicately at a club soda with lime, as if the fizz might burn her lips.

"Any luck?" she wants to know.

"Not really," he admits. "They could have landed here—plenty of private charter jets use DIA—but I haven't been able to confirm an incoming flight from Rochester, New York, within the time frame. They could have come into one of the other commercial airports, of which there are at least five within fifty miles of Denver. They could have landed at a private airstrip, of which there are scores, possibly hundreds. There are thousands of private flights into Colorado in any given time period. Rich folk come for the sights or the skiing or to tailgate the Broncos."

"Tailgating on a fifty-million-dollar Gulfstream?"

"Hey, flaunt it if you've got it," Shane says with a shrug. "Bottom line, the plane is a dead end. No way to walk it back. I have to assume my informant wasn't fibbing and he really did overhear the perps say their destination was Denver. Which makes sense if the abduction was done by the Rulers."

"You mentioned a name."

"He mentioned a name. Missy. What he says the man called his accomplice. More than once. Missy do this. Missy do that. Missy be quiet. Possibly a nickname or a term of endearment."

"I ran it. Nothing pops on the list of known Rulers. Not so far."

"Like I say, possibly a nickname. You'll keep trying?"

"Of course. Missy and her mystery man, headed for Denver. Possibly."

Shane sighs. "I know it's not much to work with."

Maggie shrugs. "Hey, hey. We've started with less, as you know. Just so we're on the same page, you remain convinced that Haley Corbin was abducted?"

"As opposed to being killed, you mean? Yes. The answer is yes. They went to too much trouble, luring her to the airport, knocking her out, loading her into the jet."

"If your informant isn't lying," she gently reminds him.

"He was eager to share what he knew."

"I'll bet he was."

"I've never done that before, Maggie," he says, feeling ashamed in her presence. "I was desperate."

"No lasting damage to the little cretin?"

"Nothing a change of underwear won't fix."

"And he won't be pressing charges?"

"Doubtful. I impressed him with the need for silence, for both our sakes. Plus I let him keep the money. He wants to make a recording, thinks he can be the next big hip-hop star. Who knows? He's ruthless enough."

She pats his hand, smiles. "No worries, big guy. You did what you had to do."

"It's on me," he says, feeling the need to explain. "If I'd been there, like I should have been, this never would have happened."

"Or maybe you'd be dead and Haley Corbin would still be gone."

"They took her alive," he points out. "They could have shot her and left her by the side of the road, or made it look like an accident. A death, even a suspicious death, leaves fewer questions than a disappearance, so they're taking a chance abducting her. There has to be a reason. My theory is, her little boy is alive and wants his mother, so they made it happen."

Maggie says, "Not a bad theory."

"Any word from your informants?"

She sighs. "Not a word about the boy, not a word about his mother. But 'informants' is too grand a term. Our contacts inside are strictly bottom of the heap. This will be happening at a higher level and the Ruler organization is structured in layers of secrecy. That's part of their appeal. For Rulers, information is everything—the higher you go, the more you learn. All we know for sure is, there are rumors about Arthur Conklin's health declining, and a succession struggle between factions. Which you already know."

"Wendall Weems versus Conklin's wife."

"So the rumor goes."

Shane finishes his coffee. At this point in his cycle of insomnia, the caffeine barely blips. "I'm going in. It's the only way."

Maggie shakes her head disapprovingly. "And I flew fourteen hundred miles to persuade you otherwise."

"You can try," Shane says.

Maggie opens her briefcase, slips out her laptop, taps it to life. "I've done a little more in-depth research on Kavashi, the security chief. Turns out that ten years ago he was on the short list of suspects in a couple of murders."

"Oh, yeah?"

"Remember the deal new members make? By joining they agree to 'share-in' twenty-five percent of any increase in their net worth? Well, every now and then somebody gets rich and decides it was all their own doing and they refuse to pay the percentage. The contract they sign with the Rulers isn't enforceable, why give up such a big chunk of their newfound wealth? Blah, blah, blah. So they walk away. Or attempt to."

"This Kavashi guy is the collector, is that it?"

"More like the enforcer. The Conklin Institute has a forensic accounting division that enforces collections from the members. They know where every penny goes, and who earned what, and therefore what they owe. But human nature being what it is, deadbeats were always a problem, right from the beginning. Refuse to pay and you were banned, shunned, thrown out. All personal and business connections were severed, loans were called in, and a full-court effort was made to ruin you by financial means. Lawsuits, mostly. Fail to pay and you get buried in shysters. Still, some of the deadbeats prevailed, got to keep all the loot. Until Kavashi came into the picture. Then things got untidy for a while."

"Let me guess. He didn't take 'no' for an answer."

Maggie nods. "In both cases we know about, explosives were used. First victim was a car salesman from Montclair, New Jersey, who joined the Rulers and within a few years owned a chain of luxury dealerships. In his TV ads he was 'Mister Mercedes.' Until one fine day he went to start up his S600 and got blown to smithereens. That was bad. The second victim was way worse. Started up a wholesale jewelry business in Arizona, took it online, eventually sold it to Amazon or eBay, I can't remember which. Anyhow, he walked away with something like fifty million dollars for his final payday, and decided the Rulers didn't deserve their cut on this one. So he got necklaced. Cute, huh, a jewelry guy gets necklaced? Maybe you recall the one where the victim walks into a Sedona police station with a note begging the police to shoot him because he's got this ring of plastic explosive molded around his neck, with a ticking detonator attached, and he hates the idea of his head getting blown off? Parts of the video were all over cable news for a few days."

"Rings a bell," Shane says. "The cops put him in a vacant lot, evacuated the area, and sent in a robot. But the bomb detonated anyway, right?"

"It did. And somebody tapped into the video feed from

the robot, put it all over the net. The uncensored, not-for-cable-TV-version. My guess is, nowadays when any Ruler decides not to pay, they suggest he or she check out the necklace video. It's very, very gruesome, in a head-goes-into-orbit kind of way."

"And these crimes were tied to Kavashi?"

"Tied is too strong a word. He was a person of interest in the investigations. Frankly the investigators knew he did it, or arranged to have it done, but there was no physical evidence linking him to the bombs, and nobody was willing to testify. Therefore no case. Word at the time was that Arthur Conklin wanted Kavashi thrown out of the organization, but that Evangeline backed her buddy Vash and prevailed. In any case, he handles Ruler security and remains as dangerous as ever."

Shane smiles. "You're worried he'll blow me up."

"I am, yes. Or just have you shot. So you *should* be worried."

"I hate getting blown up. Therefore I'll be very careful."

"Don't be flippant, Randall!" she says, fiercely. "I don't worry easy and you know it."

He grimaces. "Sorry, Mags. But I'm worried, too, and I don't see any alternative. The FBI won't send in the HRT based on my hunch about what might have happened to Haley Corbin."

"The Hostage Rescue Team? That's pretty elite. What's wrong with a field-office SWAT team?"

"Nothing. They're good, but the HRT is better, and something tells me taking on this bunch of nut bars requires the very best. But even the field-office SWAT needs some sort of verifiable evidence before they can obtain a warrant. Therefore someone has to go in there and find evidence, help make a case. In this case a civilian. Me."

"What about Colorado Social Services?" Maggie suggests eagerly. "Concern for an endangered child usually rings the right bells."

"In Texas, maybe, when the suspected abusers are a known polygamist sect. I spoke to the DSS supervisor in one of the adjoining counties, just to see what it would take to initiate an investigation, and she said there has never been a child-endangered complaint filed against the Rulers, not as an organization, anyhow, and not in Conklin County. They're simply not on the radar. And the DSS is very, very leery of taking on the Rulers without evidence that will stand up in court. They want something solid, something actionable. At the very least I need a credible witness from inside the compound. Which is what I intend to find, once you get me inside."

"There has to be a better way."

Shane leans back in his chair, making the legs creak ominously. "I'm open to suggestions."

"Come back with me to D.C. We'll work it from there. We'll make a case. We'll get you the HRT."

Shane smiles wearily. "I'll bet you could. But how long would it take to work through channels, convince the 'crats that my hunch is good, that their butts won't be on the line, careers ruined? You're good, Maggie, the best. But even for you, it would take weeks. Weeks that Haley and Noah might not have."

"You've made up your mind."

Shane nods.

Maggie sighs. "There might be a way to get you inside."

"I'm all ears," he says, wide-awake.

4. The Futility Of Crying

Snow is falling. I know that snow is falling because there's a skylight in one of the many bathrooms, and the fat white flakes are starting to accumulate, blocking out the slate-gray sky. The skylight is the only window not obstructed by storm shutters. My only view of the world outside, and soon it will be covered.

For all I can see, I might as well be confined in a million-dollar igloo. Although, come to think of it, a home of this size and quality—the kitchen alone has more square feet than my entire farmhouse—probably goes for a lot more than a million.

Missy says that it snows frequently, because of the elevation, and that's one of the many things they love about Conklin, the perfect snow. She says the village is like a ski resort without the lifts or the lines, and she should know because she and her husband own homes in Vail and Park City, for when they want to actually ski. They also own homes in Silicon Valley, Manhattan, Nantucket, and Key West, and, oh yeah, she almost forgot, this adorable little mews in London.

The Barlows are filthy rich and, from what I can tell, about as shallow as the manufactured celebrities they seek to emulate. Missy tells me that Eldon is brilliant—and I suppose he must be, on some level—but I haven't seen it. In my presence he seems more keenly nervous than intelligent. Frightened, actually. As if terrified that complicity in my abduction will come back to haunt him.

Which it will, if I have anything to say about it.

For now I'm biding my time, holding my tongue. The strange, ugly little man with the beautiful eyes convinced me, for the moment, that calling in the authorities would put Noah's life at risk. But watching that DVD of my little boy being tutored by that snake-in-the-grass Irene Delancey very nearly drove me over the edge. On one level I was intensely relieved to see him looking healthy, if not happy. On another level I'm outraged that they've stolen nearly two months of his childhood, two months that I didn't get to share, two months I'll never get back. How dare she! How dare they! To make it worse, there's no sound on the DVD, so I've no idea what poison Delancey is spewing, or how much my little boy knows about what's really going on.

Does he know I'm searching for him, that I won't give up until he's back in his mother's arms? He must know. He's his father's son, and he knows the most amazing things.

Wendall Weems, my real captor—abducting me was his idea, obviously—claims he knew Jedediah as a child. "He was still in diapers when Arthur bought back and republished his book," he says. "Quite a handsome baby, as I recall, but given to crying when he wasn't being held. Colicky, I think they call it."

Weems is musing, trying to be friendly, and I can only stare at him in disbelief.

"Colicky? I haven't read that horrible book, but Jed did show me the chapter on child rearing. Unbelievable! His father thought it a worthy experiment to leave a three-month-old baby unattended in a dark room for twelve hours. He calculated an infant would not actually die of neglect in that time period, and that it might, quote 'learn the futility of crying.'"

Weems nods solemnly. "Barbara—she was Jedediah's birth mother—as I recall she was perfectly frantic at the time. Arthur insisted on the full twelve hours. The exercise was really as much about Barbara as it was the baby, of course. Arthur firmly believed that the mother-child bond often does more harm than good, in terms of self-actualization. He's a man of immense, unshakable willpower. Or he was until recently."

The strange little man's indifference to the notion of tormenting a child to prove a point drives me wild. Especially because that tormented baby was my own husband. It's all I can do not to leap out of my chair and slap the complacent expression off his homely face. "I was wrong about you people," I say, practically spitting out the words. "You're not just greedy and selfish, you're unspeakably cruel! This great man you so admire. You know what he did? When a homesick boy wrote home from boarding school, saying that he loved and missed his parents, his father cut him off. Told him love was weakness, and that he was not to contact his mother again until he'd grown up."

"Granted, that may have seemed cruel at the time. But in the long run—"

"In the long run, *what?*" I interrupt, almost shouting. "In the long run Jed's mother died! He never saw her again. And his father never even bothered to let him know she was dying. That's the man you admire. That's the man you revere. A monster!"

Weems studies me, as if aware that he's miscalculated. "You're angry," he observes. "It's a natural enough reaction."

"You think? Your people blow up a school, steal my son, kidnap me, all because years ago some cranky professor wrote a book on the importance of being selfish? And I dare to be angry?"

The little man regards me with great solemnity, exuding infinite patience. "No one dares to be angry, my dear," he points out. "Anger originates in the atavistic part of the brain, not the cognitive. You can dare to risk everything, you can dare to be great, but you can't dare to be angry or afraid. Anger and fear being linked, of course. Manifestations of the same instinct."

I can't stand it anymore. Leaping up, I grab the front of his shirt, yank him close, and scream into his startled face, "Give me back my baby! Give him back or I swear I'll kill all of you!"

Then I'm flat on my back, the wind knocked out of me, held down by the Barlows, both of whom look sick with fear but nevertheless determined to protect their precious leader.

"Ruler Weems," gasps Eldon as I squirm and struggle to get free. "Are you okay? What do we do? Tell us what to do."

His voice is utterly calm. "Let her go."

Instant obedience. My arms are released.

"If Mrs. Corbin wants to attack me, she is free to do so. I will not defend myself, and you will not interfere."

Hands relaxed upon the arms of his chair, Weems awaits my reaction. I crawl to my feet, shooting venomous looks at my so-called hosts.

I'm shaking with adrenaline, so wobbly I can barely stand. "Do not speak to me of Jedediah," I say, boring in on the strange little man. "My Jed was worth a thousand Arthur Conklins. He was good and true and loving. He was smart and funny and kind. His father tried to wreck him, but Jed couldn't be wrecked. He had a heart of gold, and if his stupid plane hadn't fallen out of the sky none of this would be happening. Jed would have known what to do. He always knew what to do."

Then I'm sitting on my butt—how did that happen?—and bawling into my hands, crying for my dead husband, crying for my little boy, crying for me.

"Your husband's plane didn't fall out of the sky," Weems says gently. "Not by accident. He was murdered."

5. Gouda Like The Cheese

Shane considers himself lucky there were no Lincoln Town Cars available for rental at Denver International Airport. Indeed, his request for such a vehicle had prompted much rolling of eyes. "You'll need the four-wheel drive," they kept saying, and they were right; he does need the four-wheel drive. And if the Jeep Grand Cherokee feels bumpy and windblown compared to his precious Townie, it proves to be surefooted on the snow-slicked highway out of Denver.

Two hours later, on sharp curves straddling the Rocky Mountains, it's all that keeps him from sliding off the road into a steep ditch or worse.

Having gone to college in upstate New York, Shane thought he knew about snow, but this is another world entirely. The scale here is much, much bigger. The sheer mass of the mountains makes him feel insignificant, a bug clinging desperately to his little path in the wilderness. Plus it seems to have messed up his orientation. In the flatlands, near large bodies of water—areas like, say, the East or West Coast—he always has a pretty good sense of direction. In the midst of high mountains, with hard-blown granular snow diffusing the waning sunlight, he has to rely on the in-dash GPS unit. Couldn't on his own have pointed north if his life depended on it.

According to the GPS, Conklin is a mere seventy miles from Denver as the crow flies. But crows don't fly at this altitude, certainly not in this weather, and by geographical necessity the actual road distance between the two points is about double that. Snow and caution, and the desire not to plummet uselessly to his death, means that by the time Shane finally arrives at the Conklin security checkpoint, night has fallen and he's creeping along like some old geezer in the go-around-me lane.

He powers down the window of the Grand Cherokee, grins into the chilly darkness.

"Good evening, sir. Welcome to your prosperity," the guard recites without a trace of irony. "Please state your name and your business."

"Ronnie Gouda, like the cheese," Shane says. "RG Paving, out of Dayton, Ohio. Here for the seminar."

He hands over his ID and charge card—fully functional duplicates kindly supplied by Maggie Drew—and waits as the guard returns to the checkpoint, a structure that resembles one of those titanium wave-front museums by Frank Gehry. Fully illuminated, fully staffed, fully armed, the BKS logo prominent on all uniforms. Shane has seen international border crossings that look less imposing. The security officers are cool and cordial, bearing no resemblance to the usual bloated rent-a-cops employed at most gated communities.

There are two lanes on either side of the checkpoint, one for civilian vehicles, the other for tractor trailers, and as Shane waits, peering through the windshield wipers, guards actually open up a trailer and inspect the cargo, carefully matching it against a manifest.

Disturbingly thorough.

A few minutes later Shane is asked to step out of his vehicle.

"Is something wrong?" he asks. "I already paid for the seminar. Thought it was all set."

The guard, a broad-shouldered young female of about thirty, gives him a thin smile. "Nothing wrong, sir. Just procedure. We need to scan your picture, issue a visitor badge, and so on. Please step out of your vehicle."

Shane steps out of his vehicle. Shivers as a blast of wind rattles his brand-new parka. Like icy hands finding his warmer spots, making him flinch.

Inside the brightly lit checkpoint, all is well. Computer data indicates that Ron L. Gouda, having attended an introductory "What the Rule of One Can Do for You" seminar in Dayton, Ohio, and having paid in full the five-thousand-dollar nonreturnable initiation fee, has qualified for a three-day, all-inclusive Level One seminar at the Conklin Institute.

Obviously they're not yet aware that the real Ronnie Gouda has just been secretly indicted for rigging state highway contracts, and is playing nice with his new friends in the Justice Department.

Which is a good thing. A very good thing.

Shane gets his picture snapped, is issued a clip-on face badge, plus an electronically coded card that will key open the door to something called a domicile unit.

"Domicile unit?" he asks, genuinely befuddled.

"Bed, bath, study area. You'll find the D.U. cozy and comfortable. The code card also allows access to the Hive. That's the cafeteria for the Level One seminars. The Hive has a four-star chef. You're in for a treat, sir."

"For five grand I hope so," Shane says, playing the part of a successful, self-made contractor, figuring the guy would be just a little mouthy, a big dude used to running his own show.

The security guards don't react to the comment, or to his attitude. No doubt they've heard it all before. Their vibe is professional, by the book, and Shane is thinking that if this is how they run the show in the village, breaking through security is going to be a real challenge.

"You'll need this," the female guard says, handing him a small plastic device. "Clip it to the visor."

"What is it?" Shane asks innocently, although he has a pretty good idea what the device is and how it functions.

"Smart tracker," the guard responds. "We track all vehicles within the village boundaries. No exceptions."

"Oh yeah?" says Shane, allowing a touch of belligerence to sound in his contractor's voice, feeling his way into the role. "What if it falls off or gets lost?"

The guard gives him a don't-mess-with-us look. "If the signal is interrupted, that will be detected by our sensors, sounding an alarm. We are obliged to respond in force."

"Like what, a SWAT team?"

"A little like that, yeah."

"Are you kiddin' me? Really?"

"We take security very seriously, sir. Enjoy your stay."

They wave him through the checkpoint.

Three miles farther on down the road, Shane comes around a steep, dramatic curve, and just as he does so the night sky clears, revealing a bright canopy of stars behind the soaring mountains.

Beautiful but a little spooky, truth to tell.

The whole village is laid out before him, subtly illuminated, as if the architects had the amazing night sky in mind. Nestled into the base of the mountain peaks is what appears at first glance to be a small college campus, attractively frosted by the recent snowfall. The Conklin Institute, no doubt. Higher up the mountainside, he can make out ski lodges and luxury condo complexes of the type he has seen in Aspen. Steep, snow-shedding metal roofs, walls of glass and shingle, some of the windows illuminated by guests-in-residence.

Road signs point him to Domicile One, situated on the lower level, directly across from the campus. Despite the name it looks very much like a chain hotel, and the folks at the front desk look like ordinary hotel employees, uniformed in sky-blue blazers, neat haircuts, and well-trained smiles.

Overnight bag in hand, Shane scuffs the snow off his boots before stepping into the lobby. Wanting the staff's first impression of him to be favorable. Never know when you might need a favor.

"Amazing stars!" he booms, grinning heartily. "Is it always like that here?"

He presents his coded card.

"Welcome to Conklin, Mr. Gouda. May your stay be profitable."

"Excuse me? Oh, I get it. Yeah, yeah, I hope so. That's the idea, right?"

"They'll explain it all at the seminar, sir."

"Uh-huh, yeah. Let me ask you, I couldn't get a signal out there in the parking lot. Is there a problem with cell phones? I gotta make some calls."

The desk manager, baby-faced and as generically friendly as a battery-powered puppy, smiles happily. "Cell reception is spotty, Mr. Gouda. There's a telephone in your unit. Feel free to use it—there's no extra charge."

"Yeah, okay," says Shane the contractor, thinking that a place as well-organized as this would have a cell tower if it so desired. So if visitors are being directed to a locally wired phone system, there has to be a reason. The security service likely monitors the guests' calls. Ah, paranoia.

"The Hive opens for breakfast at 6:00 a.m. Don't miss it—they make a mean pancake. Your seminar begins at 8:00 a.m. sharp, in Profit Hall. Just follow the signs. And a reminder—the doors to the hall close at precisely eight. No one is admitted after that, and failure to attend means your invitation will be automatically revoked."

"Meaning I get the old heave-ho?" Shane says affably. "You folks play rough!"

"Your time has measurable worth, sir. So does ours."

Shane shrugs. "That seems fair enough. I'll have my butt in the seat, don't you worry."

The 'domicile unit' is, as promised, cozy, in that it's quite small. Certainly not the typical motel room he expected. No TV, no broadband or wireless connections, further limiting access to the outside world. The single bed is too short for his elongated frame, but he's used to that, and in any case doesn't expect to be getting much sleep, or to spend much time in this little room. The only entertainment on offer is a freshly minted copy of *The Rule of One,* situated on a bedside table in roughly the spot that you might find a Gideon Bible in a regular hotel chain.

He decides the room has the feel of a monk's cell, except that he supposes monks don't get their own showers or toilets, or fluffy fresh towels.

Shane unpacks, placing his shaving kit within reach of the shower stall and sink. He takes a long, pleasantly hot shower and then dresses in dark clothing. Figuring on taking a midnight stroll, getting a feeling for the layout of the village, maybe a sense of when the security patrols come through, and how they might be avoided. Maybe get a glimpse of the so-called Pinnacle, if the stars stay bright.

You never know what you might see when the rest of the world is asleep.

His gut instincts tell him that Haley Corbin is being held somewhere in the vicinity. Probably not in the village itself—it's unlikely that her captors would risk her being seen by visitors—but definitely somewhere within Ruler territory. He's mindful that although Conklin County comprises something like two thousand square miles, most of the occupied part is right here.

She'll be somewhere close.

Shane checks the time. Barely nine, much earlier than he thought, considering the starry depth of the night, or the general sense of slumbering quiet within the motel, or the domicile, or whatever. Maybe he doesn't need to wait until midnight for his walk on the wild side. Eleven will do. No problem.

Shane lies down on the narrow bed, fully dressed. His feet extend well beyond the foot of the bed, but the mattress has a pleasing firmness and the pillow is, to his surprise, pure heaven. He's thinking the room is a bit stuffy, maybe slightly too warm—is there a thermostat? He can't recall seeing a thermostat—and the air has a faint medicinal odor—what is that exactly, and why does it seem so familiar?

He closes his eyes.

In three deep breaths he's sound asleep.

6. How Can You Improve On Perfection?

"We were never able to develop any proof," Weems says. "Not actionable proof."

The man is explaining how he knows that Jed and twenty-six other equally innocent passengers were murdered, and yet he remains utterly calm. It makes me feel like screaming, or scratching his eyes out, or both.

How can they be doing this to me? First stealing my little boy, then making me relive the horror of my husband's death all over again? How can they be so cruel and yet remain so calm? How can they be so cruel, and yet remain so cool about it? Weems acts as if he's delivering a lecture. Missy and her husband sitting there like toads, blinking at me, as if they've heard it ad nauseam. And maybe they have.

"Monsters," I say, my throat thick. "Jed always knew what you were. That's why he cut himself off from you horrible people."

Weems nods sagely, as if anticipating my every response.

"Great men often have problems relating to their children. It goes all the way back to the ancient kings. In the animal world, male lions will sometimes destroy their own cubs, rather than risk competing with them when they're fully grown. Arthur is—was—a genius, a transcendent thinker, but like all humans he's not without faults. He drove his only child away, and that is a terrible thing, even if his intentions were otherwise. Even if he later regretted what he had done."

"Jed never even knew his mother was dying! How could anyone do that to a boy? His own father!"

Weems sighs, shakes his head. "As I said before, I can't believe that cruelty was Arthur's intention. He thought he was protecting the boy."

"By not letting him see his own mother?"

He shrugs, conceding the point. "As I said, even the great Arthur Conklin is not without fault. The point is, he changed his mind about Jedediah. After he suffered his first heart attack, when his mind was still reasonably clear, he asked me to make contact with the boy. Sorry, I continue to think of Jedediah as a boy, since that's how I knew him. By the time his father expressed an interest in reconciliation he was, of course, a full-grown man, with a wife and child of his own—indeed with a life of his own, a man in full."

A man in full. Not a phrase I'd ever thought about, but it described Jedediah exactly. Out of necessity, out of the emotional cruelty of his own family, he'd been forced to grow up when he was still very young. When most boys his age were still having their boxers washed and folded by their indulgent mothers, Jed was living entirely on his own, working his way through college.

My man in full.

"I did manage to contact Jedediah," Weems says. "It was a few months before he was killed. Did he mention that to you?"

I shake my head, ashamed that Jed felt he had to keep secrets from me. Although he had alluded to something going on in the Ruler organization, and joked that if he ever disappeared it would be because of his father. The truth is, I hadn't wanted to know. Hadn't wanted to think about anything disrupting our life, and assumed it was just some sort of residual paranoia, understandable when dear old Dad runs a cult.

"He made it clear he had no desire to have any sort of contact, that it was too late to mend fences. I said something about how we could make things better for him, if he came back into the fold, and he said, and I'll never forget this, 'How can you improve on perfection?' He was quite serious. Jedediah felt that his life was perfect exactly as it was. Those were his words. 'I have the perfect wife, the perfect child. All my father could do is mess things up. So thanks but no thanks.'" Weems heaves a sigh of regret that sounds almost genuine. "I must confess, Mrs. Corbin. I truly did not understand what he meant until I met you and had a glimpse, however brief, of your little boy."

By then I'm bawling so hard, so convulsively, that I barely notice Missy fussing anxiously, trying to blot my flood of tears with a wad of tissues. If Weems is troubled by my reaction, he doesn't show it. He simply waits until the crying abates, then continues where he left off. "Whatever I believed his motivations to be, Jed made it abundantly clear that he would remain apart, no matter what pressures might be brought to bear," he says, sounding philosophical. "I broke the news as gently as I knew how to Arthur, who by then was beginning to fail—his mind was no longer clear—and I'm not sure he even truly comprehended the situation. But Evangeline assumes that everyone shares her lust for power and wealth. She convinced herself that Arthur was going to name Jedediah as his successor, cutting her out. So she arranged to have him killed, and to make it look like an accident. Somehow she made it happen. I've never been able to determine the details. Some clever, undetectable form of sabotage, no doubt."

In the back of my mind, the image of a plane falls from the sky, tumbling like a bird with a broken wing. It's more than I can bear. I have to force the image back into its little box or it will drive me mad.

"I'm sure it's distressing," Weems says, "but you need to understand what she's capable of. At the moment she believes that controlling Arthur's only grandchild is somehow to her benefit. The moment she no longer believes that, he'll be a liability, and, as I say, Evangeline's liabilities have a way of vanishing without a trace."

He seems so calm, so matter of fact. Maybe he's making it up about Jed's evil stepmother, trying to get me on his side. This sounds horrible—it feels horrible to think it—but at the moment it doesn't matter how Jed died, whether it was an accident or on purpose. Knowing the truth won't bring him back. All that matters is Noah. Getting him away from these people. That's what Jed would want. Get Noah away from people who think like this—lions killing their cubs, women who steal children because it gives them some advantage, men who arrange to kidnap mothers as if it's some clever move in a game of chess.

My little boy has to be rescued. I'll fight for that to my last breath. As I blot up my tears with Missy's tissues, I'm certain of only one thing: I'll do whatever it takes to get my child back. Including murder.

Does that make me as bad as they are?

Maybe, but I don't care.

7. Whatever She Likes

Evangeline in the starlight, watching her lover sleep. Although, in truth, her handsome Vash is both more and less than a lover. The sex is good—he's as strong as a horse, dutiful in his devotion to her pleasure—but there's no emotional connection, no mental sparks passing between them. Not like Arthur in his heyday, obsessed with getting into her mind as well as her pants. Ah, now *there* was a lover! She would not, in truth, consider Mr. Bagrat Kavashi an actual friend, let alone a lover. More like a companion whose interests frequently converge with her own.

A convergence, that's what they have. A useful convergence, with benefits. Besides, she has little use for friends, in the normal sense of the word, as people you care for and who in turn care for you. Evangeline truly cares only for herself and that, she sincerely believes, is as it should be. It's the source of her focus, her power, her strength.

She plops onto the enormous bed, making the mattress bounce. "Wakey, wakey," she trills.

Bagrat Kavashi sits bolt upright, eyes wild. He looks, in this moment, fully capable of hot-blooded murder, which makes him all the more attractive.

"So where's Wendy?" she asks sweetly. "He's not at home. I checked."

"What?" says Vash, still groggy with sleep. "What is wrong?"

"Wendall Weems. He's up to something, darling. I can feel it in my trim little tummy. I checked the cameras. He's not at home."

Vash grunts, reaches for her. She backs away, smoothing the hem of her silky, thigh-high chemise.

"I want you to find him," she says. "Where's Wendy? That's the game. Like Waldo."

"Who is this Waldo?"

"Never mind. Come with me, chop-chop."

She more or less drags him down the hall to the nearby war room. What had once been a mere office suite, now converted to a state-of-the-art intelligence-gathering hub. On its multiplicity of screens she can monitor activities in the village, on the campus, and, thanks to recent work by BK's clever technical operatives, she can now look around inside the fully compromised residence of her rival.

"Drink this," she says, handing Vash a cold can of Red Bull.

Muttering curses in his native language, her chief of security drains the slender can, wipes his mustache with the back of his hand, and burps loudly, aggressively.

"Feel better?" she says. "Good. Let's get to work."

"Work? Is time for sleep!"

"Exactly. Except Wendy isn't sleeping, which I find suspicious. He's a man of regular habits, always in bed no later than ten, up no later than six. Out of curiosity, I checked his bedroom, to see if he was asleep—I mean, why should he sleep if I can't?—and he's not there. So I checked his office. Then I checked every room in the Bunker. No Wendy."

"You crazy woman. So what, he's not in bed? Maybe he's got girlfriend."

Evangeline has a good laugh. "You're cute when you're cranky, you know that? Wendy with a *girl?* That bag of wrinkles?"

"Okay, a boy, a goat. Who cares?"

She curls up in her big chair, hugging her bare legs. "Vash? Think about it. Haley Corbin is missing, right?"

He shrugs, acknowledging the unpleasant fact. A miscalculation he hasn't wanted to factor into the present situation. "Maybe she runs away. I tell you we find her, don't worry. Not a problem."

"Runs away right after she hires an FBI agent to help her find her little boy?"

"Ex-FBI," he corrects her. "A big nobody. Once you leave FBI, you have no power, no authority. But okay, maybe she don't run away. You think, what, Wendy steal her? Why he does this, exactly?"

"Because we were going to make her go away. It makes sense if you think about it. We have the boy in our possession, so he takes the mother, right from under our noses. A countermove."

Vash shrugs, but he looks interested, and not just in her legs. "Is possible. I check it out, okay?"

He cinches the sash on his black silk robe—a gift from her, one of many—and sits down at the console. Using the scrambled line, he puts the word out to his night shift captain. Be on the lookout for Wendall Weems, total discretion required. And now that his mind is more or less fully functional, he decides that Eva the Diva may be onto something. The woman is crazed on several levels, but she has remarkable survival instincts. Plus she's right about Ruler Weems being very methodical, a man of well-established habits. Given the precarious situation—an undeclared war of succession—any deviation from the norm is suspicious. There's nothing on Weems's schedule about a sudden trip, and in any case there's no way he could leave the Bunker, let alone the village of Conklin, without Kavashi being informed. Weems is supposed to be under constant surveillance, and yet he's managed to vanish from his residence without triggering alarms. Something, indeed, must be happening.

Question: if Weems or his agents spirited away Mrs. Corbin, right under the noses of the BK operatives in New York, would he be dumb enough to bring her back to Conklin? Hiding her in plain sight, as it were?

Cold hands slip around his neck, producing an involuntary shiver. "Have you found him yet, darling?"

"Not to worry Eva's pretty little head."

"Mmmm. Still, I do worry. Wendy is an ugly little man, but he's very dangerous. It would be a huge mistake to underestimate him."

"No mistake. We find him."

Evangeline begins to nuzzle him, unaware of the faint twinge of revulsion that her touch produces. "Which brings us to the next question," she says huskily, kissing his throat. "Once we find him, what do we do with him? How do we make Wendy and all his followers go away?"

"Whatever you like, that's what we do."

"Really?" she says, straddling his lap, her nimble fingers reaching for the bathrobe sash. "Let me show you what I like, you great big bad boy."

Kavashi does his duty. Toward the end he almost begins to enjoy it.

8. One Rinse Cycle

Shane wakes up feeling strangely refreshed, and, by the time he rolls off the bed, entirely suspicious. No way he fell asleep unassisted. Not, as in this case, deeply and without dreams. And for that matter fully clothed.

He's trying to recall exactly what he may have ingested the night before when the telephone begins to bleat.

"Yes?"

"This is your wake-up call, Mr. Gouda," a personalized recording announces. "The Hive is now open for your breakfast needs. Follow the green line from the Hive to Profit Hall. Doors close at precisely eight, so don't be late!"

Very cheery, in an insistent sort of way. Setting the tone: we instruct, you obey.

Shane decides that to maintain his cover he must, at the very least, be semi-obedient. Ron Gouda might stray from the line now and then—he's a bit of a rebel, is Ronnie Boy—but there's no point in getting himself ejected from the village before he's had a chance to scope it out. Plus, he's famished.

As he passes through the reception area, one of the staff members helpfully points the way to the underground passage that leads directly to the Hive.

"No need for the heavy coat, Mr. Gouda!"

His first reaction: there's a new shift at the desk, so how do they know who he is? Then he sees them furtively consulting computer screens as guests stumble into the lobby, and Shane recalls his picture being snapped for the ID badge.

He hates that they're so well-organized. That's not going to make his task any easier.

"Can I leave this here?" he asks, handing over his puffy down jacket.

"Not a problem," says a cheerful young woman with gleaming white teeth. She whips out a plastic coat hanger, deftly suspending the jacket on a partially filled clothing rack. Practiced and efficient, all part of the routine.

Probably some discreet security staffer will go through my pockets later, he thinks. Through everybody's pockets. Which might explain why the connecting tunnel wasn't mentioned when he arrived last night. An opportunity for security to see what telling items might be left in all that bulky clothing. Clever, and it confirms his assumption that his 'domicile unit' will likely be examined in his absence.

Maggie's data file, downloaded to a flash memory stick about the size of a postage stamp, has been secured upon his person. He's resolved that any attempt to retrieve it will result in broken limbs, and not his own.

As to the room itself, they can search it to their hearts' content. He left not a fingerprint behind. Mr. Gouda being meticulous about hygiene, wiping the taps and so on. Not that a print would do them much good. Like all current and former agents and employees of the FBI, his fingerprints are stored in supposedly unhackable files and not available to unauthorized inquiries. His laptop, purposefully left in place for their perusal, has been scrubbed of everything but

RG Paving spreadsheets and estimating software. They might, he supposes, harvest some DNA from his pillow—even a healthy scalp sheds a little dandruff—but that won't get them anywhere because he's made sure his DNA is not on file. Not at the FBI, not anywhere.

Professional paranoia, perhaps, but it has saved his life more than once. He has to assume that whoever abducted Haley Corbin will know she had been consulting with a former FBI agent who specializes in child recovery cases. Will they be expecting an intrusion from Randall Shane? Print and DNA data are covered, but facial recognition software would make an easy distinction between the ersatz Ron Gouda and the real one, so there's always the possibility that he was flagged at the checkpoint and is now under surveillance.

Not that he's seen any sign of it. So far he's been treated like all the other 'guests.' That is, like cattle being gently but firmly funneled down the old chute. According to Maggie, the real genius of the Ruler organization is in knowing precisely everything about the financial status of all potential members, as well as other personal details that may prove useful for maximum extraction of cash. Five grand for a three-day seminar is just the beginning.

At that price, Ron Gouda expects a damn good breakfast, and Shane finds himself in total agreement.

The Hive is—and he hears the joke more than once—buzzing. Shane counts twenty-seven other guests filing into a spacious, glass-domed cafeteria. Sorting themselves out by choosing tables, then wandering up to the sumptuous buffet. Shane, who feels like a bear coming out of hibernation, picks up the commingled scents of bacon, eggs, pancakes, maple syrup. He loads up a plate. A big plate.

He's here to mingle, and so homes in on an occupied table. "Hey there, mind if I join you?"

Of course they do, but the Gouda doesn't take 'no' for an answer. Shane, far from an extrovert in real life, is rather enjoying the hail-fellow-well-met persona of the man he's impersonating. He introduces himself and shakes hands, making it impossible that his tablemates fail to respond in kind.

An attractive young couple from Duluth, currently "doing good" with an Amway franchise and looking to move up in the world. A lean, hungry-looking term-insurance salesman from Kentucky who doesn't say much but looks to be measuring Shane for a policy pitch. Last and most interesting to Shane, a forty-year-old woman with flinty, intelligent eyes. Quickly sizing him up, she lets everyone know she started a chain of trendy convenience stores in Southern California. That explains the slim platinum Rolex on her sun-freckled wrist, and the self-confidence that makes her push back at the biggest, loudest male at the table, if not the gathering.

"So what do you do, Mr. Gouda? Whatever it is, I'm guessing it keeps you outside a good deal. Construction?"

Shane grins. "Got me. You want a road built in the state of Ohio, a mall parking lot, whatever, you go to RG Paving and we'll get 'er done, if I have to drive the machine myself. Which normally I don't, not anymore."

He gets the impression the grab-and-go queen wants to establish where he fits, statuswise, and that in her mind outdoorsy construction is somewhere below her own level of success.

The term-insurance guy, sensing an uneasy standoff, says, "I always liked the smell of hot asphalt. Weird, I guess, but it reminds me of summer."

"It's an honest smell," Shane says, chuckling heartily. "Just be glad I'm not in the Porta Potti business. Oops! Sorry, didn't mean to spoil your appetites."

But the woman with the flinty eyes hasn't given up. "I'm curious," she says. "What prompted your interest in joining the Rulers?"

He shrugs. "Haven't joined yet," he points out. "Just checking it out. Fact is, some of the most successful people in my state are in the program. Contractors, politicians, entrepreneurs. So I've been told. Folks don't advertise they're Rulers, exactly. My impression, it's like a private club."

"And you like private clubs?"

"If the club is to my advantage, I do. And make no apologies for it, neither! Thing is, I heard about that little introductory seminar they give in Dayton, thought I'd give it a shot. I liked what I heard. Enough to get me to sign up for a look at the real deal. We'll see. If it makes sense and it puts me ahead, why not?"

Satisfied, the woman with the flinty eyes works on her fruit salad. Not a big breakfast kind of person, apparently.

The others make small talk, and Shane manages to introduce his recollection of a Ruler—one of those at the little old intro seminar in Dayton—whose first name is Missy. She made an impression on Ron Gouda, but not so much that he can recall her last name, or where she was from. Did any of the others happen to run into the little lady?

Nobody had.

When Shane finishes his plate, he pushes it back, gives a sigh of satisfaction, and says, "I don't know about anybody else, but I slept like a baby last night. Must be this mountain air. Normally I'm an insomniac kind of person—too much going on in my head, I guess. Can't recall the last time I fell asleep before ten o'clock, and slept right through."

The others admit, the couple somewhat shyly, to falling asleep almost instantly, and all at about the same time. Shane leaves it at that, not wanting to share his own suspicions about airborne sedatives contributing to the situation. Which makes sense, in a perverse, mind-control kind of way. Casinos pump in oxygen to keep the gamblers wide-awake, why not do the reverse if you want to make sure potential Rulers are well-rested and amenable to recruitment? No uncontrolled fraternization between 'domicile units' in the wee hours. Everybody sleeping, waking, and eating in unison. It fits with what Shane has been able to glean from Arthur Conklin's unreadable book. Insect and animal behavior patterns as they relate to individual success, and how establishing new thought patterns enables the motivated individual to establish a new 'rule of one.'

Shane learns a little more about the process when, as promised, the doors to Profit Hall close at 8:00 a.m. precisely. He's been expecting something like a grand cathedral, or at the very least a modern auditorium. But it turns out there's more than one assembly hall in the complex, and the thirty or so new recruits have been confined to a relatively small theater equipped with a variation on stadium seating. The difference being that each seat is separated from the next by cubicle-height walls.

You enter in a group, but experience the seminar alone,

as an individual. All of the group watching the same images on a big central screen, but listening to the audio part on individual headphones, so that the voices seem to be speaking to you alone.

Pretty clever, Shane admits to himself. The tension between individual and group being part of the whole Ruler spiel. Which begins in total darkness with a lush, swelling soundtrack—he's put in mind of Holst's *The Planets* as interpreted by John Williams of *Star Wars* fame. The first image is of the famous cover of *The Rule of One,* some thirty feet high on the screen. Size alone makes it appear totemic, important. Next there's a clever, almost dizzy dissolve into the author photo, and then the viewer seems to break through into a neatly ordered study or library, and Shane finds himself in the presence of Arthur Conklin himself.

Conklin is somewhat older that the author photo on the original book, but he can't be more than sixty, so the seminar had to have been recorded more than twenty years ago. And yet it has a convincing 'live' feel, as if Professor Conklin were in a nearby studio. The video quality is uncanny—no scratches or static or faded colors to give away its true age—and seems to have been somehow rendered in high definition, although surely HD didn't exist when this particular lecture was recorded.

Shane gives the production values an A+ and wonders if Industrial Light & Magic had a hand in refreshing the imagery. If not ILM, then some entity with a similar skill set. But what really seals the deal is the audio part of the experience. Conklin's book might be difficult to comprehend, but the man himself knows how to talk. He has an attractive voice in the middle register, neither so low as to drone, nor so high as to whine. It's a perfect FM radio voice, well modulated and compelling, and it makes you want to listen and learn as Arthur recounts his early years. His struggles to improve himself both physically and mentally. His confusion as to the motivations of human behavior. The long years he spent away from the human sphere by recording the orderly patterned behaviors of the insect world—specifically ants and honeybees—on-screen are some remarkable film clips of ants and bees toiling away—and ultimately his discovery that the human brain can be rewired by a process he calls 'deep thinking.' Before his brilliant, charismatic new friend Arthur can explain about 'deep thinking,' the lecture pauses for a lunch break.

Shane, who thinks of himself as impervious to sales pitches and other forms of indoctrination, is stunned to discover that nearly four hours have gone by.

How did that happen? Was it something in the pancakes, or was Arthur Conklin simply that good? And how could Shane, who has never met a self-help book he cared to finish, find the lecture so fascinating? On an intellectual as well as a gut level, Randall Shane is pretty sure of himself. He knows who he is and what he believes. At this stage of the game he has no interest in 'rewiring his brain' or 'evolving to the next level.' He's comfortable in his own shoes, as it were. And yet he had listened avidly to Arthur Conklin and found that after four hours of one-way conversation, some essential part of him really did want to know what 'deep thinking' was, and how it might affect his own powers of concentration.

Bloody hell. He'd been brainwashed, and all it had taken was one rinse cycle.

9. Because We Want To Stay Alive

For the first couple of weeks after his father died, Noah clung to me. Physically clung to me, his arms around my legs if I happened to be standing up, snuggling up to my breast, thumb in his mouth, if I was lying down. It helped me to keep such close physical contact—I could feel how alive my son was, feel the fierceness of his small heart beating, somehow in sync with my own. We were adrift in the same powerful current of grief. In my mind Noah and I were being swept along by a great and terrible river, and people along the river-bank kept waving to us and urging us to come ashore, but we had each other and we didn't want their comfort because it was right for us to be carried along by torrents so deep, so powerful, that they opened up canyons in the earth, eroding the world, making new landscapes of sorrow and loss.

Three days after the funeral—it had been a nightmare, getting Jed's remains released, and seemed to have taken forever, although it was only about ten days—Noah stopped clinging and he was no longer sucking his thumb, and he said to me, "It's really real, isn't it? Daddy's really gone and he's never coming back?" I said yes, it was really real, his Daddy was really gone, and Noah thought about that for a few moments and he looked me straight in the eye—we were at the kitchen table, pushing our food around but not really eating—and he said, "Daddy wants me to grow up and be strong for you, so that's what I'm going to do," and there was something about his tone that made it seem he was speaking with his father's voice, as if Jed was looking at me through our little boy's eyes and saying goodbye, and the amazing thing is, I didn't break down. I didn't burst into tears. Just hearing him say that gave me so much strength and confidence that I was able to reach out and take Noah's hand and say, "You're already strong. You're my superhero. But I'd rather you didn't grow up too fast, okay? I need you to be my little boy for a while."

After that we were okay. The emptiness was still there, of course—sleeping was especially difficult for me—but somehow we'd come ashore without me noticing, and we were both in the world again, doing what you do to get through each day.

Remembering how Noah had shown me the way, how an eight-year-old's inner strength had far surpassed my own, makes me believe that he'll be strong enough to keep his own mind, no matter what poison is being spread by those who want to use him. Missy keeps warning me about Evangeline, what a terrible, evil person she is. For all I know, that's true. But what sticks in my craw is Noah's teacher, Mrs. Delancey. That bitch! Her I know, or thought I did, and it seems to me unutterably cruel that she must have moved to Humble for no other purpose than to ingratiate herself with Noah and with me. All the while planning to steal him away.

That's who these people are. Never forget.

Meanwhile, after the strange little man leaves us, Missy Barlow wants to show me around. I'm not kidding—the woman who helped abduct me wants to give me a tour of her house—in effect my prison—and show off all the cool stuff she and her weirdo husband have accumulated.

"The design had to be approved by the Ruler council, of course, but Eldon really did most of the design thinking himself."

'Design thinking,' it turns out, is when you think of something—in this case a Really Rich Ski Lodge—and then hire someone who actually designs it. In Missy's world, apparently, buying the *Mona Lisa* is the same as painting it. That sounds crazy, but I'm not about to defend her sanity. It's as if her life is unraveling, and she thinks if she talks fast enough the trend will reverse itself. You don't go from being a successful, law-abiding citizen to a felon-in-hiding without it having some pretty strong effects on your mental status. And who knows, maybe she was always a few bricks shy of a load, as Jed liked to say.

"We're the only Fives with a house anything like this one," she brags, as we tour the shuttered, shaded interior. "Fives, that's for Level Five, there's seven levels altogether, and the only one who's ever reached Seven is Arthur Conklin. There's only like about ten who ever made Six. Ruler Weems is a Six. So is Evangeline, although some of us sort of assume she cheated because she's Arthur's wife and nobody dared to tell her she didn't pass. So being a Five is, like, really high in the organization. There's maybe fifty Fives, and you have to share-in a million a year, minimum, to stay a Five. Until you're like sixty years old and then you're an Honorary, and you can stay at your level even if you don't make as much money."

"Share-in" is the Ruler version of tithing, and Missy is really proud that she and Eldon share-in way more than a million a year. Which Eldon calls "the price of genius," at least according to his chatty wife. His particular genius being in gameware design, whatever that is, exactly. My first thought is Guitar Hero, like maybe he designed the fake guitars—isn't that gameware?—but Missy rolls her eyes and explains that Eldon's genius is way, way more impressive than Guitar Hero because, artificial drumroll please, he designs technologies for cell-phone gamers. Plus with the money he earned from his first patent he had the foresight to buy a ring tone subscription service, and that's turned out to be "like, a superinvestment."

"Ring tones?" I ask. "That's how you got rich?"

Missy must sense that I'm less than impressed, because she huffs herself up and goes, "Me and Eldon own some of the most famous ring tones in the world!"

"Great. Listen, Missy, I appreciate the tour, you and your husband have a fabulous house, even if we're sort of hiding in it with the shades drawn, but I'm really not in the mood for *House Beautiful,* okay? Maybe later, but right now all I care about is how you can help me get my son back."

"We're doing all we can," she protests, getting all sulky. "You heard Ruler Weems. This is a really difficult situation. Not to mention dangerous. Me and Eldon, we're risking our lives to keep you safe."

"Okay, you're risking your life. You're my angel. Where's Noah? Where are they keeping him?"

"I don't know. Someplace we can't get to, that's all I know. Probably the Pinnacle."

"The Pinnacle?"

"Yeah, the Pinnacle is where Arthur lives. And Evangeline. It's way up the mountain, sort of like built *into* the mountain, you know? Everybody says it's fabulous and amazing, but I've never seen it. You can't get to the Pinnacle unless you're a Six. It's supposed to be superfortified. Eldon says if the world ever blew up, like in a nuclear war, the Pinnacle would survive."

"So he's seen the Pinnacle?"

"No, but he knows people who have. Eldon knows everybody important."

"Does that man who came to see us, Mr. Weems, does he live in the Pinnacle?"

"He used to, but not anymore. Not since Eva decided to take over."

"Missy, listen to me. I'm going to assume you're a good person, okay? And that your involvement in this is well-intentioned. But I want you to do me a favor. I want you to persuade Eldon to take me to the Pinnacle, okay?"

"I don't think he can do that," she says, reluctantly. "Ruler Weems might, but not Eldon."

"When is he coming back, Ruler Weems?"

A shrug. "Dunno. In case you haven't noticed, nobody tells me anything," she adds, sounding petulant.

At that moment her husband appears on the grand stairway. He doesn't seem at all pleased that Missy is conducting a house tour. "Upstairs, both of you."

"But the place is all closed up from the outside," Missy protests. "Why do we have to hide in the bedroom?"

"Because we want to stay alive," he says. "Upstairs, now!"

10. Bad Little Gnome

In his private sanctuary deep inside security headquarters, Bagrat Kavashi finally finds time to think for himself. He hates to admit that a woman has the power to overwhelm his powers of concentration, but Evangeline is no ordinary female. She is, after all, the consort of the great leader, a transcendent genius, and has herself reached a level of oneness to which he can only aspire. At the same time he fears for her judgment, if not her sanity. Her lust is not restricted to the flesh, but extends to all the levers of power within her grasp. Money. Greed. Manipulation. Fear. These are, as he well knows, intoxicants that can overwhelm rational thought. So he takes it with a grain of salt when Eva the Diva rants about purification and purging of the Rulers. In his homeland, regular purges are a useful tool for maintaining power. Stand those you mistrust up against a wall and shoot them. Nothing could be simpler. But as the head of a small but increasingly influential U.S. security firm, Vash is keenly aware that even in a remote corner of Colorado, wholesale slaughter is bound to attract the kind of attention that could destroy the Ruler organization, as well as his own company. A missing person here or there—truly missing—is one thing, and a task he's well equipped to handle, but making an entire faction disappear—scores of citizens, some of them very wealthy—that remains difficult, if not unthinkable. And yet he must find a way to satisfy Evangeline; his own power and wealth, his fate, is commingled with her own.

A problem to be solved—but what a problem!

Vash pours himself a drink of Georgian vodka from a bottle he keeps in a freezer. An American affectation—a true Georgian would drink vodka at any temperature below a full boil—that he's grown accustomed to since he arrived on these welcoming shores. In truth, not so welcoming at first—the rival Chechens were already firmly established in Brighton Beach and had little respect for a country lad from Pshavi, Georgia. But with a little luck and a steady hand upon his straight razor, Vash established himself as a force to be reckoned with and soon part of an uneasy alliance between the most ruthless factions of the bratva, the brotherhood of criminals who had elbowed the American Mafia out of their own rackets. Vash's specialty in Brighton Beach was protection and extortion, just as it had been in his home province. But in the good old U.S. of A., the ambitious young immigrant discovered the usefulness of computer surveillance. Before he broke into the life of, say, a prosperous Russian businessman, he first hacked into the man's computers, establishing exactly what resources could be reasonably extracted, and what personal habits might make the target vulnerable. From computer hacking, Vash got into advanced surveillance techniques—hidden cameras, tracking devices, all the little toys of espionage—so that by the time he made his move he was eight or ten steps beyond whatever ham-fisted security the target mistakenly believed would keep him safe.

It was like taking candy from babies. Big, murderous babies, some of whom had to be disappeared without a trace. Which meant leaving not so much as a filthy fingernail behind. He'd developed a special technique for such in his native land, and perfected it with the help of American technology. By then Vash had become educated in law enforcement. Although grand juries sometimes indicted criminals when there was no dead body to introduce into evidence, they were loath to do so. Missing persons had a habit of turning up on the other side of the earth, alive and well and drawing from their offshore accounts. And even if the victim really was deceased, the lack of physical proof could be exploited by clever defense attorneys to make it look like good old Boris was living the high life in Säo Paulo or Shanghai. Wink-wink to the jaded juries, who in New York tended to distrust the government almost as much as they did those under indictment.

All things being equal, no dead body means no prosecution. Exceptions are made if there was a witness to the crime, and the witness is willing to testify, but no one had ever been foolish enough to testify against Bagrat Kavashi. Not and survive. The last eyewitness who attempted to give testimony in the province of Pshavi 'caused' an explosion in the courthouse resulting in the death not only himself, but the entire team of prosecutors.

Vash—for a while thereafter known as "Boom-Boom"—survived the explosion by hiding behind the judge's steel-plated desk, as planned. Unfortunately the judge, an engagingly corruptible fellow, did not make it. There wasn't really room for two under the desk. Too bad, he'd rather liked the judge, but when a bomb is about to detonate, a man has to trust his instincts.

He sips at the vodka, savoring the ice-thickened alcohol. Back home the habit was to pound the stuff down, shot after shot, but Vash prefers to take it slow, maintaining control. In the old days he used to secretly dispose of his drinks while the others slammed and roared and eventually fell senseless to the floor. He'd be the only sober man in the room, indeed the only conscious man, and sometimes took advantage by strangling a rival or two.

Soothed by the warmth of the vodka, he activates a surveillance screen and begins to tap the keyboard, coaxing up images. Both live feeds and the recorded backup. Vash knows the programs inside and out. And while his private sanctuary does not have the flash of Eva's multiscreened command center, he's a professional while she is, at best, an enthusiastic amateur.

Ten minutes later he's located Wendall Weems. The ugly little man is right where he should be, inside his multiroomed bunker, where he believes himself to be protected, if not invulnerable. So did Eva simply get it wrong—did she neglect to check all the rooms? Or does Ruler Weems have, as the Americans say, something up his sleeve?

Vash makes a few adjustments to the motion-detecting software, then begins to run the digital video back over the last twenty-four hours, searching for an anomaly. Which obediently pops up after a relatively short interval.

He sits back in his chair, puzzling it out. At exactly 1205 hours, the Bunker is completely empty. Not a creature is stirring, not even the mousy Mr. Weems. Vash scrolls it back another twenty seconds, and the motion-detecting software pops up, providing an image of Weems entering the bathroom adjacent to his bedroom.

His men had not bothered to plant a surveillance camera in the bathroom. Moisture from the showers tended to fog up or short out small cameras, and besides, no one wanted to see Weems on the potty. It was enough to document him entering and exiting. But exiting is the problem, because Weems never does. The next time his motion is detected almost four hours have passed and Weems is ambling down a hallway toward his library, looking preoccupied.

Convinced there must be something wrong with the

software, Vash calls up the files for the device positioned outside the bathroom. As he recalls, it's a model SDR35, a fully functional smoke detector equipped with a covert video camera, utilizing a Sony CCD image sensor. Simple, reliable, and effective. And true to form, there's nothing wrong with the camera or the video feed. It faithfully records the closed door of the bathroom from the moment Weems enters until the present, and never does the ugly little man emerge, nor does anyone else enter. A bathroom that, according to the blueprints, has only the one door. And yet the next time Weems trips a motion detector, hours have passed and he's in another part of the Bunker.

Impossible, on the face of it, but nevertheless true. Clearly something is truly amiss. Ruler Weems has been a bad little gnome. He has secret passageways that don't show up on the blueprints. But where do they lead? Where was he for the missing three hours? Somewhere within the Bunker, maybe perusing some until-now-unknown collection of illegal porn? That would be delicious, and might even be useful. But what worries Vash, what furrows his handsome brow, is the possibility that Wendall Weems has a way to leave his Bunker without being seen, and thus the ability to confer with his supporters without being monitored by BK Security.

Bad little gnome.

11. His Master's Voice

Much as he'd like to hang around the Hive and socialize, Shane skips lunch and hurries back to his domicile unit, intent on checking in with Maggie Drew.

Housekeeping has made a visit, leaving fresh towels on

the rack. No sign that any prints have been lifted—fingerprint powder is messy stuff—but he's assuming his water glass has been bagged as part of the security routine, because if he'd been in charge, that's what he'd do. Just as he assumes they've copied the files off his laptop, strictly as a precaution. In fact, he hopes so, as it will confirm that Ron Gouda is just another ambitious contractor looking to get ahead. More numbers to crunch for the Ruler database, and no indication—not yet—that his impersonation has been detected.

With cell phones not functioning, Shane has no choice but to use the landline thoughtfully provided by his hosts. In full confidence that will he be recorded, if not actually monitored, he punches in the agreed-upon number, which begins with the area code for Dayton, Ohio.

"RG Paving, how may I direct your call?"

"You're talking to the big cheese, honey babe."

"Mr. Gouda! How are you, sir? Is the skiing good?"

"Ha! Nobody believes me when I tell 'em this ain't a skiing vacation. Like nobody seems to believe old Ronnie's interested in improving his mind. Why is that? Never mind. Thing is, I only got a short interval before I got to get back. But I really need to cross a few t's on the bid for the I-75 grade-and-pave. Hate to lose that one just because I didn't give it the hairy eyeball one last time. Can you send the PDF to my e-mail? Thanks a mil, honey babe."

He disconnects, opens the laptop, and waits for the link to activate on the encrypted messenger software. His old pal Charley Newman calls it 'Instant Messenger For Spooks,' which pretty much sums it up, but you don't have to be a spy to want your personal e-mails to remain private, and that goes triple for federal employees. It does mean that Maggie will have to use her personal computer, not the office terminal, but that's probably for the best, too. Her message pops up on the screen.

Honey babe?

That's what the big cheese calls his Gal Friday.

So, how goes it, Mr. Cheese?

Weird but interesting. Very slick operation. Security level extremely high, verging on paranoid. Cells don't work. My guess is, all communication filtered through security. Plus, I think I was drugged last night.

WHAT?

Can't be sure, but other guests report falling deeply asleep at exactly the same time. Possible airborne sedative. Fentanyl or something equally effective.

FENTANYL HIGHLY DANGEROUS !!!

Anything on our friend Missy?

ACKNOWLEDGE FENTANYL DANGEROUS!!!

Okay, acknowledge. Don't worry, I won't be in my room tonight when they pump the stuff in, if that's what they're doing. Now what about the mysterious Missy? Any luck?

Yes, indeed! Mysterious M. identified as Melissa G. Barlow, spouse of Eldon Donald Barlow, gameware designer. A Level Five member and a big-time contributor to Ruler coffers, associated with the Weems faction. Eldon owns many, many toys, including a Gulfstream G-450.

You are my sunshine! Address?

Sorry. Barlow residence not specified as to street address, just listed as 'ski lodge, Conklin.'

That'll get me started. Anything else?

Leave while you can. RIGHT NOW.

Soon, honey babe, soon.

If the morning session was impressive, based on the sheer persuasive charisma of Arthur Conklin, the afternoon session is, for Shane, more than a little strange. This time they're seated in regular auditorium seats, not the individualized cubicles, and yet they've been instructed to don the same wireless headphones from the earlier session.

Despite the oddity of wearing individual headphones while in a group—what's next, 3-D glasses?—the session at first seems straightforward, and very old school. The instructor, a trim, slightly nerdy fellow equipped with a headset, uses a pointer and a series of charts as he explains each of the Ten Reasons to Rule Yourself, taken from the first chapter of the founder's famous book. It all feels eerily reminiscent of the Bible classes Shane attended as a child, which he supposes makes sense, since *The Rule of One* is, for this group, a kind of scripture guiding them along the one true path to self-improvement.

"Rule One," the instructor intones. "'There is only the one of you.' Okay, so what does it really mean? Your first reaction may be to think the answer is obvious, that we are all individuals, unique to ourselves. But as with everything Arthur Conklin writes, there's more to it than that. Much, much more. What he's referring to is—and you'll find this in the glossary—a concept known as *the singularity of mind.* It is the idea, fundamental to *The Rule of One,* that *you are your mind.* Does that sound obvious? It's not. It bears repeating—*you are your mind.* You are not your heart. You are not your soul. You are not a bag of skin filled with bones and organs. You, the distinctness of you, exists entirely within the electrical field generated by the human brain. So before we can take a step along the path laid out by Arthur Conklin, we must first accept that there is a difference between the *mind* and the *brain.* The brain is just another organ, albeit a rather amazing one, containing billions of distinct cells, each cell linked to billions of other cells by synaptic connections. For purposes of this lesson, try thinking of the *brain* as a radio set and the *mind* as the electrical field that comes into existence when the radio is turned on. We accept that the mind cannot exist without the brain, just as blood cannot circulate without the heart. But the mind is not the brain, just as blood is not the heart."

Listening to the warm, strangely familiar voice in his headphones, Shane experiences an unsettling disconnect. Word for word it sounds like a typical self-improvement narrative—unlocking the power of the human mind to overcome life obstacles—but the nerdy, earnest dude on stage just doesn't seem to fit the powerfully persuasive voice.

And then he realizes why the voice doesn't fit. He slips off the headphones and confirms his suspicion: the speaker has a thin, reedy voice with a slight lisp, whereas the voice in the headphones belongs to none other than Arthur Conklin himself.

So how is it possible that Nerdy Dude is so perfectly limning what must be a recording? Right down to the timing, the pauses, the rhetorical flourishes? It can't be a variation on lip-synching, the execution is too perfect for that. The only explanation Shane can come up with is some sort of software that runs the speaker's voice through an Arthur Conklin filter.

Shane is put in mind of that nostalgic magazine ad, with a dog listening to an old phonograph recording of His Master's Voice. The Rulers had taken it several steps further, by finding a way to make the institute lecturers speak in their master's voice.

Bizarre, but actually very effective—why mess with success? If Conklin himself is no longer available, keep his image alive in updated videos, let his voice be replicated and repeated, endlessly and intimately, through the mouths of his acolytes.

Plus, and Shane knows a thing or two about programming, it must be really cool software. Now that he understands the mechanism that drew him in, he loses interest in the content—a lot of lofty-sounding stuff about using the hidden powers of the mind to find the One True Voice that will lead, essentially, to the pot of gold at the end of your personal rainbow. He tunes it all out and concentrates on the problem at hand: finding the power couple who snatched Haley Corbin from the airport.

Shane's gut tells him Haley is alive, and that she's somewhere nearby. Locating her begins with locating Mr. and Mrs. Barlow, whose ski lodge must be among those that overlook the campus. There are hundreds of condos and lodges, so he can't simply go door-to-door, not without triggering a reaction from BK Security. He has to find another way. If he had weeks or months he might pull off a direct infiltration, posing as a Ruler wannabe with big pockets, or maybe by infiltrating the security force. But he doesn't have weeks or months. From what he's seen of BK Security, they'll twig to him sooner rather than later, possibly before the three-day seminar concludes. He has to make a move in the next few hours, before all the doors slam shut.

The session concludes with a fairly brief description of the Ruler hierarchy. New members enter at the lowest level, of course, and gradually proceed upward through a series of 'graduations,' ultimately achieving the "seventh level of oneness." Each level requiring a considerable investment of not only time, but increasingly hefty initiation fees. By level five, qualification includes having a net worth of no less than five million dollars. The implication being that by the time you've gotten that far along, money will be sticking to you like stink on a monkey. Not that the lecturer, speaking in Arthur Conklin's voice, puts it quite so indelicately, but that's what Shane hears beneath all the smooth talk. Join the Rulers and become a money magnet. Revel in your selfness. Empathy is a weakness. Guilt is for losers. Celebrate the glorious oneness of you, and grab all the loot you can with both hands.

After the session concludes, and most of the new recruits have stumbled out of the auditorium looking somehow both stunned and energized, Shane lingers behind and seizes the hand of the speaker, shaking it enthusiastically.

"Heckuva talk, partner! You could sell ice to the Eskimos, and coming from me that's a compliment. Ron Gouda, Dayton, Ohio, pleased to make your acquaintance."

"Thanks," says the startled speaker, attempting to extricate his hand from Shane's big paw. "If you'll follow the others to the Hive, there's free hot chocolate."

"I'll do that, sure, you bet. Lemme tell ya, friend, when they told me the fee for a three-day seminar was five grand, my first thought was, for that kind of money I can go to Club Med, soak up the sunshine and the piña coladas. But now I been here and heard the presentation, I'm thinking it's worth every penny. Five hundred thousand pennies, to be exact."

"I, um, they have cookies, too. In the Hive. To go with the hot chocolate. Just follow along with the others," the man urges, trying to step around.

"Can I ask you a personal question?" Shane says, blocking his way. "What level are you? I'm betting a guy who talks as good as you must be at least a Level Six."

"Level Six is very high," the man says uneasily. "Most of the instructors are, um, Level Two."

"You're a Two? Well, I'll be darned. That raises my appreciation of the whole enterprise, if a fella as accomplished as you is only got that far along. My opinion, they need to bump you up to at least a Five! I met a Five and he's a pretty smart dude, but no smarter'n you. You know him? Eldon Barlow? Something to do with them computer games, I don't know what, exactly. But I do know he's got himself a beautiful aircraft, 'cause that's where I met Eldon, him and his wife, Missy, they were at Dayton Airport, that's the birthplace of American aviation in case you didn't know, on account of Wilbur and Orville Wright are from Dayton, and there's this gorgeous Gulfstream G-450—are you familiar with the 450?—and I just had to go over and admire it and that's when I run into the Barlows. Really nice people. They got a ski lodge here and told me to drop in and say howdy, was I ever in the vicinity. But wouldn't you know, I misplaced their number and my cell don't seem to work worth a darn. I don't suppose you could point out where the Barlows live? Or if there's a phone book or directory where I can look 'em up?"

The speaker, by now trembling with nerves, is staring at Shane the way an unarmed hiker might look at the sudden appearance of a grizzly bear on the trail. His eyes flitting to the exits, calculating where to retreat and how fast he has to run to get there, all the while not wanting to antagonize the bear in his path.

"We're, um, not allowed to give out any personal information," he says.

"Sure, a course. But you know the Barlows, right? At least you heard of them?" A flicker in his eyes confirms that he has, indeed, heard of the Barlows. "Are they home by any chance? Maybe you could call 'em yourself, tell 'em Ron Gouda from Dayton happens to be in the vicinity. They want, they can call me. No loss of privacy, we do it that way, right? Whattaya say, Mr. Two Level, can you help me out? Can you call the Barlows?"

"Um, not directly, but I'll, um, see what I can do."

"Fantastic! Tell you what, you're ever in Dayton I'll buy you the biggest steak dinner you ever seen. Thirty-two ounces of prime, grain-fed steer. Or we could do the pork rib barbecue. Your choice."

"Sure, I'll keep that in mind. Could you excuse me? I'm, ah, running late."

"Eldon and Missy Barlow! As a personal favorite to me."

"Yes, yes. If you'll just go along to the Hive."

"Absolutely," Shane says, letting the man get by him. "Free hot chocolate, cookies. Wouldn't miss that for the world."

Five minutes later Randall Shane has found an exit from Profit Hall. As he steps out into the beautiful, frozen landscape of the Conklin Institute, his eyes scanning the mountainside residences for activity, he's thinking two things.

One, there's a pretty solid chance that a security cruiser will be dispatched to warn, and/or question the Barlows about the presence of a potential troublemaker, and with any luck he'll be there to see it happen.

Two, he really, really regrets leaving his new down parka at reception, because if something doesn't happen in the next fifteen minutes he'll be frozen solid.

12. When The Night Turns Blue

He's trying to dance the cold away, stamping his feet and flapping his arms, when the flinty-eyed grab-and-go queen shows up, all decked out in an ankle-length parka, fake-fur earmuffs, and long and very pink wool scarf.

"What in the name of God are you doing out here?" she wants to know, clapping her mittens together "We're having a cold snap! You'll get frostbite!"

"Just clearing my lungs! Stuffy in there!" Teeth chattering, Shane tries to respond cheerfully.

"I thought we got all the nuts in Southern California," she says, staring up at him. "Apparently they kept a few in Ohio."

Shane grins like a madman. Maybe if she thinks he's crazy she'll leave him alone. Whatever, he's invested now. Has to stay out in the open ground where he's got a clear view of the surrounding community, the terraced streets rising above the campus. Looking for any sign of security response that might lead him to the Barlow residence.

"You know what the temperature is?" she demands, her California tan turning almost as pink as the scarf. "In the last hour it's fallen to five degrees! That's without the windchill. With the wind it's below zero."

"Feels good!" Shane tells her, hugging himself. "Gets the old heart pumping!"

What gets his heart pumping is the sight of a BK Security cruiser speeding along one of the upper streets. The cruiser stops, dome light strobing, beneath a massive, multilevel ski lodge. His eyes are watering so badly that he can't see much more than that. Does the responding officer get out and ring the bell or whatever? Is the lodge even occupied? He can't tell, but it's a place to start.

"You're right, I better get inside!" he says, abruptly excusing himself. "It's c-c-cold out here!"

Then he's running in huge, loping strides, across the hard-frozen ground, heading for the entrance to Domicile One.

There's a new crew at the reception desk, but Shane manages to retrieve his parka with a minimum of fuss.

Although he's again disconcerted to find that staff people he's never seen before seem to know him by sight.

"Did you enjoy the seminar, Mr. Gouda?"

"Yeah, yeah, it was great. Opened my mind to a whole new way of thinking."

"Wonderful. You don't want to miss the welcome party. They're expecting you."

"Me personally? Really? That's great. Just got to get something out of my car."

"One of the staff can take care of that, Mr. Gouda," the desk clerk says, holding out his hand for the keys. "That way you won't miss the party. Just follow the arrows back to the Hive."

Really, it's like dealing with robots. Polite, personable young robots who won't take 'no' for an answer. In open defiance, Shane zips up his parka. "It's a personal matter," he says, striding out the door, car keys in his fist.

A glance back reveals that the desk clerk has already lifted a phone, no doubt reporting an uncooperative guest.

Shane hurries out to his vehicle, hoping it will start. Fortunately the Grand Cherokee is equipped with a good battery—plenty of cranking amps—and although it hesitates and then shudders sluggishly, the engine somehow manages to chug to life on the first try. Not waiting for a warm-up, he guns the beast a few times, watching the tachometer spike, and then puts it in gear. No squeal of tires—the Big Cheese is just going for a little old sightseeing ride—but a firm application of the throttle pedal.

He's keenly aware of the tracking device clipped to the visor, and would dearly love to heave it out the window, but doing so would automatically alert security, and that will happen soon enough, thank you. He's also thinking he's never before in his life been in such a controlled environment. This is the kind of total surveillance the old Soviets and Maoists only dreamed about. Call it a silicon curtain, with every obedient citizen reduced to a pulsing dot on a monitor, guided from one indoctrination to the next. Not for nothing was Arthur Conklin an expert in insect hive dynamics. His followers might preach a kind of Darwinian individualism—the self above all—but when it came right down to it they were obsessive about instilling group behavior into would-be Rulers, from the very get-go.

The interior of the Cherokee has all the warmth of a walk-in freezer—how long does it take these things to warm up?—but he doesn't have time to fully appreciate his discomfort before decisions are upon him. There's a circular road around the campus, and no immediate clue as to where it joins the road that rises up the mountainside, providing access to the residential area. Should he go left or right? He decides to retrace the way he came in, figuring the residential access must split off somewhere back before the signs that had so helpfully guided him down into the campus the night before.

Speaking of night, the shadow cast by the setting sun is rapidly crawling up the mountainside, leaving the valley dimmed. Ominous, somehow. Four in the afternoon and already the lights are coming on. No doubt the temperature is dropping even further. All of which confirms his decision not to attempt a recon on foot.

Randall Shane, human Popsicle. We found him after the spring melt, your honor, no idea how he wandered off, or what he was looking for.

By the time he's found his way back to the entrance to

the valley, the interior of the vehicle has warmed up sufficiently for his breath to stop showing. And there, unmarked, the road does indeed split off, a narrow fork of well-sanded tarmac curving away, and upward. Grateful to the rental agent who suggested he opt for four-wheel drive, he sets out on the elevated road. After the first steep rise the roadway levels off, hugging the mountainside, and he's able to see down into the valley below, where the lights of the campus beckon like a nagging teacher. *Return to your seat, grasshopper. Drink your hot chocolate, nibble your cookies, and obey, obey, obey.* Well, screw that. He's not here to expose some money-sucking self-improvement scheme, however cleverly presented, he's here to develop enough evidence to justify a search warrant, hopefully bring in the FBI, or at the very least the Colorado state detectives. Some law enforcement entity that can cut through the crap, find Haley Corbin and her kid before the whole place goes Jonestown.

He comes around a curve and encounters the first residential complex. Condo units, from the look of it. Slowing down, he tries to picture where he is, relative to how it all looked from the campus. If he's not completely disoriented—and there's no guarantee of that—the big ski lodge is considerably farther along, in an area of stand-alones, not condos.

Shane speeds up, telling himself not to outrace his own headlights. The shadow of night has already found its way far up the mountainside, and although low-pressure sodium lights mark the edges of the road it would be fairly easy to make a mistake, find himself vaulting into eternity.

A couple of switchbacks farther up, he starts to see single residences. As if the smaller condos are starter homes for the lowly Level Ones and Twos, the impressive ski lodges reserved for high-ranking Rulers. He keeps eyeing the campus below, trying to get his bearings—it can't be much farther—when he comes around a corner and finds his windshield painted by a flashing blue lights.

He immediately slows, gives a wide berth to the security cruiser parked at the curb. As he passes he can see the officer yakking into a handheld. A quick glance reveals that the large residence is shuttered, without lights.

Damn. He keeps going, not wanting to attract the cruiser's attention—small chance of avoiding that, in this neighborhood, but what the hell—and waits until the flashing lights are out of sight before pulling over to assess the situation. Is it possible that he's got it all wrong? That the mysterious Barlows either have nothing to do with Haley's disappearance, or they've stashed her someplace else, maybe far removed from Conklin?

Unless deploying the storm shutters is to keep away the prying eyes.

Only one way to find out.

Shane is trying to find a place to park his vehicle, somewhere it won't be noticed, where he can recon the shuttered ski lodge without freezing to death, when the night turns blue with lights.

13. Ruler Weems Says It's Up To You

There was this show on A&E once, about the Stockholm syndrome. You probably already know what that is, but in case you don't, that's when people taken hostage start to identify with the bad guys who are holding them. The term comes from this incident in Sweden where bank robbers kept people hostage for five days, and by the end the victims were defending the bad guys. It sounds totally whacked, but apparently it has do with what happens to people under stress, and how they gravitate to those with power.

In my particular situation, I seem to have gotten it backward. Missy Barlow, who helped abduct me, and who is holding me prisoner in her own home, has got it into her silly little head that we're best friends.

When the cop first rings the doorbell, she clutches me and whispers, "Oh my god! They're coming! You've got to help us!"

We're hiding upstairs in the master bedroom—way too many mirrors, if you ask me—pretending the house is unoccupied. Shades drawn—electronically activated, actually—lights on low, we're sealed inside. Which means, obviously, that no one can answer the door. But we can see the cop on the monitor, leaning on the buzzer and shouting into the intercom, wanting to know if anybody's home.

"What do they want?" Missy whimpers. "Eldon, make them stop!"

Her husband, who is slender and somehow heterosexually effeminate, looks to be on the verge of tears. "How do you suggest I do that?" he hisses. "Just be quiet, maybe they'll go away."

Missy clings to me like a long-lost sister. "Tell him to make them stop," she begs, then turns plaintively to her husband. "Oh my god, I wish we were somewhere else! Eldon, why can't we be somewhere else?"

That makes Eldon roll his eyes, and glance to me as if

he expects sympathy. What's with these people? Can't they get anything right? Have they forgotten what they did to me? And why do they think I'd share their desire to have the cops—okay, the local security officers—go away?

"It's Eva," Eldon says. "Somehow she knows about you."

"I don't know Eva from a hole in the ground," I remind them. "But that's a cop ringing your doorbell, not some high priestess."

"Eva's not a high priestess," Missy corrects me. "She's…she's Eva, okay? She's dangerously crazy, okay? People she doesn't like, people who get in her way? Bad things happen to them. Plus the cops are on her side. Right, Eldon?"

The doorbell stops ringing, and on the monitor we watch as the cop walks away and is swallowed up by the darkness. My captors collapse like a couple of rag dolls, gasping with relief.

"Oh my god!" Missy whimpers, flopping back on their enormous bed. "Oh my god!"

"Maybe I should go out before he leaves," I suggest. "Give myself up."

"Are you crazy? They'll kill you!"

"You don't know that."

For his part, Eldon shrugs, never meeting my eyes. "You can do what you like," he says, speaking very carefully. "Ruler Weems said it's up to you."

I'm angry enough to do it, just to spite them. On the other hand, the strange little man they call Ruler Weems made an impression. He's manipulative and charming and obviously can't be trusted, but he did seem genuinely concerned for my safety. What if they're right? What if my life really is in danger? Part of me wants to reject everything they say—they *kidnapped* me!—but some other, cautious voice in my head urges me not to be too hasty. Despite the uniform, that wasn't really a cop at the door. It was a Ruler security officer, supposedly controlled by the very same people who blew up Noah's school. The same people holding him captive, feeding him lies, grooming him to be their new Messiah. The New Profit, that's what they call him. How sick is that? And according to Weems the same people killed my husband. They must know that given the chance I'll blow their ugly little world to pieces and do everything in my power to see that they spend the rest of their lives in prison.

To do that, I have to survive. I have to live for my son.

"Relax," I tell them. "I'm not making any hasty decisions."

Eldon, crouched by the security-cam monitor, goes, "Uh-oh, what's this?"

Missy whimpers, "Shit, shit, shit!"

What has attracted their attention is more flashing cop lights. Not stopping outside the lodge, but speeding past, heading down the road at high speed. No sirens, just the lights. As if the cop—excuse me, the henchman—has been distracted by some other, more critical event. We can't see where he's going, just that he's leaving in a hurry, following the other cars.

"I counted four vehicles," Eldon says softly to himself. "That's just about the entire force. Not exactly a center of criminal activity, Conklin."

I beg to differ—how about kidnapping, isn't that a crime?—but don't bother saying so because there's something about the last-minute distraction of the officer, pulling him away from our hiding place, that makes me think of Randall Shane.

Could he be out there, setting up a diversion? Are his old friends in the FBI about to stage a rescue?

Get a grip, Haley. Fantasizing about rescue attempts is probably part of the Stockholm syndrome. How could Shane know where you are? How could he even know you've been abducted rather than, say, murdered and left in the woods? Remember, he warned you to go back home and lock the doors. He knew you were in danger, and like a stubborn fool you ignored him. You hired a professional and then ignored his advice, how dumb is that? So don't assume that after you screwed up that he'll somehow figure it out and arrive with the cavalry. You're on your own. If anybody is going to find a way to rescue Noah, it will have to be you.

Eldon gets up, looking resolute. He still won't look me in the eye—is he ashamed? He should be!—but he has the appearance of a man who has come to a difficult decision. "We need to call Ruler Weems," he tells his wife. "He'll know what to do."

"Not on the regular phone," she warns him. "He said never to use the regular phone."

"I know that! I'm not a fool. I'll use the Iridium. Ruler Weems thinks the satellite phones are still safe."

"I'm sorry!" Missy whimpers, bursting into tears.

"Oh for God's sake, stop it. I can't think if you're blubbering."

"I'm s-s-so afraid they're going to kill us. You know what they're like, Eldon. They won't h-hesitate."

He sighs and then embraces his wife, who shudders

against him like a terrified child. "Stop it now. Just stop," he says soothingly. "Nobody is going to kill us."

"How do you k-k-know?"

For the first time Eldon Barlow looks directly at me, with eyes as cool as chips of black ice. "Because they want to kill her."

14. The Forever Jolt

The holding cell isn't a whole lot smaller than his so-called domicile unit. Similarly furnished in what he's come to think of as 'postmodern monk,' except in the holding cell the bed, chair, and small desk are bolted to the floor. Bare lightbulb out of reach in a metal cage. No windows. A single door, heavy steel, equipped with a viewing slot. No shower, of course, just a remote-flush stainless steel toilet commode of the type common to modern detention centers. You want it flushed, you have to ask the guard nicely.

The four security hacks who wrestled him into the cell—Ron Gouda wasn't in a mood to be manhandled—called it "Gitmo," making jokes about waterboarding him. Very funny. Hilarious. But the good news, they didn't seem to have a clue about his real identity, even if they didn't believe his "I was just out driving around" explanation of what he, a mere visitor, was doing in a restricted residential area.

He's in the holding cell for maybe fifteen minutes—his watch has been confiscated—when the viewing slot in the door slides up.

"Mr. Gouda?"

In character, Shane responds like an outraged citizen.

"Hey, are you guys nuts? Get me out of here! What kind of resort is this? You think I paid five grand to get arrested for driving around?"

"Hello, Mr. Gouda. Very nice to meetcha. I have Taser, you know what Taser is?"

Shane's feigned indignation turns to a cold sweat. The man on the other side of the door speaks with an Eastern European accent, and with a forceful authority. Has to be the big enforcer that Maggie mentioned, Bagrat Kavashi, CEO of BK Security, suspected assassin and all-round bad guy. But Gouda wouldn't have any idea who Kavashi is, nor would he be overly impressed or frightened by what he would consider to be rent-a-cops.

"Yeah, Taser, sure, so what?" Shane says, approaching the door, trying to get a clear view of who he's speaking to. "Don't tase me, bro, right? Is this a joke?"

"No joke," says Kavashi. "Back away from door, Mr. Gouda."

Meester Goo-dah. Distinct accent, but no problem making himself understood. All Shane can see is a dark mustache and a killer smile.

"Seat on bed," says the mustache. "Hends on knees."

Sit on bed, hands on knees.

"Are you freakin' kiddin' me?" Shane barks, feeling Gouda's rage. "Get me a phone so I can call my lawyer!"

"Seat on bed, be good boy, we talk."

"You the good cop, is that it? I already met your bad cops."

"I am good cop, yes. Seat on bed."

Shane sits on the bed, big hands on his bony knees. The door opens. Kavashi steps into the cell, a rakishly handsome man, and with no more ceremony that he might swat a fly, fires an X26 police-issue Taser directly into Shane's chest.

Fifty thousand volts of electromuscular disruption turn the former FBI special agent into a quivering jellyfish. Neuromuscular incapacitation occurs the instant the darts enter his flesh and continues for ten seconds, or an eternity, whichever comes first. At the academy some of the instructors referred to tasering as 'giving the perp a lift,' as in 'lifted into heaven,' because the subject typically feels as if he's dying. Lighting up every muscle and nerve in the human body tends to do that.

By the time Shane recovers from the near-death experience—way, way worse than he ever imagined—the darts have been yanked free from his chest. He's flat on his back, gasping for breath, and Kavashi is grinning down at him from a distance of maybe ten feet, too far for a lunge even if Shane felt himself capable of such, which he doesn't. He has all the strength of a kitten. Besides that, he can't think straight.

"Stay down," Kavashi suggests. "Be good boy or next time I pull three times."

Shane's brain is processing the experience through a deep layer of fuzzy cotton, but even so he knows what "pull three times" means. Pull once on the trigger and the jolt lasts ten seconds. Pull twice more, after the darts have entered the flesh, and the chaotic electromuscular disruptions last for thirty seconds, or possibly longer, until the battery completely discharges.

Forever, in other words.

"You didn't piss pants," Kavashi points out, keeping the reloaded Taser aimed at the middle part of his body. "Next time I give you personal promise, you piss pants."

Shane can't think of what Ron Gouda might say at a

time like this, so he doesn't say anything, he just stares at Kavashi with bugged-out eyes. The security chief has effectively established dominance and Shane can't fight it, not until his head clears and his strength returns.

"So, Mr. Ron Gouda from Dayton, Ohio, you are fake person. Carry fake ID like terrorist. Is that what you do, come to nice town of Conklin to be terrorist?"

"What are you taking about?" Shane manages to say. Every muscle on his upper body feels weak, whipped.

"You come to study our books, make yourself into a better person? You come to listen and learn? I don't think so. They find stupid man where he has no business to be, first thought, maybe you want to break into big house, steal things. So I run a Google search on Mr. Ron Gouda of Dayton, Ohio, and you know what I find? Interesting item with nice photograph. Mr. Ron Gouda belongs to Shriners, helps raise money for sick kids. They put his photo in the newspaper, holding big check for new hospital. What a nice man, Mr. Gouda. Short, but nice."

"It's a mistake. Another Ron Gouda."

"Two men with same name, both owning the same company?"

There's something about having his cover totally blown that makes the blood flow to Shane's brain. "Okay, you got me," he says, holding up his shaky hands. "My name is David Johnson, okay? From L.A. I borrowed Gouda's name so I could get inside, check on my wife."

"Your wife is here, too?"

"Maybe, I don't know. But I think she's having an affair with one of your members. I don't even know his name, but he's a rich guy with his own personal jet. Linda always had a thing for pilots."

The gun never wavers as Kavashi backs up a couple of feet. Still well within Taser range, but now way beyond even the wildest lunge on Shane's part. The security chief seems genuinely amused by Shane's new story.

"Man from L.A. with slut for wife, what do you do for a living? What is your job?"

"I'm a cop," Shane says. "LAPD."

When making it up on the fly, best to stick as close to the truth as possible.

Kavashi takes a seat in the bolted chair, nodding his head, as if in appreciation. "Very good story, Mr. David Johnson. Cop with cheating wife, maybe I believe you someday. But not today. Today I believe you are man who used to be FBI. Big man, six foot four, beard like you, eyes like you. Randall Shane, yes?"

"Never heard of him."

"He's big stupid man who made big stupid mistake. You come here looking for someone, make lots of noise, very clever, and my men show you where he lives."

"I told you, I'm looking for my wife."

Kavashi smiles. "Randall Shane has no wife. He has nothing. One small house, one big car. No wife, no children. They die, very sad. Randall Shane has nervous breakdown, can't sleep, quits FBI, or maybe they fire him, who knows?"

"I demand a lawyer. You have no right to hold me."

"Why are you here, Mr. Shane? You cheat to get inside. You pretend to listen to very good wisdom of Arthur Conklin. You ask about Eldon Barlow, where he lives. Why? What do you want?"

Shane thinks about it. Kavashi has managed to find, if

not a photograph, a physical description of Shane on the Net, undoubtedly from one of the missing child forums. So, given his reach and resources, he knows pretty much everything. Except, possibly, the identity of whoever snatched Haley Corbin. Although Shane has helpfully led him to the front door, so to speak, and undoubtedly put the Barlows in danger, wherever they are.

Nice move, he thinks. Could I possibly screw it up any more?

Shane figures he has, at best, one last chance to convince Kavashi to let him go. The convincer is, he'll come clean, or as clean as he dares.

"The FBI knows I'm here," Shane says.

Kavashi seems unimpressed. "So they know you cheat and lie and pretend to be someone else? Means nothing. Do you have warrant, Mr. Shane? Does FBI have warrant? Answer is no. Rulers good people, we have nothing to hide, no reason to lie. You are the one who is hiding, lying, and breaking law."

"So kick me out," Shane suggests. Figuring now that he's seen the layout he can find another way back in. Go dark this time, do a creepy-crawly, starting with the shuttered ski lodge.

"Maybe tomorrow," Kavashi says, getting to his feet.

"You can't hold me. This is a private security company, not a legal police force."

Under the mustache, Kavashi's lips curl. "We have compact with State of Colorado. Means we can hold suspect of crime until state troopers come and take away. Maybe I call troopers tomorrow morning, bring you out to checkpoint, hand you over. All legal. All correct."

Kavashi looks as though he's in a mood to maybe continue the conversation, lord it over his captive for a while, but he's interrupted by a security officer who comes in the door, whispers something to the boss.

Kavashi's expression changes. He's all business, no longer amused. "Right away," he says to the officer.

Then he steps forward, fires the reloaded Taser into Shane's prone body, and gives him the full thirty seconds of fifty-thousand volt electromuscular disruption. The forever jolt.

15. Missy Helps

Missy Barlow thinks the world is about to end, and for all I know, she's right. The monitors show a number of cruisers parked on the street below the house, and some of the cops, all of them warmly dressed, seem to have fanned out, covering every possible exit.

Clearly they know someone is hiding inside.

"It's a SWAT team," she decides. "They're going to shoot us."

Her creepy husband glares at me, as if the whole thing is my fault. He's been trying to raise Ruler Weems on his handy-dandy Iridium satellite phone, but so far no luck. Maybe that's my fault, too.

"I didn't see any rifles," I point out. "Don't SWAT guys have rifles?"

"They'll storm inside," she insists, savoring her fear. "Shoot us down like dogs."

It's sad, but she's stopped turning to her husband for comfort. His solution to all problems is to ask Ruler Weems what to do, and since Weems is unreachable, he has nothing to recommend. Though he seems to be leaning in the direction of sacrificing me for the common good. More accurately, for his own good. And the weird thing is, I'm not exactly opposed to the idea.

Not getting shot, of course. Quite the reverse. What will happen if I appear at the door, hands raised? These may be private security officers, but from what I see they look like normal people. Will they really shoot an unarmed woman? Do they even know who I am, or that my son is being confined elsewhere in this crazed community? Or have they simply been dispatched to kick down the doors and round up whoever happens to be inside?

All things considered, wouldn't it be safer to surrender before the shooting starts?

Given the way I was treated after Noah's school blew up, I have no great love for law enforcement organizations. Too rigid, too narrow-minded, and despite what they say, too unwilling to see things from the victim's point of view. But certain individual cops had been fine, had helped me get through the worst of it. Troy Hayden, the acting police chief. Tommy Petruchio, the young State Trooper. Randall Shane, not so young, perhaps, but stalwart and dogged, and the first to really believe me. Maybe there's one out there like them. Willing to listen, willing to help. What are the odds?

Not good, according to Missy.

"They're not even Rulers, okay? They're certainly not cops. They're more like mercenaries, guns for hire, and they answer to Kavashi. He signs their paychecks. They may not shoot you on sight, but they'll turn you over to the big boss, and believe me, honey, you don't want that. Eldon knew this guy who wouldn't pay his share-in? Vash broke both his knees and then framed him as a child molester.

Planted stuff on his computer, confiscated his accounts, ruined his life. Supposedly the guy committed suicide, and who knows, maybe he did. But it was Vash made him do it."

"Lovely."

"Missy, don't," Eldon says, looking up from his sat-phone.

"What, don't share? She's here with us, she should know what can happen."

"She's not a Ruler. That's privileged information."

"Eldon, they're getting ready to kill us, okay? Is *that* privileged?"

"Look at the monitors, Missy! At the moment all they're doing is standing guard. They're just regular security guards, not his special-ops people. We still have time to fix this."

"If Wendy answers his phone."

"Don't call him Wendy. That's an insult."

"Okay, Ruler Weems. Did you ever think maybe there's a reason he's not answering? Like maybe Vash already got him? It's over, Eldon, they're just prolonging the agony."

Her husband rolls his eyes, returns to his precious phone. Sweat beading on his Botox-smooth forehead, rolling down from his hairline. I'm almost positive he's had a permanent so he and Missy can have matching hairdos. Maybe not the worst thing in the world, but given the circumstances, far from reassuring.

"We'll be okay," he mutters.

Meaning, I'm convinced, that he and Missy will be okay. Whatever 'we' means to Eldon Barlow, I'm not included. He doesn't strike me as a cold-blooded killer, but if bullets come our way, he'll duck behind me, if not hold me out front. And whatever he's risked for Ruler Weems—

pretty much everything, from what I can see—he's surely regretting it now.

"Why don't they just do it?" Missy mutters, staring at the monitors. "What are they waiting for?"

"We're the bigger faction," Eldon reminds her. "It may not feel that way sometimes, but Evangeline represents a fairly small minority."

"But look who," Missy says plaintively. "All of them really important, really powerful. Plus almost all of them are Sixes. How are we supposed to fight against that?"

"We must keep our minds clear. This is a test of our resolve. We face the new day with a new mind. Never forget."

Missy says, "When this is over, I never want to see snow again."

While they bicker and whine, I try to concentrate on what to do if the worst happens. A full-fledged assault with guns. Where to hide, how I might escape. I've sort of figured out the hide part—the Barlows have a cast-iron tub in one of the guest bedrooms that looks bulletproof—but I'm having trouble picturing *escape.* Escape to where, exactly? Into the frozen night of the Rocky Mountains, in the dead of winter? Where would I run to, over the snow and ice? How would I stay alive?

Better to give myself up, if possible, and take my chances.

Thinking long range, maybe I can pretend to be a Ruler. Convince them I believe all their selfish, control-your-mind-and-you'll-control-the-world nonsense. Why not? Plead my case to be reunited with Noah. Make them think I'll help Mrs. Delancey with the tutoring, or the indoctrination, or whatever it is. Be a good little Ruler and agree with everything they say. The important thing is I'll be with my little boy.

Beyond that, I can't think or even fantasize about what might happen. How do you survive a civil war without taking sides? Because that's what this feels like, a war between the wackos. Arthur Conklin's wife and her followers, Ruler Weems and his, and me and Noah caught in the middle, pawns in a game we can't possibly understand.

"Oh my god," Missy says, her voice piping with fear. "Look, it's him. Oh my god, we're all going to die."

They both stare at the new presence on the monitor. A tall, rangy-looking guy in a hooded, fur-lined jacket. The way the security guards respond—they do everything but salute—it's obvious he's the boss.

"Kavashi," Eldon says.

Then he wrestles me to the floor—stronger than he looks, the bastard—and slips a heavy plastic fastener around my wrists, pulling it tight. And when I tell him he's scum of the earth, and I hope he really does die, the sooner the better, he slips a gag into my mouth.

Missy helps.

16. Scene Of The Crime

Shane lies on the floor of the holding cell, attempting to gather his thoughts. A full blast from a Taser doesn't make you lose consciousness, it makes you *wish* you'd lost consciousness. Aside from anything else—the fear, for instance—the experience is totally humiliating, both physically and mentally. You go from being a strong, physically fit individual to a bag of twitching Jell-O in the time it takes to squeeze a trigger. Individuals deranged by drugs or psychosis were sometimes able to overcome a Taser attack, ripping out the darts, but a normal person is rendered totally helpless. On an intellectual level you're aware that a Taser jolt is low-amperage, nonlethal, and that you're not going to die. But on a physical level it feels exactly like death, a horrible, humiliating death where you lose all control of your dying body.

The only reason he didn't wet his pants is because he'd used the toilet shortly before Kavashi arrived. Small favors. Of greater concern is the fact that he can't seem to think straight. Did Kavashi blast him two times, or was it three? No, wait, it was the three trigger pulls, prolonging the experience. Something must have malfunctioned, because it lasted, much, much longer than the thirty seconds it usually takes for the battery to discharge. Or did it? Maybe his perception of time got all messed up. Is that possible? Did it scramble his brain? But—and this comes back to him in bits and pieces—according to the instructor at the Academy, a Taser doesn't affect the brain directly, it subdues a perp by short-circuiting muscles and nerves, more or less locking the brain out of the process.

So why can't he think straight? Did something go wrong, did the Taser short-circuit his mind, as well as his muscles? Can't think, and physically he feels totally spent, as if he's just run a marathon, or endured a flood of adrenaline, or both. Shaky, shaky. What he really wants to do is escape into sleep, let his brain recharge. If a Taser can recharge, why not his brain? Does that make sense? But he can't let himself sleep because something bad is happening, only he can't seem to remember what, exactly. Something Kavashi knows. Something that can hurt Haley Corbin.

Right. Kavashi knows who Shane is, and why he's here. He knows Shane is looking for Haley Corbin and her little boy. He knows Shane has been asking about a Ruler named Eldon Barlow. And just before blasting Shane for the second time—or was it third?—he put it all together. Something in his eyes, a glint of triumph.

Stupid, stupid. You assumed Kavashi knew all about Mrs. Corbin, but he didn't, not until you helped him find her.

Sit up, you stupid man. Think of something. Do something.

Without warning, the door to the cell opens.

Before Shane can stop himself he rolls under the bed, curls into a fetal position, wanting to hide from the Taser.

"Mr. Shane?"

Out of a bleary, bloodshot eye, he sees, not his tormentor Kavashi, but a strange little man. Something wrong with the man's face, as if he's been badly sculpted in kindergarten clay. Wearing black like a priest, but without the collar.

"Randall Shane? I'm Wendall Weems. I know where Mrs. Corbin is hiding. We've got to get you out of here, Mr. Shane. You're her only hope."

Something about the man's manner and voice is strangely calming, and the tension leaves Shane. He's still afraid of getting zapped with a Taser—physically terrified—but he's able to pull himself together, drag his body shakily upright.

"Okay," he says. "I'm great."

He's far from feeling great, but Weems leads him from the holding cell, and then he's out in the cold clean air and suddenly his mind is clear and he knows what to do. More or less.

A few minutes later, as they load gear into a borrowed BK Security van—okay, stolen—Shane asks Weems how he managed to get inside the security station without being seen, let alone into the holding cells.

"I have my little secrets," Weems says, handing Shane body armor and a police-issue tactical shotgun.

They've already loaded in the smoke canisters and the flash-bang stun grenades, borrowed—okay, stolen—from the BKS armory.

"Are you going to tell me?"

"Of course," the little man says. "That's part of the plan."

"So you do have a plan?"

"Oh, yes."

"Good," says Shane. "Always helps to have a plan. Get in, fasten your seat belt."

"Where are we going?" asks the little man. Although he already seems to have a pretty good idea.

"Scene of the crime," says Shane.

"What crime?"

"The one that's about to happen. That's *my* plan."

17. Men Like Big Scary Bugs

It's weird. I'd been thinking of the cast-iron bathtub as a possible refuge and that's where Eldon decides to stow me. Bound hand and foot with plastic ties and some sort of ball-rubber gag in my mouth, like a pacifier only much bigger. He slips me into the cool dry tub without ceremony. A moment later Missy lifts my head, provides me with a pillow.

"There you go," she says, as if the pillow will make it all better. "I'm really sorry, but Eldon's right, we can't have you running away. What if we need to trade you? I mean, in a funny way you're all we've got right now, okay?"

No, it is not okay. If looks could kill, Missy Barlow would be a smoking pool of melted protoplasm by now.

Leaving me helpless in the tub, they return to their master bedroom suite to watch the monitors and, from the sound of it, to bicker and whine like a couple of overbred whippets.

I told you so! No you didn't! Shut up! No, you shut up!

F. Scott Fitzgerald—I read *The Great Gatsby* in eleventh grade and loved it; go Daisy!—had it partly right. The rich are different than you and me: if the Barlows are any example, they're really, really stupid. If that's what you get after years of improving your mind, I'm happy to remain unimproved. And relatively poor, just as a precaution.

After a couple of minutes obsessing on revenge—Missy Barlow hanging upside down with fire ants running down her skinny legs—I decide it makes more sense to concentrate all my energy on my present situation. My hands are behind my back, so there's no way to gnaw on the plastic tie. No obvious sharp surfaces to rub my wrists against.

And writhing my ankles just seems to make the bind tighten. More than anything I'd love to spit out the awful-tasting rubber gag, but it's held in place with a strap that goes around the back of my head.

Come to think of it, what were they doing with an item like that, right at hand in their bedroom? The thought of some sort of sexual kink makes me *really* want to gag. Don't go there, don't even think about it. Breathe through your nose, remain calm.

Testing the limits of movement, I'm pretty sure I could flop myself out of the tub, but decide to wait. As I'd been thinking, the heavy cast iron may afford some protection if the bullets start flying. Happy thought. It conjures up a scene from an old classic movie Jed rented from Netflix, *Bonnie and Clyde.* The only actor I recognized was Gene Hackman, and he looked absurdly young. Like just about everyone else in the movie, he gets shot, but the worst is the end when the two knuckleheads, Bonnie and Clyde, get totally riddled with machine-gun fire. Just so you get the message, it's in slow motion. By the time its over they look as though they're made of bloody Swiss cheese, which is not a picture you want sticking in your mind when you're holed up in a shuttered house and the cops are outside loading shotguns and putting on vests and helmets.

So I'm in the tub thinking about stupid Bonnie and her stupid Clyde when Missy starts shrieking. "Oh my god, Eldon! Here they come!"

First, the power goes out and we're plunged into

darkness. Missy's pathetic whimpering makes me almost feel sorry for her. Almost.

Next thing, the sounds of shrieking metal—the shutters being pried off—and then breaking glass, and men shouting, and the sting of something in the air, maybe tear gas. I can hear the Barlows coughing and wailing.

Then a window smashes in the guest bathroom, right over the tub. Something hits my legs, nearly stopping my heart. I can't see, but it hisses madly—a canister of noxious gas—and suddenly my eyes are tearing and I'm choking around the gag.

Coughing, coughing. Can't breathe.

I manage to roll out of the tub and lay gasping, facedown on the cool tile floor. Whatever the gas or smoke is, it scalds my sinuses, induces fits of convulsive coughing. I'm desperate to get the damn gag out of my mouth—can't breathe! can't breathe!—but nothing works, and then I'm out of control, convulsing, as if my body is trying to vomit out the intrusive rubber gag in my mouth.

White pinpoints of light in my eyes—am I passing out from lack of oxygen?—and the lights become powerful flashlights. Muffled shouting, "Got her! Got her!" I can see just enough to recognize dark uniforms, men looking like big, scary bugs with their glistening gas masks, and then they're carrying me out of the bath, into the smoke-filled bedroom, and down the grand staircase.

The air improves as we descend, although my eyes still sting, my throat and nose continue to burn. I kick and writhe—take the gag out of my mouth, you bastards!—but they've got me and I can't get away.

The power comes back on and through my tears I see the Barlows facedown on the foyer floor, bound hand and foot with plastic ties, just as they had bound me. They're crying and begging for mercy—We didn't know! We didn't know!—and then the handsome, hawk-nosed man with the mustache looms in, checking me out, and for the first time I'm truly terrified, rather than merely frightened.

Something in his eyes. Cold, calculating, dismissive.

He jerks his chin. "Outside. Put in van."

As if I'm a piece of noxious garbage to be dispensed with.

The men who carry me have slipped off their gas masks and somehow it's shocking to see how young they look, how perfectly ordinary. There's no particular animosity in their eyes—indeed, they avoid making eye contact with me, ignoring my muffled pleas to remove the awful, choking gag—but no connection, either. I'm a task to be accomplished, a bundle delivered, but I'm not making it easy for them.

We're at the front door when the sun explodes.

Night, I'm thinking. Can't be any sun.

A concussive blast follows the hot, white flash, compressing my lungs, squeezing out the air. People are screaming, shouting. I'm completely blind, the flash still burning deep behind my eyes. Has the house exploded? Am I dying? Already dead?

More than anything I want to scream, but can't.

I'm on my back in the doorway, completely blind,

writhing for air. Then strong arms lift me up, cradling me like an infant, and fingers gently pry the gag from my mouth, holding me as I suck in the cold air of night—we're outside now, how did that happen—and I hear his deep and gentle voice saying, "I gotcha, Mrs. Corbin."

Then he flips me up onto his big shoulders and runs away from the shouting, into the night.

Shane.

He doesn't run far, less than a hundred yards, I'm guessing, but by the time he puts me down I can see again, although dimly. We're on frozen, windswept ground, next to a metal shed or structure. The Barlow place is some distance down the mountain from where we're crouched. It looks to be almost completely consumed by black smoke. Uniformed men run in and out of the smoke looking panicked, though somehow furtive.

"A flash-bang grenade, a few smoke bombs," Shane explains as he clips away the plastic ties, freeing my arms and legs.

Behind me the shed door opens and a familiar voice says, "Quickly! We don't have much time!"

Ruler Weems, urging us inside.

Shane helps me stand—my feet are still numb from the binding—and hobble into the deeper darkness of the little shed. Barely room enough for the three of us to stand, and so dark I can't see my hands in front of my face.

Weems clicks on a powerful flashlight, aims it at the concrete floor. "Keep your hands at your sides. This is a transformer station. Touch the wrong thing and you'll die instantly."

Following his instructions we press our backs to the metal wall, inching along until he tells us to stop. Personally I wouldn't trust the little man to guide me across the street. I'm following Shane, who came and got me, just as he promised.

Weems crouches, fiddles with something on the floor. It makes a faint hydraulic sound, the sigh of pressure released, and then a portion of the concrete floor lifts, bathing our legs in a greenish light.

Beneath, steel rungs go down into an illuminated shaft.

"We must hurry," Weems says.

"You think Kavashi knows about the tunnel?" Shane wants to know.

"He'll figure it out eventually," Weems says. "Right now I'm worried about the boy. What they'll do to him when they realize we've escaped. Let's go! Ladies first."

I drop into the tunnel. Praying it will lead me to Noah.

Part V
The Pinnacle

1. Something About The Boy

As it turns out, torture isn't necessary. Or not much of it. The Barlows have seen the error of their ways and are eager to cooperate. If Vash understands them correctly, and the whimpering makes it difficult, their defense is that Ruler Weems made them do it. They're clueless about Randall Shane, or how he happened to escape from a locked holding cell, and have no idea where he might have taken Haley Corbin. All the Barlows know for sure is that whatever happened, it isn't their fault, and to make up for it they'd like to become part of Eva's faction, please. Pretty please with millions on top.

"Not my decision," Vash had informed them. "Maybe Evangeline forgive you, maybe not."

That had provoked much weeping and whining. Vash has a low tolerance for whiners—there's something about a pleading voice that sets his teeth on edge. Had it been entirely up to him, the Barlows would have perished in their own home, victims of an unfortunate fire. Not as punishment, but because he finds them to be as irritating as they are untrustworthy. As it is, their fate remains undetermined—Eva has too much on her mind, and seems eager to blame Vash for not having the godlike powers to know everything and be everywhere at once.

"Let me see if I've got this right," she says with her acid tongue. "You had him and you let him get away? This so-called nobody, this supposedly harmless man who used to be with the FBI? And then the harmless nobody steals one of your tactical vans, waits until your men retrieve the woman from the house, then steals her away and they both vanish in a puff of smoke. Is that about right?"

"Somebody help him, obviously."

"Obviously."

When Evangeline gets like this, frustrated because things haven't gone her way, she looks as if the only thing that would make her feel better is the opportunity to kill someone with her own hands. Vash would be sympathetic—when he was slightly younger he often indulged in such excessive reactions—except that in this instance he's the someone Eva would like to kill. Something to keep in mind, when it comes to long-term survival strategies.

"Any idea who helped him?" she asks sweetly.

"We review the video. Takes two hours, maybe three. Many cameras, much data."

Eva the Diva gets up close and personal, bumping her hips into his pelvis, and not in a friendly way. More like the sexual aggression of a praying mantis, eager to be off with his head. "You don't need to find it on the cameras, darling. We both know who it was."

Vash shrugs. "Could be Weems, yes. Is possible. Or maybe he bribes one of my men."

"Trust me, Wendy did it. And you know how I know? *Because I was watching.* You can't be bothered, apparently, so I've been keeping an eye on Mr. Ugly. And guess what, he wasn't at home. Again. So I guess he must have borrowed that invisibility cloak from Harry Potter, huh? The one that lets him come and go without being seen?"

"Who is this Harry Potter?"

"Don't be dense, darling." She hooks her fingers in his belt, tugs him even closer. "The point is, we can't control Wendy if we don't know where he is. Silly me, I thought I stressed that. I thought I made it clear. But apparently you don't think it's important to keep my most dangerous rival under surveillance. My blood enemy. The wretched little man who would happily dance on my grave, given the chance. No, you let him come and go as he pleases."

"I have men looking at blueprints. He must have hidden exit from Bunker."

"How is it possible that you wouldn't know about it?"

"No one can know what they don't know. This is point. Okay? Maybe he makes modification in Bunker before I take over security. Some way to get out of Bunker without being seen. Yes, that's what I believe. He comes, he goes, we can't see."

Vash is fairly certain he knows where Weems's secret exit terminates—inside a bathroom, out of camera range—but decides not to share until he's certain, and has a plan to deal with it. Eva's inclination is to go in with guns blazing, but Vash is keenly aware that the Bunker is well fortified and that Ruler Weems will have a plan of defense. Plus, with a former FBI Special Agent on the loose, now is the time for caution.

"This nobody who got away," Eva says. "Tell me how you're going to catch him."

"Road has been closed, campus being searched. Also private residence. He can't get away. Only way out is to hike through mountains. Thirty miles, winter conditions. Impossible. So maybe they freeze to death."

"So you think they're trying to get away?"

"Yeah, of course," he responds, surprised by the question. "They know they can't get to boy."

"And what happens if they make it?" she says teasingly, her fingers at work beneath his belt.

"Bad things. Not good. The mother give testimony, Feds get search warrant from judge, come here looking for child."

"That's what you think?"

"What else?"

Eva smiles with her teeth. "I looked this man up, this nobody you said not to worry about? I read the blogs, darling, testimony from grateful parents, and I came to my own conclusion. I don't think he's trying to get away. He's going to try and rescue the boy. That's what he does."

Vash disengages her questing hand, steps away. "Good," he says, clearing his throat. "If he does that, we catch him for sure. Nobody gets into Pinnacle."

"Like Wendy can't get out of the Bunker without us seeing him?"

Vash has no reply.

"Let's do something about the boy," Eva muses.

2. Bulldog, He Mutters

For a while after Jed died, I kept having this dream about a long dark corridor. I was in a hospital or mortuary and somewhere at the end of the corridor was a room where I would be asked to identify the body of my dead husband. I wanted to get there, wanted to see Jed one last time, but the corridor seemed to go on forever and I could never get to the room before the dream ended. It wasn't a nightmare, exactly. There was no fear, just a great longing. Then the walls would begin to close in and I would wake up in a cold sweat, missing Jed so bad that my whole body ached.

The dream comes back to me as we hurry along the tunnel in single file, Weems leading the way, with me in the middle and Shane following in a crouch. The tunnel, Weems explains, is made of fiberglass pipe, six feet in circumference—plenty tall for me and the strange little man, but not nearly big enough for Shane to stand upright. He can touch both sides of the tunnel with the palms of his hands and does so, to help keep upright as he scoots along, hunched over. The escape tunnels were installed when Arthur Conklin was worried about criminals who might be drawn to the Ruler's wealth. Apparently there was a time when the cult leader feared he might be kidnapped and held for a billion-dollar ransom. The tunnels were a way out, as well as a place of refuge. They appear on no blueprints, their existence known only to Arthur and his trusted associate, Wendall Weems. The cult leader, recently remarried, did not even inform his new wife of the secret escape tunnel, lest she be part of some plot against him.

"That was during his paranoid phase," Weems explains. "He got over it, of course. The thing about Arthur, he was always learning, exceeding the limitations of the ordinary mind."

I'm still feeling a bit stunned, not so much by the flash of the stun grenade itself as by the rapid turn of events. Only a few days ago I'd been snatched from the airport, caged like a dog, flown across the country, confined to a shuttered house, tormented with video images of my son being brainwashed, and told there was nothing I could do about it. True, I'd been clinging to the notion that Shane would find me, but it was the kind of hope that keeps people buying lottery tickets. What were the odds?

In his laconic way he makes it sound like no big deal. "You were the one who told me about the Rulers," he points out. "So I came to where the Rulers live and started poking around. Just basic investigation."

My joy at being freed lasts about as long as it takes for a deep breath. There's no room for joy in my heart until I have Noah in my arms. And if Weems is right, freeing me has put my son in immediate danger.

"We've started the clock ticking," he says, his melodious voice booming in the tunnel. "Kavashi knows about Mr. Shane's connection to the FBI. He'll be expecting a raid, and taking precautions. That means destroying evidence, and, Mrs. Corbin, your son is evidence."

All the more reason to hurry. Shane, crouching and in constant danger of bumping his head on the tunnel lights, is having trouble keeping up, despite his long legs.

"I feel like a bug in a straw," he complains. "How much farther?"

"We'll take a short break to catch our breath," Weems announces, halting. "To answer your question, there are more than three miles of tunnels. One branch goes to my bunker, the other to the Pinnacle."

"Your bunker?" I ask. "What, like Hitler's bunker?"

"Most assuredly not," he says huffily, turning to look me in the eye. "And what would a woman your tender age know of Hitler and his bunker?"

"The History Channel."

"Of course." He nods to himself. "What we have long called our bunker, for lack of a better term, was originally constructed in Arthur's paranoid period, like these very tunnels. Built mostly underground, as an impregnable fortress—although nothing is, of course, truly impregnable. Later he moved to the Pinnacle, which is higher up the mountain. The Pinnacle is quite spectacular, really. A great cathedral of glass and steel and stone, and unlike the Bunker it looks outward. Arthur liked to say it greets the world. He thought of it as a great ship sailing upon a sea of clouds. Of course this being Colorado, most of the time there aren't actually very many clouds, but you get the idea."

Shane, resting his long body against the curve of the pipe, says, "You're sure the boy is in the Pinnacle?"

"I'm sure."

"You have spies there? Someone from the Evangeline faction who reports to you?"

"I have my sources."

"We need to call in the cavalry," Shane says emphatically.

"The cavalry. How very romantic. By all means, alert your colleagues."

"You have no objection?" Shane asks, sounding surprised.

"No. The time has come. As I say, the clock is ticking, and Eva herself is the time bomb. No one knows when she might go off, what she might do, but I have no doubt she's capable of unleashing great violence, if she thinks that is what it will take to secure her position."

"And you'd like her out of the way," Shane points out.

"Absolutely. She's been a disaster. We are a small organization. There are less than ten thousand full-fledged, dues-paying members. We can't afford to be divided, fighting amongst ourselves."

Shane nods, studying Weems, whose face always seems to be averted, conveniently shadowed. Partly it's his simian, jutting brow and his deep-set eyes, but I can't help thinking that the strange little man reacts to light like a creature who doesn't want to be seen.

Shane says, "So Evangeline gets arrested and you become the big cheese, the ultimate Ruler."

"What I will do," Weems responds, with great dignity, "is see that things continue as Arthur would have wanted. Strengthening the organization. Building connections into the mainstream. Continuing to interpret Arthur's writing and teach Arthur's lessons. Spreading the word."

Shane says, "And you'll do the interpreting. You'll decide what words get spread."

"Who better than me?"

Shane stands up, as best he can. "We'll need a phone, an Internet connection, or a radio. Some way to make contact with the outside world."

"Kavashi will have cut off landline and broadband by now," Weems says. "There's a satellite phone in the Bunker. You can use that."

Shane takes a deep breath, touches my shoulder. "You hanging in there?"

"Yup."

What else can I say? My fate, and my son's fate, is in Shane's hands now. His and the FBI, if we can make contact.

"I thought you were delusional," Shane confesses. "That first day. Bonkers with grief."

"Why did you stay?"

He shrugs his big shoulders. "Something about you, I guess. You looked so ferocious."

"Me?"

"Like a little bulldog. I knew you'd never let go, never give up."

"Bulldog, huh? Is that meant to be a compliment?"

His eyes slide away from mine. "Just an observation. I certainly didn't mean you look like a bulldog."

Weary and frightened for my son as I am, I can't help but grin. "Whatever," I tell him. "That was a lucky day. The best in a while."

Weems clears his throat. "We need to keep moving, folks. It's only a matter of time before Vash figures out the tunnels."

We trudge along for what seems like a great distance, the tunnel inclining steadily upward, then abruptly switching to double back in the opposite direction. Weems suggests we think of it as an underground switchback road, which doesn't mean much to me. Every yard is bringing me closer to Noah. That's what I cling to.

At one point we come to a vertical shaft. It contains an open elevator car that has the size and heft of an oversize toy, but Weems insists that it has been rated for a thousand pounds, considerably more than our combined weight. It is, he assures us, perfectly safe.

"How old are these tunnels?" I ask.

He shrugs. "Twenty years or so. Something like that."

"So the last time this perfectly safe elevator was inspected was twenty years ago?"

"It's the only way up," he says. "I'm afraid there's no alternative. If you like, we'll send you up in the car alone. Mr. Shane and I will follow."

"No way!"

There's barely room for the three of us in the car, which sways a little as it slowly ascends, bumping the shaft walls. Shane notices my complexion going green and says, "So you're not fond of elevators."

"Not little swingy ones, no."

He takes my hand. "Try closing your eyes."

That makes it worse. My hand is sweaty, his hand is cool and strong.

"We're going to be fine," he says, his voice calm and reassuring. "We'll make a call to my friend Maggie and she'll make sure that help is on the way. You'll be safe in Mr. Weems's Bunker, won't she, Mr. Weems?"

"Most certainly," Weems says. "I've taken every precaution. Vash can't touch us."

"And where will you be, while I'm being all safe and cozy?"

"I'll be having a look around the Pinnacle."

"Searching for Noah."

"That's right."

"I'm coming with you."

He shakes his head, dismissing the idea. "I'll bring him to you. That's a promise."

"He doesn't know you. He'll be scared."

"We'll discuss this after we make the call," Shane says, sounding stubborn.

"There's nothing to discuss."

He grunts. We come to the top and the little elevator bumps to a stop, rises an inch, and settles at the correct level. Back in the relative stability of the tunnel, my knees stop trembling and the relief makes me almost giddy.

"Wait here," says Weems. "I have to disable Vash's cameras."

He climbs up a set of rungs protruding from another, much smaller vertical shaft—remarkably agile for a man of his age—and a moment later he's gone, having sealed the hatch at the top of the shaft.

"I'll be moving fast," Shane says, continuing the conversation while we wait for our strange little guide to return. "There's no telling what I'll run into."

"La-la-la-la-la."

"What?"

"Means I'm not listening."

"Bulldog," he mutters.

Above us the hatch opens, and Weems calls down for us to come on up.

3. Slam, Bam, No Thank You, Ma'am

To be truthful, I don't really recall much of that History Channel show about Hitler's bunker. Jed was the one with an interest in World War II, not me. But I do remember the Spartan interior and, of course, the total lack of windows. My sense is that Hitler and his cronies were living in a concrete hole in the ground, with air supplied by a ventilation tower that looked like a witch's hat. In the end it was cyanide and pistols, and the bombproof bunker became a gruesome tomb, with death coming not from above, but from the people themselves.

Weems's bunker isn't quite that desperate, but he does have the Spartan part down. Actually it's more like a monastery without windows. Small, sparsely furnished rooms that could be cells. Bare concrete floors with a few thin rugs here and there. The only thing decorating the thick, concrete walls are framed photographs of his hero and mentor, Arthur Conklin. Seeing the famous author in a series of candid pictures—speaking at a podium, working on a manuscript, blowing out the candles on a birthday cake—is for me a very unsettling experience. This is Jed's father. His dad. The physical resemblance is slight, but it's there. And it says something that all of the pictures are cropped to leave out whoever else might have been present. As if Arthur Conklin lived in a universe occupied only by himself.

While I look at the photographs—they're deeply creepy if you know what was left out, namely his wife and son—Shane and Weems discuss the surveillance problem.

"Vash had a crew install new smoke detectors about six months ago, when Eva first made her move. I knew at once they were hidden cameras and began to behave accordingly. Fortunately they neglected to put a camera in the bathroom, so they never spotted the tunnel entrance. I use it sparingly, of course. For the most part it didn't matter if they monitored my movements—I'm a creature of habit, very predictable. And up until a week or so ago I came and went freely and still had regular access to the Pinnacle."

"What's regular access?" Shane wants to know.

"The Pinnacle is built into the steepest part of the mountain about a quarter mile from here," Weems explains, sounding almost professorial. "An aerial tram covers the last five hundred feet of vertical distance. It's reliable and efficient, based on a design they used in Portland, Oregon. An identical tram connects the Bunker to the same lower terminus—the original tram, from before the Pinnacle was built. Both cars can carry up to twelve tons of freight and passengers."

"So you can leave anytime you like."

Weems gives a wry smile. "Alas, no. Both trams are controlled from the Pinnacle. My tram only works if they say it does, and at the moment they prefer to keep me in the Bunker, ostensibly under their control."

"Okay, the trams are regular access. What else?"

"There's a helo pad on the upper level of the Pinnacle. Rarely used because of the wind shear, which makes landing difficult even on a calm day. I assume Vash has it booby-trapped, because that's the obvious landing place for an assault by helicopter. The access door to the helo pad is blastproof, even if you did manage to land a copter."

"You mentioned a satellite phone," says Shane, who seems eager to get on with it.

"Yes, of course. But first let me show you the layout of the Pinnacle itself. You may find it useful."

Weems rolls open a blueprint and the two men lean over it, tracing the outline of the complex. I have to butt in to get a look—why is it that men always suppose a woman can't read an architectural drawing? Okay, I'm not good with schematics, but with the help of the Home Depot clinics, and many hours studying HGTV, I've developed an excellent sense of space and scale. And I must say the Pinnacle looks really cool, designwise. The exterior drawing reveals a soaring structure with a subtly curved concrete roof extending well beyond the supporting walls, like the brim of a stylish hat. Protection from snow, I assume. Large glass walls slant inward at about twenty degrees. The whole place has the look of a modern airport terminal in some trendy city like Paris, or that famous opera house in Sydney.

The look of it aside, Weems points out that the design was about more than being stylish. "Arthur always had security in mind, even in his more open periods. The way the roof juts out and the walls slant back? He insisted on that because it makes an assault from the air extremely difficult—it's rappelproof for one thing. Plus there are blast shutters that can be deployed instantly. As I mentioned, the tram is controlled from the top, and if that fails, the cable can be manually detached at the upper terminus, cutting off all access. The only other way in is through the tunnel shaft, indicated here," he says, tapping the drawing with a thickened fingernail. "But as I say, we can expect Vash and his men to figure that out sooner rather than later. My concern is that when she becomes aware that an attack is under way, Eva will drop the blast shutters, detach the tram cable, and seal the building. You'll have a siege situation."

"That would be the nightmare scenario," Shane agrees. "We can't let that happen."

"Seen enough?"

"I think, so, yeah."

Weems rolls the prints up and produces an Iridium phone that could be a clone of the one that belongs to the Barlows.

Part of a matched set, apparently—not that it did the Barlows much good. "You'll have to stand close to an exterior wall," he suggests, handing the sleek little phone to Shane.

Shane, looking just a teensy bit nervous, punches in the number. He strains to listen and then his face lights up. "Maggie! I'm inside. Yes. I've secured Mrs. Corbin, who was being detained against her will. She has seen video images of her son, who is being held in the other building. The Pinnacle. Just like you said. Weems?" Shane glances over, makes eye contact with the strange little man. "Mr. Weems is cooperating. Matter of fact, he's the one who broke me out of jail and gave me the means to contact you. No, I'm not kidding, I'll tell you all about it later. Hold on, I've got an idea."

Shane has Weems unroll the blueprints, snaps pictures of the Pinnacle design, then takes a photo of me standing next to Weems, who does everything but tuck his head into his torso like a turtle, and sends all of the images to the FBI over the satellite phone.

Looking very pleased with himself, Shane says, "Okay, that should be more than enough for a warrant. Maggie? See if the HRT will respond to the obvious challenge. If not, go for the local, but get 'em here quick, whatever you do. Time is of the essence. We think they may be making a move against the boy. Gotta go!"

He snaps the phone shut.

"What's the HRT?" I ask.

"Hostage Rescue Team. They're the best. But if they're not available, the field office tactical team in Denver can do the job."

"So it's happening? For real?"

"Help is on the way."

Now that it's actually happening, now that the rest of the world is ready to believe me, working to rescue my son, I'm not sure how to react. Part of me is wild with anticipation, part of me sick with fear. What if we're too late? What if they hurt Noah? What if any one of a million things goes wrong and somehow it's my fault?

Shane doesn't seem to notice, as if he's already concentrating on the task at hand.

"Mind if I keep this?" he asks Weems, dropping the phone into a pocket before our host has a chance to reply.

Obviously the big guy is about to make his move. I'm ready for an argument about why I should stay behind. Too dangerous, I'll get in the way, and so on. Let him try—I'm not taking no for an answer. I can't be this close to my son and not take the extra step.

What I don't expect is that without so much as a quick goodbye, Randall Shane will take three quick strides to the bathroom door and lock himself inside.

Slam, bam, no thank you, ma'am.

By the time I persuade Weems to unlock the door—okay, I threaten his miserable life—Shane has already slipped down into the shaft and sealed the clever little hatch behind him.

4. Freaking Never

Evangeline has a new plan. This will be a short-term plan, as opposed to her long-term plan. Long-term, she becomes the voice of the Rulers, in complete control of the organization. That's a given, despite the nagging impediments that stand in her way. Short-term, she finds a way to turn the current crisis to her advantage. She must take control, bend others to her will—that, after all, is the most basic rule of one. Manage this crisis successfully, it will also help achieve her long-term goal.

Planning and execution. Which, in this case, are inextricably linked.

"Vash?"

Lover boy is busy at his desk, scrolling through the video archives, looking for evidence of how Wendall Weems is managing to move around the community undetected. He looks up from the screens, his handsome face bathed in the light from below. "Yes?"

"Irene has her instructions. She'll take care of the boy."

He shrugs, absently stroking the wings of his mustache with his left thumb. "Good."

"Any sign of Mr. Nobody and the miracle mom?"

"Not yet. They'll show."

"No doubt," she says with a tiny, cutting smile. "Probably when we least expect it."

"Could happen, yes."

He waits, knowing there's more.

"I've been thinking, Vash."

"Ah," he says, his expression unreadable.

Evangeline plants her hip on the edge of his desk. She's excited by her new idea. Even in the middle of a long winter night it makes her feel wide-awake, zoomed with the perfection of her plan.

"When Arthur passes, we enter a new age," she begins. "Everything will change, and yet we must have continuity. The organization cannot be allowed to splinter. We must continue to speak with one voice. Even more important, we must shape the truth."

"Shape truth?"

Evangeline sees that she finally has his attention. Bagrat Kavashi is familiar with the notion of a malleable truth.

"Let's assume that we can expect a visit from the Feds, sometime very soon. Within the next day or so. Do we agree that's likely, whether or not this man Shane pays us a visit here personally?"

"Very likely. Hundred percent."

"Okay, given that we'll be taking a hit, exposing ourselves to the outside world, the questions is, what do they find?"

"Not boy," he says firmly.

"Not alive, no. He's a smart little thing, who knows what he might tell them? But what if the Feds find something that leads them to the boy, and away from us? What if they find Wendy and his followers?"

Kavashi perks up, interested. "Blame the boy on Weems?" He nods, liking the idea. "The mother, too."

"Why not? I've been thinking that Wendall might be a morbid individual, drawn to death. It happens in some organizations. Remember the folks from Heaven's Gate. No? They believed they would rendezvous with an alien spacecraft after death, and be taken to a better place. An express ride to heaven, more or less. Mostly less, as it turned out. But their example might be useful."

"Explain."

"What if Wendy and the gang do a Hale-Bopp? Remember that comet that signaled the end for Heaven's Gate? When the comet passed by they all took poison or something."

Kavashi looks up. "Yes. Very useful example."

"Yes. And we'll make sure there are documents on Wendy's computer, explaining everything he did because of some signal to go to the next world."

"Ah," says Vash. "But what is Weems's signal?"

Evangeline sits on his big strong knee, very pleased with herself. "Arthur dying," she says brightly. "That's their signal."

The boy sleeps with a night-light. The light is a gift from his teacher, Mrs. Irene Delancey, and despite the fact that he no longer trusts her, he still loves the night-light, even though it's probably meant for little kids, not ten-year-olds. It's called a Twilight Turtle and it projects constellations on the walls and ceiling. Eight different constellations, to be exact, plus a whole bunch of other stars. The turtle-shaped night-light glows comfortably on the bureau in his new bedroom, a room with no windows and only one exit, which is always locked.

They call it a bedroom but Noah understands that he is, in fact, their prisoner. And when he wakes up in the middle of the night, that's the first thing he thinks about: how to escape. He's heard stories of other kids who got snatched and then made friends with the ones who snatched them. As if they never really tried to get away? That's not for Noah. No matter what they tell him about being the One True Voice, and all the neat stuff he'll learn by listening to recordings of his grandfather droning on and on, and how special he'll be when he grows up, with thousands of people hanging on his every word, Noah has no intention of staying.

No way will he ever forget about his mom, a suggestion actually put forward by Mrs. Delancey recently, who said that after a while his memories of his mother will fade away and he won't miss her because his life will be so full of learning about the Rule of One that he won't have room for anything else.

No freaking way! His mom doesn't let him use the word *freaking,* because she says it's a substitute for an even worse word, but in this situation Noah thinks it would be allowed. If he listens inside his head he can even imagine Mom with her hands on her hips, going *No freaking way, Noah, don't listen to them, don't ever forget me, don't ever forget who you really are.*

Freaking never. He's never ever going to forget. Not in a million years. Not if Mrs. Delancey makes him listen to the stupid headphones until he's a hundred years old. And when he wakes up with his eyes wet from crying in his dream, he knows exactly who to blame. Mrs. Freaking Delancey, that's who.

Mrs. Delancey who pretended to be his friend, who pretended to care, who pretended to help him with math and taught him about prime numbers, and who let Noah believe she was the second-most-beautiful-and-special person in the whole wide world. All pretend. All a lie. All so he'd trust her enough to go under the bleachers and hide in the ventilation duct. Which is where they grabbed him, just the way she planned, and put the stinky cloth over his face and made him go to sleep.

Everything she says is a lie, including the part about Mom being killed in the explosion. At first he thought it was true and then right away he overheard people saying stuff, lowering their voices if they noticed him listening, but he has really good ears, not to mention a really good brain that can figure out if they're still talking about his mother, as if they're worried about what she might do, then Mom must still be alive.

Noah clings to the idea of Mommy alive. Mommy alive gets him through the day, and helps him at night when he's so alone that it hurts inside, as though his whole body is being squeezed by a giant fist.

His mind races with thoughts about what really happened to his mom, the need to escape, to find the truth, the soothing voices in his headphones, until he's so exhausted he can't think anymore.

He's almost back asleep when something wakes him. Footsteps, ever so quiet, approaching his bed. Despite being afraid, he forces himself to open his eyes, and sees Mrs. Delancey, bathed in the stars from his night-light.

"Come with me," she whispers urgently. "We have to hide."

5. He Who Leads

The thing about being scared is, after a while you get used to it. Numb to it. It's as if there's a faint, high-pitched scream in your head, and it never stops, but you learn to ignore it, like sirens in the city. Ruler Weems—why do I keep wanting to call him Reverend?—thinks I'm making a big mistake. *Stay with me,* he urges, *keep safe for your child,* and a big part of me wants to do just that. But I keep thinking Noah will be scared when some big guy he's never met tries to snatch him from his bed. Which gets me worrying about where he's been sleeping, and does he have a nice bedroom, and does he know I'm alive or have they been filling his head with lies? Because if he knows his mother is alive he'll be wondering why she hasn't come to get him, and if he thinks I'm dead then in his head he's an orphan, alone in the world. Unless he thinks of Mrs. Delancey as his new mom. Which come to think of it must be what the Rulers had in mind, taking him away from everything he knows. Isolate the child, make him feel so alone and terrified that he'll bond with the one familiar person in his new world, the teacher who he trusted and admired. Who, to be frank, he had a crush on.

Makes me want to scratch her eyes out. Bitch.

"This is a mistake," Weems says, his big eyes imploring me from deep in his homely face. "Mr. Shane is a trained professional and he strikes me as very competent. But you—" He hesitates, clears his throat.

"But I'm what, a girl? A housewife? I plead guilty. I'm not a cop, I'm not an investigator, and I've no idea what I'm going to do. But I've got one thing nobody else has, not even Shane."

Weems raises his misshapen eyebrows.

"I'm his mother," I say. "Now show me how to open the hatch or I swear I'll bite your ankle."

The hatch is built into the tile floor of the shower stall, and at the push of a concealed button—a worn bit of tile, actually—the floor of the stall lifts open, powered by a hydraulic hinge. I can't help thinking that Noah would think it was very cool, having an entrance to a secret tunnel in your shower stall. Boys love that kind of stuff. Apparently grown men do, too.

"But you don't have a weapon," Weems protests.

"Wouldn't know how to use it if I had one. If you see

the FBI before I do? Tell them to be extra careful. Shane makes a big target and he'll have Noah with him."

"You're so confident," Weems says, marveling.

"What choice do I have?"

And then I'm slipping down the rungs and the last thing I see before the hatch shuts is Weems's little feet, clad in black Nikes.

He's no bigger than a boy.

The tunnel is even spookier on my own. Plus there are strange, scuttling noises transmitting through the fiberglass. After a moment I realize it must be Shane, scooting along and using his hands for balance, and sure enough when I call his name he curses, distant but distinct.

Nice. I'm here to help and he greets me with a four-letter word.

It's fairly easy for me to catch up. I can run, he can't.

"Bad idea," he says, hands on his knees, panting. "Go back while you've got the chance."

His forehead is bleeding a little, from where he must have bumped into a light fixture. Being extra tall obviously has its disadvantages.

"You've made your position clear," I say, forcing myself to be calm. "Now what's the plan?"

"Haven't got one," he admits. "Get inside and see what happens."

"That's it?"

He shrugs. "This kind of situation, all you can do is react. Plans never work."

"You don't want to have to worry about keeping me safe, is that it?"

"Exactly."

"Then don't. Here's the deal. I'll go first, and if they catch me I'll make a fuss. A really big fuss. While they're busy with me, you find Noah."

"Damn," he says, looking rueful.

"What?"

"That might actually work."

We move along the tunnel until we're under another vertical shaft, the connection to the Pinnacle, according to Wendall Weems. He claims to have never used it because they'd then know he somehow could evade security, and because for the last six months the Pinnacle has been Evangeline's domain. The few times he's been inside to visit Arthur Conklin's sickbed he's been accompanied by her guards, his every movement noted.

Shane looks up, peering into the shaft. His voice is a husky whisper. "You sure you want to do this?"

I place my foot on the first rung. "Shane?"

"Yes?"

"Don't stare at my butt."

He grins. "He who leads gets butt stared at. That's the deal, so live with it."

Taking a deep breath, I head up the rungs, into the darkness at the top of the shaft.

At the top, I hook one arm through a rung, reach around with the other, find the hatch release handle.

"Ready?" I whisper down to Shane, poised a few rungs below my feet. Can't see him, but I'm keenly aware of his large presence, ready to catch me if I fall.

"Ready."

"Here goes nothing."

I turn the release handle and the hatch pops up, followed by a clatter of metal. Very loud. Loud enough to chill my blood. So loud they'll know we're here.

"Quickly!" Shane urges.

Taking a deep breath I scramble up through the hatch and roll out of the way, colliding with a bucket and some awful, stringy thing that feels cool and moist and somehow dead.

A damp mop. We're in a custodial closet, redolent of ammonia and pine-scented detergent. And it's as dark as the shaft below. Surely the commotion with the bucket must have alerted them to our presence. Any second a door will open, and lights will pin us to the floor like bugs.

Shane and I lay side by side, barely breathing. Waiting.

Silence. Other than my heart slamming.

After a minute or so Shane gets up on his knees, fumbles in a pocket, and produces a small halogen flashlight. "Never leave home without it," he whispers, panning the beam around the closet. The place is a bit larger than I first thought, jammed with cleaning equipment. Considering the amount of stuff lying around, it's a miracle the hatch only disturbed one bucket. Which, obviously, sounded a lot louder to us than to whoever else might be listening.

Encouraged by his confident behavior, I get to my feet, being careful not to bump anything else. Which necessitates me more or less clinging to Randall Shane. With a pang I realize that the last time I was this close to a man it was Jedediah, and we were hugging goodbye as he left for what would be his last trip.

Don't think about it. Don't feel it. Not now. Now is for Noah. No room for anything but your son. Finding him, saving him, holding him, telling him it will be okay, because if he's alive and safe then it really will be okay, no matter what else might happen.

Nothing matters but Noah. Not even me.

"It's four o'clock in the morning," Shane whispers. "Hour of the wolf. They must all be asleep."

He sounds very pleased, eager to get on with it. I borrow his little flashlight, flash it around until I find what I'm looking for, what I know must be there.

"Not hour of the wolf," I whisper back. "Hour of the vacuum cleaner."

6. The Purity Of Fear

Go with what you know. My father used to say that, usually when he was about to do something foolish, but I guess when the pressure is on, you tend to fall back on the familiar. I may not know anything about guns—Shane has one, as it turns out—or tactical assaults, or undercover operations, but I do know from housework. Miele, Hoover, Shop-Vac, whatever the brand, I'm your girl. Take charge of renovating an old farmhouse and you do a lot of cleaning up. For sawdust you want the Shop-Vac, for the fine dust that comes from sanding drywall compound, the Miele can't be beat, provided you remember to change the filter when you change the bag.

Not that I expect to do much cleaning. But with a rag on my head, holding back my hair, and a sturdy work apron with voluminous pockets, I certainly look the part. The vacuum cleaner, a Sanitair upright carpet model, has a five-amp motor and a thirty-foot power cord. Not that I actually intend to turn it on. But it makes a good prop, and rolls easily over the carpeted floors.

Having something to push gives me confidence. As if I have a purpose, a reason to be there, and something to argue about when I am, inevitably, asked to explain myself.

Much to my surprise, the Pinnacle seems to be empty at this hour. Where are the patrolling security guards, the fanatical cultists scheming in the dead of night? Resting their little heads on their little pillows, apparently.

The place is huge. Vast. The ceiling soars so high I couldn't even begin to estimate the height. The blueprints gave me a sense of the layout, but not of the actual volume, which seems to be on the scale of a football stadium. The giant, inward-slanting windows have been sealed with what Shane says are automatically deployed blast shutters.

Not storm shutters. Blast shutters, as in able to withstand moderate explosive devices. So if they're expecting an intrusion from a SWAT unit, where are the defenders? You'd think the place would be crawling with BK Security guards armed to the teeth. And yet as I push the Sanitair through the twilight hush—the lights are very low, but more than adequate for getting around—the place feels empty.

Maybe they know the FBI is on the way and they've decided to hunker down, but not to fight. They must know what happens to cults that attempt to resist law enforcement units. It never seems to end well, and from what little I know, the Rulers strike me as fanatical but practical. They're all about self-advancement and making money, not actively defying the government. Therefore unlikely to start gunfights with the FBI.

Or that's what I'd like to believe. In that relatively comforting scenario, we find Noah sleeping in his bed, and Shane and I protect him until his FBI pals break down the doors and rescue us. All of Ruler Weems's paranoia proves to be exaggerated. His rivals are going to surround themselves with high-powered lawyers, not high-powered rifles, and everybody gets to live happily ever after. Except for those who eventually end up in prison, like Evangeline and Mrs. Delancey, and maybe the Barlows. I haven't really decided on the Barlows yet. They abducted me, true, but it's also true that they brought me very close to Noah, and that counts for a lot, even if their intentions weren't exactly selfless.

My mind races with this and a hundred other considerations, spiking on the adrenaline rush that makes my mouth dry and my knees feel weak. Got to keep moving or I'll fall to the floor and curl up in a fetal position.

The blueprint indicated that the guest bedroom suites are located on the second level, so that seems like the best place to start. There's a service elevator somewhere around the corner and down a hallway, but I can't bear the thought of getting stuck in an elevator, so I take the stairs. Not just any old stairs, either. This is a grand staircase out of an old MGM musical, fully twenty feet wide, making a majestic curve up from the ground floor. A glance at the massive but somehow elegant newel posts and balusters makes me think the stairway alone cost way more than my old farmhouse.

I'm halfway up the staircase when a shadow moves on the floor below, chilling my blood. It's Shane. He grins, gives me a thumbs-up, and with my heart banging like a heavy-metal drum I pick up the vacuum and continue. The construction feels as solid as the Rocky Mountains, and I can't help but wonder what a structure like the Pinnacle must have cost, having to transport all these exotic materials to this remote location. Unfathomable. As unfathomable as the folks we're up against: rich enough to construct vast temples at high altitude, to fly in their own private jets, build whole cities in the wilderness. People who think they can blow up schools and steal children with impunity.

I'm almost at the top when a man suddenly comes striding quickly around a corner—seemingly from out of nowhere—and almost knocks me back down the stairs.

I manage to save myself, but land awkwardly on my knees, one hand clutching a baluster and the other the vacuum cleaner, a pulse of pure fear pounding in my ears.

The man mutters something in a foreign language, one I don't recognize, and extends a hand to help me to my feet.

"Sorry," he says perfunctorily. "Apologies."

I recognize him from the Barlows' security camera. He's the cop in charge. A lean, darkly handsome guy with a neatly trimmed mustache and a dark curl of hair artfully arranged on his forehead. The movie star looks are spoiled by cold, ruthless eyes—if he's sorry about anything, it's that I slowed him down.

"I'm okay," I say, glancing away from those judgmental eyes, so as not to give myself away. Pretending to busy myself by rewinding the power cord. Knowing in my heart that I'm about to be exposed. That I'll have to start my put-up-a-fuss act, distract him long enough for Shane to slip by somehow, find his way to the guest suites.

The man with the mustache is staring at me, studying me. I can feel it.

A strong hand reaches out, lifts my chin. I find myself looking into those cold eyes, trying to keep my composure while I gather my strength.

"Is very early for housekeeper," he says.

I shrug, back away from the hand. There's something about his touch that makes my skin crawl.

"Is okay," he says, nodding to himself, as if arriving at a decision. Then without another word or glance he's turning away, heading down the staircase.

Something about the whole exchange convinces me he knows exactly who I am, but has decided not to interfere.

Why? How is that possible?

Don't worry about it, Haley. *Why* doesn't matter, not at this particular moment. The only thing that matters is finding Noah before the man with the ruthless eyes changes his mind, sounds an alarm.

Pushing the vacuum in front of me, I hurry down the hallway that leads to the guest suites, praying the layout hasn't changed since the blueprints were drawn.

Before we were married, Jed and I once wandered through the Four Seasons Hotel in Manhattan, marveling at the grandeur of the design by I. M. Pei. This has a similar feel, with a lot of light, polished stonework and a gently arched ceiling that glows with what looks like natural light, but isn't.

To my surprise there are no security guards here, either. And although relief pours into me like warm water, I'm aware that the lack of guards is not necessarily a good thing. Surely the heir apparent to Arthur Conklin would warrant protection.

What's going on? Where is everybody?

In the hushed silence of the deserted hallway, I stop at

the first door. Unlike a hotel there's no card-coded lock, and to my surprise the heavy, paneled door swings open at the push of the handle.

A glance reveals that the luxury suite is unoccupied, has probably been that way for some time, if the dust sheets are any indication.

There are six guest suites in this part of the building, and I despair that they will all be similarly vacant, ghostly sheets protecting the furniture. As indeed they all seem to be. Noah must be hidden away elsewhere, in some secret place not indicated on the drawings. But upon pushing open the sixth door, I detect a faint perfume. A tantalizingly familiar scent of a room that's been lived in, slept in.

Instantly I know that a woman has been here, and not long ago. Unlike the other suites, this shows signs of recent occupation. No dust sheets, no sense of prolonged stillness—somebody slept on that oversize mattress, and left a book on the bedside table. Somebody left faint impressions on the thick carpeting. Somebody left the door to the walk-in closet slightly ajar.

I'm about to check out the closet when a strong hand grips my shoulder.

Stifling a scream, I whip around and find Shane looking down at me, a finger to his lips.

Hand on my heaving chest, I manage to regain what little there is of my composure.

He leans down so that his beard softly brushes my ear.

"That was Kavashi, the security chief. I'm sure he recognized you."

"I don't get it," I whisper back.

"He's playing at something, I don't know what. But we

don't have much time. The blast shutters are down. They know what's coming."

"This is her room," I tell him. "Irene Delancey. I'm sure of it."

"Good," he says. "That means we're close."

He's right, and it suddenly occurs to me that these are suites, and that suites have connecting rooms, and I hurry to the wide, paneled door at the back of the room. What I had at first assumed must be another closet. And as soon as the door swings inward, revealing another, smaller room, I know, beyond a doubt, that this is where Noah sleeps.

There are stars on the walls and ceiling, emanating from a night-light on a bureau. Constellations to keep him company. He'd be able to name them, too, my brainy boy, my precious son, and then I'm flinging myself on the empty, rumpled bed and burying my face in the pillow, the smell of him bringing tears to my eyes, and a full-bodied pang of love so powerful that I fear it may stop my heart, because I know, even before we search under the bed and inside the closets, that he's no longer there.

We just missed him. The bitch has my boy.

7. The New You

Evangeline knows what the breaking dawn must look like, on a day like this. The way the first faint blush of daylight will climb down the mountainsides, putting the rough surfaces in relief. With the Pinnacle sealed she cannot, of course, actually see the glow lifting over the eastern horizon, or the stars fading from the sky, but she's fully capable of describing the familiar scene to Arthur Conklin as he lays very nearly comatose in his special hospital bed.

"It's beautiful, darling. You called it a great waltz, the planets swinging in time to the universe. That bright planet rising with the sun, that must be Venus, I suppose. And the fainter star or planet, could that be Mercury? You'd be able to tell, Arthur, because you always knew such things. Always knew exactly where you were in the world and what you were seeing. You could name the stars and the planets, and every bug I ever saw, and you made those Latin names sound like poetry. What was that horrible beetle you loved? Scarabaeus something or other? You told me the ancient Egyptians believed the beetle pushed the sun over the horizon every morning, which sounded rather beautiful. Then you told me the real beetle rolled up balls of dung, and that's what made the Egyptians think it did the same thing with the sun. A dung beetle!"

Evangeline has dismissed the medical attendants so that she and her husband are alone in the great room.

"It was so like you, to make a dirty little bug seem so grand, so important in the scheme of things. You never bored me, Arthur, not once in twenty years! Being your consort has been a great adventure. And I promise you, my darling, that you'll never die, not really. I will continue to speak with your voice. I'll be the new you."

The old man's head begins to rock from side to side, feebly but distinctly. His eyes remain closed—he hasn't opened them in two days—but there's every indication that he can hear, and that he doesn't particularly like her tone, even if he doesn't exactly comprehend her words.

"The Rulers have come to a turning point, my darling," she explains as she slips the pillow from beneath his frail head. "Mistakes have been made, all in a good cause, and the barbarians are at the gate. Literally, I am afraid. A convoy of black Chevy Suburban SUVs, filled with armed men. I believe they're called a tactical rescue squad, but really they're just ignorant slugs who do what they're told. We'll have to let them through, of course. But not before we get our little ducks in order. Not before we make sure that your vision will endure. Not before I make your old friend Wendy go away, and take his followers with him. It will be very tragic. And the boy? I'm sorry to have to tell you this, but the boy is going with Wendy. They'll think it was because the old mole was so loyal to you. Hereditary bond of the boy and all that plebeian crap people love. There's no other way. It's sad but it's all for the best. All for the Rule of One. And now, my darling, I'm sure you'll understand if we hurry things along, just a little."

Evangeline places the pillow over his face and presses with all of her strength. She's surprised not only at how much the old man resists, but by the flush of tears that come to her after it is finally over.

She truly hadn't expected to cry.

8. Good For Us

It's like *The Guns of Navarone* without the guns. That's the assessment from the Hostage Rescue Team Leader, reporting to Assistant Director of Counterterrorism, Monica Bevins, who shakes her head and asks him how old he is.

"Um, thirty-two, A-Dick. On my next birthday."

"Then *The Guns of Navarone* was an old movie long before you were born," she points out.

"Yes, A-Dick. An oldie but a goodie. Gregory Peck and Anthony Quinn on a suicide mission to save innocent lives. Same kind of deal we got here. A large, reinforced structure built into an inaccessible part of a mountain. Quite a challenge."

"This will not be a suicide mission, Team Leader, is that clear?"

"Yes, A-Dick. I was referring to the movie, not us."

"They didn't have helicopters back then. We do."

"Yes, A-Dick."

"There's also an aerial tram system, if you can figure out how to retrieve cars from the topside terminal. One car at the upper structure, one at the lower, both inoperable at the moment. Former agent Randall Shane mentioned a tunnel connecting the two buildings. We need to locate it."

"Yes, A-Dick. Working on it."

"Keep me posted," she says, dismissing him.

Bevins has never seen anything quite like the situation in Conklin, Colorado. There's been no overt resistance. Riding shotgun in the lead Suburban—strictly against protocol, but screw it, this is Shane—she had flashed the warrant at the BK Security goons and much to her surprise they'd been waved through. It soon became clear that the FBI would have full, unfettered access to the campus and the surrounding village, that the private security firm had been ordered to stand down.

The problem is the fortress the locals call the Pinnacle. The village may be open to inspection, but the entire structure of the Pinnacle has been shut up like a giant, reinforced clam, shielded with blast shutters. The landline phones have been cut off, and the aerial tramway is not responding. Nobody is responding. Getting inside will mean finding the tunnel, or, failing that, cutting through the hardened blast shutters with an acetylene torch. That will take time. Time they may not have, if the situation inside goes south.

Bevins was a rookie Special Agent when the Branch Davidian thing went down, and she watched it unfold on TV like everyone else. The disaster at Waco, in which many innocent children died, haunts the FBI to this day, and agents working a cult situation have it in mind as an example of what can go badly, horribly wrong. But the cult headquarters in that case had been a collection of ramshackle farmhouses. This is way different. The Ruler campus looks positively bucolic, the residential area could be an exclusive, gated community in Aspen. This ain't the Bible-thumpin' badlands of Texas, and Arthur Conklin is no David Koresh, preaching apocalypse. So maybe wiser minds will prevail. Bevins certainly hopes so.

Her own history with Shane complicates the situation. Because she is tall, over six feet, and because she and Shane have long been close, her colleagues assume they have a sexual history. To Bevins's mild regret, that is not the case. Shane was married and faithful for most of the years when they worked together, and their friendship remains platonic, even as they quietly acknowledge a mutual attraction. Their bond transcends rank and status, and to Bevins it doesn't matter that Shane is technically retired. So when the call came in from Maggie Drew, she had to act, had to make it happen. Normally the A.D. of

Counterterrorism would not be at the scene supervising a kidnap recovery situation, but if Bevins hadn't swung weight, given the green light, they'd still be arguing about jurisdiction.

She's out on a limb with Shane, a civilian, relying on his word that the missing mother and child are being held against their will. Of the top ten priorities of the FBI, as approved by the Director, supporting missions like this one comes in at number nine. Just one level above "upgrading technology to successfully perform the FBI's mission." At some point she's going to have to justify the operation, but right now she's more concerned about having it conclude successfully, without loss of life.

"Team Leader? Where are we?"

"Chopper on the roof. They'll be attempting to breach the blast shutters with a torch. A dozen agents on the ground, searching for the tunnel entrance. Sonar detectors have been deployed—if there's a tunnel, we should be able to detect it up to a depth of fifty feet or so, depending on the density."

"Good," she says. Keeping in mind that an Assistant Director or 'A-Dick' can't be seen to be chewing her fingernails, however much she might be tempted as a stress-reliever.

"The thing about *The Guns of Navarone?*" he says. "It was an impossible task but they got it done."

"Forget the movies, Team Leader. No Hollywood heroics, please. Go by the book. Nobody dies. You are to take no unnecessary risks."

He grins. "We're the HRT. We eat risk for breakfast."

"Speaking of breakfast, is there any coffee available?"

The Team Leader hands her a Thermos flask. "High-test," he promises.

Inside the Pinnacle, in the perpetual twilight of the closed blast shutters, word spreads from Ruler to Ruler, many of whom weep inconsolably.

Their great leader, the One True Voice, is gone.

No one seems to be quite sure what will happen next. With Arthur Conklin dead, who will speak for them? Many favor the homely familiarity of Wendall Weems, the founder's closest friend. Others prefer the fiery approach of the founder's wife—his widow now—Evangeline Dowdy Conklin.

Eva the Diva makes the first move, speaking from her late husband's studio. Throughout both the Pinnacle and the Bunker, flat-screens come to life, and Eva appears, dabbing at her eyes, her voice thick with sorrow.

"Arthur has taken flight," she announces. "Early this morning his body ceased to function and he removed himself to the next level. Before he went, Arthur spoke to me at length. I am still processing his many revelations, and will share them with you in the months and years to come. But for now, hear this. Arthur's last wish is that his transition be an occasion of reconciliation between the factions. Therefore we will gather in our respective areas to mourn his passing, and to prepare ourselves for the future. Only then will we open our doors to the outsiders who have come here in their ignorance.

"A few moments ago I spoke with Ruler Weems. Our conversation was cordial. He will be convening a special meeting with his people, and I with mine. There is no profit in fighting amongst ourselves. Between us, we will come to an equitable solution. Rest assured that we will find a way to face the new day with a new mind."

Evangeline shuts off the camera and exits the studio, heading for her war room. Her plan is falling neatly into place. Within the hour she will have solidified her grip on the organization. Wendy and his people will follow Arthur into the next world, wherever that might be, and trouble her no more.

"Vash!" she calls out. "Is everything ready?"

He's been busy in the war room, calmly programming a complex portion of the system's software. He looks up, his expression betraying no emotion.

"Is good," he says. Then he smiles, his cool eyes warming up, drinking her in. "Bad for them. Good for us."

9. Good Night, Irene

When the flat-screen TV came to life in Irene Delancey's empty bedroom, announcing the death of Arthur Conklin, I nearly jumped out of my skin. Not just because it startled me, but because of what the announcement might mean. When a cult leader dies—excuse me, is "removed to the next level"—"outsiders gather"—that must be Shane's FBI friends—it can't be good. An organization in crisis, factions fighting for control, the whole place in lockdown, it all sounds as if it's spiraling out of control. That can't be good for us.

The woman making the announcement had seemed serene in tone, but I don't believe her for a second. Something about her is off, way off. She has the look of madness; confident, chilling madness.

As soon as the screen goes dark again, Shane tries to make a call, but with no view of the sky, not to mention all the concrete and steel between us, the fancy satellite phone can't get a signal. No phone, and therefore no way to know how long it will take the FBI to find a way inside. And in my mind at least, if we don't locate Noah in the next few minutes, something terrible is going to happen. Call it mother's instinct, or plain anxiety, but there it is, the absolute need to find my son now rather than later.

"Two possibilities," Shane says, surveying the empty bedroom. "Either she heard us coming, or something else frightened her. Same result, whatever the cause. She's hiding and she took your son with her."

"How do you know that?"

He holds up the book left on Mrs. Delancey's bedside table. "Noah told me," he says with a gleam in his eye. "He left a message."

"Oh my god! Let me see!"

The book is, no surprise, Arthur Conklin's *The Rule of One.* Apparently the true believers keep it close at hand, like the Bible. The surprise is the scrap of paper tucked into the book, hastily scrawled in pencil:

WE ARE HIDING.
NOAH CORBIN, AGE 10
P.S. TELL MY MOM

I know that handwriting! No question, it's Noah, and aside from the brief glimpse of video provided by Ruler

Weems, the first real tangible proof that he's not only alive, but well. Despite whatever poison they've been feeding him, he knows his name is Corbin, not Conklin. Plus he wants his mother to know where he is. That's a good sign, right? Right?

"S-sorry," I blubber, totally losing it, clutching the little note to my heart.

Doubtful a big strong shoulder would help, but there's no way of knowing, because Shane isn't offering. He's not being unkind or uncaring, but neither is he offering to comfort me. It's clear that he shares my concern about finding Noah right away, and that must take precedence. No time for emotional meltdowns, save the tears for later.

"I suspect she hasn't gone far," he says, waiting for me to get it together. "If she wanted to hide, her options would have been limited."

"But we checked all the rooms on this floor," I say, frantic.

"No," he says firmly. "We didn't. You looked in the doors, saw the dustcovers, and backed out. Very quietly, too, I might add."

He's right, of course. We'd been searching for rooms that were lived in, not places to hide. Stupid! In an instant I'm back in the hall, racing for the next suite, housekeeper disguise forgotten. Bursting through the door, I run to the adjoining room—all the layouts are the same—and find it just as empty. Dustcovers, stillness. My instincts telling me the air in here has not been disturbed recently, that the mustiness has been honestly come by.

Check everything. Look everywhere. Bathrooms, closets, under the bed.

Whipping back a shower curtain, I come face-to-face with a madwoman. Her hair is a mess, her eyes are red, she looks as frantic as me. She *is* me.

What kind of place is this, putting mirrors behind the claw-foot tubs?

By the time I get to the last of the guest suites, every door has been opened, every closet looked into, every shower curtain whipped back, and still there's no sign of Noah, no clue as to where he's been taken.

My head is light with the pounding of my heart. In despair I fall to my knees and cover my face as it all comes crashing together. The conflicting tides of fear and frustration and just plain old need, the need to have my child in my arms at last. I've come this far, the madwoman of Humble, the crazy mom who won't give up, because somehow I can feel that my child is alive, and where he might be, but whenever I almost get there somebody moves him farther away.

I can't take it anymore. This ends now, or I really will go stark raving mad.

"Noah!" I scream. "Where are you!"

Shane, startled, reaches out to caution me, but I duck under his hand and fling myself out into the hallway, bellowing at the top of my lungs, "NOAH! NO-AHHH! IT'S MOMMY! NOAH! NOAH! NOAH!" chanting and screaming with all my strength, with everything I've got, and to give him credit, Shane doesn't really try to stop me.

"NO-AHH!" I cry, running back and forth, doing my best to shout the walls down with the sound of my voice. "NO-

AHHH! NO-AHHH! NO-AHHH! I WANT MY SON! GIVE ME BACK MY SON! NO-AHHH! NO-AHHH!"

I scream his name until my throat is so raw I can't get out a sound, until the air is out of my lungs, until the strength is fading from my body, and hope from my heart.

And then I hear it. Very faint. Not Noah, not his voice, but something. A tiny thump no louder than the thudding of a single sparrow wing. But it's enough to get me flying down the hallway, through the open door, and into one of the empty guest suites that we've already checked twice. And exactly as I enter the room, there's the faintest flutter of movement under one of the dust sheets, a simple white cotton sheet covering an unused desk.

Hands extended like eager talons, mama bird zeroing in, I rip away the dust sheet and there under the desk is Irene Delancey, who looks almost as terrified as I do. Struggling in her arms is a desperate little boy. She has her hand clamped over the boy's mouth, and her face is bleeding from where's he's scratched her, and his feet are kicking.

That's the thump I heard, that's what made the dust sheet flutter. Noah, my son, my beautiful true-blue boy, responding to his mother's cry.

"Let him go," I tell her, my voice hoarse and croaking.

"I saved him," she whimpers, pleading for forgiveness. "They want to kill him and I saved him. You've got to believe me."

"Let him go."

She does, she lets him go, and then he's in my arms, hugging me as if his life depends on it, crying *Mommy, Mommy, Mommy,* clinging with all his might, and everything is good. I am made whole again and everything is right in the world.

Except for one thing. Cradling Noah with my left arm, I lift my foot and stomp Mrs. Delancey right in the nose.

10. Run For Your Life

For weeks I've dreamed of this moment. Dreams so palpable, so real that I awoke convinced my son was back home, and I'd find myself staggering into his empty bedroom and realize that the real nightmare was in being awake.

Now that it has finally happened, now that I can feel Noah's heart pounding against my own, all the pain and grief starts to melt away, and it is as if I'm finally, truly, wide-awake to the world. Strangely, my rage at those who stole him melts away, too. It's as if there's only room enough in me for love. Maybe that will change over time, but right at this moment, this wonderful, wonderful moment, all I feel for Irene Delancey and her Ruler friends is pity.

They are so utterly pathetic. Worshipping a mean old man who encouraged them to be selfish, is there anything more sad?

Cupping her hands to her bleeding nose, Irene looks at me imploringly. "We have to get out of here," she whimpers. "She'll find us."

"Evangeline?" asks Shane. "Is she the one?"

I hadn't even noticed that he'd come into the room. He's been standing apart, letting me hug Noah, who is clinging to me as if he never intends to let go, his wet face buried against my neck, his legs locked around my hips just as he used to do when he was three or four and still wanted to be carried.

"Something has happened to her," Irene says. "She was always dangerous, but lately it's gotten worse. I think she must be delusional. All of her Sixes have seen Noah, so why does she think she can make him disappear? Everybody already knows he's here, she can't just make him disappear. It doesn't make sense."

Shane goes into the bathroom, returns with a cold cloth. "You may need to have that cauterized," he says. "This will help with the swelling."

"I never wanted to do this," she says, pleading with me. "You've got to believe me."

Her nose may be broken, but there seems to be no way to stop her from babbling on, making her excuses. How her husband got in trouble with the Rulers for cheating on his share-in, and how Evangeline and her horrible boyfriend were about to ruin them—leave them virtually penniless, imagine!—and the only way out was to do what they demanded. Take the job in Humble, befriend the child, bring him to Conklin. She'd never known that the police chief would be killed in front of the children, or that the school would be blown up, honest! And she'd only agreed to continue as Noah's tutor to make sure he was okay, blah blah blah.

"Let me get this right," I say. "You're given a choice—lose money or kidnap an innocent child—and you choose to kidnap the child? *That's* your defense? That's the best you can come up with?"

Noah, clinging to my neck, whispers, "She's lying, Mom. She's a liar, liar with her pants on fire."

"I know that, sweetie. Hush now. It doesn't matter. We don't have to listen to her anymore. Not ever again."

"No," agrees Shane. "But she's right about one thing. We do need to get out of here, and fast. If I'm not mistaken, the entire building, or most of it, has been evacuated."

I'm really too busy comforting Noah to pay close attention to what he's saying, but I can see from his expression that he's very worried, that in his mind we're still in immediate danger.

"You were yelling loud enough to rattle the walls," he points out. "No security response? There's only one explanation—nobody comes to see what's going on because they've already left."

"Evangeline is still here," Irene says, talking around her clotted nose. "She and her Sixes. At the top level, in the private residence. They're holding vigil for Arthur."

"But the guards are gone," Shane says, pondering. "Rats deserting the ship."

He decides we can't wait for the Hostage Rescue Team to breach the building. The fastest way out is the way we came in—through the tunnel.

"Follow me," he urges. "No sneaking around, we'll run for it."

"Don't leave me!" Irene begs, following us out the door, into the deserted hallway.

Shane is right. I was yelling to raise the dead, that should have attracted attention. And if the building has been abandoned by the security chief and his men, there has to be a reason.

"Mom?" says Noah, releasing his grip on my neck. "Put me down. We can run faster that way."

Holding his hand, we run for the stairs. Shane in the lead, his long legs eating up the yards, and Irene whimpering and stumbling as she tries to keep up.

Part of me is frightened—who wouldn't be?—but part of me can't help noticing how fast Noah can run. He's nimble and balanced, physically healthy. So they must have fed him okay. My mommy gut tells me he hasn't been damaged beyond repair. Whatever else he's been through, whatever mental traumas he's suffered, we can deal with all that.

He clings to my hand, though, and won't let go, as if he can't bear to lose physical contact. I expect he'll be back sleeping in my bedroom for a while, as he did after his father died. That'll be okay. That'll be fine. And if he doesn't want to sleep in my bedroom, I just might move into his. For a little while. Just until I get used to the idea that he's safe, that no one will come to take him away in the middle of the night.

Making plans, even as we run for our lives.

The custodian's closet is just as we left it, door unlocked. Shane is the first inside, and he doesn't even bother to flip on the lights, he drops to his knees, pushing away mops and buckets, searching the area of floor where the hatch had popped open.

"Got to be here somewhere," he mutters. "A pressure switch."

The lights come on. I assume it was Irene because I don't even know where the switch is, and besides, Noah has climbed back into my arms and I quite literally have my hands full. But it isn't Irene, she looks as startled as me, and then in an instant her face drains white with fear. Not just fear—terror.

"Nobody move."

Standing in the doorway is the handsome guy with the killer eyes. The man with the mustache. The man who stopped me on the stairs and let me go. The man they call Vash, which is short for something else, I can't remember what, now, exactly. Doesn't matter what his proper name is, he's pointing a funny-looking gun at Shane, who remains on his knees in the middle of the crowded custodial closet. Looking, and this scares me, very spooked, if not exactly frightened.

"Nobody move," Vash repeats with a humorless chuckle, as if applauding his own cleverness. "They say that in American westerns, yes? Okay, Mr. FBI man, you got gun in belt, I can see that. Pistol you stole from BK vehicle, you naughty boy. You think you draw fast like in westerns, blow bad guy away. No, no, no."

"Go ahead, tase me," Shane says, not making a move for the pistol. "See what happens this time."

Vash laughs. "I already see. Two times, already. Third time, you pee pants for sure."

"Maybe I learned how to take it. Maybe the third time, you're the one who wets his pants."

"Ha! Not possible. While you flop around, I take pistol you stole and shoot you," Vash promises. "Bang, bang. Self-defense."

What I want to do is put down Noah and grab a bucket and throw it in this horrible man's smug, handsome face. But before I can think it through, Shane gives me a warning look and says, "Don't. I'll handle this."

Which Vash thinks is very funny. "You handle? Big joke for big man. Where you going, huh? Escape into tunnel? I don't think so. We find the entrance, toss in a little boom-boom, make part of tunnel collapse. Forget tunnel. Forget escape. You are safer right here, trust me."

Shane snorts. "Trust me. From a war criminal? I'm guessing most of those who ever trusted you are dead."

Vash shakes his head, disappointed. "I'm wishing I had time for this," he says. "Could be lots of fun."

"What's your hurry?" Shane says.

Taunting Vash. Daring him to fire. Which doesn't make sense, with Shane more or less helpless on the floor and Vash holding the Taser. I know enough from what I've seen on TV that getting hit with a Taser may not be fatal, but it does turn you into a nonfunctioning slab of twitching muscle.

Is he planning to sacrifice himself while Noah and I get away? But where can we go that Vash can't find us? It doesn't make sense.

"Is the place going to blow up?" Shane asks him, pushing. "Is that why you're in a hurry to get away? Like you blew up the school?"

"Stupid penny man blows up school, not me."

"So you knew Roland Penny. I'll bet it was you that filled his head full of nonsense about ruling the world, and then pointed him in the right direction. Is that how you did it?"

"Never mind the penny man," Vash says dismissively, no longer smiling. All business, and in a hurry, too. "You lie down! Everybody lie down! I put plastic ties on wrists, not too tight. Then I give myself up to FBI, okay? I explain everything. You be fine, don't worry."

Irene whimpers and collapses to her knees, holding out

her wrists like a child who knows she deserves to be punished. With one hand, cocky Vash whips a tie around her wrist, cinches it tight. "Good girl," he says. "Lie facedown. Nothing bad happens, I promise."

Eyes streaming, she obeys. Obviously convinced she's about to be executed, but too frightened to resist.

Meanwhile Shane is staring at me with great intensity, as if trying to communicate something, though for the life of me I don't know what. Has he changed his mind, does he want me to make a move, distract the man with the mustache? No, that's not it. He wants me to stay where I am, he'll make the first move. So we're back to sacrificing himself to help us get away. Or else he has something else in mind entirely, something I can't quite fathom, and I'm hoping that's it, because I've run out of ideas.

"Out the front door, huh?" he says, sneering at Vash. "Give yourself up? Might work, if there's nobody left to testify against you. What happened, did you and Evangeline break up? Did you decide to sacrifice her before she sacrifices you?"

"Facedown," Vash insists, taking aim with the Taser. "Now."

"Now would be good," Shane says, standing up.

Vash's eyes widen in surprise, but before Shane can reach for the pistol wedged into his belt, he fires the Taser.

It all happens so fast I can't be sure what I'm seeing, but it looks like a couple of little wires attach themselves to Shane's chest, and then his whole body begins to twitch and convulse in the most awful way.

I instinctively turn so Noah can't see what's going on, and then a truly astonishing thing happens.

Shane's face is horribly distorted by the twitching muscles, but somehow he's grinning like a maniac. His eyes, alive in the midst of quivering facial muscles, are triumphant. As if this is exactly what he planned.

Shane, through sheer force of will, does the impossible. The supposedly impossible. He regains enough control over his flailing limbs to tear the wires out of his chest. He then yanks the Taser out of his assailant's hands, and with a roar takes the stunned security chief by the neck and smashes him into the wall like a rag doll, wham, wham, wham.

It's all over in a few seconds. A moment later the semiconscious Vash is being cuffed with his own plastic ties, trussed up like a calf at a rodeo and pushed to the side of the closet.

Irene, staring with bugged-out eyes, says, "Wow."

Wow is right. He's amazing. Magnificent, really. The only reason I don't applaud is because my son is squirming around, getting an eyeful.

"Who is the big man, Mommy?"

"He's our new friend, sweetie."

"I'm glad," says Noah.

Me, too, I'm thinking. Me, too.

Shane isn't done. He pops open the escape hatch, gives me a grin. "We better get a move on. Time's a wasting."

"He said he blew up the tunnel."

"The man is a liar—it looks okay from here. We'll be fine. Let's go."

He holds out his hand. I take it.

11. The Button Is Pressed

A temporary helicopter landing site has been set up in the parking lot of the Conklin Institute, and that's where Maggie Drew lands, amidst a cloud of fine snow kicked up by the blades of the McDonnell Douglas 530, affectionately known as a 'Little Bird.'

The affection is not shared by Maggie. She hates helicopters, and they hate her. It was a two-barf-bag trip from Denver International, and the crew is glad to see her go. They keep their snarky comments to themselves, however, when they realize Assistant Director Monica Bevins, the on-site commander herself, is waiting to personally assist the lame little puker out of the aircraft.

"Any news?" Maggie shouts over the whirr of the turbines.

"Lots of news," Monica says, holding out an arm for her limping friend. "None of it good."

"He hasn't made contact?"

"Not since that call to you."

Maggie hugs the much taller woman's arm as they approach the black Suburban that will take them up the mountain, to the forward offensive position. "I've got a bad feeling about this one," she admits. "I've been working up a profile for Arthur Conklin's wife, Evangeline—she's the leader of the more radical faction."

"I know who she is, Mags. I downloaded your file on my BlackBerry."

"Sorry. Didn't know if you had time to read it."

"I'm a multitasker. You know that."

The doors lock as the driver accelerates out of the parking lot.

"So what's the new angle?" Monica prompts.

"Oh! Sorry!" Maggie says, staring out the tinted window. "I've seen this place in photographs, but they don't do it justice. Really spectacular." She gives a worried sigh, makes a brave smile for her friend. "Okay. Back to Evangeline. Eva the Diva. The psych data is not exactly encouraging. Taking prior behavior patterns into account, and similar cults that depend on a single, charismatic individual, I think there's a pretty good chance she'll go off the deep end. She may trend into an apocalyptic scenario and not be able to see a way out."

Monica nods. "With their leader dying and the factions struggling for power, we've been assuming the worst. Unfortunately it's taking a lot longer to break their defenses than we anticipated. Can you believe they have weapons-grade blast shutters? Acetylene won't cut the stuff. Had to send for a hi-temp plasma torch and even that's slow as hell."

"So we've no idea what's happening in the Pinnacle."

Monica nods. "Or the other building, the one they call the Bunker. Unfortunate name. Can't help but think of Hitler. Speaking of apocalyptic scenarios."

"What about the tunnel Shane mentioned?"

"Yeah, well, that's part of the bad news, I'm afraid. We finally located the entrance, but somebody rolled an explosive device into the lower part of the tunnel—we're thinking modified RPGs—and blew it up. Collapsed at least a hundred yards of the tunnel, which is just your basic six-foot diameter fiberglass conduit, and not capable of withstanding any sort of explosion. We can dig it out, but it will take time. Days, not hours."

Maggie looks sick, and not from the helicopter ride. "They blew the tunnel? Who, exactly, do you know? Which faction?"

"All I know, it was probably somebody with the security service. We found a van nearby with traces of the explosive."

"Eva's people," Maggie says.

"Is that good or bad?"

"It's all bad," Maggie says. "But Eva is worse. She isn't just keeping us from getting in. She's keeping them from getting out."

The Suburban slows to a stop. The women step out into the frigid air and look up to the massive structures built into the mountain.

"It's so quiet," Maggie marvels. "I hadn't expected that."

Monica glances down at her much shorter companion. She's about to make a comment, then thinks better of it.

Quiet as the grave, she almost said.

Evangeline decides she's waited long enough. She'd been delaying until Vash got back—he'd been fussing like an anxious schoolboy, very unlike him—but she simply can't wait any longer. He'll miss the big moment, but that's just too bad. Weems has been assembling his Sixes, those who were already in residence at the Bunker, just as she has gathered her own people, ostensibly so they can cut a deal and get on with the sad business of mourning the Profit. What would the One True Voice think of all this Sturm and Drang, she wonders. What would Arthur do?

Easy answer, as far as Evangeline is concerned. Whatever the situation, when given a choice, Arthur always selected for the survival of the organization. Even if it meant that not every individual member would survive. As a scientist he understood the importance of culling, of cutting away the deadwood, and had structured the Rulers accordingly. Many drones at the lowest level, feeding the hive, and only a select few at the top, to reap the benefit.

What's going to happen is, Weems and his followers have decided to join Arthur in the afterlife. At least, that's what his latest blog entry says, courtesy of Evangeline. Best thing: when the Feds bring in their forensics experts, and they will, they'll discover that the fatal command originated on Wendy's personal computer, as if he, not Evangeline, pushed the fatal button.

A shame, really, how grief made poor, ugly little Wendy delusional. But totally believable. Pure genius.

Eva decides to make one last attempt to raise Vash on the intercom. No response. Odd, she assumed he wanted to share in the moment, but then it occurs to her that lover boy would rather not be in the room when she presses the button. He prefers to operate from the shadows, maintaining plausible deniability. Which, come to think, isn't a bad thing in this case because if worst ever came to worst, he can't be called as an eyewitness to the event.

An event, not a crime. Crime is for those at the lower levels.

The screens show that all is ready. Weems and his Sixes—a small group of the wealthiest, longest-serving

Rulers—have gathered in his conference room in the Bunker. The sound quality is terrible—all booming echoes and static—but it's not necessary to know what they're saying. They'll be discussing her offer, coming up with counteroffers. The visuals tell her all she needs to know: they all look so somber that it really isn't that much of a leap to conclude that a final solution might be on the agenda.

Eva has her finger over the screen, about to make the one little touch that will turn the Bunker into a death zone, when the most extraordinary thing happens. Wendy actually leaps out his chair, exclaiming something.

Does he know?

And then, a miracle. The completion of perfection. Because three more people enter the conference room. Three people and a child. The big man Vash identified as the former FBI agent, Shane, accompanied by—who is that?—is it Irene Delancey? Yes! Why it looks like someone has blacked her eyes, or is that her makeup running? And then, the icing on the cake, that little pest Haley Corbin comes into view, hugging Arthur's grandson to her side.

Eva is stunned. Vash delivered! He found a way to get all of her enemies into the Bunker, where the sad event will take place. This is way better than having to make the woman and the boy disappear somehow later. They'll be among the victims blamed on Wendy. Too bad about the boy—she had such high hopes, but he hadn't worked out, and sometimes you just have to acknowledge a mistake and move on.

She has to pause for a moment and wipe away the tears. Tears not of grief, but of joy. This has to be a sign from

Arthur himself, his way of letting her know that she's made the right choice.

"Bless you, Arthur," she says.

She presses the button, releasing the gas. Fentanyl, a favorite from Vash's old killing grounds. The lethal effects of high doses of Fentanyl had first been established by Russian security forces, who had used it against Chechen terrorists holding hostages in a Moscow theater. Indeed, it was so lethal that almost everyone died, hostages included. It had been particularly effective against the children.

To fall asleep and never wake up. Is that so bad?

12. This Is The End, My Friend

Maggie keeps shuffling between the heated, idling Suburban—your tax dollars at work—and the frigid cold of the Colorado morning. If she wasn't so worried she'd be able to appreciate the stunning beauty of the setting. The clear air, the awesome majesty of the high country, the illusion that you can see forever. But at the moment the mountains and the altitude are the enemy, making it difficult to execute the mission. Helicopters have been coming and going from the roof of the Pinnacle, which turns out not to be booby-trapped, as Shane had warned in his brief call. Thank God for small favors. There haven't been many. The blueprints that came through from the sat phone have been helpful, but even so, no one anticipated the difficulty of breaching what turns out to be a modern fortress.

Under typical circumstances, the Hostage Rescue Team would have been inside minutes after arriving on-site. As it is, a couple of hours have passed. An eternity, given the volatile circumstances.

Maggie's hoping for the best—Randall Shane has been surviving on guts and luck for years, why should these run out now?—but she's got a bad feeling. This is about as far from a typical hostage scenario as you can get, complicated by a cult leader in close alliance with an individual, Kavashi, who has been getting away with cold-blooded murder for years, and who has ways of making his victims vanish, never to be seen again.

Pacing the area as A.D. Bevins confers with the rescue team by two-way, Maggie concentrates on walking without a limp. No cane today, the latest flare-up of her RA having subsided, and she had wanted to demonstrate her physical well-being to Shane, if only because he'd looked so stricken when she came off the plane in Denver leaning on her cane.

She's hoping against hope that Randall Shane's luck will hold, but what gnaws at her is the unspeakable fear that when the rescue team finally does get inside, Shane and the mother and child he's trying to save will be gone without a trace. Torn from the world.

She hates that it might all end here, in this way. And then she admonishes herself not to give up. This is Randall Shane. He can't die, not like this, not with a child's life at stake. Buck up. Think positive.

At precisely that moment Monica Bevins comes striding up, clutching her two-way. Her face is ashen, her eyes desolate.

"Oh, Maggie," she says, choking up.

"Tell me."

"They finally broke through into the Pinnacle. The entire structure has been flooded with some sort of lethal gas. They're all dead, Mags. Everyone inside is dead."

So that's it, Maggie thinks, that's how it ends. Strange, but when she'd envisioned such tragedies in the past, she had always imagined that when the moment came she would collapse or faint, and yet here she is, standing on her own not-so-sturdy legs.

Maybe this is what shock is, standing in one place, unable to speak, when you should be running around and screaming your head off.

Slowly, she becomes aware of a humming sound. Is that in her head? No? Has the wind come up? Instinctively she looks around, expecting to see some evidence of a storm approaching—that seems fitting: a violent electrical storm—and then she sees it.

"Monica, look."

High overhead, the tram cable is turning. A tram car comes into view, slowly descending from the Bunker. Without a word, Assistant Director Monica Bevins takes off in a sprint, heading for the lower terminal.

Maybe a hundred yards uphill, at a steep incline. No way can Maggie run that distance without blowing out her hips. But she can walk fast, and she doesn't falter, and when the tram finally arrives at the terminal, she's there waiting with Monica. Her hands clasped over her heart to keep it from leaping out of her chest.

"We don't know who it is," Monica warns, drawing her Glock 23, holding it at the ready position.

"Sure we do," says Maggie. "Are you kidding?"

But when the car shudders to a stop and the door slides

open, the man who emerges is Wendall Weems, recognizable from his photographs as perhaps the homeliest individual Maggie has ever laid eyes on. Except for his eyes, which are startling in their intensity. He spots Monica with her weapon at the ready and says, "Thank you, but that won't be necessary. If you wish to arrest me, I shall go willingly."

Monica lowers her gun. "Good. You'll be taken into custody. Please turn around."

"Kidnapping the boy wasn't my idea."

"We'll let the lawyers sort it out, shall we?" Monica says, pulling out her handcuffs.

As she clicks the cuffs on his wrists, Weems looks around and says, "I wonder, has anyone seen Mr. Kavashi? The security chief? I expected him to be here. He was supposed to meet me outside, at the terminal."

Monica looks startled. "I'm confused. We thought he was your enemy."

Weems shrugs his misshapen shoulders. "Until very recently. The last hour or two, actually. But he indicated to me that he wanted to change sides. I got the distinct impression he intended to betray Eva and cast his lot with us."

When Monica informs him that Evangeline and her followers are dead, the victims of a toxic gas released into the Pinnacle, Weems's face turns a whiter shade of pale. "So if Vash remained on the premises, he is among the victims?"

"It looks that way, yes."

To Maggie's eyes, he appears genuinely shaken by the news.

When Weems is finally clear, several frightened-looking individuals emerge from the tram, among them a woman with raccoon eyes and a swollen nose who Maggie barely recognizes as Irene Delancey, the bond-trader-turned-schoolteacher-turned-kidnapper.

Then, ducking his head, Randall Shane steps out into the clear light of day.

"Hey, Mags."

"You okay?"

"I'm good."

He looks exhausted, but somehow happier than she's seen him in years. Clutching his left hand is one of the most beautiful women Maggie has ever seen, scared but gorgeous, and somehow radiating strength, and attached to Shane's big right hand, like he doesn't intend ever to let go, is a ten-year-old boy with a big smile on his face.

They look like a family.

EPILOGUE

Five Months Later

Things don't always work out the way you want them to. Nobody knows that better than me. You meet someone, fall in love, imagine you will be together forever and always. You tend to forget the 'until death do we part' part. And when it happens you're sure, you're absolutely certain, you will never love again.

Sometimes, if you're lucky, you're wrong.

That's what I'm thinking as we drive back from Donnie Brewster's Humble Mart Convenience Store with a pound of hot dogs, and a dozen buns, and Noah's favorite pickle relish.

Plenty of mustard at home. Again, the kind Noah likes.

Okay, hot dogs may not be the healthiest food, and I know I shouldn't be indulging his every whim, but it's a warm summer evening and he's a growing boy, and how much harm can a few tube steaks do?

Tube steaks. That's what Jed used to call them.

In the backseat Noah has the window rolled down and the wind is fluffing his hair and he looks as blissfully content as any kid who is about to stuff himself with delicious nitrates could look. He's had an amazing recovery, all things considered. For the first couple of months he did share my bedroom, in his own little bed, and he insisted on a night-light. He was leery about going outside, didn't want to see any of the kids from school. Indeed, he stayed home for all of the semester, with me acting as tutor and feeling, to put it delicately, challenged. I don't know squat about prime numbers, which may have something to do with Noah's recent decision to return to school in the fall. I'm hoping he still feels that way when September rolls around, but you never know. One day at a time.

As to the events in Colorado, they managed to prove that Bagrat Kavashi, the horrible man with the mustache, had perished in a scheme of his own devising when he rigged the poison gas for the Pinnacle instead of the Bunker. He thought he had the perfect way to lay all the blame on Evangeline, who would be conveniently dead via 'suicide,' but he failed to escape his own trap. I don't think of myself as a vengeful type, but, really, the scum bucket deserved it.

Noah leans forward in the seat belt harness, taps me on the shoulder. Apparently unaware that I've been watching him in the mirror.

"Are you happy, Mom?"

He asks this regularly, checking in. And I always answer the same way. "Most of the time, sweetie. Nobody is happy all the time."

He nods, satisfied, and resumes his look out the window, blinking into the wind.

It's Noah who first spots the plume of smoke when we

come around the last corner to our modest-but-if-you-ask-me-perfect farmhouse.

"Mom, smoke!"

"I can see that, sweetie."

And I can see Shane tending his new Weber grill, looking as serious as any man who ever prepared to burn a hot dog for a soon-to-be-eleven-year-old boy.

He insists on charcoal. No propane gas for Randall Shane.

I know, I know. He's fourteen years older than me, and that can be a big deal if you let it, which we don't. Also he's far from rich, he doesn't drive a cool car, and his work sometimes takes him far from home. For that matter there's always a chance, however small, that he won't come back, that he'll die trying to save someone else's little boy or little girl.

I know all that.

But I also know this: we live on borrowed time, all of us, and wasting a day of it—or a lonely night—is a crime. Besides, I love the big guy to pieces. It's different from Jed, but just as intense. So get out of my face with this he's-too-old-for-you stuff, I don't want to hear it.

Sorry…you can take the girl out of New Jersey but…you know how it ends. Happily ever after, if I have anything to say about it.

And I do.